THE HIGH-KING'S HARP

THE WARRIORS OF TIR NAN OG

BY ALISON SCOTT

Pro Christo Domino

South winds,
Far now my fathers' shores!
I sail an un-sailed sea;
Jeweled birds, fish with wings; oars
Splash wave-bound stars.
Some, by summer won, seek farms;
Figs, olives, wine.
Some dream of Odin's Stone;
Winter, women, home.
I dream of Rome,
City of saints and swords,
A lass in chains, my heart enchained
Long winters past. A sword
Beneath my pilgrim's cloak,
I kneel to Peter's bones.

from *The Saga of Floki Magnusson*
circa 900 (?) AD

Of you are told glorious things,
O city of God.

Kethuvim

PROLOGUE

The wind shifted as the sun set. Watching his sail, Gil signaled to Ragi to tighten the sheet. The ship heeled, white foam breaking from her bow wave. Janetta pointed over her shoulder, "We leave Hakon behind."

"Of course," Gil grinned as a ship's length of sea opened between his stern and *Sea-Raven's* curving prow. *Silver Dragon* sailed her best on a broad reach, and at her best, nothing could catch her.

"The earl says ...."

"I know. I know. Stay together." He cast a quick glance at Floki, sitting cross-legged on the deck between Ulf and Grimhildr, all three bent over a map of Hrolf's Isle charcoaled on the weathered boards. The young Northman never looked up, but Gil adjusted his tiller, anyhow, spilling enough wind to allow Hakon to close the gap. "Spoil sport." He grinned again. "If it were ponies, you'd be miles ahead."

"Ponies aren't alone in the middle of the sea," she said primly. Her eyes, sparkling like sun on water, undid the effect.

"*Our* ponies are." He nodded toward Lionheart and his three Hrolf's Isle companions, shaking flies from their hot Northern manes and twitching their ears. As the wind strengthened, carrying warm scents from the dim blue coast, they stamped restless hooves, eager for land. Nightfall would be soon and sudden, with no long Northern twilight. That, as much as the warm breeze over his shoulder, told him how far they'd come from Hrolf's Isle, where now the winter sun would scrape the southern hills, and from dawn to dusk was a handful of hours.

Gil ran his gaze along the distant shore and glanced again at Floki. The earl was absorbed in his map of the farm he would grant Grimhildr and Ulf as his wedding gift. He added a line to the map and Grimhildr shook her head sharply and gave his shoulder a shove. Gil winced, not wanting to think what would happen to a man who did that, but with a patient smile, Floki re-drew the line. He looked up then, met Gil's eyes, and pointed inland.

Uneasily, Gil returned his gaze to the shore. The coast was rocky and challenging, hazed in spray. He sought a smooth strand to beach for the night and found none. Signaling Hakon, he turned seaward, sailing out beyond the next headland, secretly wishing Floki would take the helm.

Janetta stretched and yawned, and leaned comfortably against his shoulder, more confident of his skills than he was himself. Grimhildr, who had eyes in the back of her linen headdress, looked up, snapped her fingers, and pointed left and right. Gil sat up straight at the tiller and, with a reluctant sigh, Janetta moved a few inches away. Grimhildr shook her head and pointed again, and only turned back to her companions when a clear foot of helmsman's bench showed between them.

Despite her girlish pink cheeks, Grimhildr, as tall and sturdy as her brother Bjorn, was as strong as a man on the oar and as skilled with her throwing axes as any warrior. Even Gil had to admit she made a perfect chaperone. Janetta glared at the white headdress, as the dowry conference re-convened. "Why does she wish to marry at *all*," she whispered, "if she so disapproves of love."

Gil ducked his head when he answered. "Uh, maybe she's like … a … vigorous woman?"

"And is that not love?" Janetta gave him a smile that made him marvel again that she ever managed to live with nuns. She inched defiantly closer along the bench, until her bare, sun-freckled arm touched his again.

"Tell me more," he said.

"More? I tell you everything! Everything from when I was a child in Francia, too small to remember. Even the very day we came first to Camelot you know, and how the queen gave me this psalter." Her hands closed on the prayer book resting on her knees, "That I treasure still. And all the games and tournaments, and the great knights and their beautiful ladies ...."

"Tell me again," he murmured, his eyes on the nearing headland. "I like hearing it." He thought wistfully of her carefree childhood, lost, when Camelot fell. "It's like a beautiful dream that you wake up from and for a moment you still think it's real."

"It *was* real," she said sadly. The sadness vanished and she smiled joyfully. "And it will be again. You will make it real!"

"Me," he grinned. "All by myself."

"Well, not you alone," she conceded. "But there are so many who hold our cause – my father and his kin, all the exiled knights of Caledon. Your own good father, Lance'lot! And the mighty Palamedes. Surely Arthur will return and all will be well!" Her eyes lit on Floki's blond head, bent over the dowry map. "Even the good Northman holds true to Arthur's cause. And he is as fierce as a lion!"

Gil looked quickly up the deck at the earl and said quietly, "The only cause *he's* true to is Floki Magnusson."

She shook her head. "Then why does he sail to Rome?"

"For Danni," Gil answered at once. "And if the Golden Knight hadn't taken her, he'd never be here."

"Then it is not true he cares for none but himself," she said stubbornly. "I am glad for Danni, that she has so fierce a protector. I fear for her, all alone."

Gil looked away, squinting at the misty horizon. He couldn't let himself think of Danni, a prisoner in chains. His eyes strayed to Percy and Eirik, constructing a fort of cloaks and oars beneath the creaking mast. Oblivious of the adult game in which they were pawns, Danni's brother and the sea-king's hostage son turned the warship into their own happy playground.

"I would be so frightened," Janetta said. "But she is brave."

"*You* are brave," he said.

She shook her head again. "No. I ran away from my betrothal and hid with the Grey Sisters. Were I brave, I would have stayed and bought my father's favor."

"*No,*" he cried, slapping the tiller hard. "He betrothed you to the *Golden Knight* ... a usurper, a *monster* ...."

"Yes. And had I followed his wish, my father, my good stepmother, my small brother, would sleep on linen sheets in a fine hall. Instead, they are in Francia with only the forest for shelter. It is my fault."

Gil slapped the tiller again. "But even your father knows he was wrong, now. And your stepmother *helped* you escape. And Sir Alisander and Grania ...."

"My good fosterers," she murmured. "To live so many loyal years and die in exile."

Gil thought sadly of the grand old couple's last winter, with stones for pillows, on the heights of Hrolf's Isle. "It was their choice," he said.

She was silent. "You know everything about me," she said at last. Even my failings. I have no secrets. And still, I know nothing of you. You are all puzzles. *All* secrets. I do not even understand how you are here. Only, that I am glad you are."

"I'm glad too." He tightened his free arm around her and she leaned against his shoulder. *How am I here? How am I, Gil Lake from Greene Mountain Falls, at the helm of a longship on the sea-road to Rome? With a girl from King Arthur's Court?*

The wind shifted again as they rounded the headland. He adjusted his tiller and looked to the masthead where Floki's golden pennant fluttered royally. A surf pounded the rocky shore; spray glistened on the dragon figurehead. Gil listened to the slapping of the choppy sea against the bow and the familiar thrumming of wind in the rigging and glanced down at Janetta's dark head. "I crossed a sea no man can sail," he said.

"More puzzles!" She looked up, laughing in defeat. "Tell me one thing. One simple thing that I can understand. Your father's hall. Tell me of it. That can be no secret, and Lance'lot surely would have a fine hall. "

Gil shook his head. "It was just a little house."

She clapped her hands together, surprised and charmed. "A little house? Like the house the earl builds for me on the Holy Isle?"

"Well, bigger than *that*. But it wasn't a hall. Just a house."

"Where did his warriors sleep?"

"He didn't have any warriors. He wasn't Lance'lot then.

Only Laurent Lake." Gil shrugged. "Dad," he whispered. "He was just Dad."

"That is how you addressed him?" He nodded. "What was he like?" she asked shyly.

Gil stared ahead, over the ship full of lazing Northmen, the restless, head-tossing ponies in their pen, to the hazy sea beyond the headland. He tried to picture his father; not the weathered, battle-scarred face of Lance'lot, when he parted from him, in Francia, but Laurent, twenty years younger, in another world. "He was fun," he said at last. He shook his head abruptly. It was so long since just having fun was what life was about.

"Fun?"

"We played ...."

"Games? Like King's Table?" She gestured toward Rachel and Ismail, their heads bent close together over their gaming board. Gil suppressed a grin. Deep in soft-voiced discussion, they hadn't moved a piece since None.

"Sort of," he said, wrinkling his forehead as he strained to grasp the fading future. "We had a kind of window and we saw things through it, maybe warriors, or dragons, and we could make them move with ... with ...." He shook his head. "It's gone," he said.

She touched his arm, sharing his loss if not understanding it. He closed his free hand over hers and then laughed. "We had ships!"

"Longships!"

"No. Little ships."

"Like the skiff you sail to the Holy Isle."

"Littler. Tiny little ships, big enough just for one man. And an oar, with two blades," he said. Suddenly he was back on the river at home, kayaking with his dad and Crazy Ivan. She laughed gaily.

"Imagine, the mighty Lance'lot in so small a ship! And a little house for a hall. Had he taken vows, like the good father, Aidan, to live in poverty?"

"No," Gil said, sharper than he intended. "We weren't poor."

"Forgive me."

"It's not your fault. It's mine. I *thought* we were poor ... the house was so small and my bedchamber ...."

"You had your own bedchamber?"

"Yes. And it was bigger than the earl's." Her eyes widened. Gil's own swept the deck, resting on Ismail's frizzy dark head. Ismail, whose home in Africa was a mud-floored hut. And here, even the earl roofed the half-built hall that sheltered his household with old sails and slept in a room as bare as Aidan's cell. "We were rich," he said simply.

She absorbed that thoughtfully. "Then, surely, even though there was no hall and no great ship, you must have had fine horses. Tell me of the horses."

"No horses." She sat up to stare incredulously. "We didn't have horses."

"But how did you travel?"

How? He raked his mind for images, while his eyes raked the unpromising shore for a strand. At last a picture came, and, searching for words, he began, "Ivan had a sort of horse. Armored. Only, the horse and the armor were one thing." Gil could almost see it, and himself, riding pillion behind Ivan, fleeing Dr Fairchild's clinic. "It roared," he said.

"How fearsome a horse!" she gasped.

The image blurred and blended with another that eclipsed it: himself and Floki Magnusson galloping away from Merlin's Tower on the great white monkish plough horse. "I can't remember," he whispered.

She watched him sadly. "I understand. It is secret."

"But it's secret from me, too! Look, ask Rachel. She forgets things about home, too."

"But we went to her home. It was Deer Bay."

"Jorvik. She calls it York. And it was all different. Everything was different. And anyhow, Deer Bay is very old. My home is newer. If we sailed there, now, we'd just find forests and rivers and mountains and animals."

"No people?"

"Sure, people. But *other* people. They had their own kingdom, before ours."

She sat up straight, her eyes widening again. "You are usurpers?"

Gil sat silent, thinking suddenly of something he'd almost forgotten: Danni's story of Indian magic and the whirlpool of the Underwater Bridge. Uncomfortably, he said, "I guess we were."

A flash of white sand on the shore jerked his mind back to the present. He half-rose at the helm, studying the distant strand. It looked wide and open, curving along the dusky coast, the surf smooth and even. "Ace," he murmured. He sat back on the bench, turned to signal Hakon, and froze.

A dim shape had materialized directly ahead of the spray-drenched dragon. Huge and blue, it blotted out the darkening sky, as if dusk and mist had, by some alchemy taken solid form. Gil sprang to his feet, hands clutching the tiller.

"A fortress!" Janetta cried, "Like Mont Tombe."

Gil shook his head. It looked far bigger than the Frankish Viking's island-top hall. And it was smooth and featureless, more like the hunched back of some mythical animal, than anything built by man. His eyes glued to it, he called, barely turning, "Floki!"

The earl was already on his feet, striding down the deck to the helm. Gil looked up an instant and saw his white smile. "Look, Warrior," he said, pointing to the hulking form seeming to bar their way. "A sight to please your eyes."

"What is it?"

"What are they," Floki corrected. He pointed far out beyond where Hakon's prow shadowed their stern. "Look, with your good young eyes."

Gil peered into the mist and saw dim land there, too, low and dark, like Pentland, on the long-ago day they sailed first from Einar's Holm. "Africa," said Floki. He stretched both arms wide. "The Great Pillars, Warrior. The gates to the Roman Sea. Find us our strand. Tonight we drink ale."

"That one?" Gil said uneasily. He cast a hopeful eye at the streak of white off his load board. The distant rumble of surf grew louder in his ears.

Floki smiled. "Beyond here I know no more than you. An un-sailed sea, Warrior. Like a woman, the first night." He smiled again, dreamily, then slapped Gil's shoulder. "You say. Your eye is as good as mine."

Gil tightened his grip on the tiller. "Only," Floki leaned close, "Not there," he pointed to a barely visible line of ripples in the dark blue sea. Gil nodded and adjusted his course around the shoal, wondering if Floki knew he hadn't seen it. He'd learned so much since they left Hrolf's Isle. But always the sea had more to teach him.

When he was sure he had cleared the sandbar, he signaled again to Hakon and swung *Silver Dragon's* prow toward land. They beached smoothly, with only a whispering scrape of oak on forgiving sand. Janetta smiled proudly. "Well done, helmsman," the earl murmured over Gil's shoulder. "You tame that woman yet."

CHAPTER ONE

Twenty days on from the Pillars of Hercules, they swung due south and left the coast behind. "Sail for the sun, Warrior." Floki smiled, his eyes on the misty horizon. "In two days, we see land."

Gil obeyed the command with uneasy heart. They had no map and not even their bold young earl had sailed this southern sea. From Mont Tombe to the Great Pillars, they had hugged the shore, riding only far enough out to avoid rocks and shoals. The stormy Frankish sea gave way to warm green waters until, flanked by dolphins and sword fish, they slipped between the mighty rock sentinel and the hazy African coast, into the Roman Sea.

Here, too, they clung close to the shore, past vineyards and pine-topped bluffs, and hillsides dotted with sheep and goats. Each night they beached on narrow gravel strands, loosed the ponies to graze on the bleached grass, and replenished their supplies from the countryside.

They took no more than what was needed; a sheep or two, grapes and figs, flagons of oil and sacks of meal, and they killed no one who did not stand in their way. And if they chanced upon a village market, Floki paid for their provisions, willingly, in silver. But markets were few and there were sixty mouths to feed. *Now you are a Northman,* Floki had said once to Gil. *A true warrior,* he had meant. But a Northman was also a murderer and a thief.

The villages, when they found them, were small clusters of white houses grouped around a courtyard and a well. In narrow alleys between the houses, market stalls sheltered beneath dark Moorish tents. Rich with color and scent, they were filled with marvels for Northern eyes and treasures for Northern wives.

Floki allowed the crews ashore only in small peaceable groups and bargained courteously with farmers and merchants. Even when, bright hair shining in the gloom and sword at his side, he strode through the dusky alleyways, men stepped quietly aside and women gathered their children close. A Viking, even with his own two small boys in tow, was still a Viking.

Behind him, his sea-weathered warriors dug deep in their purses for silks and jewelry for the women of Hrolf's Isle. Percy and Eirik emerged from the tents clutching toy horses plaited from reeds, or miniature Saracen swords, and once, a bright green parrot that sat now, squawking splendidly in *Silver Dragon's* rigging.

Gil no longer argued when Floki divided silver between himself and his friends. His calloused hands and sun-burned face told him he had earned it. Besides, even Hakon Sea-Friend accepted coins from his cousin, calmly, as if it were his right.

In the first market, Gil and Ragi bought necklaces of glass beads for Janetta and Rachel. But Ismail also gave Rachel a gift, a bracelet set with colored stones that he had purchased secretly. Surprised, Gil watched Rachel adorn herself with both. Ismail smiled his happy white smile. Ragi's face darkened. Now, at every chance, new, competing ornaments were presented to Rachel, until she jingled when she walked, like Grimhildr, weighed down with Ulf's many pledges of love.

"You can't marry them both," Gil whispered to her, in the dark of a fire lit camp.

Rachel shrugged and admired one silver-laden wrist. "It's the way the game's played. And I'm not marrying either of them."

"Don't be so sure. Floki can give you to anyone he likes," Gil grinned. "It's the way the game's played." Rachel's eyes flashed and she swung a punch at him. He ducked his head. "Don't hurt Ismail," he said solemnly.

Aside from provisions for his ships, and a straw hat to shield his head from the sun, Floki himself ignored the bounty of the markets. Instead, he sought out men of the sea – fishermen, traders, any who shared enough of a common tongue to be understood – and gleaned from them what they knew of the sea-road to Rome. Then, just a day before, a man approached them as they filled water casks at a courtyard well, a man whose blond hair belied his eastern dress and marked him as a Northman. A Danish Viking called Halfdan, he had served the emperor in the Great City of the east and he knew the Roman sea as Floki knew the waters of his boyhood.

Crouching amid curious dark children, he scratched out their course in the goat-trampled dust. Now, trusting his word and the stars, they sailed on, far beyond the sight of any land, into blue emptiness.

"I thought it was small," Gil murmured to Ismail. The African boy looked up from the hook he was baiting and laughed.

"Is big sea," he said. He tossed the hook over the side. In moments he had a shining fish to join the heap at his feet.

"I had a map, once," Gil said. A dim picture rose of the globe on the bookshelf in his room. "It looked small on my map."

"The Mediterranean!" Rachel lifted a corner of the silk veil she and Janetta had draped over their heads for shade. "Odysseus sailed here for twenty years."

Gil's eyes strayed to Janetta's swift brown fingers, nimbly braiding Rachel's hair. Her sun-tanned arms were bare beneath the pleated sleeves of her linen under-dress. Cloaks and woolen tunics were folded away in sea-kists. The Northmen lounged bare legged in the sultry heat. At night, even the girls slept on the open deck. Gil returned his gaze to the dragon prow slicing the silken blue waters. "Who?" he said.

"Odysseus," Rachel sighed. "Did you ever learn anything at school?"

"Not a lot," Gil grinned. School seemed as far away as the cold seas of Hrolf's Isle. "What was he? A Viking?"

"No. He was not a Viking," Rachel said wearily. "Other people sail ships."

Gil nodded. This wide southern sea did not belong to Northmen. Now and again, ships appeared, out of the blue haze; strangers' vessels with curious rigging, manned by traders and fishermen in foreign clothes, speaking foreign tongues. Most, they ignored. But a few, with well-dressed crews and well-laden hulls, Floki plundered with casual ruthlessness, adding their Arabic coins, hack-silver, and even gold, to Grimhildr's treasure chest.

Ismail baited another hook. "Big sea," he said again. "I think not even Floki swims across it." He tossed his line over the side. The baited hook made a little splash, echoed by a bigger splash ten yards off their steering board; Floki swimming with strong, lazy strokes, between the two ships. Raising his head, he shook water from his plaited hair and waved playfully.

"Throw him a fish," Rachel said.

"I work hard for these fish!" Ismail protested. "He can catch his own."

Gil looked up at the sail. "Someone tighten that sheet," he grinned. "Let's leave him."

Ragi tautened the sail, but it sagged languidly in the heat. The ships were barely moving. Floki kept up with them easily.

"Call for oars," said Rachel, prodding Gil's leg with a bare toe. He grinned but shook his head, his eyes on *Sea-Raven*, gliding, sleek as a swan, through the morning mist. Erling, stripped to the waist, his hair and beard bleached white, sat half-dozing at the helm. Back propped again a sea-kist, Hakon shaded his eyes and squinted at his cousin in the water. They knew, as Gil knew, the wind would rise after None as it did every day and were content to wait.

A grey line of ripples drifted across the blue sea. At the masthead, the golden pennant fluttered briefly, before falling still. In a moment, it rose again. Gil smiled at the first touch of wind on his cheek and drank in a breath of air that smelled of sea and not of ponies and manure. Lionheart, leaning sleepily against the posts of his pen, raised his head and snorted, as if he, too, was weary of his own heavy scent. Ragi adjusted the sheet again. A ripple spread out from *Silver Dragon's* bow and broke gently around her swimming master's head.

Floki dove under the water and disappeared.

"Quick!" Rachel cried gleefully. "Now's your chance."

"You'd miss him," Gil said placidly, his eyes searching the

sea. Rachel laughed, but Janetta rose to her feet, and laid her fingers on the tiller beside Gil's hands.

"Do not leave him!" she cried. "He will drown."

"No such luck." Gil shrugged and pointed ahead of *Silver Dragon's* prow, where a sleek dark animal head had appeared. "You won't drown a selkie. Even here."

Hakon peered into the hot, white light and shook his fist. "Will you cease playing, so we can catch this wind?" he shouted. The dark animal shape disappeared in a splash of bright water. Hakon glowered at where it had been, until suddenly Floki's blond head appeared just off his load board. "And will you stay one thing or the other? I have enough of this changing about."

Floki flicked water at his cousin and then turned in the sea and swam smoothly to his own ship. Gil nudged the tiller, heading up into the wind. *Silver Dragon* slowed and settled gently into her modest wash. Bjorn leaned over the rail and extended his huge arm. Gripping it, Floki hauled himself, naked and dripping, half over the rail, and gestured to the deck. "Warrior! Throw down the cloak that I may cover myself."

Gil leaned and gathered a fold of the garment Floki had left draped across a sea-kist, lifted it, and held it aloft. He grinned suddenly. "Why? the women will not see. And if they do, they'll only laugh."

Rachel giggled behind him, but Floki only rested his chin on his bare arm and regarded Gil thoughtfully. "Warrior. The wind and sea make much noise. I do not hear that." He held his free hand out again and smiled sweetly.

"Right," Gil muttered. He tossed the cloak. Floki swung himself over the rail, wrapping it quickly around his body. He smiled again at Gil, as he pulled on his breeches and tunic.

"You grow bold, helmsman," he said. "Is it the southern sun? Or this Saracen you commune with?" He nodded politely at Ismail and his fish. "Or," he leaned over for his sword belt and buckled it around his waist. "Is it those Moorish sails beyond our prow?"

Gil stretched up and stared out to the misty sea. Red smudges marked the horizon. He shook his head. "I didn't see them," he whispered.

Floki gave the side of his head a quick light slap. "Make course for them."

"You sure? I think there's three of them."

"There are four. And hounds pursue the hare that runs. Go." He signaled *Sea-Raven* to follow them, and called out to his crew, "Come, my friends. I would have these Southerners see you in all your splendor."

The dozing Northmen aroused themselves and then, catching sight of the sails on the horizon, raced for their swords and shields. Floki bowed suddenly to Rachel and Janetta. "Your splendor, however, I would not reveal. Nor yours, Troll-Maiden." He beckoned Grimhildr and hurried all three into the black tent. Then he took his place beside Gil, with Percy and Eirik at either side.

Heeling before the strengthening wind, they sailed on; their rails lined with warriors bright with shields and steel. Floki laid his hand on Gil's shoulder. "What see you? Fishermen?"

Gil peered into the heat haze. The strangers' ships emerged from the mist and grew tall, with high sterns and triangular sails rigged from steeply slanting booms. Gil shook his head. "They look like us," he said.

Floki grimaced. "Not as pretty."

Gil stared at the rapidly approaching vessels, whose crews also lined their rails. "They're warships. But they're turning," he said hopefully, as the strange booms swung abruptly across the hulls.

"As they must," Floki said mildly, "They sail against the wind." He watched disapprovingly. "They are clumsy," he said. "But four, regardless." He laid his hand on the hilt of his sword, as the four ships returned to their course. "Are you afraid, helmsman?"

"What do you think?

"That is well. Your stupidity lessens. But do not show it, Warrior. All that stands between us and death is a story." Gil looked briefly at the approaching warships.

"What?"

"Remember, now, the two guards by Odin's Stone, the day I welcomed you home?" Gil nodded. Some welcome. "Two powerful warriors," said Floki, "Running from a fishing knife. Why? Because I tell them a story, and they believe. Now," he leaned close, "Another story.

"We, these sixty men on two slender ships, are as powerful as Odin. The winds obey us. The gods avenge us. Our swords are forged by giants. No steel can resist us. We are Northmen, Warrior the terror of the world. We look at death and laugh."

"We do?" Gil murmured.

"Yes!" Floki grinned and suddenly lunged at Gil with both hands, closing his strong fingers around his ribs.

"Ow! That ...."

"Tickles. Yes! Laugh, Warrior."

Gil laughed, gasping for breath. Beside him, Percy squealed and Eirik giggled happily. "Yes! It is funny! Laugh! Bjorn!" Bjorn blinked and then roared gleefully. "All of you!" Mirth swept down the deck and was echoed by Sea-Raven's crew across the water. Floki released Gil and suddenly raised his strong clear voice in a rowing song. A chorus instantly joined him, and fierce with shouts and thumping of shields, the singing swept across the warm sea like a wind from the fabled North.

The oncoming ships drew close, their ruddy sails lined four abreast, their hulls looming high above the water. Then two broke away, veering outward. "They surround us," Floki said lightly. "Hold course."

Gil could see figures aboard, now; men in loose white robes, crowding the decks. Several looked down from the raised sterns of each ship. In the hand of one, he caught the glitter of a grappling iron. "They're going to board us," he said.

Floki shrugged. "The taller the ship, the easier that is done. King's Son," he turned suddenly to Eirik. "Ride the dragon."

Eirik's eyes lit with pleasure. Dashing forward, he pushed his way through the throng of singing Northmen, scrambled past the girls' tent and the pony pen with its nervous, neighing beasts, and clambered up onto the curving figurehead.

"Show them steel!" Floki shouted.

Happily Eirik drew his sword, and riding the dragon like a rearing pony, waved the blade in a circle around his head. The Northmen cheered so loudly that the approaching strangers also heard, leaned over their rail, and craned necks to see. Gil saw the dark faces suddenly brightened by smiles.

"A wolf cub always delights," Floki said softly. "But it is yet the child of wolves."

As the leading ship glided past their prow, a tall, black-bearded man rose to his feet beside the helmsman. He pointed at the boy on the dragon and his rich laugh rolled across the water.

Floki signaled for silence from his crew. "Respect our new friends!" He bowed to his Saracen counterpart and his oarsmen all did the same. A light cheer arose from the white-robed men and, smiling broadly, their captain drew a fierce, curving sword and raised it high in salute. Floki drew his own and both leaned out as the ships slid by, making an arc of steel over the peaceful sea.

And then they were past. Gil watched the high sterns sinking lower and the red sails fading to smudges on the opposite horizon. His sweaty hands eased their grip on the tiller and he sat down heavily on his helmsman's sea-kist.

"You are well, Warrior?"

"Fine," Gil gulped. He forced a grin. "That was really smart," he said. "Really, really smart."

Floki smiled. "They had other prey," he said quietly.

Gil nodded, trying to stop his hands from shaking. Then he said, "So have we."

"Northman!" Floki's lean face broke into a grin and he slapped the top of Gil's head delightedly. Then he turned and shouted forward, "Down off there, now, King's Son! Before I must swim for you."

Floki took the helm himself, then, steering intently by the sun. Eirik, proud of his triumph over the Saracens, took up a stance at his side. Released from his duties, Gil sank wearily down on the sun-warmed deck, propped his aching shoulders against the load board rail, and was instantly asleep.

When he awoke, the sun was low and Janetta was curled beside him, her head resting on his shoulder, a forgotten spindle clutched in her hand. Gently, he untangled the new-spun wool and laid it on the deck. Then, boldly defiant of watching eyes, he enfolded her in both of his arms and returned to blissful sleep.

He awoke again at twilight. Floki was yet at the helm, steering now by the brightening stars. Beyond their steering board, the blue, cloud-draped peaks of an island floated in the amethyst dusk. A soft white surf broke against a curving strand. The scent of flowers drifted from the shore.

Gil sat up straight. "Look," he whispered to Janetta, "Land." She murmured something, but remained steadfastly sleeping, her head heavy on his shoulder. Lionheart whinnied suddenly and from the dim hills came an answering neigh. Janetta awoke and stared at the passing shore.

"Where are we?" she cried.

"Tir nan Og," Floki said, without turning. "I have crossed the sea no man can sail."

Her eyes widened. "This is so?"

"No," he laughed. "It is not so. But it is better. There lies Halfdan's Island Mountain. There," he gestured to the wave-washed strand, "We rest this night. And there," he swept an arm out to the darkening east, "But a day's sail further, lies the Port of Rome. We near the end of our journey. Then, only the best part remains."

"What is that?" she asked innocently.

"Battle!" Eirik crowed.

Floki ruffled his flaxen hair. "No, King's Son," he said with a smile. "The best part is the journey home." He stepped back from the steering oar and beckoned Gil. "Helmsman, take her in."

They camped, one more time, on an empty strand, building a driftwood fire on the wet sand between the two beached ships. Ulf and Erling led a hasty raiding party into the deepening dusk and returned with three sheep and a small, bleating, black goat that Floki refused to let them slaughter, because Percy cried.

Still, they feasted well on mutton and fish, and a basket of figs from the last market. After, Ulf stretched out with his boots to the fire and his hands clasped on his full stomach, looking up at the hazy southern sky. "This is a good land," he said. "I make a farm here and stay."

"Until the Moors steal Grimhildr," Erling said, grinning.

Ulf shook his head slowly. "Many, many Moors it will take to steal Grimhildr." He raised his head sharply, "And then," he said, "A year passes and they send her back!" Laughter rumbled around the fireside, while Grimhildr spun her spindle and pretended not to hear.

Floki smiled. "We are Northmen, Ulf. We belong in the snow." He stood up. "Come," he said to Hakon, "Where there are grazing beasts, there are shepherds. We set a guard." Two men from each ship were sent off to the surrounding high ground, over-looking the camp, and the girls were escorted to the safety of *Silver Dragon's* deck.

Gil went out to check once more on the tethered ponies and found them in the darkness by the gentle jingle of bridles and the snorts and grunts accompanying Lionheart's inner litany of complaints.

The grass is dry.

Think of it as hay. You like hay.

There's salt on the grass.

Soon we'll be in Rome. They have great grass, Gil lied.

I want my field.

Right. You're a North-pony. You belong in the snow. Which, by the way, you hate. He slapped Lionheart's dusty rump and walked back to the camp.

Just beyond the circle of firelight, he glimpsed a quiet dark figure standing alone at the edge of the sea. He paused; hand instantly on the hilt of his sword.

"Put away your blade, Warrior. Battle is over for the day." Gil remembered suddenly a night on Pentland, long ago; the first night of a journey grown longer than he could have imagined.

"How did you know it was me?"

"The way you walk. I hear that. Come, sit." Floki gestured to a smooth rock.

Gil took his seat beside the Northman, studying him curiously in the faint starlight. Something gently shining was tangled about his fingers. He held it up toward the unseen eastern sea, and Gil recognized the necklace he carried for Danni.

"Ulf is wrong," Floki said. "Ah, Warrior. Think of Odin's

Stone. And below, the white tides of the Holy Isle." He swept his hand left to right, as if they were standing on that Northern hill again, the tide race below them. "There, look, the little house where your lady shelters," he whispered, and Gil could almost see it. "And above," Floki looked up at the misty sky, "The winter stars so close, you bow, lest you strike your head upon them." He stared up a long time and said, "It is but days to Christ's Mass. Aiden makes his winter fast there, in the snow. And it will be winter yet when we return. Good!"

He turned to Gil. "A good time for a wedding. The harvest in. Little light and little work to do. He turned the amber beads in his hand, his fingers playing lightly with the jeweled golden cross. "It will be cold. But there will be ale and fires and feasting. Eoin will sing of us. Aidan will bless us. A cold night for a wedding, Warrior, but, ah, she will not be cold." He smiled quietly and slipped the necklace carefully into its leather pouch.

"And then," he whirled and grasped Gil's shoulders in a friendly hug. "Then you! Three years you work the farm I give you. Your first harvest: a betrothal. Your second harvest: a wedding. Your third harvest, ah, your third: a son. *Twin* sons! One you raise. One I foster." Floki's grip tightened in fatherly warmth and he laughed aloud, silencing for a moment the voices at the distant fireside.

Gil shook his head. *I can't. I'm just a kid. And I don't belong ....* But he looked down at the hands he had raised in protest. They were broad and calloused, a child's hands no longer. *I'm fifteen.* Again he shook his head, this time in amazement as a vision arose of Janetta and himself, reaping the silver barley of Hrolf's Isle.

He was fifteen. He was a man. And that cold Northern land was his home.

CHAPTER TWO

A t dawn, the wind failed them. Only the ripples cast by fish and birds stirred a sea of pearl blue silk. With lowered masts, they set out under oars toward a horizon lost in mist. The blurred white disc of the sun rose higher but no wind rose to meet it. Past Saxt and past None, the oarsmen rowed on, sweating and grumbling and slurping thirstily at the ale horns filled by Janetta and Rachel.

Floki took turns at the oar, and between them paced the deck or stood at Gil's shoulder adjusting his course. The sun tipped westward, casting their shadows forward onto the glassy sea. Hakon called from *Sea-Raven's* deck, "Enough, cousin. We would rest."

"And while we rest, our quarry makes his unholy reverence to Saint Peter, and turns again on the road North?"

"Men cannot row both day and night," Hakon shouted.

Floki smiled and shrugged. "Men of Shetland, perhaps not. But men of Hrolf's Isle?" He looked up and down his own rowing benches, grinning, and his weary oarsmen cheered.

"Men of the High Island!" Ragi shouted and raised a fist.

"Men of the Horse Island!" two others returned, lowering eager oars.

Hakon threw his hands in the air and signaled his own oarsmen.

"But wait!" Floki called, "We lend you Grimhildr! With one hand, worth three Shetlanders on the oar. With the other, she spins fine wool!" Hakon flung a curse over his shoulder as both ships surged on into the dusk.

Darkness fell, the sky cleared overhead, and the wind came, at last, with the stars. Bruised, aching hands raised masts and freed the long-furled sails. Ghostly beneath a velvet sky, the two ships rode on through the night.

Shore birds came with the dawn, circling their masts and crying a plaintive welcome. Percy's parrot raised its green wings and squawked in protest. Gil peered blearily into the reddening east, eager for the sight of land, but still he smelled the port before he saw it. His nostrils twitched at the sweet scent of wood smoke, soon joined by the salt and seaweed stench of a tidal shore, and then the rank odors of manure and middens and rotten fish, all heavy on the sultry air.

The sun burned bright overhead, but a low mist yet cloaked the sea. Then suddenly a ship appeared, off their steering board, and then another, and then many, all around; squat purposeful silhouettes of traders and fishermen through which the longships glided, exotic as dragons.

Gil looked about warily for signs of threat, or indeed of fear, but no one seemed to notice them. At his shoulder, Floki laughed. "We come to Rome, Warrior. We are not the first strangers to ground our keel here."

The mist thinned and broke apart in wisps and streamers, revealing the walls and towers of a fortified port, and red-tiled roofs of jumbled buildings beyond. In their midst, a great river opened into the sea, trafficked by ships of all sizes, bare masts gliding above roof tops as they rode inland under oar. Wharfs lined the riverbanks, bristling also with masts and crowded with men and beasts; bony brown cattle, flocks of goats, and lean horses pulling laden carts. Aboard *Silver Dragon*, the four ponies neighed nervous greetings to their southern counterparts.

In the lee of the shore, Gil called for his oarsmen and sent Ragi and Ciarnan to lower the sagging sail. Alerted by the slowing of the ship, Janetta and Rachel tumbled sleepily from their tent and ran to Gil's side. "This is Rome?" Janetta cried, staring at the port.

Floki shook his head. "It is to Rome as Hrafn's Ayre is to Deer Bay," he pointed to the river mouth, "and by the sea-road, there, as far from it, as Deer Bay from that strand." He studied the well-defended harbor and then abruptly stepped beside Gil and swung the steering oar, turning *Silver Dragon's* prow up the coast. "We take that, however, on Halfdan's word," he said, signaling Hakon. "For we go overland."

"Overland!" Gil cried in dismay, his eyes yet on the inviting sweep of the river.

"Ah, the Viking!" Floki said happily. "He scorns the dust of the road on his boots!" Still, he kept his hands firm on the tiller, as the coast glided past. Then suddenly, he stepped back, relinquished the helm again to Gil, and pointed at the harbor wall. "There, Warrior, on the near shore, and again on the far. You see them?"

Gil shaded his eyes against the glare. A broad wooden capstan, rimmed with protruding wooden poles, surmounted the massive stone wall. From it, heavy metal links ran down into the water. Across the river, an identical device mirrored it. "What are they for?" he asked.

"For that," Floki indicated the dark wet links. "They lay a chain across the river, Warrior. With those machines, they raise it. They use horses. Or slaves. They will have many of both."

Gil imagined the great cylinders turning and the chain rising, like a sea serpent, across the flow of the river. "It's like a gate. They can close the harbor."

Floki smiled. "This is not the Northlands, Warrior," he said quietly. "Here there are laws and rules and men with armies to see they are obeyed. We might find ourselves unwilling guests; our ships forfeit. Or sold into slavery, to pay some tax invented at the moment."

"But there are laws, you said," Rachel protested. "And this is Rome."

"It is Rome. And with as many earls as it has laws, all at each other's throats. Again, the word of Halfdan, but he knew and liked the place. The Great City, under the Emperor's eye, was less amusing." He paused and smiled at Rachel. "He is a Viking, Pretty Hawk, beneath his gorgeous robes. He likes battle."

"Good!" Bjorn shouted from his oar. "I like battle."

"And I," Eirik echoed, worming his way under Floki's cloak. "We fight them!"

Floki closed his hand on the nape of the boy's neck and shook him like a mother cat shaking a kitten. "No. We have our own battle, King's Son. We have no time for theirs. We travel overland. There will be traders and pilgrims and farmers, and we may hide among them, like the poor farmers we are." He paused, his eyes yet on the harbor wall. "Nowhere on that river can I hide two ships."

Bjorn groaned in frustration, and his groans were echoed by others as the weary oarsmen left the port behind and drove on, past the last remote farmhouse to a barren gravel beach amid dark marshes.

The moment they grounded their keel, Floki jumped down to the strand, signaling Gil to follow. "Come with me, helmsman. We go hawking."

"Hawking?" Hakon glowered down from his own beached craft. "We row all day and half the night. No one eats. And now you play?"

Floki smiled innocently. "What, Sea-Friend, are there none among you who can lay a fire?" He turned and saw Janetta watching and smiled again. "Here. This child will show you how." He reached up to the deck and lifted her down, and then did the same for Rachel, setting her lightly on the wet shingle. "Now, Pretty Hawk," he murmured, "We seek our road." He strode off down the strand, with Rachel at his side. Lionheart's frantic whinny of abandonment pierced the morning air as Gil trotted guiltily after.

In the shelter of a muddy stream bed, just out of sight of the ships, Floki tossed his sword belt on the ground and called Rachel to him. "Fly high and swift," he said. "We are not among friends." Intent already on the sky, she stepped within the circle, spoke the blessing, and vanished in a blur of wings.

The wind fell still and the sun rose higher, warming Gil's back as if it were spring. Small insects floated over the oily waters of the stream. Wood smoke from Hakon's campfires stained the blue sky, and Gil sniffed hungrily at the scent of it, dreaming of breakfast. Floki shaded his eyes and peered at the sky. "She flies too long."

"No wonder," Gil said. "We're miles from anywhere." But then a church bell rang out suddenly in the still air, marking the hour and undoing the illusion of isolation. Gil scrambled up

the crumbling bank of the stream and scanned the horizon for
a roof or a tower, but the swaying grasses hid all. Then, high in
the perfect sky, a tiny dot appeared and homed unerringly on
their refuge. "She's here!" Gil cried.

Floki leapt to the bank beside him and held up the looped
sword belt for his returning hawk. Sure as an arrow, she
swept through it and landed, a laughing, red-haired girl amid
the marsh grasses. "You fly too far, Pretty Hawk," Floki said
solemnly. "One day, you lose your way back to me."

Rachel sat up. "But surely women find you as the Falling
Star finds the North?" She giggled as he reached down for
her hand and lifted her to her feet, but then she straightened,
smoothed down her skirt, and grew at once serious. Turning
to face inland, she stretched out her slender hand to the
encircling marshland. "All around, on every side, there's
marsh and swamps. They go on as far as I could see, with
the river running through them. But over there," she pointed
to the right, "A road runs inland, filled with people; soldiers
on horses, pilgrims, traders, farmers with mules and carts; a
whole world of people."

Gil squinted in the bright sun, staring at the silent waving
grasses. "We heard a church bell."

"There's a monastery. I flew over the cloister. There were
monks, like at Hy. And a lovely bell tower full of doves." She
looked aside, suddenly, and Gil suspected she, at least, had had
breakfast. "I flew higher, then," she said. "And I saw the road
going on, with marshes all around. But beyond, there were hills,
and on them, a white city."

"A city on a hill," Floki said.

"A city on seven hills," Rachel whispered, her eyes aglow.
"Rome."

The ships were secure above the tideline, awnings stretched
over lowered masts, when they returned. Parties of Northmen
trudged up the strand, gathering sacks of driftwood. Bjorn,
shouldering a water cask, passed them on his way to the stream.
Ismail cantered by on Lionheart, leading the three Hrolf's Isle
ponies out to grass.

Floki nodded approvingly and then strode to where Hakon

sat gutting fish by the fire. "A fine camp, Sea-Friend." He smiled at Janetta kneading dough beside Grimhildr, "She teaches you well."

Hakon glowered and cast fish guts into the flames. Grimhildr dusted flour disdainfully from her hands. "No strength in this meal," she grumbled.

"Ah, Troll-Maiden, soon you are home with the fine barley of Hrolf's Isle." Floki raised his gaze, took in his sea-weary crew, and beckoned them closer. "Soon you are all home, with silver for your women and stories for the hearthside, stories until your heads grow grey." They grinned and gave a tired cheer, proud, and homesick, at once.

"But first," he nodded to Gil, "My helmsman and I have business in this city." His eyes swept the ranks of men. "Those I would have with us: Ciarnan, wise in the ways of churchmen. Ragi, Man of the High Island, cliff-climber. My Saracen," he nodded at Ismail. "Calm head, swift sword." He paused. "Now, who likes battle?" He smiled at Bjorn.

"Me!" Eirik pushed in front. Floki moved him aside, but said, "Yes. A tale for your father's hearth. But only if you guard Bjorn, as before."

Percy ran to join Eirik on Bjorn's other side. "Yes," Floki smiled. "And you."

Hakon stood up and shook his head.

"Troll-Maiden," said Floki. "We make a pious nun of you, and Ulf's hopes are in vain. And you," he smiled at Janetta, "Who know the ways of nuns. And last," he beckoned Rachel, "You who speak the tongue of churchmen."

"Cousin!" Hakon exploded. "With women and children you fight a king's army?"

"Yes, Sea-Friend." Floki smiled. "A king's army. And with sixty Vikings I do not defeat him. So, I use my wits instead. A thing, I know, you do not understand." He turned to Janetta. "Go to my sea-kist, little nun, and bring the garment I wear at Mont Tombe."

Janetta ran to the ship and returned with a bundle of rough cloth. Floki wrapped it around his lean body and solemnly raised its hood, covering his bright hair. Gil grinned and snatched up a long, thin piece of driftwood. "Here!" he said, "Do battle like the brothers of Hy."

"Staff and penitent's robes," Floki said, taking it with a smile. "Now, on the road, I am a pilgrim. They," he gestured to his chosen companions, "A pilgrim's family. With them, I disappear. No one sees me or speaks of me. Which is good. For when word of us reaches our quarry, the hound becomes the hare." He paused, and added quietly, "And word will reach him. But with Odin's help, I reach him first."

"Very holy," Hakon said drily. "Aidan rejoices."

"A day to come," Floki said, "I make Christian penance. This day belongs to my father's gods." A rough cheer rose from his crew and he smiled. "Ah, Vikings all. Even you who wear Christ's cross," he nodded to a tall Shetlander's silver pendant. "So be it. As Vikings we come. And as Vikings, we take our leave. But on this shore you must live peaceable as monks. Sea-Friend," he turned to Hakon, "I leave you Grimhildr's bridal kist."

"What?" Hakon's black brows drew close.

"The silver, cousin. Use it, all of it if you must. Trade at the port for food, tools, any needs. But ride at anchor, always, beyond the harbor wall. Still, word will spread that you are here. Should any ask, say only you await a pilgrim. Let no man speak my name, and, no matter how provoked, let no man draw steel, until I return."

"And if you do not return?" Hakon said quietly.

"Cousin! I am Floki Magnusson."

"Who is not immortal." Hakon met Floki's playful gaze with a bleak, humorless glare. *"How long do I wait, Cousin?"*

Floki sighed and looked at the blue southern sky. "Sea-Friend," he said. "You weary me." He shrugged. "Here: should fortune fail us, then with my last dying breath, I send you my hawk." His gaze strayed to Rachel and softened. He reached out and lifted her chin with his fingers. "When you see her, raise sail for home." Rachel drew back and he let his hand slip from her face. Suddenly serious, he said, "Find her a gentle mate in the North." He turned to Gil, "Helmsman, the ponies ...."

But Rachel thrust herself between them. "Stop it!" she shouted. "Stop giving me to people."

"What?"

"Just stop it. Leave me alone!"

"Leave you alone?" Floki stepped back, stunned. "And let any man who wishes clip your wings?" He shook his head. "Hakon is kind," he said reasonably. "He will choose well."

"No!" she stepped closer, and raising a fist, shook it in his face. The circle of men stared open-mouthed. "He will not choose. *I* will choose. Me!" Whipping around, she strode away, her small hands still balled into fists at her side.

"Right," Gil murmured. Cautiously, he edged backward, but Floki's hand suddenly fell on his shoulder and remained there as Rachel mounted the ship's gangplank and disappeared inside her tent.

"Warrior," he said at last. "Can women ever be pleased?"

Gil shuffled his feet. "The ponies?" he said hopefully.

The bell of the hidden monastery rang Saxt as they set out. Floki led, following the sound into the trackless marsh. Bjorn guarded the rear. Grimhildr shepherded Percy through ditches and bogs. Rachel and Janetta hauled Eirik out of pools. Ciarnan, Ragi, Ismail, and Gil struggled behind, leading the recalcitrant ponies.

Laden with provisions and clanking with shrouded arms, the beasts skidded on haunches into streams, danced around tussocks of springy turf, and whinnied in dismay as marsh water splashed their bellies. Gil tightened his grip on Lionheart's rein. *It's a bog. Like on Hrolf's Isle. It's not like you come from the driest place on earth.*

Lionheart flared his nostrils and rolled his eyes. *It smells.*

No worse than you. Gil swatted at flies and thought longingly of the smooth waters of the great river, winding inland from the sea.

Ahead, Floki retrieved Eirik from a chest-deep pool and swung him up onto his shoulders, without breaking stride. Gil took pity on Percy, then, and boosted him onto Lionheart's back. Already, his own boots were sodden, his trousers caked with black mud.

Squinting at the sun, he strove to orient himself in the baffling landscape and yearned for the compass he had given to Floki, who never seemed to need it at all. Weaving his way through bewildering channels and featureless meadows, the Northman struck as sure a course as he did at sea. Before the bell rang for None, the tile roof of its bell tower was in their sight.

They came out onto a roadway of ancient stone slabs. A boy was driving goats along it, and at once Percy wanted down to run and play with them. Floki set Eirik down, too, and smiled as both children plunged into the jostling flock, shouting to their boyish keeper in their alien tongues. "When grown men are as children," he said to Gil, "Sword smiths will go hungry." He smiled again, and then turned his eyes to the road ahead. "But that day is not here. Come, Warrior, we learn what these churchmen have to say."

The land rose slightly before them, and the modest summit of the road offered startling views over the flat countryside to where a great bend in the river glistened in the sun. Below, the monastery appeared a small oasis in a desert of marsh grass. But as Gil studied its gardens and vineyards, he saw that the oasis was once much larger. Traces of field borders remained. The ruins of much grander buildings were scattered, half overgrown, amid encroaching wilderness.

"A Roman villa," Rachel said. She pointed to a row of marble pillars, gleaming white in the sunlight, which formed a long, roofless rectangle. One end wall yet stood and snugged against it like a lamb beside its mother, was the monastery church. Bits of re-used marble framed its doorway and enhanced the tall brick bell tower with bands of white.

"It was big," Gil said, his eyes seeking out the shadowy lines of walls and ditches beneath the marshland. "Look, the fields ran right to the river. And here," he pointed a dozen yards beyond the road to a jumble of fallen stones, worked and carved with figures and designs. More great pillars lay among them like half-buried dragon bones. "What happened to it?"

Rachel smiled. "'*Sic transit gloria mundi.*'"

"What?" Gil raised an irritated eyebrow.

"History," she said, with another smile.

They were greeted at the roadside by a brother in black

robes, holding out both hands in welcome. Smiling kindly, he shepherded them into a courtyard bounded by the walls of church and cloister on one side, and two low, thatch-roofed buildings on the other.

From within the open doors of one came the flicker of a cooking fire and the scent of wood smoke. Long plank tables stood before it, in the open air. A crowd of people waited nearby; men and women, children playing noisily or solemnly guarding bundles of belongings, old men, turning their faces to the winter sun.

Many were dressed, as Floki, in penitents' robes and leaning on road-worn staffs. But others looked like farmers or merchants, with their goods bound for market. A small flock of black sheep milled beside the church. Red hens clucked in wicker cages. Beneath a sheltering tree, two donkeys brayed and shifted their mountainous burdens of pottery and rolls of silk. Amid the noise and clamor, the black-robed brothers slipped back and forth, offering water from cool jugs and patting the heads of children as they passed.

The second building stood well apart, its door closed and windows shuttered. None of the crowd approached it, but two brothers came from the kitchen with baskets and earthenware jugs, and entered, drawing the door closed behind them. Rachel's smooth brow furrowed as she watched and she plucked at Gil's sleeve. But Floki drew her attention to the smiling monk. "He would speak with us, Pretty Hawk."

Rachel stepped forward then, conversed with the brother in Aidan's church Latin, and turned back to Floki. "He offers us food and drink for our journey." She pointed to the tables where more brothers were setting out pottery dishes laden with vegetables and bread.

Floki cast his eyes over the monk's fraying robes, his lean face, and bare feet. "They are poor," he said to Rachel. "We do not take their food."

"It is their duty to feed pilgrims," she said simply. "They are bound by their vows."

"But we are not pilgrims," Floki shook his head. "Tell them we have eaten." Gil gave the bountiful table a wistful glance and resigned himself to another meal of dried fish, as the man turned regretfully away. But Floki called him back, suddenly. "Ask him where I would seek a pilgrim," he said carefully. "A brother from the North who travels from Francia to Rome."

Again, Rachel translated. The monk smiled, burst into a cheerful flow of Latin, and then nodded happily as she recited: "'Seek him where Northerners enter, by Saint Peter's Gate. Seek him in the Saxon quarter, or among the Franks. Seek him at the tombs of the martyrs and the saints. But first, and last, seek him at the shrine of Peter. There, every pilgrim is found.'"

Floki nodded gravely. "I thank him."

The monk smiled innocently in return and gestured, once more, toward the laden tables. But a sudden shout drew the attention of all away. Two men in pilgrims' dress had entered the courtyard, leading a mule on which was mounted a third. Hunched over the animal's neck, the rider swayed awkwardly with each step, clutching his cloak and shaking with cold. One of the brethren ran to assist him before he fell.

Helped down from his mount and supported by his friends, the shivering pilgrim was led across the courtyard to the shuttered building standing alone. As the door opened to allow him entrance, a shaft of late sunlight lit the dim interior, revealing blanket wrapped forms huddled on straw mattresses on the floor. Silent monks moved among them and one turned to welcome the newcomer into their midst.

"What's wrong with them?" Gil asked uneasily.

"Fever," Janetta said. Her eyes were wide. Beside her, Ismail nodded.

"Can we, like, catch it?" Gil whispered to Rachel. She was looking past the building and over the courtyard wall to the fading sky. He caught her arm. "Can we?"

"Not from them," she shook her head. But before he could feel relief, she waved toward the rough, wet land surrounding them on every side. "From that. The marsh. It's malaria, Gil."

"Malaria?" he blinked. "Like in Africa?"

"Like anywhere there's swamps and mosquitoes," she said sharply. "Come on," she grabbed his arm.

"Where are we going?"

"To tell Floki we have to stay here until morning. We can't travel through the marsh at night."

They found the Northman coaxing Percy and Eirik away from a cage full of hens. Rachel shoved Gil forward. "What about you?" he hissed.

"Women don't choose campsites. You're his helmsman. He'll listen to you."

Floki listened distractedly, struggling with the two giggling children. He swung Eirik up onto a pony's back and shook his head as Percy ducked under Lionheart's belly to escape. "When he kicks you, you know not to do that," he said mildly, and then, turning to Gil, "No, Warrior. We trouble these good men no further. They have work enough without us. We travel until Compline and camp until dawn. I would be in Rome before Saxt."

"Floki, it's not safe," Rachel burst out. He looked surprised.

"What ruffles the feathers of my fearless one?" He grinned and touched her cheek playfully. "Does someone threaten her with a husband?"

She ignored him. "That man. Those people," she waved to the shuttered building. "They're sick and they'll probably die. It's the marsh. The marsh is full of sickness."

Floki smiled. "They are Southerners. Weak."

"No!" she shouted. "Anybody. You. Me. Even Bjorn can get sick in the marsh."

He shrugged. "Then it is Odin's will." He turned away, pursuing Percy. Gil blocked his path. "Warrior. We lose the light."

"Wait," Gil said. "Remember the little animals? The ones under the rocks? The ones that frighten you?" He took a deep breath and made creeping feet of his fingers in the air. Floki flinched. "Centipedes. Remember?"

"The marsh has those animals?"

Gil glanced quickly at Rachel and said, "No. Not those. Something else. Something worse."

But Floki laughed, then. "There is nothing worse. Warrior, I go now. Come if you please." He hoisted a re-captured Percy up onto Lionheart's back. Gil turned to Rachel and raised his hands in defeat. She looked around desperately, and suddenly dashed across the courtyard to where the silk merchant's laden donkey grazed beside its dozing master.

"Floki!" she called. "I want these." She tugged loose a length of silk and smiled, first at Floki, and then at the awakened merchant. Floki paused at the gateway and then handed the reins of the animals to Grimhildr. He looked puzzled but was already reaching beneath his pilgrim's robes for his purse.

"Which pleases you, Pretty Hawk?" he said, smiling gently.

"All of them."

"All! So many veils!"

The merchant, fully awake, began pulling length after length of silk from the donkey's panniers, his own smile broadening the while. "This, this, and this," Rachel said, marking them off, one by one. "Eight. Nine. Ten." Floki stood as patient as a browbeaten husband, as she turned and, with another bright smile, said, "Eleven."

Counting on his fingers for the merchant, he said, "Twelve. We take twelve." The merchant unfolded his scales and grinning from ear to ear, crouched in the dust of the courtyard and weighed Floki's silver. The deal concluded, Floki beckoned Gil and Ismail to his side and loaded the silk on their shoulders. He looked happier, even than the merchant. "Warrior!" he leaned close as Gil transferred his burden to a pony's back, "I have the answer! *Silver* pleases women! Even those who want no husbands." He cast a cheerful glance at Rachel. "A little silver and they smile."

Beyond the monastery, the road ran broad and straight, its ancient stone slabs worn smooth by centuries of travelers. When they stopped at last, to eat, the way they had come stretched far back into the dusk. Peering across the endless marshes, Gil strained for a glimpse of the distant sea. Still, Floki ruled they had not gone far enough, and, as the moon rose, they prepared again to set out. Rachel watched and then ran to the pony bearing her bundles of silk.

Shaking out the first roll, she draped it over herself like a tent, and grinned up at Percy, seated already on Lionheart's back. "Your turn!" She unwound the silk veil and tossed it over his head. Percy giggled and flailed about happily and made ghost noises at Gil. Lionheart stamped and tossed his frightened head and Gil steadied him with a tug on his rein. "You, too!" Rachel flung him a bundle of silk. Clutching it, he stared at her dumbly. But Ismail caught the length of cloth she threw to him and swiftly veiled his dark head.

"All of you," said Rachel, waving to Ciarnan and Ragi. "All of you. Cover yourselves. Gil," she urged, "Do it."

He lifted the silk veil. "Mosquito nets," he said quietly.

Rachel gave him a weary look. "What did you think?" He shrugged and self-consciously covered his head with the silk. It was stuffy inside, but he could see clearly through the fragile weave; clearly enough to pick out the black specks of circling insects.

"Janetta!" he cried, "Quickly!" But Rachel was already draping a length of emerald veiling over her black hair.

"It is very beautiful," she said helpfully, though she cast Gil a baffled glance.

Grimhildr seemed quite taken with her new veil, raising it proudly over her linen headdress. But Eirik shoved his away. "I am a man."

Rachel spun and thrust the silk at Floki. "Show him," she said. "Put it on."

He drew back. "I veil myself like a woman?" He smiled at Bjorn and Bjorn laughed his rumbling laugh. Eirik planted himself between them and glared at Rachel, his chin jutting in defiance.

"Okay," Gil muttered. He strode forward, raised both hands and brought them together with two sharp claps. Eirik jumped and Lionheart snorted. Gil opened his hands and searched the palms, and then thrust them in front of Floki. "There," he said, pointing with the forefinger of his right hand to the two squashed insects on his left. "The animals."

Floki peered at the black smudges on Gil's grubby palm. "Those?" Gil nodded. Floki shook his head. "No, Warrior," he said reasonably. "I do not fear them. They are small. And they have not the legs." He smiled and shrugged.

"But they kill you," said Ismail suddenly. Bjorn laughed

louder, pointed at a whining insect, and drew his sword.

"I kill him first!" he roared, mightily slicing air.

Floki laid his hand on Bjorn's shoulder and gently moved him aside. "What say you, Saracen?"

"The animals bring sickness." Ismail raised his hands in apology. "It is so."

Floki stood in silence. Then, without speaking, he took the rest of the silk veils from Rachel. Ignoring the child's protests, he spread one over Eirik's head. "Bjorn," he beckoned, "Do as I say." As Bjorn draped himself in voluminous silk, Floki veiled his own head and bowed to Rachel. "Is that well now?"

"Yes," she said grimly. She turned away and then spun back to face him. "Why?" she demanded. "Why do you believe him, and not me?"

Floki smiled beneath his silken veil. "You know from books," he said. "But he knows from living, Pretty Hawk." His smile broadened. "Still, you are more beautiful in your veil, than he in his. Indeed, very beautiful." Rachel turned her back, but he called after her, "Behold, I am a pilgrim no longer, but a Saracen with his harem of brides. And here," he slung his arm over Bjorn's shoulders, "Is the most beautiful of all!"

They camped that night in the ruins of another villa. The moon was long down, the ponies stumbling with exhaustion, and the children asleep on their backs. Floki lifted them down without waking them and covered them with his cloak. Rachel stretched their silk mantles over the boughs of a cypress tree, making a secure little tent.

"Ah, they sleep like Vikings," Floki said. "Beneath a green mast." He laid his hands on the dark tree bough and looked up at the stars. "And do you make an awning for me, now, my hawk?"

"Make your own," Rachel snapped. Gil grinned. He cast a futile glance at Janetta, but Grimhildr was already hastening her far away. Resigned, he joined Ismail, Ciarnan, and Ragi, making their beds in the roofless house, and spread his mosquito net over two broken pillars.

Floki flopped on the tile floor beside him. "Am I a troll, Warrior?" he said. "Do I drink the blood of children?"

"Try more silver," said Gil.

At dawn, Gil woke to the whinny of a horse. Thrusting aside the dew-sodden silk veil, he leapt to his feet. The sound came again, Lionheart's frantic neigh. "Ismail! Ciarnan!" he prodded his sleeping friends with his foot, as he buckled his sword belt around his waist. They stirred beneath their mosquito nets. "The horses!" Gil cried. Not waiting for a response, he ran from the roofless villa.

Beyond lay the row of cypresses that marked the road, and across it, the open meadow where, last night, they had tethered the beasts. Spurred by images of wolves and horse thieves, Gil ran, weaving around heaps of masonry, his feet skidding on broken tiles. Climbing the steep banking of the roadway, he stumbled to a halt.

Where the road crested a small rise, a man stood, surrounded by all four of their ponies. Lionheart turned his head, and seeing Gil, reared. *He's taking me away.* Gil broke into a run, his hand reaching for his sword hilt, and then, abruptly, stopped and peered at the figures silhouetted against the pink sunrise sky. The man stood motionless, leaning across the back of a Hrolf's Isle pony, his attention fixed on something far away. The cowl of his pilgrim's robe hung loose, revealing a golden mane.

Gil dropped his sword hand and resumed walking at an unhurried pace. *And you've never seen him before in your life.* He mounted the crest of the hill and gave Lionheart's rump a resentful slap. *Thanks a lot for waking me up.*

"Warrior," Floki beckoned him without taking his eyes from the distance. "Behold."

The marsh below was shrouded in morning mist, but beyond, floating as on a sea, lay orchards and vineyards, cultivated fields and pastures dotted with cattle. Gleaming in the first light of day, the river wound through them, flowing down from the great walled city surmounting the crests of its seven hills.

The city wall itself dwarfed the ships on the water and

the dawn traffic of the roads that ran on all sides to its gates. Within, stood buildings of a grandeur Gil had not seen in all this world. Amid the white shining monuments of the ancients, clustered churches of every size, their bell towers catching the early sun. Around and among them were other towers, sturdy fortifications, so tall and so many that the horizon bristled like the back of an angry boar. "Halfdan's delight," said Floki. "A city at war; every earl his own emperor."

Gil shook his head, too caught up in his awe to speak or to hear the footsteps approaching, until a slim hand slipped into his own. "Janetta," he whispered. "Look." He turned and saw the city and the dawn reflected in her eyes, and for a moment all of it existed just for them.

Then Eirik and Percy blundered into his side, swords drawn, squabbling over who would take Rome first, and in moments, all of their party were there, pointing and exclaiming over the sights before them. Then, suddenly, a bell began to ring, the sound carrying clearly over the still air. It was joined by another and another, and then hundreds, as all the churches of Rome called their faithful to prayer.

"Lauds," Gil murmured, and Janetta crossed herself and slipped to her knees in the dust of the ancient Roman road. Still clasping her hand, Gil did the same. Floki looked from the city with its chiming bells to the boy and girl by his side. Then he, too, sank to his knees and bowed his head over his pilgrim's staff. One by one, their companions followed. Only Bjorn remained, standing alone like a forgotten child, until, with a puzzled shake of his head, he knelt beside his earl at the threshold of Saint Peter.

CHAPTER THREE

"Rome stinks like a byre!" Grimhildr wrapped the tails of her linen headdress over her nose and turned her face from a man urinating in the gateway of the city wall. "And Romans have the manners of cattle."

Floki lowered the rain-soaked cowl of his robe and grinned cheerfully. "You are spoiled by Viking courtesies, Troll-Maiden. Where else is man or beast to go in such a place?" He waved a hand to the mass of people and animals sheltering together beneath the soaring arch.

Outside, a grey, winter downpour cascaded down the ancient walls, puddled the roadway, and splattered sullenly on the grey waters of the river beyond. The bright dawn had dulled to cloud and rain. Long before they reached the city, their garments were soaked, the ponies' coats steaming. Their fellow travelers, who grew in numbers as smaller roads joined their own, trudged stoically beside them.

Many were farmers, up with the dawn to bring produce into the city. But many more were penitents, bringing only themselves and the burdens of their souls. Staggering with exhaustion, or stumbling with excitement, they hurried on; some staring up at the city in tearful ecstasy, others chattering happily in a dozen different tongues.

At the foot of the wall, two men dressed like brothers of Hy stopped and fell to their knees in prayer. Floki also halted and laid a restraining hand on Gil's shoulder. Raising his gaze to the rain-drenched stone, he looked left and right, as if in pilgrims' wonderment. But Gil caught the sharp, cold battle light in his eyes. "Take care, Warrior," Floki murmured. "Behind doors, in the shadows, above our heads. By chance, our noble friend precedes us."

Gil wiped rainwater from his nose with the back of his grubby hand. "Even if he has," he said, "How would he find us?" He stared around at the close-pressed crowds. "How will we find him?"

"I find him." Floki smiled. He turned to the others. "King's Son. Walk at my side."

Eirik's happy white grin spread across his dust-smeared face. He jumped down from his pony and took his place proudly, small hand on the hilt of his sword. Floki smiled again. "Another tale for your father's hearth. At ten winters, you set foot in Holy Rome."

Two strides into the gloomy arch, Lionheart balked and reared. Percy shouted and clung to his mane. Gil tugged impatiently at the lead. *What is it now?* Lionheart's eyes rolled in terror, as two men, mounted on enormous iron-shod horses, clattered through the arch, leading a dozen slaves. Fair, blond and far from their Northern homes, they clung to the chain linking their neck collars, stumbling desperately at the horses' heels.

Penitents, merchants, and farmers all scurried aside, falling over each other in their haste to escape. A frail, white-bearded pilgrim staggered and fell to his knees. Janetta cried out in alarm as the crush of people swallowed him.

"I help you, grandfather!" Floki dashed forward, parting the crowd with his outstretched arms. "Come." He leaned down and lifted the old man to his feet.

Still playing the penitent. Gil smiled, but the compassion gentling the Northman's face seemed real, as he wrapped an arm around the old man's shoulders and went on. Tall and forbidding in his austere robes, he cleared a space before him as men stepped prudently out of his way.

Gil moved to follow and was drawn up short by Lionheart's lead. The pony stood, head and tail drooping in despair. *I want the ship.*

It's okay. Gil patted Lionheart's neck and leaned his face against his rain-soaked mane. Suddenly, he, too, wanted his ship and the cool, clear empty sea, far from this place where men were chained like beasts.

Ismail, Ciarnan, and Ragi pushed by with the Hrolf's Isle ponies. Lionheart whickered desperately. *I'm alone.*

Gil shook his head. *If you'd move, you wouldn't be.* He hauled on the lead, and dragging one hoof at a time, Lionheart inched through the arch and out into the street beyond. His ears pricked forward at the sight of the others waiting while Floki sent the old pilgrim gently on his way.

But then a terrible sound shook the air, a cry, half roar and half scream, and an animal lurched into view, setting Lionheart trembling with new terror. With its mountainous back piled high with flagons, and its shaggy neck and scornful head adorned with bells and fringes, it swayed high above men's heads, lordly as a cathedral. Lionheart skittered wildly sideways with Percy clinging frantically to his neck. *Horrible horse!*

Gil gripped the lead with both hands. *He's not a horse. And he won't hurt you.*

His feet are horrible.

No. Just not hooves.

He smells horrible!

Gil screwed up his face. *Not arguing. If you just move, we won't smell him anymore.* With all his strength, he hauled the pony's head around. But a hand closed on his shoulder, holding him back.

"Warrior! Behold!" Floki cried. "A horse with toes!" Lionheart flung his head up breaking free. Gil lunged, re-capturing the lead. Floki pulled him back. "A hunch-backed horse with toes!"

"It's a camel, Floki." Gil wrestled Lionheart back in line, propping Percy up as he slid sideways.

Floki's face lit with delight. "What is this camel-horse?"

"Not a horse. Another animal." Gil wrapped his sleeve over Lionheart's face, shielding his view of the beast.

"Ah!" Floki cried. "I know this! Gorilla! Gorilla-horse." He smiled. "I am right?"

Gil dropped his sleeve and looked the Northman in the eye. *"It's a camel, Floki!* Will you please …?" He froze. Over Floki's shoulder he glimpsed a rush of movement as five armed men burst out of the crowd. Backing against the rearing pony, he gripped Floki's forearm and hauled him out of the way.

The swordsmen closed, swarthy faces contorted with fury, scattering the terrified crowd. Then six more emerged from an alleyway behind Gil, flinging bright capes back from their sword-arms. Gil lunged for Janetta, shielding her with his body. But the newcomers barged by, one slamming into Lionheart's rump in his haste. Another brushed past Floki as if he wasn't there and fell upon the first group, weapon in hand. In moments, a battle was raging, growing in ferocity as more men shoved through the terrified crowd, joining one side or the other.

Others gathered, shouting encouragement, until the narrow street was a mass of clashing swordsmen and roaring supporters. Hemmed in by the walls of houses, Gil and his companions could only watch.

The fighters tired; some stumbled and fell. One collided with the camel and went down in a shower of broken pottery. Laughter rang down the street and the shouts turned raucous. A slender, handsome youth ran out, bellowing like the camel, and the crowd cheered his mockery. He flashed a white smile, and strutting past the exhausted swordsmen, suddenly paused, as his gaze fell on Janetta.

Gil thrust her behind him. The youth smiled and lifted his chin slightly and gave it a little jerk. Two of his companions rushed in, pinning Gil's arms to his sides. The handsome youth bent his dark head and kissed Janetta on her lips. Then, with a boyish giggle, he turned and fled. Gil broke free from the restraining hands and lunged after him, drawing his sword but a powerful arm caught him around the waist, and hauled him back. "We are pilgrims," Floki whispered, "And this is not our battle."

"It's mine!" Gil shouted. Viciously, he kicked out, struggling to free his sword arm.

"There are thirty of them, helmsman. Raise your sword to one and you raise it to all. Both sides join against you." Floki dropped his voice further. "And she pays the price of your pride." He loosed his hold, then, and stepped aside.

Still seething, Gil looked up. Janetta was watching him imploringly. "Please. Do not fight. He does not harm me." He nodded roughly, sheathed his sword and turning his back on

Floki, took up Lionheart's lead rein and went on.

The rain had stopped and watery sunlight lit the buff walls and red-tiled roofs above them, though the cobbles beneath their feet were yet in shade. Gil skidded on a smear of fresh manure, carrying its stench with him. Rank with its own odors, the crowd surged around him, a relentless tide of pilgrims flowing onward to the shrine of Peter. Swept along by it, they had no need of map or guide.

Their street petered out beyond a crumbling house. Before them were fields, a church standing alone, and cattle grazing. A fresh breeze came up from the river. Stragglers from the street battle pursued each other onto a bridge.

The open space revealed a vast vista of the city's churches and towers and monuments spread out across its hills, the enclosing wall dwindling into the distance. "It is as big as the High Island," Ragi murmured fearfully.

"And as full of idiots," Floki waved at the chaotic swordsmen. One had fallen into the river. Two splashed to rescue him. The rest gave up the battle and stood shouting from the bank.

The doors of the church opened and a mass of people came down its steps, followed by black robed monks, and clerics in purple vestments, carrying banners and singing. The pilgrims stopped and waited patiently for them to pass.

Lionheart tugged at his lead and when Gil loosened it, he dropped his head and began to graze. Hungrily, the other ponies joined him. Gil rubbed his stomach and grinned. "Wish I ate grass." Ismail and Ragi grinned back. But Ciarnan stood, leaning against his pony, his face soft and young again, like the day they had played with sticks and ball beneath the high cross of Hy.

"They sing 'De Profundis,'" he murmured. Gil shook his head, uncertain. Ciarnan's voice fell lower and he stared after the monks. "I am beneath the floor of the church. Donal lies bloodied with the beasts. Above my head, my brethren sing as they go to die ... *De profundis clamavi ad te....* Out of the depths, I cry ...."

They followed the procession onto the bridge, crossing to an island in the midst of the ship-thronged river. Floki's gaze swept the myriad vessels, and he pointed to one, moored to the island's shore. The ship's flaxen-haired crew stood out boldly among the dark southerners. "Northmen," he said. "Danes." He sent Gil and Ragi to speak with them. But the men were traders, not pilgrims, and knew nothing of the pilgrim road, or of a king from the North.

Across the island, a second bridge took them to the far shore, where they plunged back into the maze of ancient streets. The procession of worshippers turned aside, entering another church, and the street fighters dwindled to a handful of youths jeering at each other in an incomprehensible tongue. But the pilgrims grew in numbers, joining from the side streets, or emerging from half hidden chapels and shrines, until they filled the narrow roadway from wall to wall.

Jostled by the press of bodies, the smaller and weaker struggled to keep their footing. Floki lifted Rachel and Janetta up onto ponies' backs and pulled Eirik beneath the shelter of his arm, while Bjorn and Grimhildr forged head, twin longships on a human sea.

Then suddenly they rounded a corner and sunlight flooded down from a wide expanse of sky. Before them, the city was cleft by a vast open space; a long, narrow oval, curved at both ends and bordered by crumbling walls rising in broken, vine-tangled tiers. The crowd broke and spilled outward, through gaps in the ancient stonework, into the over-grown interior.

The ponies pushed eagerly toward the scent of grass. Gil trotted beside Lionheart, inspired, too, by the smell of food. Wood smoke drifted overhead, rising from beneath the stone arches at the base of the walls, where cooking fires flickered in the shadows.

When they reached the center of the huge enclosure, they stood amid grazing sheep and little encampments of travelers, looking up at the great, broken ramparts surrounding them. Only then did Gil realize they were within a building.

"What was it?" he whispered in awe.

"A stadium," said Rachel.

"Like a baseball stadium?"

Rachel laughed. "For the games. The Romans loved games. All sorts. Races. Athletics. *Not* baseball," she added drily. "Look," she pointed to the stepped brick of a wall. "That's where people sat to watch."

"A grandstand." Gil ran his eyes over the tiers of seating and then dropped his gaze to the supporting arches below. Massive and unmoved by centuries, they sheltered, now, whole houses and stables and storerooms piled with hay or wooden casks, all crammed ingeniously into the foundations. Directly across from him, a little church was snugged into the wall, the curved stonework of an arch forming its roof. He thought suddenly of Deer Bay and the Northmen's rough houses amid the Roman ruins. Here, Romans, too, crept like small animals beneath their fathers' stones.

"There is war?" said Ismail.

Rachel shrugged. "Many wars. And many years."

"I always thought things just got bigger and better," Gil said.

Rachel smiled. "So did they."

Outside the little church, priests distributed food to the pilgrims. Floki allowed the children to accept bread soaked with oil and bowls of broth. But he sent Gil and Ismail to the merchants' stalls lining the sides of the ruined arena, with silver to buy fodder for the animals and cabbage and coarse bread for themselves.

Their meager meal finished, they went on, deeper into the city. The bells all around were ringing Saxt when Rachel suddenly stopped before a pillared portico fronting a huge circular building. "Wait," she murmured. "I know this."

Gil stared up at the domed roof looming over the crowded narrow streets. Floki leaned close. "What is it, pretty one? A silk merchant with more veils?"

She shook her head solemnly. "It's Maria Rotunda," she said. "I've been here before."

Floki looked up at the massive columns. "Here? Here also? How far you fly in Tir nan Og, my hawk. Tell us of it."

"I can't. I was four. My father bought me a toy, a little unicorn." She shrugged. "I remember that."

"Ah, my fearsome hawk. So small that a father's toys delight her." He looked into her eyes and then he, too, was solemn. "Where is that child, now?"

Where? Gil thought. *Is she there, somewhere, in that place that hasn't happened yet? Am I? And Danni ... two children at a river ....* For a shadow of a moment, he could smell the cool water and hear Danni's triumphant laughter. *Where was she now? Who was she now?* He thought of the veiled girl in the Golden Knight's grand pilgrimage. A girl in chains.

"Come," he said to Rachel. "It doesn't matter. We're just losing time."

But Floki wanted to hear more and she shrugged again. "It's all I remember. Except ...." her face brightened, "Yes!" she cried. Leaving them behind, she ran up the steps and through the portico, into the building beyond.

"Not without me!" Floki ran after her, and thrusting Lionheart's lead into Ismail's hand, Gil hurriedly followed.

Pushing through a crush of dark-skinned pilgrims in the entranceway, he emerged in the dim interior and stumbled to a halt. High above him, the domed roof floated in shadow, lit only by a single shaft of sunlight pouring through a circular opening at its center. Beneath it, the marble floor glowed, but the curved walls of the immense structure were barely visible. Clusters of pilgrims moved like ghosts in the golden dusk. "Rachel!" Gil called. He glimpsed movement and a flash of Floki's yellow hair, as the Northman sprinted through the shaft of light, seeking her.

Then Gil's eyes, adjusting to the dimness, fell upon a small girlish figure, crouched in the center of the floor. "My hawk!" Floki bolted to her side and flung himself on his knees beside her. "You are no child, and I, no father. Do not leave my side unguarded again."

She nodded happily. "Look, Floki. The holes. See? For rainwater." She pointed above. "The rain comes in because the roof is open. So they made drains. My father showed me. I was here." She traced the holes in the floor with her finger. "See? It's real."

Floki shook his head and said again, "Where is that child, now?" He stood, and taking her hand, lifted her to her feet. Raising his eyes, he seemed to see the great roof for the first time. "Warrior," he said. "Men build such a thing?"

Gil nodded.

"The Romans built it long ago," Rachel said. "It was a temple to all their gods. They had many gods. Like Northmen."

"But it is a church," Floki pointed to an altar, where candles flickered beneath a painted crucifix.

She smiled. "They've borrowed it. Like the Northmen borrow Odin's Stone."

Floki studied the crucifix. "So many gods," he said softly. "And Aidan's god-who-dies defeats them all. Come. We must go on." But he paused suddenly and then grasped Rachel's hand again and, gripping Gil's arm as well, dragged them hurriedly toward the curving wall. There, he thrust them both into a niche holding a small side altar, in darkness but for the flames of an oil lamp. Slipping in beside them, he stood in the wavering shadows, gazing intently across the huge church.

"What is it?" Rachel whispered.

"There, at the high altar," Floki gestured toward three men standing before the crucifix, dressed in grey robes like the brothers of Hy. "They are Irish," he said. "And he, there, with the black beard?" Gil nodded, peering through the shifting mass of pilgrims. "I know him," said Floki, "and he knows me."

"*How?*"

Floki shrugged and smiled. "He lends me a boat. But I do not return it. So you must speak with him, not I." He laid a hand on Gil's shoulder and the other on Rachel's. "Go together. Ask if he hears of a king from Alba, travelling the road from the North."

The scraps of Irish Gil had learned from Ciarnan won only a baffled smile from the black-bearded brother. But Rachel's church Latin brought a gleam of understanding to his eyes. He spoke rapidly in a soft, low voice. Rachel nodded and the brother smiled again and raised his hand in a parting blessing for them both.

"What did he say?" Gil whispered as they retreated to the side altar.

Hidden again, with Floki, in the shadows, she said excitedly, "He and his brothers were caught in a blizzard in a high pass through the Alps. They came upon an encampment of great noblemen, sheltering from the snow. They were rich, with many horses and even wagons. There was a fire, and food. But they turned the brothers away."

"That's him," Gil said grimly. "Who else would do that?"

Floki shrugged. "There are other evil men in the world."

"They heard a harp," Rachel said then. "Within the camp. An Irish harp, playing so beautifully that they struggled to leave before they froze."

Floki's pale eyes glinted triumphantly in the lamplight. He nodded toward the Irish brothers. "How many days are they here?"

She shook her head. "They were at Peter's Shrine yesterday. That's all I know."

"Then they came yesterday. 'First and last, the Shrine of Peter.'" He turned to Gil. "He is close, Warrior. Many men together travel more slowly than few. But he is close." He returned his gaze to the Irish brothers, making their way from altar to altar. "Here," he said, drawing silver from his hidden purse and passing it to Gil. "Give it to him. Tell him, 'For the boat.'" He repeated the phrase in Irish. "Quickly. We wait beyond."

Outside, Gil found them again with the others, soothing the restless ponies. "He is pleased?" Floki asked.

"I didn't stay to find out." Gil took Lionheart's lead from Ismail and studied Floki curiously. "What was that about?"

Floki glanced back at the portico of Maria Rotunda, as they went on. "I meet him on that Irish shore when I am in a hurry to leave that place. I ask for a crossing. He leaves his work and takes me to sea, and then I strand him on an island and take the boat." He looked affronted by the shock on Gil's face. "A good island, Warrior!" he protested. "He does not starve." He shrugged and smiled. "And Viking scoundrel though I am, I pay my debts."

But Gil thought then of that other Irishman, the Irish warrior Padraic Njalsson, and Floki's other unpaid debt. *He, who lives by the sword, dies by the sword.* He shrugged. That would hardly worry Floki.

They pressed on, leading the ponies through a tangle

of streets, until, at the end of a dark alleyway, Gil glimpsed sparkling water. Abruptly, they emerged again at the river that wound through the city. Sunlight flooded down on its wide expanse. A bridge, crammed with jostling pilgrims, crossed beneath a brooding fortress on the opposite shore.

Janetta ran around Lionheart's rump and caught Gil's hand. "Look. There beyond the river." Gil's eyes traced the high roof of a mighty basilica rising above a jumble of buildings. A great wall enclosed all, its stones bright and barely weathered. The road from the bridge led through its open gate. "Surely it is Peter's Church."

"It has to be." Gil felt numb. The end of the journey. Whatever happened, they would go no farther than this. *Then the best part: A white strand on a Northern shore. The Holy Island in its lace of white seas.* He twined Janetta's fingers in his own, and wondered who among them would live to see home.

On their first step from the bridge, they were met by eager merchants proffering spiritual treasures: candles, and small vials of hallowed oil, and badges and icons portraying Saint Peter with his keys. More worldly goods, bread and dried figs, cheese and sausages, stout new staffs, and shoes were offered by stalls that lined the roadway.

The air was filled with the clamor of voices, shouting in foreign tongues, and the bells of the basilica ringing the ninth hour. The devout fell to their knees in the street. Over their heads, Gil saw a cluster of wooden buildings, roofed in smoking thatch. Two fair-haired men were sawing wood before the nearest. Again, he thought of Deer Bay. "Are they Northmen?" he asked.

Floki studied them and shook his head. "Saxons," he said. "Or men from Frisia." Then he stopped and smiled. "But there," he indicated a tough-looking old man sitting on a bench before an open door. "He is a Northman."

The man wore a threadbare tunic over crudely patched britches. Faded blond hair fell to his shoulders. Scarred hands rested on his knees and his greying beard blew softly in the wind. A silver Thor's hammer hung companionably with a Christian cross, from a cord around his neck.

"Grandfather," Floki addressed him. "What ship brings you here?"

The Northman squinted up in the bright light and shaded his eyes. "*Star-Seeker*, sailing from Hedeby. Ten years past, she sleeps beneath the southern seas. And I sleep here." He slapped the wooden door post of the rough house behind him.

"Would you return?" Floki asked gently. "My ship lies not far from here. I give you passage."

The old sailor smiled. "My bones like the southern sun. And Peter's Church gives me my bread. The Northlands see me no more. And what of you, young pilgrim?" he said amiably. "Have you sins enough already to lay at Peter's feet?" His face creased with amusement. "At your age, I sought the arrow-storm, not the cloister."

Floki smiled. "The days of the heroes are done, grandfather. I am but a humble farmer. I need shelter for my people and fodder for my beasts. Would you guide me?"

The old Northman's eyes crinkled with delight, and proudly heaving himself to his feet, he set out at a sprightly pace into his Northern enclave in the heart of Rome. "Here, the pilgrims come from Saxony," he said, "And there," he pointed to a different, though still Northern architecture, "Those from Francia."

"They stay long enough to build houses?" said Gil.

The old man shrugged. "Some make their pilgrimage, honor every saint and set foot in every church, and are gone by Lentron. Others stay a year. Two years. Others, with souls more burdened than yours, young friend," he nodded to Floki, "Stay all their remaining days."

He led them then to a hospice whose priests spoke many tongues. The dormitories, with their straw-filled pallets, reminded Gil of Hy and he felt at home, making his bed beside Ismail, with Ciarnan and Ragi at either side. Bjorn prodded his mattress distrustfully and then lay down with his head and feet hanging over the ends. "A bed for dwarfs!"

Gil imagined Grimhildr, sheltered with the girls in the adjoining women's house, suffering a similar fate. He grinned at Bjorn and raised his cloak, as if a veil, over his head. "But look! No little animals!" Lying down, he stretched luxuriantly, but at once, he felt a small sting, and then another. He sat up, swatting at his legs.

"Is okay," Ismail smiled. "Just fleas."

Gil sighed and stood up. "I thought we left those on the ship." Scratching resignedly, he went out to the stables behind the hospice, where Floki and the children were spreading hay in a trough for the ponies.

The three Hrolf's Isle beasts munched peacefully in a row. Lionheart cowered in a corner of his stall and rolled terrified eyes at two donkeys, dozing in the next. *Those? You're afraid of those?* Gil rolled his own eyes.

They're too small.

Yeah, yeah. He climbed into the stall and shoved Lionheart toward the food trough.

Their tails are too ropy.

Gil stopped and cast a weary glance at the donkeys. *HOW is that a problem?* He threw his hands in the air, climbed out of the stall, and followed Floki and Percy and Eirik out of the stable. In the sunlit doorway, he paused and looked back at Lionheart hunched in the gloom. *Who needs penance when I have you?*

"Gil, quickly!" Janetta waved from the corner of the stable building, her face turned excitedly toward what lay beyond. He jumped over a heap of manure and ran across the broken cobbles to her side.

The stable ended in a collapsed heap of rubble where some other, older structure had stood. Through the gap remaining, Gil saw an open, uneven square, a *piazza*, lined on one side with pale brick houses. A bright, sparkling fountain stood at its center. Merchants' stalls, shaded by red, blue, and yellow awnings clustered about it. Others clung to the side of a long low building, festooned with bedding and clothing drying in the sun.

Beyond, half hidden by fluttering linen, a flight of steps rose to the pillared portico of the basilica that soared above the square. Its roof and bell tower glowing in the late sun, its walls in shadow, it stood amidst the clutter of the square like a placid mother surrounded by her children.

A flight of doves whirled and circled the fountain, catching the fading light on their wings. Janetta caught Gil's hand.

Behind him, he heard Percy's excited shout, and both children burst by, running to the fountain. Holding their hands up to its sun-washed spray, they dashed gleefully amidst birds and rainbows. "It is so beautiful!" Janetta cried. Gil smiled and leaned to draw her closer, but a rough hand slapped his head.

"Follow them, Warrior!" Floki shoved him toward the children. "Do not forget why we are here."

Chastened, Gil ran out into the square and stood at the side of the fountain, watching while the children played, until Ismail, Ragi, Ciarnan, and Bjorn appeared from an alleyway beside the hospice. He waved as they hurried to join him, followed by Rachel, and then, Grimhildr, smoothing her headdress and walking with the solemnity of a nun. Floki stepped forward from the shadows, with Janetta at his side. "Trust no man," he murmured to Gil, as he passed.

"But it is Peter's Shrine!" Janetta cried sadly. Floki smiled down at her.

"Yes. And every man here is as innocent as I." He laughed and called the children to him and let them lead him from merchant's stall to merchant's stall, as if he were their indulgent father. Bjorn shadowed them, a stride behind, while the others watched every entrance of the crowded *piazza*.

Percy ran to Gil, tugging at his sleeve, and showing off a lead pilgrim's badge pinned to his tunic. "It's a true one," he said, "Because we're here." He pointed to the image of Saint Peter and then up at the church. Eirik poked the new badge with an envious finger.

"You would be a pilgrim, too?" Floki said. Eirik nodded hopefully and with a wry smile, Floki bought another badge and fastened it to the collar of the boy's cloak. "I do not think your father thanks me," he said. "Come, now. Play is over." With an arm around each child, he mounted the steps. "Helmsman," he called, "Beside me. We call upon royalty, once more."

At the top of the steps, they entered a vast, roofed courtyard lined with columns and as crowded with people as the *piazza* outside. Beggars plucked at Gil's tunic. A merchant thrust a tray of badges before Janetta. Gil pulled her to one side and stumbled to a halt.

At his feet, rows of sick pilgrims lay shivering on low couches, tended by black robed brothers. Their moans joined the shouts of the trinket sellers, the excited cries of travelers, and the insistent clanging of bells. "This is a church?" Gil murmured to Rachel.

"It's only the atrium. The forecourt." She pointed to the five huge, gilded doors in the far wall. "The church is there."

"Helmsman!" Floki turned and beckoned him forward without releasing his grip on the children. "Stay with me. These are rough seas." He paused until his small band of Northerners clustered around him again and then led them together through the center door.

Beyond, the broad central aisle of the nave swept away between glistening rows of marble columns, toward a great arch at the far end. More columns flanked further aisles on either side like a forest of many colored trees. Above, the gilded roof beams soared three times the height of *Silver Dragon's* mast and the great ship could have tacked from wall to wall with ease.

Red-gold sun, flooding through windows high above the nave and shimmering in the silken veils that draped the column arches, was rivalled below by the flickering of countless oil lamps and candles. Lampstands, candelabra, reliquaries, side altars, and the tombs that lined the distant frescoed walls, glittered with precious metals and jewels.

Bjorn looked around with a child's wide eyes and closed his huge fist on Floki's shoulder. "This is gold?"

Floki grinned. "Enough to sink a king's longship, and should you touch one piece, I bury you." He slapped Bjorn's mighty forearm, and pointed down at the marble floor, "Here, with the bones of popes." He turned sharply to the young Vikings behind him, "And you as well."

But both Ismail and Ciarnan looked shocked by even the thought, while Ragi only stared in awe at the thousands of pilgrims filling the enormous church from wall to wall. "All of the Northlands have not so many people," he said.

The two children clung to Floki's robes, peering warily from the shelter of his arms. Eirik chewed his sun-burned lip. Percy put his fingers in his ears as the bells rang on, whimpered, and closed his eyes.

"Come," Floki smiled down. "There lies Peter's Shrine." He crouched and directed the children's gaze through the milling crowds toward the altar in the apse beyond the arch. "We go, now, and kneel before his bones."

Eirik's eyes lit with ghoulish interest, but Percy squeezed his own more tightly shut and shook his head. Floki handed Gil his pilgrim's staff and lifted Percy up in his arms. "Look, now," he smiled, "It is but a church, like I build for Aidan."

"A little bigger," Gil muttered, picturing how many Cille Aidans he could stack beneath the gilded roof.

"And they, there," Floki showed Percy a column of clerics progressing up a side aisle, chanting Vespers, "But holy brethren of Aidan himself." He raised his gaze to the roof where doves circled in an enclosed heaven. "Birds seek their nests. All is well."

Carrying the child, he joined the flow of pilgrims up the nave. Before the high altar, he bowed and turned to see all were safely at his side. Then, still holding Percy, he crossed to the steps leading down to the tomb. Clutching Floki's staff and shepherding Eirik between himself and Janetta, Gil followed.

The staircase was narrow and cut in stone. Cool air rushed up from below, stirring the blue haze of incense drifting from the altar. Walls of stone muffled sound. The voices of the descending pilgrims dropped to a hush. Percy whimpered again and Floki began to sing, a bairn song from the North, until the boy giggled and fell quiet.

Then there was no sound but the shuffling of feet along a curving corridor, no light but a feeble oil sconce. The smell of earth arose, dank and cold. Ahead, the line of pilgrims slowed to a halt and the lamplight flared in a fresh burst of damp air. A new light glowed from a second passage, and where it joined their own, pilgrims fell abruptly to their knees. *We kneel before his bones.*

Fear, colder than the tomb air, gripped Gil's heart. In his mind, he saw already the white bones of the saint, scattered like the bones of the knight in the briarwood of Pentecost …

the bones of the prisoner in Merlin's Tower ... the bones of his father in the Indian Kettle Pool. *But he's alive. My father is alive!*

Gil summoned Lance'lot's tired face, smiling down at him in the forest in Francia. But the vision faded as the oil lamp behind him flickered again and went out. In the darkness, the pilgrims moaned in fear or ecstasy.

I bury you with the bones of popes. Gil thought wildly of the tombs beneath the marble floor, all around him now in the earth. The whole beautiful church rode like a ship on a sea of bones. "But my father's alive," he said aloud, his voice a hoarse croak.

Which would you believe?

"Dr. Fairchild!" Gil whirled, staring behind him and around. But there was nothing but the dim faces of pilgrims, straining toward their goal. And their relentless, gentle pressure forced him on until he, too, stood suddenly apart, before the entrance of the tomb.

"You must kneel!" A small hand slipped urgently into his own. "Here is Peter." Janetta pulled him down beside her, onto the stone floor.

"Where ...?" he gestured in confusion to the corridor, lit at its far end by a single flame.

"Beyond. In the earth. Far below." She smiled. "See?" She pointed to the walls of the passage, embellished by richly painted seascapes. On one side, the fisherman raised his full nets. On the other, he strode across the waves to his master. *Helmsman.*

A light scent filled the air, like early summer on Hrolf's Isle. With it came a peacefulness so sweet that once again Gil wished time to stand still. But the eager faithful pressed forward, crowding them on toward another curving passage, and then steps again, rising to light.

Blinking and still clutching Janetta's hand, Gil stumbled up into the immense nave of Peter's Church. He turned quickly, seeking his companions. Janetta touched his arm and pointed. "The earl is there."

Floki knelt on the marble floor, the children standing on either side. Eyes closed, the sunset lighting his mane of yellow hair, he raised his face to the high altar, as serene and remote as the frescoed angels on the walls beyond. Respectful pilgrims stepped aside to leave him at peace in his prayers.

Gil, too, waited in silence until at last Floki bowed his head, crossed himself, and rose to his feet. "Warrior," he said softly.

Gil nodded, feeling he should not speak, but Floki beckoned him closer. "Here, each man comes. First, and last, the Shrine of Peter." He gestured to the line of pilgrims entering and exiting the shrine in single file. "And, here, each man must come alone." He looked calmly again at the altar, "Here, we take him down."

"Here?" Gil whispered. "In the *church*? You can't …."

Floki's eyes took on their cold battle light. "Warrior, I am a Northman," he said. "I do as I wish."

Chapter Four

"**N**ort-mon."

Gil shook his head and looked uneasily at Ismail. "Me?" The dark-skinned Roman youth flashed a brilliant smile, dropped his horse's reins, and tossed his purple cloak over his shoulder. He wore a short white tunic, but also britches, like the Franks. Gil saw the glitter of silver on the hilt of his sword.

"Nort-mon! You sell?" Silver glinted, too, on the young man's palm. He gestured with his other hand toward the hawk perched on Gil's leather-wrapped forearm.

"No!" Gil cried.

The dark youth laughed. Then, with a knowing wink, he drew more silver from a velvet pouch at his waist and counted it dramatically onto his palm. Extending it to Gil, he reached for the bird, as if she was already his.

Gil backed Lionheart quickly out of reach. Ragi, Ciarnan, and Ismail turned their ponies too. The youth shrugged, shook his head, and with a touch of disdain, put his money away. Turning his own horse, a tall, lean animal with a fine arched neck, he rode off.

Gil grinned uneasily at Ismail. "Wonder what Floki would say if I told him I'd sold Rachel."

Ismail grinned back and drew a perfunctory finger across his throat.

"The man is very wealthy," Ciarnan said, his eyes following the Roman youth. "He thinks everything belongs to him."

Gil, too, watched the young Roman until horse and rider disappeared behind a looming tower, constructed extraordinarily on top of an ancient arch.

"Northern hawks are prized above all," said Ragi. "He

could sell her again for twice as much."

Gil drew the hawk close to his chest. She turned her head and fixed him with her unfathomable yellow gaze. "It's okay," he said. "It won't happen." She blinked and looked away, deep in some bird thought. He shrugged. It was hard enough to get inside Rachel's head when she was human.

"Come on," he said. "Let's get away from that." He gestured toward the fortification from which the haughty youth had appeared. Floki had warned him to avoid the towers, but they were everywhere, dotting the empty countryside, overseeing fields and vineyards, dominating all but the mightiest of the ancient ruins.

Each fortress held an earl and each, indeed, granted himself the authority of a king. Twice before they had been stopped by well-armed youths, and once required to pay some kind of fine before they could pass.

Gil turned in his saddle and looked back over the broad expanse of open farmland to the wet roofs of the distant city. He picked out the dome of Maria Rotunda, lit by the morning sun, and beyond the river, the roof and bell tower of Peter's Church where Floki kept guard at the shrine.

But here, amid cattle-grazed pastures and fields of grain stubble, only fallen marble ruins remained of the city that once lay within the ancient walls. Huddled now around its river, Rome was dwarfed by its own past.

He raised his eyes to a steep hill crowned with a half-fallen structure of gleaming marble. Dark cypresses enfolded stray columns. Grass grew high around marble porches. "Up there." He indicated an open space grazed by three spotted goats. "We'll fly her from there. I want to be able to see where she goes."

Lionheart picked his way amid crumbling brickwork, shying at the marble head of a statue staring blankly up from the ground. In the center of a faded mosaic floor, Gil reined him in, slipped down, and held the hawk high. "Go," he whispered. "And don't get caught."

She raised her wings and, with a savage cry, took to the air. Circling once, she set out, swooping through rows of columns, rising over the domed roof of a temple, and dwindling to a speck above the city itself. He lost sight of her as she crossed the river and could follow her only in his mind, soaring over Saint Peter's mighty church and its newly built wall and beyond, out into the empty countryside, following the road to the North.

"She flies home to the Northlands!" Ragi cried. "She does not return."

"She returns," Ismail said quietly.

"Yes! With his throat's blood in her beak!" Ciarnan stretched out his hands like a bird's talons and made a snarling face.

Gil grimaced and shook his head. Fierce she was but still just a bird, small and fragile and no match for the Golden Knight. But she would tell them where he was.

When she did return, he saw by the sheer triumph of her flight, that she had been successful. Grinning, he held up his leather-wrapped wrist for her, and in the same moment, he saw the riders. "Ismail," he murmured. But the African boy had seen them already.

"Look. In the middle. Our friend."

There were five altogether, mastering their fine horses with arrogant ease. The youth who had sought to buy Rachel smiled graciously. His four companions reined their mounts to left and right.

"He returns for his hawk," said Ciarnan.

"My hawk," Gil muttered, as her talons slapped into the leather. He drew the bird close. Ciarnan reached for his sword. "No. Not our battle," Gil heard himself echoing Floki. "Run."

Ciarnan growled an oath and Ragi protested, "On hill ponies?"

But Gil slammed his heels into Lionheart's ribs and spun him toward a steep bluff descending to the grassland below. *Down. Over the edge. Or they eat you!* Cascading loose stones, they plunged downward, leaving the angry shouts of their pursuers behind. Hill pony agility won them a hundred yards, but on the flat ground below, they quickly lost their lead.

Hooves thundered behind Gil. Shadows closed, left and right. He hunched over Lionheart's neck. *Run! Run!* Lionheart snorted and showed a white-rimmed eye, as two riders drove their rangy mounts up on either side. "Nort-mon!" The Roman youth grinned insolently down on Gil, and restraining his galloping mount with one hand, reached with the other for the hawk. "Now you sell!"

A hand closed on Lionheart's bridle. Laughing, the second youth dragged the terrified pony to a halt. Trapped between the two big animals, Lionheart reared, pawing air. Gil raised his left arm, flung the hawk skywards, and with his right hand, drew his sword. "Fly to Floki!" he cried, but the hawk swooped low, instead, streaking across yellowing meadow grass toward a stuccoed church. He just glimpsed her tail feathers vanishing into its round, domed vestibule, when bright steel flashed to meet his own.

In moments he was absorbed in a chaotic battle on horseback, fending off both Romans. Ciarnan galloped to his rescue, barging between Gil's opponents, the Hrolf's Isle pony shouldering their mounts aside with his sturdy weight. Gil struggled for a glimpse of the church with the domed entranceway, but a third youth rode in between. Then, above the clanging of clashing steel, he heard Ragi shout, "Rachel! No! Go back!"

Whirling Lionheart, he saw her standing in the church's open door, her sword belt circling her linen dress, her red hair hanging loose to her knees. His stunned opponents lowered their weapons with shouts of surprise and then yelps of admiration. The hawk was forgotten, the girl now their prize.

But Ismail was already galloping to her refuge. He leapt from the saddle and, abandoning his horse, raced to the doorway, spun Rachel around, and with her, vanished inside. The clang of the tall bronze doors slamming shut behind him brought shouts of laughter from the young Romans.

"The Saracen hides like a woman," Ragi muttered in disdain.

"Not likely," said Gil. But he urged Lionheart on toward the church.

Still laughing, three of the Romans dismounted and hauled at the doors. Without resistance, they swung open, revealing the dark interior of the vestibule. The laughter died. One youth edged back. Gil peered into the gloom. Light glinted on branching bone and flashed in a dark animal eye. "Yes," Gil murmured, as a hoof scraped the ancient tile floor.

The two bolder Romans also backed away, reaching blindly behind them for their horses' reins. Then, with shouts of horror, they turned, scrabbling aboard their mounts as the hidden beast leapt into the light.

White antlers raking the air, the Ismail-Stag charged out into the sunbaked ruins, with Rachel, red hair flying and arms linked around its shaggy neck, riding astride its back. Gil at once gave chase, fearing the Romans would do the same. But they had seen enough. Babbling wildly in their own tongue, they fled back the way they had come.

The Stag ran on, leaping fallen pillars, darting amidst shrubs and rubble, toward a huge circular building towering above churches and ruins. Its curving stone walls were pierced by tiers of arched openings, some thick with vines, some with whole trees sprouting high in the sky. At the lowest level, the earth had swallowed the building's foundations, half concealing the entrance ways, but the Stag made straight for the nearest, and bending its antlered head low, scuttled within.

When Gil reached the truncated archway, he dismounted to enter, leading Lionheart, with lowered head, behind. Ragi joined him, and Ciarnan followed, with Ismail's abandoned pony beside his own.

"The Romans?" Gil asked.

"Still running!" Ciarnan laughed. But Ragi looked grim.

"They'll be back with twenty more." He hunched his shoulder toward the far end of the archway. "And thanks to the Saracen, we are trapped."

Gil shook his head. "You're used to Change-Things. They aren't. Ismail knew what he was doing." He turned his back and hastened through the long dim tunnel toward the bright sunlight beyond, emerging in a vast circular space, an amphitheater of enormous proportions. Tiers of stone seating rose to the sky, as thick with grass and flowering plants as a mountain meadow.

More grass filled the interior, but apart from a scattering of nimble goats, the huge structure appeared empty. Then Gil's eyes fell on the two figures, alone in the center of the arena, a slim boy and girl, her arms yet linked around his neck.

Grinning, he ran forward with Lionheart trotting at his heels, his hand raised in a triumphant high-five. *"Ace* circle!" he greeted Ismail, as the boy's brown fingers slapped his own.

Ismail grinned back and accepted his pony's reins from Ciarnan. "Thank you. Now I need him again," he smiled shyly.

"Why?" Ragi said. "With such a Change-Thing, you can always run away faster, yourself."

"What does that mean?" Rachel said.

Ragi shrugged, his eyes straying to Ismail, locked yet in her embrace. "Change-Things are all different. Some fly. Some fight. Some run."

"Stags can fight." Rachel tightened her hold. "Running worked better. They're gone, aren't they?"

"For now.

"Forever. Didn't you hear them?" She laughed, "'It is the devil! It is the devil!'"

"Is no problem." Ismail gave Ragi his gentle white smile. "I know you are there to fight them. So I am safe to run."

"I think everybody did the right thing," Gil said levelly. "And now the right thing is getting out of here."

"And back to Floki," Rachel released Ismail. She allowed herself a proud smile. "To tell him I found the Golden Knight."

They found the earl keeping his vigil at Peter's Church; not within shrine or altar, but in the atrium, among the clerics tending the sick. Kneeling in his pilgrim's robes, beside a feverish traveler, he looked so like one of the brothers that Gil had to tap Rachel's arm to draw her notice. "Pretty convincing," he said with a wry grin. But as Floki gently held a cup to the penitent's lips, he thought suddenly, startlingly, of Aidan.

The earl looked up, spoke softly to the sick man, and rose to join them. He gave Gil a strange, quiet smile, as if he had read his thoughts. "I am young and strong, why should I not help?" Then he smiled again, and added, "Here, where I see all who come and go?" He turned quickly, as a group of pilgrims entered the atrium, and the creak of his leather sword belt beneath his loose cloak, and the sharp light in his eyes, dispelled any illusion of holiness.

"He won't be there," Rachel said calmly. "He's still beyond the Wall."

Floki whirled. "You've seen him." She nodded. "Come," he clasped her arm and led them all from the atrium and down the long flight of steps to the *piazza* beyond. Percy and Eirik were playing by the fountain, creeping up on Grimhildr to dip the tails of her headdress in the water. Bjorn watched, benign as any pilgrim. Floki looked carefully around, and then, keeping his voice as soft as the murmur of the fountain, said, "Tell me."

"They're camped an hour's ride beyond the gate. In a grove of cypress trees, beside the road."

"Pretty early to be camped," Gil said doubtfully. "Why there? So close."

Floki smiled. "A king does not end his pilgrimage in the dim light of Vespers. But the next day, at Lauds, so all can see his glorious humility, shining in the morning sun."

"Perhaps it rains," said Ismail.

"Ah, wise Saracen!" Floki gripped Ismail's shoulders and shook him, happily. "Rain indeed! A rain of sword blows on his head, before the day is done." He turned again to Rachel, his voice softened. "Did you see her?"

Rachel shook her head. "I heard her."

"Singing!" Gil remembered the voice that drew Cat to the locked door, at Mont Tombe.

"Yes. And there was music, a harp, like she used to play at Cille Aidan."

"But you did not see her," Floki said.

"Nor the Knight," Rachel shook her head again. "But he must have been there. There were pavilions – three, and one with his pennant flying – they were all inside, except for the few tending the horses – many horses and four wagons – and two others tending the fire where they roasted an ox and a pig." She paused. "That's how I knew they would stay there. Why would they leave such a feast?"

"Why, indeed," Floki said drily. "Well might he enjoy his meat, out-with the walls of the holy city, when all within keep the winter fast. Let us hope he wipes his lips well, before he kisses Peter's ring." He laughed but was at once serious again.

"Still we cannot be sure of what could not be seen. I must know how many he rides with, how well they are armed. And how many guard her."

Rachel looked down. "I should have flown into the tent," she said unhappily. "But I didn't dare. It felt like a trap, with no way to the sky."

"Very wise, my pretty one!" he said instantly. "Hawks so fine are much prized here, as indeed are fine women."

Gil winced, recalling how close he'd come to losing Rachel, in either guise.

"But still," Floki said softly. "We may yet learn more. Another animal may help; one more common, and of less value. Indeed, an animal so common that the streets of Rome fair seethe with them, and the smallest Roman coin would purchase twenty. Though why one would want twenty, I cannot think."

Gil sighed wearily. "You *do* mean me, don't you?"

"You!" Floki looked aghast. "My treasured helmsman? Never. But your Change-Thing ... that is another story." He looked up at the sky and smiled. "There is time, yet though. Cats walk at night." He clutched the hair at the nape of Gil's neck as if to lift him off his feline feet. "And, this night, this Cat will walk."

———

Gil met Floki in the stables as the Compline bells rang. Ismail held a small clay oil lamp, while Floki led their largest pony from its stall and flung a saddle on its back. Gil slipped by him, reaching for Lionheart's bridle. Floki laid a hand on his arm. "One horse makes less sound than two. One man draws less notice than two." He drew his sword, marked a circle in the earthen floor, and smiled. "Cats walk at night."

"I'm supposed to walk the whole way? It's an hour's ride!"

"So? You have four feet, the same as he," he pointed to the pony's shaggy fetlocks.

"They're this big!" Gil protested. He held up outraged fingers, an inch apart.

Floki pointed the sword at Gil and at the ground. "In." Gil

sighed, stepped within the circle, and grumbled the blessing. Cat arrived with tail swishing and ears flat.

Mounting the pony, Floki rode out of the stable, into the *piazza* of Peter's Church. Light flickered from the fires of pilgrims gathered around the fountain, and from a thousand candles within the basilica. The streets beyond were inky black. Cat slunk in the shadows at the pony's heels as Floki rode to the city wall. Soldiers swung open the Gate of Peter, and Cat followed the trotting pony out into the night.

Stars lit their way on the dusty road. Sweet scents filled the air: flowers, sleeping birds, mice, and rats in the fields. A moon rose beyond a stand of dark cypresses, brightening the landscape and revealing a rubble of fallen buildings at the roadside. Here and there, a marble column or a headless statue softly gleamed. Campfires showed where night had fallen upon pilgrims just short of their goal. Three times they passed dark entranceways into modest hillsides; burial sites where candles flickered at the doorways of the dead.

Half a mile from the Wall, they came upon one more. Floki's pony shied and Cat glimpsed a figure huddled in the shadows, among the votive lights. It smelled human and female and neither shouted nor hissed. Floki rode by with an exchange of gentle greetings. Cat sat down. His paws stung. Also, he had forgotten where he was going, and why.

The woman saw him and bent and stroked his head. Cat purred and listened contentedly to the receding hoof clops until they stopped and then resumed again, returning. "Warrior. We are not there yet."

Cat sniffed the edge of the kind woman's veil and then batted at a heap of small coins, piled among the candles and cut flowers. The woman patted him once more and began murmuring softly, fingering a knotted cord on her wrist.

"This is not the camp we seek, Warrior." Floki shook his reins sharply. "It is a burial place. One of the saints. A saint noted for ridding the city of unnecessary cats," he said, with another shake of his reins. The necessary cat licked a paw. "*Warrior.*"

The woman smiled benignly at the young Northman

addressing the cat; the frail of mind came often to the shrine. Floki leaned down, caught Cat by the scruff and swept him, paws rigid, up to eye level. "Will you walk?" Cat hung, staring balefully and thinking about how he would walk with all four paws flailing the air.

Floki abruptly gave up. With two hands, he swung Cat onto his shoulders. *"No claws."* Then he gathered his reins, paused to hand coins to the woman tending the shrine, and rode on. Pleased with his new situation, Cat settled into the cowl of the Northman's robes, and began to purr, kneading his claws happily in Floki's hair.

He was asleep when the pony stopped next. Awakened, and missing the peaceful rhythm of hoof beats, he kneaded harder, hoping to start them again, and was rewarded with two firm hands gripping his middle. Swung over the Northman's head, he was dropped unceremoniously to the ground. "We are here," Floki said. "And now you *will* walk."

Cat sat down and washed off the offending finger marks. Looking around, he saw dark trees, and beyond, a ruddy glow of fire. Voices and laughter drifted through the trees, and two sweet scents: wood smoke and roasting meat. He sniffed eagerly, and then smelled a scent sweeter still: cat. Not the rank challenge of tomcat, like at Cille Aidan, but something new and powerfully appealing. Turning from the fire glow and ignoring the nudge of the Northman's foot, he sought the source.

He saw a building, not far away, its tile roof outlined in the moonlight. Devoid of human smells, it was yet rich with feline scents, old and new. Nearer still, fallen marble pillars made a pleasant jumble of nooks and crannies, and from within one little cave, two eyes glowed green.

The scent drifted closer. Half-rising on his haunches, Cat raised an uncertain paw. The green eyes blinked, and as Cat blinked gently back, their owner stepped from the shadows; small, sleek, black, and waving an enchanting tail. Like a ship's prow to the North Star, Cat's nose swung to meet her.

"Warrior!" A firm hand gripped his scruff. "No! You are too young. And on pilgrimage! What do I tell the good father, Aidan? *What do I tell your lady?*"

Swept ignominiously into the air, Cat could only scrabble helplessly with his paws as he was carried away through thickets of dark branches to the far side of the grove. There, Floki set him on his feet and pushed him into the circle of firelight. "Go! And if they catch you, they can keep you, for all I care."

But, presented with another new scene, Cat forgot the feline distraction among the pillars and remembered his human purpose. Low and wary, he crept toward the fire lit camp.

A line of horses was tethered at the edge of the trees, and one, a splendid charger, shook its mane and snorted, scenting him. Cat shrank low as a man came, calmed the animal, and returned to the fire; then he rose out of his crouch and made a wide circle around the stamping hooves.

Remembering Floki, he dutifully began counting the horses. He gave up at four, the number of his paws. Undeterred, he counted the wagons; three with bowed cloth covers and one, open and empty; and then the tents. Two were round but one was a grand pavilion with two peaks, the Knight's golden pennant floating above the highest.

He caught the longhouse scent of ale, as he crept behind the three men drinking from goblets by the fire. Unnoticed, he walked by the empty wagon and up the lowered shaft of a covered one and slipped between the cloth flaps.

Sacks of meal, smelling of mouse urine, filled most of the interior, but hams hung from a rod at one end, and three wheels of cheese were stacked beneath them. He licked a ham, which tasted unpleasantly of mold, but the cheese was nicer, and he nibbled a small hole through the rind and made a hollow with his rough tongue in the creamy insides.

Then a mouse crept stupidly into view and for a while took his full attention. When he had finished eating it, except for a paw and the tail, he washed carefully and, remembering his purpose, jumped down from the wagon and up into the next. It was disappointing, no meal, nor mice, only stacks of shields and bundles of swords and bows. He left it untouched and trotted up the shaft of the third.

At once, two new human scents brought him belly low, and slinking silently, he peered through a gap in the canvas with one eye. The scents were stronger and female, and the floor of the wagon was filled with bedding. A human memory tugged at his cat mind – Floki and his boy self, cat-like in the tree in Francia; below: the wagon and two women in veils. Tail swishing, he jumped to the ground and trotted on resolute paws to the tents.

Both of the smaller pavilions were dark, though noisy snoring came from one and, from the other, a man's soft voice and a woman's low laughter. He sniffed the air and caught one of the human scents from the wagon, but not the other. He stood for a while, one paw raised, and then, turning, made a quick decisive lick at his shoulder blade and went on to the long tent with the pennant, and the fire-glow within.

He found a gap between two pegs and burrowed under the stretched cloth on furry elbows and haunches. Raising his head, he was assaulted by light, scent, and sound. Torches bound to the tent poles cast a ruddy light over two long lines of men seated at rough wood tables. Goblets thudded on boards; knives scraped metal plates. Raucous voices filled the air. Cat found a place beneath a bench and peered out through a forest of human legs. His ears twitched nervously as, through the rich scents of roasted meats, he caught a rank whiff of dog. Still, he had eluded the terriers at Mont Tombe, and success made Cat bold.

He crept forward until the trampled grass between the tables was in view, and saw, beyond, one more table, a high table with places only for three. At cat eye level were three pairs of human feet, one, in the center, in sturdy boots. A boy's bare feet, rough and bony, scraped the grass nervously at one side. At the other, toward Cat's steering-board whiskers, were a girl's, also bare, slender, and brown. Pooled around them were links of metal. A small, plaintive meow rose in Cat's throat: Danni.

He stretched up and made his neck long, raising his gaze above the table's height to see her face, and then shrank back into the shadows. Pious in pilgrim's robes, the Golden Knight sat between the boy and girl, smiling graciously at his followers. Cat hissed.

Stilling his swishing tail, he flicked his head eagerly toward the girl's face but saw only a gossamer web of white cloth. Veiled as she had been on the wagon in Francia, she appeared a simple nun, but for the long braid of glossy dark hair eluding the veil and hanging down over one shoulder.

Human memories flitted through his cat mind – Danni with her shining plaits at the river. Danni at Cille Aidan, holding her flaming torch. Danni challenging him with her forbidden swords in Aidan's church. A small chirrup of welcome escaped his tense, furry throat, and he turned reluctantly away to study the barefoot boy.

The youth was dark-haired and dark-eyed, with a thin sad face that seemed in need of a few comforting cat rubs. He sat as far from the commanding figure of Jocelyn Guidbairn as the bench would allow, clutching a small, worn harp to his chest. The food on the plate before him was untouched.

Cat would have liked to help him out there, but he had duties. Slinking back beneath the table, he crept forward on silent paws. He was five cat bounds from Danni's shackled feet, when he saw the terrier. Stretched out behind its master's boots, with only its white muzzle in view, it snored, stretched, and yawned. Teeth gleamed and its foul breath bushed Cat's tail.

Whiskers twitching in frustration, Cat sat down. Aware that the smallest attempt to win Danni's attention would win that of his canine enemy first, he began thoughtfully to wash. Then he settled in a hunch, waiting for the situation to improve. Dimly, he thought of Floki, also waiting, and then of the night passing at the slow pace of stars. He twitched his fur but did not move; waiting was a cat's tactic of choice.

He hardly noticed when the music began, so soft and so ethereal it sounded, as if some feline angel had begun to purr. His mind flitted briefly to the enchantress among the pillars, but then his thoughts stilled. All around him, the sounds also stilled. Men no longer spoke, nor even moved. Knives ceased to scrape plates. Goblets rested forgotten in quiet hands. The music grew louder, and so sweet that the air trembled, as if even the wheeling stars stood still to hear.

"*The Harp! The High-King's Harp!*" His human mind struggled to remember, but something stronger than sleep overwhelmed him and his eyes slitted closed. Cat slept, and the harp that heddled the threads of time, played on ….

He woke with a start, in darkness. Sound had lulled him; sound again roused him; a fierce growl as if the Golden Knight's terrier was an inch from his ears. He leapt to his feet, back arched, tail high, every hair erect. But there was no terrier, and the growl was fading, as if somewhere beyond his sight, a great roaring monster was hurrying away. Competing with the roar was another sound, a wild jangling, as if all the bells of Rome were ringing above Cat's head. And yet, through all, he heard still the sweet soft notes of the High-King's Harp. And fearsome as it was, the roaring voice was familiar.

Baffled, he sat down, the tip of his tail flicking in alarm, and looked around. The tent was gone, but there was no sky above. He was within a building. In one wall was a window, with open curtains. Cat jumped up on the broad sill and peered out, his whiskers twitching against glass. Brilliant light flooded a wide expanse of grass and cast huge shadows from dark trees. Further away, another bright light flashed, piercing the night, then disappeared, taking the roaring with it. The beast was outside, beyond the dark trees and shadowy wall.

He turned his head. The clanging bell continued. That sound, too, was familiar, and the darkened room was familiar too, tugging first at his cat memory, then his human. There were two beds, one empty, where some human had risen in haste. In the other, a slight figure huddled, as if asleep. Small, tense breaths betrayed wakefulness to sharp cat ears.

The space beneath the bed glowed slightly, at Cat's eye level. He jumped down, darted across the room, and batted aside a crumpled piece of cloth. The glow brightened and took form: a miniature human figure. With wings. *An angel. Sophia's angel!* Cat let out a yowl of astonishment. *I'm back. I'm in Safe Haven.* Outside, Ivan's motorbike roared away. *With me! I'm there. But I'm here, too.*

The figure in the bed sat up. Cat jumped back. Boy feet landed on the carpet where he'd been. *Aaron!* Cat chirruped. "A cat!" Aaron shouted. Dropping to his knees, he swept Cat up into his arms. Only Janetta had held him more gently. "A cat," Aaron crooned happily, and Cat began to purr.

The door burst open in a blaze of light. Aaron shrank back against his bed as a tall figure strode into the room. "I'm sorry, Dr Fairchild," Aaron cried, "I heard a noise, so I got up ...." Fairchild's eyes fell on the animal in his arms. Aaron clutched Cat tighter. "It must have gotten in when Gil went out," he said. "Out to the bathroom," he added hastily.

Fairchild looked once at Gil's empty bed and back to Aaron. "Gil's in the bathroom," Aaron said again. He backed away further, trying to hide Cat with his arms. "It's okay," he whispered. "It's friendly." Cat slitted his eyes.

Fairchild held out his hands. "Give me the cat, Aaron."

"No."

"It's feral. It may have fleas."

"You'll hurt it," Aaron said.

"Or course I won't."

Of course he will, Cat yowled. He wrapped his paws around Aaron and clung tight.

Fairchild lunged forward. Cat felt rough hands close on his scruff and the loose skin of his back. Aaron cried out and kicked at the psychiatrist's legs, but Fairchild was too strong for him. With a sob of despair he let go and Fairchild wrenched Cat from his arms.

"Don't hurt him!" Aaron begged, "Please don't hurt him," as Cat scrabbled with four desperate feet, clinging yet to the boy's pajamas. Fairchild cursed and pulled harder and ripped him free, a patch of blue flannel yet snagged in his claws. Twisting with all his sinuous strength, Cat sank sharp white fangs in Fairchild's wrist and bit down hard.

Fairchild shouted, swung Cat over his head, and flung him brutally. Cat flipped in mid-air, landed on his feet, and dashed for the door. "Run!" Aaron cried gleefully. With Fairchild's footsteps thundering behind him, Cat streaked down the corridor and out the open fire exit at the end.

Lights blazed all around him, blotting out the stars. But over the shouts and the jangling alarm, he heard two sounds: the throaty roar of Ivan's motorbike, far away, and farther still, the clear sweet notes of the High-King's Harp. Fairchild's feet rang on the metal staircase and his hand brushed Cat's tail, as Cat leapt from the stairs, into the darkness beyond ….

His dozing eyes flicked open. Torchlight cast fluttery shadows on the canopy above him. Wood smoke teased his nostrils with the tang of roasting meat. Dry grass rustled beneath his stretching paws.

The terrier yet snored at its master's feet. Beside it, Danni's chains glinted at her ankles. The bare toes of the harper scuffed the dusty ground. The last notes of the harp died away. Benches creaked as men stirred, shifting booted feet, and above Cat's head, goblets thudded softly on the boards. Voices rumbled pleasantly. Cat blinked. *A dream. A cat dream. So real, he could yet feel Aaron's comforting arms* …. He yawned and then suddenly his eyes narrowed to slits.

Something blue lay on the ground in front of his nose. He reached a tentative paw and batted it closer: cloth, a small, ragged patch of blue cloth. It smelled pleasantly of air and also of boy. *Aaron*, his human mind cried. *It was real. I was there.* But Cat had lost interest; the cloth neither moved, nor promised food. With a bored paw, he batted it aside.

He looked up again at the row of feet beneath the table, and at once his ears flattened. Where Jocelyn Guidbairn's boots had rested, there was now only an empty space. And the terrier was gone. Cat's hackles rose and with a small, involuntary hiss, he turned to creep away, just as an iron hand clamped on his scruff, yanked him from under the table, and held him up to the light. Hanging helplessly, he stared into the cruel, handsome face of the Golden Knight.

Shouts of surprise arose from the tables and sharp yapping; the terrier bounced at its master's feet, snapping eagerly. "Pretty Pussikins," Cat's captor murmured. "Where is your lady now?" He held Cat high, displaying him to all. "Shall we make you into fine gloves for her to wear? That she may never be parted from you?" Guidbairn laughed and his minions hurriedly laughed, too. "Ah, Pussikins," he said, his face a mask of sorrow, "the pity, that I must skin you first."

Still laughing, he reached with his free hand for his sword, brushing disdainfully by Cat's fiercest fighting weapon: his powerful hind paws. With a lightening thrust, Cat raked the knight's arm from bicep to wrist, splashing the white coat of the terrier with blood.

Guidbairn howled in rage, swung Cat above the dog's nose, and threw him to the ground before its waiting jaws. Cat landed on his feet, and rolled on his back, a spitting ball of teeth and claws. One caught the beast's bare pink nose, slashing it cruelly. Yelping, it drew back, and Cat flipped upright, bolted to the tight-pegged tent wall, and wormed his way under the cloth.

Behind, the terrier yelped again, as Guidbairn booted it after him. It emerged, snarling, into the night, as Cat plunged into the darkness of the cypress grove. Catching his scent, it barked triumphantly and crashed after him, into the trees.

Cat ran for his life. Around him, the cypresses offered refuge but, once treed by the terrier, he could only wait for the Knight's vengeful arrival. Better to die running, or turn and die fighting, like a Northman. *Like a Northman.* An image of Floki arose in his mind; tall, climbable, and, unlike a tree, able to fight back. Treed on Floki, he might survive. Buoyed with fresh hope, Cat raced faster, through the thinning grove, to the ruins of the villa, beyond.

Behind two standing pillars, he saw the shadowy form of the Hrolf's Isle pony, and, standing watchfully beside it, the Northman. With the terrier snapping at his tail, Cat dashed through the cat-infested rubble scattering surprised fellow felines, leapt over a fallen statue, and onto Floki's leg. Behind him the terrier wheeled in stunned circles, bombarded with the scents of myriad fresh cats.

"Off!" Floki shook his pinioned leg. Cat scrambled obediently higher, clung to his thigh, and then, digging his hind claws in deep, sprang up to his arm. Climbing messily to his shoulders, Cat settled in triumph, fore-claws embedded in the Northman's hair.

The terrier leapt and snapped but whirled away yelping as an enormous striped tomcat jumped, hissing, into the fray. Tail bushed as broad as a human arm, ragged ears flat and yellow eyes flashing, it charged the terrier like a knight in the lists. Ducking for cover beneath a marble slab, the dog met an outraged hiss from a hidden occupant and whirled, whining.

Then, small, black, and dainty, Cat's feline lady stepped out of an over-turned urn and advanced, utterly fearless, on the cornered terrier. Tail between its legs, it turned and ran. Cat yowled proudly and kneaded Floki's scalp.

"*You.*" Floki unbuckled his sword belt, held up its rough circle, unpeeled Cat, and hurled him through it.

Gil landed hard and sprawled on the dry, rough grass. "Ow!"

"That hurt? Good," Floki growled. Gil sat up, rubbing a bruised elbow. "I have fared better in sword fights, Warrior," Floki held out a lacerated arm and wiped his clawed forehead. "And bled less."

Gil gulped. "He was scared."

"*He* was? *He*, Warrior, is you."

"He's a cat, Floki, I can't ...."

"He is your Change-Thing. And he is *this* high." Floki held his hand at cat level and a new and opportunist feline gave it a hopeful rub. "*You*," he batted Gil's head hard, "Are *this* high. *Who wins*?" Gil shook his head. "I do warn you," Floki reminded him.

"I know, I know. Don't hide behind my Change-Thing," Gil sighed. But his mind was already elsewhere. *The cloth. The blue cloth.* He saw Aaron's blue pajama top through cat eyes and heard the ripping fabric through cat ears.

"Floki," he said uneasily. "I'm not a saint ...."

Floki leaned back and glared at him in the starlight. "I do know that, Warrior. And I am sorry. Were you a saint, I could bury you here and be done with you."

"No," Gil said. "You don't understand ...."

"I do not *ask* you to be a saint," Floki said wearily. "I only ask that you not be an idiot."

"I'm not a saint," Gil said again clearly. "But I think I've just been in two places at the same time."

"What say you?" Floki was suddenly still.

"Aidan said it's only the saints can do it. But then *Ciarnan* said Finn MacCoull could, because of his harp ...."

"Time-Heddler," Floki said. "The High-King's Harp."

"Guidbairn has it. He stole it. He murdered the king's harper and took the harper's son hostage, too."

"A story, Warrior. A longhouse tale."

"It's true. There's a harp in the camp, and a boy playing it. A sad boy."

"There are many harps, Warrior. Men seek amusement on pilgrimage. Other, of course, than their prayers," he added drily.

"But this one's different," Gil insisted. "Cat heard it playing and he, *I*, fell asleep. And then I dreamed. I *thought* I dreamed. I was Cat, still, but in Tir nan Og, with my friend, Aaron ...." he paused, "But I was there, too, outside. Outside, I was riding away with my father's friend, Ivan."

Floki leaned close, suddenly intent. "You *see* this?"

Gil shook his head, "I heard it. I heard his horse. His roaring horse ...." Gil's voice trailed off. Floki raised his eyebrows. Gil said hurriedly, "My enemy fought with my friend over me and I hung on with my claws in his clothes and I pulled a piece off ...."

"Dreams are dreams, Warrior. All men have them. And no doubt all cats. Few mean anything." He reached for the pony's bridle.

"Floki, the piece of cloth was with me, when I woke up."

"This cloth? From Tir nan Og?" Floki stared hard at him. "Where is it?"

Gil looked over his shoulder. "Back there. Cat didn't think it was important." The Northman gave him a black look, but Gil ignored it. He said evenly, "Floki, my enemy in Tir nan Og is my enemy here. They're the same man."

"Guidbairn?" Floki's eyes widened in amazement. "In Tir nan Og?"

"His name is different, but he's the same. So," he paused again and swallowed hard, "If he saw Cat there and saw Cat here ...."

"He knows we are here."

"I'm sorry," Gil ducked his head miserably. "I'm sorry I let him catch me."

Floki shrugged. "I send you to him. The fault is mine. Come." He mounted the pony and leaned down to offer Gil his hand. "You ride behind me now. I must hear," his face was intent in the starlight, "My lass? She is there?"

Gil swung himself up behind the saddle. "Yes," he said uneasily. "I saw her."

"What troubles you?"

"He keeps her right beside him. With her ankles in chains."

"Lest she fly," Floki whispered. "I will wrap those chains around his throat, Warrior. And she will be free." He paused, "She saw you?"

Gil shook his head. "I'm not sure. Her face was veiled, still, like in Francia. I couldn't see." Floki only shrugged.

"No matter. She will see us all, soon."

Gil told him then about the wagons, with their arms and supplies, the tents, and the horses.

"How many?"

Gil strained his receding feline memory. "Four?"

"*Four*? With four horses they ride from Francia to Rome?"

"Well, maybe more. He's just got four paws. He can't count any higher."

Floki twisted around on the pony's back. His eyes glinted ominously. "Can *you* count?"

"Sure."

"So *count*. How many 'four horses' did Cat see?"

Gil grimaced, summoning a cat-view of the tethered animals, arranged in foursomes. "Maybe nine? Thirty-four horses?"

"Thirty-six, Warrior," Floki murmured wearily. "Thirty-six horses. Two for each man. Eighteen mounted knights. And at the tables – how many?"

"He just saw their feet!" Gil protested.

"Divide by two!" Floki raised furious hands in the air; then caught the reins as the pony shied suddenly. Dim lights flickered beside the road ahead. Floki nudged the pony toward them. "Think of the longhouse, Warrior," he said. "As many men?"

"More."

"Eighty, maybe a hundred," Floki murmured. "Or is that just the feet?" he added as he slowed the trotting horse.

The small lights beside the road were just ahead, and Gil recognized the tomb where the woman had patted Cat's head.

She had gone, but clay oil lamps and the stubs of candles, yet burned before the shrine. Floki drew the pony to a halt.

"Why are we stopping?" Gil asked.

"Down."

"I've got to walk from here?"

"No. You stay here. I take you no further." He gave Gil a shove.

Gil slipped from the pony's back and stared at the tomb and the dark groves of trees all around. "Just because I'm crap at math?" he cried.

Floki laughed softly. "No, Warrior. Though when we are home, I send you to Aidan to learn. A farmer, a merchant, even a Viking must at least know how to count." He swung down off the pony and bent to lift one of the pottery lamps. "Now, Guidbairn knows we are here. Before he enters the city, he sends knights to deal with us. We are seen among the Saxons, there: Bjorn, impossible to hide, nor Grimhildr, a woman as tall as a man. The children, our Saracen ... and myself, a pilgrim who walks like a Viking, however humble he would appear. Rome is safe for us no longer. I leave you here and ride to bring the others."

"Now?" Gil cried. "There's no time. It'll be dawn in a moment."

Floki shook his head. "It is not yet Vigils – look, Frigga's spindle rides high." He pointed to the three stars of Orion's Belt, glowing in the black southern sky.

"But I was so long," Gil said. "In the tent, and in Tir nan Og ...."

Floki shook his head again. "You were barely gone before you returned. Well accompanied," he added drily. Stepping over a row of guttering candles, he approached the dark entrance of the tomb. "Come, now. We shelter you among the dead and keep you, thus, alive."

"What?" Gil whispered, stumbling in the shadows, behind.

A passage sloped steeply downward to a heavy bronze door which swung open, creaking on its hinges, beneath Floki's hand. He beckoned Gil into the blackness beyond, closed the door behind them both, and held up the guttering lamp.

The light leapt along the corridor beyond, revealing a moss-grown stone roof and rough-hewn rock walls pierced with dozens of shadowy crevices. In each, white bone glinted like hidden treasure.

Gil muffled a cry and shrank back against the dripping stone. Something scraped against his shoulder and he struck out in alarm, sweeping it aside. The severed bones of a hand fell, with a rustling clatter, to his feet. "Floki!" he shouted. The Northman turned and sighed.

"Respect the dead, Warrior." He lifted the skeletal hand, returned it to its niche, and then studied Gil's face in the flickering light. "Bones have power," he said gently. "But not to harm. A saint lies here, like at Peter's shrine. You will be safe." He held the clay lamp out. "Here. I give you this. You will have light. But stay here until I return. It is the living, out there, you need fear. Not the quiet dead."

Gil nodded shakily and reached for the lamp. But then he shook his head, unbuckled his sword belt, and dropped its circle on the stone floor. "Keep the lamp," he grinned. "I'm not going to need it."

"No, Warrior."

"But cats *like* dark places!"

Floki snatched up the sword belt and thrust it back into Gil's hands. "Yes. And they creep into crevices and sleep. And when I call you, you will ignore me. *No!*"

Grudgingly, Gil re-buckled the belt around his waist and then took the lamp with trembling hands.

"Take care! Spill the oil and you will have darkness enough, even to frighten a cat." Bidding Gil a cheerful good night, the earl stepped softly away, opened the door, slipped out, and slammed it shut.

The lamp flared, sending eerie shadows dancing. Gil groaned, sliding to the floor and covered his face until he could bear the deeper blackness no longer. Letting his fingers slip from his eyes, he looked warily around.

The lamp burned quietly now. Darkness once more shrouded the bones. *A saint lies here, like at Peter's shrine.* He thought of Janetta's hand taking his own as she bade him kneel. Clasping his fingers around the memory of hers, he closed his eyes and sank wearily into sleep.

CHAPTER FIVE

When Gil awoke, what seemed like moments later, the imagined hand was flesh. A voice whispered his name. He cried out, but small fingers pressed his lips to silence. "Janetta?" He opened his eyes a slit, fearing a dream that would turn into a nightmare. His lamp was cold, its wick doused. But a soft blue light filled the tomb. The door stood open on the dawn. A breath of wind touched his face, carrying the scent of flowers.

"Who would it be, but me?" she asked innocently.

"No one." He smiled sleepily and reached for her with both arms.

"No. The earl calls you." Floki stood in the doorway. The others filled the narrow corridor beyond. One by one, they trooped in, crowding the dead for space. Bjorn and Grimhildr ducked beneath the low lintel. Ciarnan and Ragi swaggered uneasily. Ismail smiled at Gil. "You are brave," he said. "To sleep here." Gil shook his head.

Rachel grimaced. "At least you didn't get dragged out of your bed in the middle of the night." She wrapped her arms around herself and leaned sleepily on Ismail's shoulder.

When all were inside and Eirik was tormenting Percy with a loose skull, Floki beckoned Gil, and Gil followed him out into the grey early dawn. The four ponies cropped grass a few feet away, saddled and loaded with arms and gear. Lionheart raised his head and whickered happily as Gil approached. Floki clamped a hand on his muzzle. To Gil he said, "Take the beasts up there, into the trees, and tether them where they cannot be seen from the road."

Gil nodded, gathering reins. "Wait," Floki said as he released Lionheart's nose. "*Whatever* this one tells you is a lie, except for this: I did promise and I *do* promise that if he makes one sound up there, *one*, then he returns to Hrolf's Isle as the lining of my cloak. Now, go." He shoved Lionheart's rump. "When you return, join me there," he pointed to an ancient olive tree on a little rise overlooking the road. "In silence."

Four steps away, Lionheart nudged the small of Gil's back. *He beat me.*

Lie.

He took away my food.

Lie.

He took away my friends.

What friends? They're all here.

The donkeys.

YOU HATED THE DONKEYS.

I want the ship.

Gil sighed.

Tethering the ponies behind a thick screen of poplars, he ran back to where Floki waited, stretched on the ground beneath the olive tree.

"Down," the Northman whispered, his eyes on the road beyond. Distant hoof beats rang in the still air. Gil flattened himself out of sight and lay barely breathing as a party of knights trotted purposefully into sight. Mail coats jangling, saddle leather creaking, they passed, two by two.

"Ten," Gil breathed as they rode on toward the city wall. Floki turned and smiled.

"Ah, the scholar." He stood, watching the knights' distant backs. "Ten he sends to slaughter us. Eight remain to guard him." Gil started to rise, but Floki waved him down and stretched out again on the grass. "Patience, Warrior. Soon the sun rises and he makes his holy way to Rome."

A horse whinnied in the distance as the grey olive boughs turned rosy above Gil's head. He lay rigid, willing Lionheart to silence. Hoof beats sounded, and the shuffle of many boots. Two knights trotted into view, golden light glinting on upraised lances. Behind, uneven ranks of men followed on foot.

"Eighty and more," Floki whispered. "But still less than we see in Francia."

"Where are the rest?" Gil asked.

Floki was quiet, thinking. Eventually he said, "The journey overland is harsh for all pilgrims. Some fall ill. Some die. Some turn back." He paused. "Still, eighty is enough. We are eleven. And two are children."

"Right," Gil murmured. *Great time to think of that.* His eyes were on the road where the four carts creaked into view. In the lead was the open wagon piled high with the wood of the feasting tables and the cloth of the tents. Perched on top, and dozing in the sun, was the terrier, looking harmless as a lapdog in Gil's human gaze.

Two covered carts followed, one clanking with hidden arms. He ignored them, his eyes fixed on the third. Its cloth covering was reefed at each side, revealing the bedding Cat had sniffed, but only two people rode on the bench at the front, the sad-eyed boy, clutching his harp, and a big, heavy-set woman in nun's habit. Her veil pushed back from her face, she casually munched an apple as they passed.

"Where's Danni?" Gil whispered, despairingly. But Floki touched his arm and pointed.

"There," he breathed, his voice made tender by longing. "She is there."

Six more knights rode behind the wagon; two side by side, two outlying, and two at the rear; guarding a tall man in fraying pilgrim's garb. Walking barefoot and carrying a battered staff, he was indistinguishable from the humblest penitent, but for the plain band of gold adorning his head. At his side strode a slim young girl, veiled head bowed, bare feet scuffing the dust.

"She's free!" Gil whispered. "The chains are off."

"Of course," Floki murmured grimly. "Would he have her irons tarnish his golden sanctity in Rome?"

The knights drew closer, passing only yards from their hiding place. Gil held his breath as the man and girl followed. Beside him, Floki lay still as a crouching lion until the fly-flicking tails of the last knights' horses were far in the distance. Farther still, the bells of Rome were ringing, light as birdsong on the dawn air.

"Lauds," Floki said. He rose and stood beneath the drooping

olive branches, his hand on the ancient wood. "By Vespers, he is a dead man, and she is in my arms." He gripped Gil's shoulder with a comradely hand. "One last battle, helmsman. And then to sea, and home."

By the time they set out from the shrine, the road was crowded with travelers. Mingling with them, they became, once more, a Northern pilgrim and his motley kin, and in that guise came within sight of Peter's Gate.

Floki paused beside a small stucco building, with a clutter of doves on its tiled roof. A faded brick wall enclosed a scrap of grassland and a barn. Seven black goats grazed within, tended by a small child. Percy shouted happily and jumped from his pony to embrace the nearest. Floki drew him back. "You will have goats, I promise, but these are his." He smiled at the child goatherd and beckoned him, holding out a silver coin. To Rachel he said, "Tell him, if you can, we would leave our beasts with his."

"Leave them?" Gil said, hearing Lionheart's protest building already in his head.

"We may depart from Rome in haste, Warrior, when our business there is done. In those narrow streets we are quicker on foot. We leave them here, safe beyond the wall, until we need them."

The goatherd nodded happily at Rachel, his eyes on the coin, which he clearly understood even if her church Latin eluded him. He dragged open a cross-pole gate, but as they led the four ponies in — Lionheart stiff-legged in terror of a goat kid that came up to his knees — a shout came from the dilapidated house. An old man with a bald head and a grey-streaked beard appeared.

The child held up his coin proudly, but the man began to shout and argue, pushing the ponies back to the gate. Floki stepped quickly in between. He took another coin from his purse and then drew his sword. Holding up both, he said to Rachel, "Tell him, he chooses."

But the bald man backed off, shaking his head, before she could speak. Floki tossed the second coin to the child and turned to Ragi and Ciarnan. "Your pilgrimage is over," he said.

"Arm yourselves properly. Mail on your backs and shields on your arms. Kill anyone who lays a hand on the beasts."

Both boys stared, stunned. Ciarnan stood stiff and proud, almost as tall as the Northman, every inch the king's son he was. "I came to Rome to avenge my cousin," he said, his lip trembling with outrage, "Not to herd ponies."

Floki swung the sword in a savage arc, pointing it at Ciarnan's chest. "You came to Rome to do my will. Do not make it my will that you die in Rome." His eyes were cold, his voice calm, as if killing Ciarnan would be only a minor distraction.

He'll do it, Gil cried silently. *Give in.*

But Ragi shouted angrily, "Leave the Saracen and his Change-Thing to tend the animals. They may all run away together, like he ran before."

Rachel grabbed Ismail's arm, drew him close, and cried, "He didn't run away! He saved me!"

Floki suddenly laughed. He stepped back and sheathed the sword. He nodded toward Ciarnan, and said to Ragi, "Vengeance muddles his head, and love muddles yours. Neither makes a wise warrior." He smiled, softening the words. "Without the ponies, the children never return from Rome. Our cause rests as much on you as on any."

He turned to the others, "Come. No more delay. Our quarry is well ahead."

Lionheart whinnied desperately as they left the goat pen, stretching his neck and following Gil with wild eyes. Gil steeled himself, closing the pole gate behind them. *Ragi and Ciarnan will keep you safe.*

When he looked back, he saw the boys donning their sturdy hauberks and felt a twinge of envy. But no pilgrim entered Rome jingling with mail.

Just within Peter's Gate, the throng of travelers had come to a milling halt. A herald's horn sounded ahead. Three tall horses emerged from a side street, bearing soldiers, and behind them, another, carrying a Roman nobleman wrapped in a purple cloak. Clerics and well-dressed nobles walked behind.

Pressing forward, the riders cut a swathe through the pilgrims, opening a vista of the square beyond. Gil caught

Floki's long sleeve and pointed at the golden pennant fluttering above the crowd. "Guidbairn."

But the Northman was already drawing them into the shelter of a church portico. From its shaded steps, they watched the Romans approach the procession. A small girl carrying flowers was brought forward and her wreath of blossoms presented to the pilgrim king. A cheer arose from the watching crowd, and then another, as a sparkle of thrown coins caught the sun. Children scurried to gather them and the procession went on, accompanied now by the Roman chieftain and his followers.

The mass of penitents joined in behind, but as Floki led his party from their hiding place, he turned suddenly aside, into the shadowy alley from which the Roman nobleman had appeared.

At times so narrow that the occupants of the ancient buildings could lean from their windows and clasp hands across the roadway if they chose, the alley twisted and turned, leading to an empty cobbled square. A pink stucco building commanded it, its sweep of stairs and tall, half-shuttered windows proclaiming it the Roman chieftain's palace.

Both the building and the square were deserted, their silence broken only by the distant shouts from the crowded streets they had left. More alleys opened on every side, and without hesitation, Floki chose one and led them on. "Come, a few more rabbits in this warren will not be noticed."

So many, and so crooked were the narrow alleys that Gil felt certain they were lost, doubling back toward the gate or wandering aimlessly in the tightly packed maze of streets. Then, suddenly, he was confronted with a wall he recognized and then another. "The hospice!" he cried. "We're right behind it!"

Floki grinned, "Helmsman, have I lost my way yet?" Glancing first left and right, he led them cautiously along the rear wall of the hospice and then crossed the cobbled yard to the stable and the ruin beyond. In the shelter of its crumbling wall, he paused and called Gil to his side. Together they scrambled over a heap of fallen brickwork to the gap that opened on the *piazza*.

It was quiet in the early morning, the merchants still setting up their stalls. A robed brother draped linen over wash lines stretched above the cobbles. Weary pilgrims washed their feet in the fountain, while others flowed up the steps to the atrium. There was no sign of the Golden Knight.

"Where are they?" Gil peered uncertainly into the shadows of the atrium.

"Approaching at the stately pace of kings. We cut across his bow. Good." He turned to summon the others, but a sudden commotion erupted behind the hospice. A brother emerged from the door and with him, an armored Frankish knight, shouting angrily. The brother shook his head again, calm, but unmoved. Then he looked up and saw Floki and Gil, and attempted a desperate small gesture of warning, but it was too late.

The knight turned. Gil shrank back, but Floki strode suddenly forward, the cowl of his robe raised and his cloak drawn close around his face. "Seek you the Viking, Floki Magnusson?"

Gil stared at him; then looked quickly to the others across the stable yard. Janetta met his eyes, her own wide and frightened. Bjorn stepped forward, hand on sword hilt. But Floki had taken the knight's arm. "With silver," he said, "You shall see him."

The knight shook the Northman's hand off and reached, with a sigh, for his purse. Floki stepped toward the stable and beckoned. The knight sighed again, weary of bartering with beggarly penitents. He counted out the expected coins as he followed through the low door. Before he could close it behind them, Gil bolted across the stable yard, slipped in, and took up a wary place at Floki's side.

The stable was dark and warm with the breath of beasts. In the stalls along the walls, new occupants had already replaced their ponies and a line of tethered pilgrim's mounts filled an open central aisle. Floki stepped back into the shadows beyond the door and beckoned the knight closer.

The man glanced uneasily at Gil but obeyed. When he and the Northman were standing face to face, Floki flung back his hood and cloak. "You have seen him," he said. He drew his sword. "And here is silver." Dropping his coins, the Frankish knight reached wildly for his own blade, but Floki's free arm was snaking already around his neck, grasping his hair, and snatching his head back. The sword flashed and was lowered so fast, Gil thought no harm had been done. The man's eyes opened wide and were glazing before Gil saw the blood from his slashed throat reddening the links of his mail.

Floki released the knight and as the body collapsed on the dung-stained earth, wiped his sword clean with a hank of straw. He looked up and saw Gil standing with his face frozen in shock. "Play is over, Warrior," he said gently. "We have work to do."

In the stable yard, the hospice brother hurried forward, hands held out in supplication. "Pax," he whispered, "Pax Christi."

Floki raised the sword and pointed it at his chest. "You do not see me." Then, sheathing the blade, he collected the children from Grimhildr, and with a hand on each of their shoulders, entered the *piazza* of Saint Peter.

Spying the fountain, again, and the doves, Eirik and Percy broke free and ran, shouting, to play. Floki strode quickly after, and Gil and Janetta followed. Then Percy shrieked suddenly, in terror, and Gil broke into a run. But Floki was beside the children already and the only threat was Eirik, grinning demonically and waving something thin and white in the air.

Floki reached for the thing in Eirik's hand, but the boy jerked it possessively against his chest. "A bone," Janetta murmured, and Gil groaned, remembering the severed hand in the tomb.

"King's Son," Floki said wearily. "From the Northlands to Rome, you are trouble, and now you defile the dead."

"Oh, he is gross," Rachel said, wrinkling her nose. Grimhildr stamped into their midst, holding out her broad, calloused palm for Eirik's treasure.

Percy jumped up and down shrieking, "Take it away!" Curious faces turned to watch.

"No. Leave them," Floki said suddenly. Eirik's surprised grin spread across his face, and he bore down on Percy, once more, extending the bone like a miniature sword. Percy looked at Floki in dismay, and then ran, shrieking and crying, around the fountain, with Eirik in pursuit.

Penitents and trinket sellers jumped out of their way, and an old man raised a fist at Eirik. Then the monk by the wash lines abandoned his laden linen basket and hurried to intervene.

"Now, Warrior," Floki nudged Gil and pointed at the line where, among the bedding, the black woolen robes of clerics hung drying in the winter sun. "Take the largest you find."

"Steal them?" Gil protested. "From monks?"

"*Never,*" Floki mimed horror. "Barter for them with the angels and saints."

With Janetta giggling behind him, Gil sprinted to the wash line and hauled down the habit, cowl, and scapular he judged the most voluminous. Janetta caught up the ends of the trailing garments and together they returned to the fountain, where Floki had added to the diversion by spilling a dozen small coins on the ground. Surrounded by eagerly scurrying children, he accepted the stolen robes. "May the Lord forgive you." He grinned and called, "Bjorn!"

In the shelter of a merchant's tented stall, Floki hurriedly wrapped the huge Northman in the black habit, slipped the scapular and cowl over his head, and smiled. "I vest you, Bjorn Break-Neck, a holy canon of Saint Peter." Then he stepped smoothly in between the squabbling boys, caught Eirik around the middle, divested him of his bone, and handed it to Grimhildr. "Lay it on an altar," he laughed, "That its owner not haunt your sleep."

Then suddenly, he froze, the laughter dying, as a horn sounded in the streets beyond.

"The herald," Gil cried. "He's here."

"Come." Floki gathered the children and led the others swiftly up the basilica steps, past the sick and their carers in the atrium, and through the great doors of the church. He chose a side aisle and, packed tightly together, they wormed through the praying, chanting crowds, toward the distant shrine.

At one of the many side altars, where a priest was singing Mass, Floki suddenly halted and summoned Bjorn. Backing him against a marble column, he said, "Stand there, holy canon, and watch." He pointed through the rows of pillars to the high altar. "I go there. Guard the children until I return. If there is fighting first, fight."

Bjorn grinned, his black beard bristling and his hand caressing his sword hilt beneath his churchman's robe.

"Troll-Maiden," Floki turned to Grimhildr. "You are a pious mother hearing Mass." He directed her toward the priest at the side altar and pushed Percy and Eirik after. "You and you, beside her; obedient to your mother."

"She's Grimhildr," Percy squinted doubtfully.

Floki knelt and looked into his puzzled eyes. "It is a game, Percy. In the game, she is your mother. Here, take my staff," he held out the worn wood, "And give it to me when I return." Percy carefully took the staff and then ostentatiously accepted Grimhildr's hand.

Eirik stepped closer to Bjorn.

"With Grimhildr," Floki repeated, rising quickly.

"She took my bone."

Floki's eyes flicked to the rear of the church, where the excited crowd flowing through the five tall doors announced the arrival of the penitent king. He placed his hand firmly on Eirik's neck. "It is not your bone, but a dead man's. Touch it again and I take one of yours in its place. This one that binds your head here." He slapped Eirik's shoulder. "Go."

Drawing Rachel and Janetta close, he hastened them forward, until the aisle opened onto the great space before the high altar and the twin flights of steps leading down to the shrine. "You, now, are my family, at your prayers, one on either side." He turned then, facing Ismail and Gil.

"You, there," he directed Ismail to a marble column, "and you," he pointed Gil to another. "There." Each pillar, like Bjorn's station, gave a clean sight line to the altar. "When I move," Floki said, "you move. You," he smiled at Ismail, "Take the boy and his harp. And you," he faced Gil, "Take my lass." His eyes met Gil's with absolute trust. "Then take my family," he drew the girls close again before offering them to Gil, "And run."

"Run?"

"Run from the church, to the streets, and back the way we came."

"And you?" Gil said uneasily.

"I follow."

"Alone," Gil said, his unease growing.

Floki grinned. "Warrior, I do not come to Rome to lie with saints. I finish with our friend and find you. With the ponies, beyond Peter's Gate."

"He has friends of his own," said Gil.

Floki's grin broadened. "And so have we!" He raised a hand to the pious paintings gracing every wall. "When blood is spilled in Peter's Church, the very angels cry out! And every voice shall answer: pilgrims, clerics, beggars; shouting, crying, running, falling over each other in fear, down on their knees before every altar. And we, among so many? A few rabbits fleeing the warren. Who will see us? Who will care?" He nodded suddenly, "Quiet now. He comes." With a courteous arm around each of the girls, he went forward and knelt between them, raising his face to the altar, a penitent lost in prayer.

A bell chimed, and a hush fell over the crowds at the rear of the church. Two columns of black-robed clerics filed through the doors, chanting in Latin. With a sudden chill, Gil heard the words Ciarnan's brethren sang as Hy burned.

De profundis clamavi te, Domine:
Domine, exaudi vocum meam ....

Then the chill turned to cold rage, as, crowned head bowed in regal humility, the penitent king of Camelot entered Peter's Church.

Gil stilled the hand that reached, unthinking for his sword, and peered through the forest of columns as, surrounded by his clerics, Guidbairn advanced up the central aisle, toward the shrine, a single, black-robed monk walking just behind.

The boy with the harp, afforded the poet's place of honor, was at the Golden Knight's left hand, and, slim and graceful on his right, the veiled girl walked, freed of her shackles, less slave than penitent queen. Gil drew in a sharp breath and glanced quickly at Floki.

The Northman remained, quietly kneeling, his eyes on the painted crucifix above the high altar, as if utterly unaware that his mortal enemy and the girl he loved were but a few paces away. All around him, penitents murmured their own prayers, awaiting their turn to descend to the shrine; the canons of the basilica progressed up an outer aisle, singing their office, and the Mass continued untroubled where Grimhildr knelt with the children. In the vastness of the teeming basilica, even the entrance of a king was commonplace.

Two young clerics hurried Saxon and Frisian visitors aside, clearing a space at the altar for the royal pilgrim. Guidbairn's Frankish supporters rushed to take their places, crowding their master from behind. But, as the Golden Knight paused before the altar to genuflect, no one troubled the young Northern penitent, kneeling in their midst.

Rising, Guidbairn bowed his head, lifted the circlet of gold from his fair hair, and placed it in the hands of his attendant monk. A sigh passed through the crowd, as, shorn of all royal pride, the pilgrim king turned toward the steps, and with the boy before him and the veiled girl just behind, descended to the hallowed darkness of the shrine.

Gil looked toward Floki, but still the Northman kept his trance-like stillness. The time stretched out, impossibly long and Gil wondered in sudden panic if there were some other, secret exit, reserved for honored guests, through which Guidbairn was, even now, eluding them. Then a slight movement on the shadowy steps from the shrine caught his eye, and the veiled girl appeared. Head bowed and bare feet padding, she passed out into the immensity of the basilica, within reach of Gil's hand. He looked wildly to Floki, but the Northman did not move, and, ethereal as a ghost, the girl slipped away into the crowd.

Then a cheer arose as the bare-headed Golden Knight stepped into view, mounting the last stone steps. His joyous followers pressed forward, driven firmly back by monks of the basilica, and his own black-robed clerics. Unnoticed, the young Northman at the altar rose to his feet; so still and solitary that he seemed to exist in another world.

With his back to the turmoil greeting the king, he solemnly signed himself with the cross, and gently ushered the two girls to the side. Then, in a move so blindingly fast that Gil, for all his attentiveness, reeled back in shock, he whirled, signaled with one hand to each of the boys, and with the other flung back his pilgrim's cloak and drew his sword.

Shouts of alarm panicked the tight-packed crowd. The two young clerics ran forward, hands raised in protest. With a sweep of his arm, Floki flung them brutally aside. Eyes alight with cold fire, he bounded across the ancient stone to the unguarded king. But Guidbairn was waiting for him, smiling slightly, his own blade already in his hand.

For an instant, Gil stared in astonishment; then he, too, drew his sword. Pilgrims and penitents scattered before him as he plunged into the throng, his eyes fixed on the girl's white veil. "Danni!" he called, but she did not turn.

At his side, Ismail had already captured the terrified boy harper, calming him with his gentle voice, even as he battled two of Guidbairn's Frankish knights. Steel rang on steel before the high altar, joined by a cacophony of bells and cries and prayers. Still smiling, the Golden Knight retreated before Floki's savage sword, his bewildered clerics crying out in dismay. Gil called Danni's name again, but she stood frozen, her veiled face fixed on the battle at the altar. Then three of the Franks closed in a circle around him.

A swift kick tripped up the nearest, and as he crossed swords with the next, a burly monk brought the third to the floor with a solid punch. "Blessed are the peacemakers," Gil muttered, focusing his attention on his adversary, while the veiled girl stood hugging her slim body with trembling arms. "Danni!" he shouted, fending the Frankish knight with two quick blows.

He swung again, a slashing down-stroke onto the man's leather-bound wrist, and his opponent's weapon clattered to the stone floor. But the fallen knight had scrambled to his feet and jumped in to replace him. Wildly, Gil kicked the weapon toward the girl's bare foot. "Use it, Danni! It's tough here."

She leapt back with a little cry, and the sword was snatched up again, by his foe. Two more knights closed in. Ismail strode to Gil's side, but there were five, now, then six, and but for the jostling clerics begging, empty-handed, for peace, they would be dead already.

He looked desperately for Floki, but the young earl was utterly intent on the embattled king. Again, Gil disarmed an opponent, and again kicked the weapon across the floor.

"Danni!" he begged. Through the blur of battle, he remembered her taunting him with Magnus' swords in Cille Aidan's church. "Danni, look at me!" he shouted, and with an angry hand reached out and snatched away the infuriating veil. She cried out again, holding up small, white fingers before a beautiful young face he had never seen before in his life. "*What?*" he cried.

Her dark eyes wide with terror, her cheeks streaked with tears, the girl fell to her knees, begging in Ciarnan's Irish tongue. Oblivious of his opponents, he swung the sword toward her. "Who are you? Where's Danni?"

She shrieked, and, spying the boy harper hiding behind a pillar, she scrambled up and ran to him. Clinging together, they shrank back against the marble, like two frightened children.

Two knights closed in, laughing. "Damn you!" Gil shouted, kicking one and slamming the other over the head with the flat of his sword. "Floki!" he looked up in despair to the altar. "Floki, it's not her!"

But Floki had seen and had understood, and he turned now on Guidbairn with such savagery that he might before have been playing. Guidbairn's triumphant laughter died, and fear entered his eyes. Stumbling backward, he fell to one knee, and staggered up, turning desperately to his fearful supporters for help. None moved.

But then, the black-robed cleric yet holding the kingly crown suddenly flung the golden circle to the floor, drawing from within his robes a short, well-hidden sword. No more monk than Bjorn, he raced into the battle before the altar, deadly blade in hand.

"Floki!" Gil shouted. "The man behind!" If Floki heard, he did not care, his entire being focused now only on the Golden Knight, battering him down to his knees in a lightening flurry of blows.

With strength he did not know he had, Gil slammed two of his opponents aside with his shoulder and vaulted the abandoned crown, landing a stride from the sword-wielding monk. Arm raised already at Floki's back, the attacker half-turned, exposing his ribs to Gil's sword. With all Gil's weight behind it, the steel pierced skin and flesh and shattered bone, skewering the man to the heart. Blood erupted from the gasping mouth, bubbled down the broken chest, and splashed, red and roiling, on the ancient holy stone.

For an eerie moment, there was silence. Then a roar of outraged voices rose to the frescoed angels above. Amid it all Gil heard one high, pure cry of anguish as if the angels had indeed replied. Hand yet on the hilt of his sword, he raised his eyes. Over the thrashing, gurgling body, he saw Janetta's face receding from him, as she backed away, transfixed by the horror of what he had done.

His sweaty hands fell from the buried blade and he stumbled back. Skidding in blood, he tripped over the fallen crown and sent it clanging across the stone. Another shout of outrage rose. Through it, Gil heard Floki's calm voice, "I thank you, Warrior," He looked up. The Northman stood still and ready above the helpless Golden Knight. "Now take your sword," he said, "We are not done."

The Frankish knights closed in. Ismail rushed to Gil's aid; Rachel, beside him, took up the dead man's sword. Eyes half-closed and face turned away, Gil forced his hand onto his own sword hilt and jerked back. The body flopped flesh and bone clinging grimly. Sickened, Gil rested his foot on the shoulder and pulled harder, grimacing as the blade ground against bone, then slipped free in a fountain of fresh blood. His head swirled, but he raised the sword in shaking hands. Men shrank back, newly wary.

He glanced behind him and saw Floki turn to Guidbairn with cold murder in his eyes. But then suddenly the earl looked up and spun around, his gaze sweeping the basilica and fastening on a turmoil at the distant doors. Pilgrims fleeing the battle at the altar halted and retreated, milling and crying out in panic as men poured into the church from the atrium.

Floki whirled back to Guidbairn and the Golden Knight fleetingly smiled. Then, dramatically flinging aside his sword, Guidbairn threw himself on his face before the altar, crying aloud, "I entrust my soul to God and his Holy Mother!"

A wave of flowing black engulfed him, as the canons of the cathedral ran forward, holding up empty hands and shielding the penitent king with their unprotected bodies. The basilica bells still thundered above their heads, as if to summon help. Gil looked back to the doors, expecting more clerics, intent on peace. But those entering, glittering with mail and armed with steel, were no churchmen.

"The children!" Floki shouted. Gil spun and saw Bjorn already engaged in battle, Grimhildr at his side. "It is a trap!" Floki grabbed Gil's shoulder and thrust him toward them. "It is a trap, and I, its unholy fool!"

In a numbing instant, Gil understood it all: the veiled girl-in-chains who wasn't Danni, the missing Frankish pilgrims, even Guidbairn's pious ruse at the altar, all one vast game of King's Table, with Percy its prize, and themselves the unwitting pawns. They, who had thought themselves the hounds, were the hares, from the first. And now, like all hares, they must run.

Shoulder to shoulder with Floki, Ismail, and Rachel, he charged Guidbairn's discomfited warriors. Deprived of their chieftain, the Franks edged back, then broke and ran. Floki followed, hacking down two before they reached the safety of the impenetrable throng. Kicking a body aside, he leapt over the next, clearing a path by his fierce presence alone.

Ismail grabbed the boy harper, and Rachel, the weeping terrified girl. Gil ran to join them, but Janetta was suddenly before him, holding her hands up to bar his way. "Come on!" he caught her wrist.

"No!" She shook her head. "You must go to the priests!" She pulled him back toward the clerics around the bloody body before the altar. "You must not die in this sin. Confess! Make peace for your soul."

Gil stared at her in consternation. Beyond, Floki and the others had reached Bjorn and Grimhildr. Bjorn had Percy over his shoulder and Grimhildr, a wildly protesting Eirik over hers. Shielded by the tumult, they ran down an outer aisle, toward the atrium. The Frankish knights pushed their way forward, impeded by frightened pilgrims and protesting monks, on every side. Then two burst from behind a marble column, shouting in their own tongue, and pointing at Gil.

Gil gripped Janetta's arms. "If we stay here," he said evenly, "They will kill us."

"It does not matter!" she cried.

He shook his head, then, sheathing his sword, he crouched down, gripped her slender legs, lifted her off her feet, and flung her over his shoulder. "It matters to me!"

With her slight weight nothing on a back hardened by the oar, he ran, dodging pilgrims, clerics, beggars, merchants, knights. He broke through to the atrium and out into the winter sunlight, then down the steps to the *piazza* beyond; a slim, strong young man in Viking clothes, scattering the doves in his flight.

Over his head, the bells of Peter's Church clamored unendingly and his heart returned a desperate discordant chant:

De profundis clamavi ad te, Domine ....
I am a Northman. I do as I wish.

CHAPTER SIX

A t the foot of the steps, Gil set Janetta down, expecting her to turn on him with her fists, as she had, once in the Mews Garden. But she only stepped back, hands clasped before her, her face sad. "I'm sorry," he blurted. "I had to …." Then, over her shoulder, he saw two of Guidbairn's knights emerge from the atrium, sweeping the *piazza* with hunters' eyes. "We have to hide." He caught Janetta's arm and dragged her with him into a cluster of dark-skinned pilgrims in white, Eastern robes.

Shuffling in their noisy midst, they reached the bright canopies of the double row of merchants' stalls and slipped between a booth selling badges and another offering vials of sacred oil. Gil crouched low, drew Janetta down beside him, and watched the knights descend into the *piazza*, pushing their way through the pilgrims to a line of tethered chargers beyond the fountain.

Mounting, they set out, crisscrossing the *piazza* at a ruthless canter, their eyes scouring the crowd. When they reached the furthest point, where the monks' washing lines flapped in the breeze, Gil pulled Janetta up again, and then froze as a hand closed in an iron grip on his shoulder. "Do not move."

"Earl Floki!" Janetta cried, her face lighting with relief. He touched her lips and nodded toward the first of the merchants' booths. Four Frankish knights were peering into the depths. Gil held his breath while they argued loudly with the merchant, pushing into the stall, mindless of his wares. At last, with an oath, they drew back and strode away.

"Come," Floki turned and led them behind the booths, into the narrow alleyway between them and the back of the second row of stalls. Cluttered with merchandise, tethered donkeys, manure, and refuse, it led away from the basilica with its thunderous bells, toward the distant streets.

Holding firm to Janetta's hand, Gil followed the Northman, ducking low at each gap between the stalls. "Where are the others?" he panted, as Floki paused at the end of the row.

"With Bjorn. All are safe. But you do not come. I fear you run too slow, and they catch you. So I come back for you. Then I see, there, on the steps," he looked up at the great church, high above them, "That you run very well indeed. So well, I think the holy nuns of Saint Peter are not safe." He gave Gil a quick grin, over his shoulder. Gil shook his head and Janetta looked away.

Floki laughed. "Come, we go there now." He gestured to where the *piazza* ended in a dusty clutter of wash houses, lean-to animal shelters, and pilgrims' campsites, beneath the aqueduct that fed the fountain. Weary horses and donkeys milled in a crude pen. The open ground before it was blackened from the remnants of night fires, some still sending wisps of smoke into the clear blue sky. "Quickly," Floki added, with another glance at the basilica steps.

Dashing across the open space, they just made the shelter of a wash-house wall, when twenty and more Franks broke from the atrium, descended the steps, and raced to their tethered horses. Shoulder to shoulder, the knights rode out, sweeping the crowded *piazza* with military precision, driving penitents, merchants, and clerics before them.

Pilgrims clambered into the fountain to escape. Others crowded the basilica steps, seeking the safety of the church, only to be driven back by more of Guidbairn's men. Children cried, separated from their parents. Old people stumbled and fell beneath the feet of the panicked crowd.

"Have mercy!" Janetta wept as the steel shod hooves of chargers bore down on the fallen. She turned to run to the aid of an ancient nun, kneeling in desperate prayer. Gil caught her and held her fiercely back.

"We can't help!"

"There," Floki pointed to the pen of donkeys and horses and ran to its rough wooden barricade. Vaulting it, he landed perilously amid the jostling animals. Gil and Janetta followed, dodging flailing hooves and darting between the sweating flanks of lunging, frightened beasts.

Beyond lay another wash house and the brick arches of the aqueduct. Ducking between them in quick, dangerous sprints, they skirted the *piazza*, circling back toward the hospice courtyard from which they had come. Out in the open, Guidbairn's knights had cornered the helpless pilgrims into huddled groups. Men on foot barged brutally among them, hauling out suspects. *Because of us.* Gil's mind was suddenly far away, in a burnt village on a Northern shore. *Because of us.*

"Once more, Warrior, and we are safe." Gil tore his eyes from the cowering pilgrims. Beyond one last stretch of cobbled ground lay the broken wall over which he had first glimpsed the *piazza* of Peter's Church. Bjorn's black head poked momentarily above the crumbling brickwork. Gil looked over his shoulder at the knights commanding the *piazza*, awaiting a moment when all were occupied.

Then, suddenly, over the cries and shouts and ringing bells, a new sound arose, from beyond in the Roman streets: the rumbling clatter of steel-shod hooves on stone. The sound swelled, drawing closer. Gil looked in alarm to Floki, and then back to the *piazza*, as from each of the approaches burst ranks of mounted men, dressed in the tunics and cloaks of Roman soldiers.

Without breaking stride, they bore down on the surrounded pilgrims from every side, blocking off escape. Bjorn ducked out of sight as a line of horsemen took up a position between the hospice and their own shelter beneath the aqueduct. Side by side, Gil and Floki surveyed the wall of horseflesh and steel between themselves and escape. "Warrior," the Northman murmured quietly, "this is not good." He gave Gil a small smile and loosened his sword in its scabbard.

Gil drew Janetta closer. The horses, with their great stamping feet, were so close to their shadowy hiding place that he could smell their nervous sweat and feel their tremors of fear. The clanging bells, alone, would have sent Lionheart into panicked flight, and as the thought passed through Gil's mind, the nearest Roman mount lifted up its forefeet in a half-rear. *Yes.* Gil thought, exulting. *Yes, run. Run from the wolves!"*

He roused up the fiercest wolf images he could imagine, grey, slathering, shaggy, yellow-eyed wolves. Wolves half the height of a pony. Snarling, sinuous, pack-hunting wolves.

The horses stamped, kicked out, strained against their startled riders' tight-held reins. But these were not half-wild hill ponies from Hrolf's Isle, nor ill-trained pack horses in Deer Bay, but disciplined, well-schooled soldiers' mounts. They reared and bucked, but held firm by masterly hands, none ran.

Wolves! Gil cried once more, in his silent pony voice, summoning white-toothed jaws from every side. One beast broke loose, shying, striking sparks from the cobbles with frantic hooves, panicking the others, and for a moment, Gil thought he had won. But the Roman turned the horse, circling it until it calmed, and brought it back into line. The others calmed, too. Gil realized, despairing, that these animals had faced down worse than wolves.

But then, a new memory flashed into his mind, ignited by the sparks of steel on stone: Lionheart at the blacksmith on Hy, and a pony-fear greater, even, than wolves. Fire. He turned swiftly to Janetta, crouching beside him. "Give me your shawl." She looked baffled, but immediately loosened the green silk veil that had shielded her in the marshes and covered her hair in church.

Gil took it, bunched up the voluminous cloth, and crawled with it across the cobbles until he found one loose. Floki cast him a quick, curious glance as he prised it free. Kneeling, Gil hurriedly wrapped the veil around the cobble, swathing the stone in layers of cloth, fine as spiders' web.

Securing it with a knot, he half-rose and scuttled a few steps to where a circle of scorched cobbles marked a pilgrim's abandoned campfire. Gingerly, he lifted a shard of blackened wood and stirred the remaining ash. Then he knelt, blowing softly, until embers flared.

"Warrior …." Floki called softly.

Intent on his new-born fire, Gil just shook his head. Then he laid the silk-wrapped cobble in the glowing ash. Wisps of white smoke rose at once, then a flicker of flames, and suddenly the whole silk wrapping flared alight. Jerking the sleeves of his woolen tunic over his bare hands, he clasped the flaming cobble and stood up.

"Warrior!" Floki rose to haul him down, but Gil was running out from the shadows beneath the aqueduct, into the winter sun. Gritting his teeth against the flames searing his hand, he drew back his arm and threw the cobble skyward. It soared over the heads of the soldiers, trailing fire, and over the fountain beyond, to the merchants' deserted stalls. Arcing down in a shower of sparks, it thudded into a sagging yellow canopy, igniting the sun-rotted cloth. *Fire*, Gil cried. *Fire, fire, fire!*

He drew his burnt hands close to his chest and dashed for the shelter of the arch. A shout pinned him to the brickwork. The nearest soldier leaned low over his prancing horse's neck, peering into the shadows. He shouted again, drawing the attention of two others.

Gil fixed his gaze on the white-rimmed eye of the snorting animal, conjuring an image of flames leaping higher and wider, racing along the rows of canopies, flaring in the refuse heaped behind, lighting the flapping linen on the wash lines ...*Fire!*

The horse reared, champing frantically at the restraining bit.

... *And beyond, into the streets, the thatched roofs of the Saxon Quarter, until all Rome was ablaze ... Fire! Fire! Fire!*

The horse whirled, skidding on the cobbles, and fell, pinning the soldier beneath it. *Fire!* Gil cried. Two more reared, and then one broke and ran, scattering the others, bolting through the trapped crowds, up onto the basilica steps. With the canopies ablaze and smoke rising to the bell towers of Peter's Church, chaos engulfed the *piazza*. Donkeys brayed, men shouted, and over all, the bells rang on.

"Now!" Gil cried. He caught Janetta's hand and ran, conscious of Floki just behind them. Scrambling over the fallen rubble of the broken wall, he leapt down into the courtyard, reaching to catch Janetta, as she jumped wildly, too.

Floki landed beside her and to Gil's astonishment, he was laughing. He jerked his head toward the pandemonium they had left behind them and gave Gil's shoulder a proud slap of approval. "I think, Warrior, they do not ask us back. Come," he ran lightly across the courtyard to the stables.

Bjorn stood, an immoveable defensive wall, just within the doorway. In the murky darkness beyond, Gil glimpsed the others, huddled against the rough planks of the stalls, their eyes on the body of the Frankish knight.

Soaked in congealing blood, it was attended already by buzzing flies. Gil turned his head away, sickened, and yet remote now from the carnage on the floor. He had seen worse. He had done worse. He reached a hand to the trembling Irish girl and brought her out into the sunlight.

Gathering them all tightly together, Floki led them, darting through the maze of alleyways, back the way they had come. The steps of the Roman nobleman's palace were busy now with visitors and servants, but none took notice. They had become again humble pilgrims and Rome was well used to those.

At the end of the last back street, where it joined the broad road to Peter's Gate, Floki held them back. "Two, now," he said, "And then another two. And then, two more."

Gil and Janetta slipped in beside a line of merchants' pack horses. Bjorn, still in his canon's robes, and with Eirik at his side, became, briefly, an imposing member of a procession of monks. The others followed, blending into the endless crowds flowing in and out of the walled city, and, untroubled, they passed through Peter's Gate under the eyes of the soldiers lazing in the winter sun.

A scant few strides beyond the Wall, and in clear sight yet of the Roman guards, Floki halted, gathered his party around him, and, crossing himself, solemnly knelt. Head bowed and eyes closed, he clasped his hands around his staff. Gil stared.

"What are you doing?" he whispered.

"Praying." Floki kept his eyes closed, but his lips quirked in a smile.

"Here?" Gil protested.

"It is what pilgrims do. We bid farewell to Holy Rome."

Gil saw others kneel, likewise, and uneasily did so as well. At last, after an unnervingly long while, Floki raised his head and calmly stood. Glancing back at the watching soldiers, he said, "Hounds follow the hare that runs." And turning for a convincingly regretful last sight of Rome, he led them on, toward the tumbledown farmstead where Ciarnan and Ragi and their ponies waited amid the goats.

Gil heard Lionheart's frantic whinny before he even glimpsed the sun-weathered tiles of the ancient farmhouse. Pressed up against the cross-pole gate, the pony stood shaking his shaggy mane, nostrils flaring with desperation. Gil braced himself for an onslaught of recrimination, but when he reached the goat pen, Lionheart only pressed his nose against his chest, trembling all over with relief.

It's alright, Gil said. *I'm here. I said I'd come back.* But the place where he heard the pony had no words, only an image of a broken tree on a far Northern hill. He stroked the warm fur under Lionheart's mane. *It's okay. We're going home now.* Around them, the goats bleated and Percy ran to pat one and then another. The Hrolf's Isle ponies stamped and snorted while Bjorn adjusted saddles and packs and swung Eirik up to ride.

In the few short hours since Gil stood here last, nothing had changed, and everything had changed. He fought back a sob lest it release a drowning flood of tears and led his pony back to the road.

"Where's Danni?" Ciarnan looked around uncertainly.

Ragi stared at the two Irish strangers. "Who are they?"

Gil shook his head, with an uneasy glance at Floki. But the earl turned to the two boys, waiting, armed and ready as he had ordered. He bowed suddenly. "Man of the High Island, Man of Hy, I beg your forgiveness. I call you fools for love and vengeance, and now I take it back. The only fool here stands before you." He smiled his white, charming smile, and walked away.

It was a harsh journey, seaward. Almost at once, it began to rain, as it had on the day they came. But this was a cold, hard rain, worthy of their Northern home. And no sooner had they left the Wall behind, than Floki led them off the road, into open countryside.

Pastures, olive groves, vineyards and wheat fields lay

between the Northern road and the Western one by which they had come. And there, their pilgrim guise wore thin: true penitents rarely strayed from the well-trodden way. Wanting no further battles, they retreated meekly from the suspicious looks of sun-darkened countrymen. But circling farm buildings and lying low as harvesters and herdsmen passed took time. Crossing rain-sodden marshland took more. The water-haloed sun was dipping low as they approached a fine villa, nestled behind dripping grey olive trees, within sight, at last, of their road.

This time, to Gil's surprise, Floki made no attempt to avoid it. Instead, he led them so close that their ponies' ears pricked toward the sights and scents of their own kin. Floki halted the beast he was leading, touched Gil's arm, and pointed to a cluster of dark horses in a field beside a tiled-roofed barn. Backs to the weather, they stood with heads close together, their coats steaming in the rain.

"How many, scholar?"

Irritated, Gil counted quickly, "Thirteen."

"Good. We leave them two. Courtesy."

"What?"

Floki pointed to the animals. "Take them, Warrior."

"Take them? *Steal* them?"

Floki gave him a pained look and waved a hand at the villa. "They are rich, Warrior."

"They still *need* them."

"We need them more. *Take them.* Call the others to help. I go there and find tack." He gestured toward the barn and stalked away, leaving Gil to his task.

Uncomfortably, he beckoned Ismail, Ciarnan, and Ragi to join him, and with a quick glance at the villa, barely visible through the rainy dusk, he unfastened the sturdy wooden gate and approached the horses, his mind instinctively filled with images of fodder and kind hands. They were docile work horses, gentle beasts, coming almost eagerly to his hand. He took two by their halters, and each of the boys took two more. Those remaining all followed freely, hopeful of the shelter of the barn.

It was so easy, and yet, when Gil reached the open gate, his hands were shaking on the halters, his feet leaden. Were not Ismail and his animals jostling behind him, he would have stopped and gone no further. *We're stealing. I'm a thief.* At his back, the others were laughing, untroubled, and a mocking voice within his own heart laughed, too. *So? What does it matter? I've killed a man. What does anything matter now?*

They drove the last two horses back into their field, slammed the gate shut, and ran together, triumphant with their prizes, into the dusk. Floki was waiting already, with an armful of bridles, in the shadows of the olive grove.

Mounted on the bare backs of the new beasts, with the children and their gear secure on their own, they circled the villa to the road, and set off at a swift pace, racing the fading light into the west. Lionheart, too wet and miserable to protest, trotted doggedly behind Gil's horse, a sleepy Eirik clinging to his mane.

Janetta rode at Gil's side, mastering her new mount with ease. Painfully aware she had not spoken a word to him since they left Peter's Church, he cast her quick, shy glances, hoping for a smile, or even an acknowledgement that he was there. But she kept her gaze fixed firmly over her horse's ears, until the darkness hid her face from him entirely.

They rode late into the night. Gil peered ahead, yearning for a glimpse of the sea, but all was darkness, the rain relentless. Despite it, mosquitoes swarmed around them. The silk veils, sodden in moments, were no protection, though Floki carefully draped them over the children's heads. Anyhow, Rome itself had been plagued with mosquitoes, as soon as darkness fell, and on the Northern road, they had even tried to bite Cat. Gil swatted them half-heartedly, too wet and cold to care.

When Floki finally called a halt, he slid stiffly down from his drenched horse and looked wearily around the abandoned vineyard the Northman had chosen for their camp. Poplar trees grew up among the forgotten plantings and the ancient vines, looping from one to another, formed a dripping canopy over their heads. They tethered the animals, built a lean-to of cut branches for the children, and gathered deadwood for a fire. Gil

labored with his fire striker over a fistful of half-dry grass, until
it won him at last a grudging few sparks.

"Take care," Floki leaned over his shoulder, "Lest you set
the countryside ablaze, O, Fire-Raiser of Rome."

"Some chance," Gil muttered, resisting the desire to punch
his earl for his insanely cheerful smile. But then his fire caught,
the wood crackled, ruddy light flickered through the lonely
vines and, warmed a tiny bit, he sat back on his heels and
managed a small grin.

"That is wise," Floki said. "We are defeated. But we are not
dead. We are not captured. And not even this rain lasts forever.
A man makes more sorrows for himself, Warrior, than the
world makes for him." He ruffled Gil's hair, suddenly, as if Gil
were still a little kid. "Come. The Troll-Maiden prepares a feast."

Grimhildr unwrapped a meagre store of provisions she
had bundled in her apron as she left the hospice: three loaves
of bread and a round of hard yellow cheese. She glowered,
dividing the bread and cheese into small portions with her
knife, then pointed the knife at Floki as if daring him to even
try to cheer her. "Some feast."

He bowed, with a wry smile, and then turned to the Irish
boy and girl, huddled together beside the hungrily grazing
ponies. The boy held his leather wrapped harp close to his chest.
The girl stood stroking Lionheart's neck, her face turned away,
seeming more at home with the horses than with themselves.
Floki addressed the two softly, in Irish, asking their names.

Gil smiled at the boy, suddenly remembering himself and
Ismail first learning Ciarnan's name, with sign language, when
they had no Irish at all.

"Niall," the boy whispered. He ducked his head and held
his harp closer.

"It is safe," Gil said, struggling for the Irish words. "We will
not take it." He smiled again.

The boy nodded and answered suddenly, in English. "It was
my father's." Gil instinctively touched the knife he always wore
at his belt, the knife that had been his own father's.

"It is safe," he said again.

"And you, lass," Floki addressed the girl. "Your name?" She

shook her head and buried her face in Lionheart's mane.

"Her name is Caitilin," Niall said. "She is afraid. It is strange here. She comes from a faraway place." Floki nodded.

"Caitilin?" he murmured, extending one hand. Slowly she released the pony and stepped closer. "Where is the home you have come from?"

"The Island Port," she whispered. "The Island Port of Yula's Isle."

He smiled. "That is not so far a place to me. I know Yula's Isle. Though," he paused, "I know no Island Port."

Her eyes widened. "But you must know it, if you know Yula's Isle. It is very famous."

Floki nodded and gave her again his gentle smile. "Then it is a fame that has not reached my ears. But I am but a poor farmer from the Northlands. Still, I will take you there. And you," he looked up at the boy harper, "I take you home, too."

For the first time, the dark-eyed boy smiled. "You know my home?"

Floki nodded again. "The fame of Tara does indeed reach the Northlands. I know it, and I take you there."

"You will be much rewarded!" the boy cried happily. "My father was *file* to the High-King. This is his harp that he played before the king. Only he and I could play it. And now," the sadness returned to his eyes, "Only I."

"You shall play it before the High-King," Floki said. His eyes took on a sudden dreamy light that Gil knew well. "And your own son after you."

"I have no son," the boy looked puzzled. "I am thirteen."

"You will die an old man with sons enough to play seven harps," Floki laughed. He shook his head and the dreamy light faded. "But that is far away. Here, now, are two hungry children. Come." He held out a portion of bread and cheese to the girl, and like a small, frightened animal, she crept closer, accepted it, and with a grateful murmur, sat down with it by the fire.

"And you," he smiled again and gave Niall a portion and then summoned Percy who took his with a happy grin and sat beside the Irish boy, staring curiously at the harp while he ate.

Floki divided up the rest of the food; himself, Bjorn, and

Grimhildr taking nothing. Ismail shook his head and said, "For the children." Gil and the others nodded agreement.

"You, also, are young," Floki said, but all again refused and he said, "So be it," with a respectful nod. "King's Son," he called. Eirik was hunched up, hands around his knees, before the fire. "Come. Eat." The boy shook his head, eyes squeezed shut. "No. You do not refuse. Children must eat."

"I am a man," Eirik mumbled.

Floki sighed and turned suddenly to Ciarnan and thrust the bread and cheese at him. "Eat."

"I say no," Ciarnan waved it away.

"And I say yes," Floki's voice hardened. "Eat." Ciarnan pushed it aside, angrily. Gil groaned inside. *I don't believe it. There's someone stupider than me.*

Floki leaned close and whispered, "Eat it or you will need no food ever again. Do you *never* learn?" Ciarnan met his eyes for a brief moment, then snatched the food, wolfed it down, and stalked off. Floki smiled slightly and turned back to Eirik. "See? He is a man and a king's son, also. Now you eat, too."

Eirik shook his head and covered his face.

Rachel stepped forward. "He's too tired."

Floki studied Eirik. "He is never too tired before," he said quietly. But he gave up then and urged the Irish girl to eat an extra portion. She smiled shyly, divided the bread and cheese in two, and gave half to the *file's* son before she ate.

She finished her own and sat back, absently rubbing the chafed raw skin of her bare ankles. When she saw Gil watching, she quickly covered her feet with her skirt. Floki stepped closer and knelt beside her. "Child, let me see."

She hesitated and then pulled back the cloth. His fingers lightly brushed the bruised flesh. "It is the chains," she said, making it sound somehow normal.

"Yes." Floki's voice took on an edge that belied the gentleness of his hands. "Bring me water," he said evenly to Grimhildr. The girl watched, torn between fear and gratitude as the earl washed the crusted blood from her ankles and wrapped them in strips of cloth torn from Grimhildr's apron. When he was done, she drew her feet close and gave him a small smile.

"My father, too, will reward you," she murmured.

Floki nodded. "I want no reward but this: that you tell me how you came to be chained."

She looked with haunted eyes at the *file's* son, and then lowering her gaze to her bandaged feet, began in a soft, emotionless voice: "It was a fine summer day and I went from my father's hall to the shielings above the White Hollow, to tend the cattle. But one cow was missing. Soon, a man appeared, handsome, in fine, strange clothing, and he had seen the cow, higher on the hill. If I would follow, he would show me.

"As we climbed, I seemed to hear music, a beautiful harp playing. And though I could see below me the loch and the Island Port with my father's hall, all else seemed strange. I had lost my way. And then, the man I followed stopped before a wood of rowan trees. A young girl was there, beautiful, with brave dark eyes and chains around her ankles.

"Five men stood behind her and I was afraid and turned to run. But the man I had followed caught me and took the chains from the girl and placed them on me. Then they took my outer garments and made me dress in hers, and she, in mine. Surely, then, he struck me, for though I felt no pain, I was, all at once, in a strange hall and it was night, as if I had fainted and awoken. And he was there," she looked quickly at the *file's* son, "Playing. And I was a prisoner and am a prisoner until this day." She cast Floki a look of passionate gratitude and said again, "My father will reward you, on Yula's Isle."

He smiled, but turned then to Niall, "Have you also seen this girl? The girl who wore Caitilin's chains?"

Niall solemnly nodded. "I have. But not on Yula's Isle. Nor at my home at Tara, but after I was taken from it by the raiders from Alba. They killed my father and took me away across the sea to their fine court in Camelot. For long they kept me there, their king, my new master. He bade me play for him and at first I refused. But then, men lay swords here," he touched his throat. "I am not a brave warrior, but I am of the *filidh*," he suddenly began to weep. "I play for him. My father's harp. It is shameful."

Floki touched the arm that still clutched the high-king's harp. "Even brave warriors wish to live. And you are a boy who carries no sword. It is they who are shameful. Continue."

The *file's* son shrugged, uncertainly. "One day, the king and all his court set out on pilgrimage, and they take me with them. There, too, along the road, I am asked to play at the halls of chieftains or at camps in the forest.

"At Deer Bay, we linger at the chieftain's hall. Word has come of a beautiful girl from the North, seen in the slave traders' camps. The king seeks her. He sends men to the slave market, but she is already gone, taken by a Northman from Francia.

"At once, we too set sail, and arriving at the Northman's fortress, are welcomed grandly. And the Northern slave-girl is there, kept apart from the other slaves, for she is indeed beautiful, and the chieftain would have her for concubine. But my new master lays down gold, and the chieftain's purse is bigger than his heart, and so my master claims her. That is when I see her, in his bedchamber."

Floki's face showed no expression, but his hand closed on his sword hilt.

"She is very frightened," the boy said. "But the king assures her that her honor is safe, for others of his court are there, and myself as well. He wishes only that I play for him and that she sing. And so I play and she sings as beautifully as the women of Tara, who sing like the wild birds.

"And, when I play, I am, as always, alone in my heart, as if I dream. And, so, then, when I finish, I raise my eyes, but the slave-girl is gone. Another girl is there, weeping, wearing the slave-girl's clothes and shackled with her irons. And though they are so alike that many at the court say she is the same, indeed a witch who changes her form and face, I know it is not so." He looked up at Caitilin watching him trustingly. "We travel together, guarded always, but we talk, and few of the king's court speak our tongue. For though she speaks it strangely, as no doubt they speak it on Yula's Isle, she is indeed an Irish girl, and the story she tells you is true."

"I know it is true," Floki said simply. "She is too gentle to lie. And your story, true as well. I thank you."

The boy smiled, and clutched his harp closer, glad to be done speaking. The girl, Caitilin, looked up and said shyly,

"The Northern girl ... she is yours?"

"She is mine."

"Will you seek her, now, on Yula's Isle?"

Floki looked out into the black, wet night with eyes already on the miles of sea that lay ahead. "I will seek her there. I will seek her at Heaven's Gates, if I must." A brief glimmer of exhausted defeat crossed his face. He saw Gil watching, then, and smiled. "It is well, helmsman. We have a good wind north." He turned back to the girl. "Come, child. Take shelter and sleep. We rise early for the road."

The circle around the fire broke up, each seeking out some place of meager cover. The rain had not stopped and, though Gil could not imagine himself wetter, he helped Ismail construct a little tent of matted vines to stave off the worst of it. His eyes strayed longingly to Janetta, building a similar structure with Rachel. When for a moment she looked up, and at last met his gaze, he seized his chance. Tapping Ismail's arm, he said, "I'll be back," and strode across the campsite to her side. "Please ...." he began.

"Away!" Headdress sagging like a windless sail, Grimhildr barged between and thrust him aside.

"No!" he shouted, wrenching himself free of her hands. "No!" All the misery of the day arose in a tide of frustration. "I just want to talk to her! Leave us alone." Grimhildr's brows lowered and she reached for her axe.

"Leave them," Floki said suddenly. He smiled at Grimhildr, courteous, but uncompromising. "He will respect her honor," he said. "Or answer to me."

Gil nodded gratefully, caught Janetta's wrist, and ran, dragging her with him into the darkness of the tangled vineyard. When the campfire was a distant glow behind them, he cautiously released her. "Please. Don't run. I have to talk to you."

"I do not run." She shook her head, tried to smile, and then buried her face in her hands to hide her tears. "It is hopeless," she cried. "All is lost."

"Lost? What's lost? We've escaped. We're together ...."

"Your soul. Your soul is lost."

"My *soul*?" Gil shook his head in baffled relief. "Is *that* all?"

She stepped back, the tilt of her face in the faint light showing her puzzlement. "Do you jest?"

"Jest? Of course not. I thought you were angry at me. I thought, I don't know, that you didn't love me anymore," he mumbled.

"I will always love you. Forever," she said at once, but something in her voice troubled him more.

"You talk like I'm already dead," he said.

"But you are!" she cried, her voice shaking with anguish. "It was mortal sin!"

"It was a battle," Gil protested. "People get killed ...."

"But in the church! You shed blood in Peter's Church. Before the altar! In the holy sanctuary!"

"He was going to kill Floki!" Gil threw up his hands in despair. "What? Should I just let him?" She didn't answer. He took a deep breath. "I don't believe this. Don't you care?"

"I care about your soul."

"What about Floki's soul?"

"I would pray for him."

"Oh, great. That would fix everything."

"It *would*. He is a good man. I pray to Our Lord for his soul ...."

"No," Gil whispered. "He is not a good man. He is a murderer and a thief. I'm glad he's on our side but he is *not* a good man." He shivered suddenly, as if the darkness of the night had seeped inside him. *And what am I?*

She shook her head. "I love you," she said sadly.

"So much that you wanted me to go back there and die?"

"But I die too!" she cried. "And we are together than forever in eternity!"

"I don't want eternity," he held both hands out to her, pleading. "I want to be with you, now. Here!" He stared through the veil of rain at her small, determined form, water streaming down his face like tears, oblivious of all around them, until a shape suddenly emerged from the darkness and Floki's firm hand fell on his shoulder.

"Come," he beckoned them both. "I have built you a shelter."

He guided them toward a dripping nest of branches. "I sleep with the Saracen."

Gil hesitated, glancing quickly at Janetta whose gentle fingers closed on his own. "Grimhildr?"

Floki laughed softly. "I am earl, Warrior, not Grimhildr." He smiled in the flickering firelight and then slipped away into the night.

It was a good shelter, low, but expertly woven. When they were together, inside, the rain tapped futilely on the leafy roof above them. There was barely room for one, much less two, and the only way to lie was locked in each other's arms.

She fit in his embrace as if she had grown there, part of him always and forever. He was kissing her before he even realized. Sweet, and tasting of rain, her mouth welcomed his instantly, bravely belying the words it had spoken. She had never been so close to him, and yet, never so far away. Dizzy with joy, and wracked with sorrow, he fell into dreamless sleep.

CHAPTER SEVEN

When he awoke, she was gone. A finger poked his chest. "Gil? Are you awake, Gil?" He sat up, his head brushing the roof of his leafy shelter, his arms bereft.

"Awake, now, Perce," he mumbled. Percy's cheerful face loomed closer.

"Eirik's sick. He won't get up." Gil shook his head. His palms stung from the fire lighting in Rome. All his muscles ached from the long, cold ride.

"He's probably just sleepy."

"He was sick *all over.*" Percy mimed vomiting down his front. "*And* he was sick at the other end!"

"Right," Gil muttered. "Got the point." He gave Percy a weak grin and clambered out of his shelter. His grin faded. Eirik huddled before the remnants of the fire, with Floki's fur-lined cloak wrapped around him. Floki knelt at his side. The others were gathered around in a solemn ring.

The earl spoke softly and the boy winced. "My head hurts." He bent his arm over his face and tried to curl up on the ground.

"No." Floki stopped him. "We must ride now. But I ride with you." The boy shook his head and then suddenly began to cry. Gil stared, astonished. Floki stroked Eirik's back. He looked up then, and his gaze settled on Ismail. "Is this the illness of the little animals?"

Ismail's brown face was still and solemn. He glanced briefly at Rachel and then back to Floki. "I think yes." Floki turned to Rachel.

"Pretty Hawk?"

She nodded. "It could be. Ismail has seen it," she said. And without any rancor, added, "I've only read about it in books."

Floki looked down again at Eirik, and then stood. "Bring the horses. We take him to the monastery." He bent and lifted the child, who did not protest, but sagged limply against his shoulder while Ragi brought the horse the earl had ridden. Floki set Eirik up on its back and mounted behind him. Wrapping the fur-lined cloak tighter around the child, he led them out of the vineyard and onto the road.

Mounted again on Lionheart, Gil followed him, leading his stolen horse behind. The rain at last had stopped and the drenched countryside shone golden in the dawn. In the distance, he glimpsed the pale glimmer of the sea and his heart soared. He turned and saw Janetta, so slim and graceful on her own mount, watching him shyly, and though she looked quickly away, his heart soared again.

The bells of the monastery were ringing Saxt when he spotted the tiled roof of the bell tower across an open field. The sun had risen warm and bright, drying their clothes and raising the spirits of all except Eirik who curled tighter against Floki's shoulder, hiding his face from the light.

Gil slowed Lionheart until Rachel's horse caught up with them. Nodding toward the distant monastery, he asked, "Do you think they can help?" She shook her head and looked away. Then, as they mounted a slight rise in the long straight road, he saw that his question didn't matter anymore.

The gates of the monastery were in sight, and before them, a dozen mounted men blocked the roadway. Sun glittered on the polished helms and upraised pikes of Roman soldiers, and on the shields and mail of Frankish knights. "They're here before us," Gil murmured hopelessly.

Floki drew his horse to a halt. He studied the mounted men briefly and then returned his gaze to their surroundings, pasture to their left, and to their right, the encroaching marshland. "Warrior," he said quietly, drawing Gil's attention. "The way lies there, left of that copse of trees. When you reach it, set your eyes on the next copse, until you reach the first running water. Cross that. You will see a broad, flat open marsh. Cross that with the sun over this shoulder," he tapped Gil's left, as Gil struggled between amazement at Floki's memory of their journey, described now in reverse, and his own desperate efforts to visualize it. "Cross two more burns, go left of the wide pool, and follow the burn that flows from it. It will take you to the strand and to the ships."

"I can't …." Gil started, but Floki cut him off.

"You must. Leave the horses we take here; they slow you in the marsh. Bring only ours. Here, my Hawk." He beckoned Rachel and pointed to a black-robed brother walking behind a small herd of brown cattle. "Go to him. Say I steal the horses and now I repent." He met Gil's incredulous stare and for a brief moment he smiled. "Aidan tells me all things belong to the White Christ. See, now, I only move His things around."

Gil shook his head and as the others dismounted and Rachel collected the lead reins of the stolen animals, he said, "Why are you telling me all this?"

"So you may lead them," Floki said simply. "I take the child there." He waved an arm toward the guarded monastery and took up his horse's reins. Gil stepped in front of the horse and caught its bridle. "Let the beast go, Warrior." Floki gave him a warning look and reined the animal aside.

"No." Gil stepped in front again. "You'll be dead and he'll be alone," he said bluntly. "How is that going to help?"

"The brothers will care for him. They have medicines." Floki suddenly drew his sword and pointed it at Gil's chest. "Now, go. Or I must use this and recite the way yet again to another. You waste my time."

"And you waste all of ours!" Gil shouted. "Can't you ever just be like other people? Like, normal, and afraid?" He heard himself echoing Hakon and threw his arms in the air. "This is pointless!" He turned then and caught Rachel's eye as she backed slowly away with the horses. "Tell him!"

"Tell me what?" Floki said quietly. Rachel clumped the mass of reins and leaned her forehead against one animal's mane.

"They haven't any medicine for this, Floki. Not here."

"Not here," he shook his head uncertainly. "Then where?"

"Nowhere. Nowhere in this world." She looked to Ismail.

"At home," Ismail said softly, "My little cousin dies of this."

"There is no medicine in Tir nan Og?"

"There is medicine," Rachel said. She looked at Ismail again and said, "For some." She paused and her gaze shifted to Floki. "Rich people have medicine."

"Rich people. Earls and kings … they have it?" She nodded, her eyes again on Ismail's solemn face. "Do they not share, these earls?" Floki said.

"Sometimes," Ismail smiled shyly at Rachel. "Sometimes they share."

Floki shook his head. He sheathed the sword he yet held and tightened his arms around the sick child. Rachel said, "I know you are willing to die to help him. And that will happen if you go there. But Gil is right. There's no point."

Taking from her what Gil knew he would never take from a man, he rested his hands on the child's shoulders and sat for a moment with his eyes closed. Then he slipped down from the horse's back, lifted Eirik down, too, and carried him to the largest of the Hrolf's Isle ponies.

"See, here is your old friend," he said gently. Eirik clung to his neck, shivering, and saying nothing. Floki set the boy on the pony's back and mounted behind him. He tossed the reins to Gil. "Take us to the ships."

Gil set out, on foot, leading the pony into the marsh. A glance over his shoulder told him the others were following. He set his eyes on the distant copse of trees Floki had shown him, his mind racing, seeking to recall the rest of the instructions.

Down in the marshland, all landmarks were swallowed by the waving grasses all around. Once again, he thought of the compass he had given Floki, which Floki himself disdained to use, on land or sea. Then a rebellious determination not to ask for help arose in his heart, sustaining him as he successfully found and passed the chosen copse.

Set your eyes on the next …. He strained upward to see further, and so great was his triumph when he spotted the waving clump of willow saplings, that he stepped blindly forward and splashed thigh-deep into an oily black pool. Marsh gases bubbled around him as he hauled himself out, halting the pony just in time. Floki, on its back, watched dispassionately until Gil was firmly on drier land. "Take my staff," he said then. "It is with Ciarnan."

The staff helped, measuring the depths of the pools and streams that lay all around. Gil crossed the first running water he found, as Floki had instructed, but in the flat marshland beyond, his confidence faded. The sun shone over the required shoulder, but that was only the vaguest guide. Each time he circled a forbidding stretch of water, or struggled with the pony through a thicket, his path grew less certain. The second running stream did not appear and the sun moved on, dipping westward.

Swatting clouds of insects, Gil came to a halt. "Okay," he said, looking up at the Northman. "Where now?"

"I tell you once. It is enough," Floki said without expression. "I am not always here."

"You're here now!" Gil shot back. "I'll deal with the future when it happens, okay?"

"You do not learn if I do not make you, scholar." Floki smiled, absently stroking the sick child's flaxen head. "But you are right. Straight on. The burn is thirty paces. Thirty-three paces for you."

It was thirty-two and a half. Gil was too glad to see his landmark to resent it. He went on, crossing the two further streams Floki had described and, skirting a wide, wind-stirred pool, turned at last to follow the black water that flowed from it.

The wind rose again, tossing the reed-heads and bringing with it the joyous salt scent of the sea. He stumbled toward it, wet and mud-covered, but exultant. A sound rose over the bird cries and splashing of hooves, the soft hush of breaking waves on a sheltered strand. And then, above the rippling reeds, he saw two slender pine poles outlined against the sky.

"The ships!" Gil cried. "We've made it!" He turned to Floki. The Northman studied the poles with narrowing eyes.

"You raise masts without my word, Sea-Friend?" he murmured. Then he lowered his gaze to Gil and smiled slightly. "Go on, Warrior. We will see what makes my cousin so bold."

Hakon met them, running up the strand as they emerged from the marsh. Gil saw the ships already afloat, their masts raised, and their oarsmen standing ready. A smile of relief brightened the Shetlander's dark countenance, as the whole of their party followed safely onto the sands. Then, as he stumbled to a halt in front of Floki and Gil, the smile faded, replaced by a frown of uncertainty. His eyes were on the Irish girl as he said, "But she ...."

"She is not my lass," Floki said drily. "I have noticed."

Hakon shook his head. "Who is she?" he demanded. "And where is the girl you sought across three seas?"

"Across another. And I seek her yet."

Hakon shook his head again and his expression softened. "Cousin, how long do you pursue this hopeless ...."

"'til time ends, if I must, but not this day."

Hakon's gaze swept all their faces, and then returned to Floki. As if seeing the cloak-wrapped king's son for the first time, he said, "Why do you ride with him? What has happened?"

"The child is ill," Floki said. He looked over Hakon's head to *Silver Dragon*, riding the gentle waves. "Why is there water beneath my keel? I bade you wait on this strand."

"We *have* waited," Hakon returned angrily. He was staring at the Irish girl and the boy with his harp slung over his back. "Too long already." Wrenching his eyes from the strangers, he dropped his voice and said, "We have been seen. From the sea and from the land."

Floki studied his cousin. "Who? Who has seen you?"

"There was a ship ... it sailed close to shore." Hakon waved his hand along the strand. "Its crew watching."

"A warship?"

Hakon shrugged.

"Fishermen are a curious breed," Floki said. "And jealous of their waters."

"And fond of talk in the ale houses." Hakon's black brows drew close in an angry furrow. "You have been seen in Rome."

"So have many, cousin," Floki smiled quietly. "And who sees us?"

"Danes." Hakon jerked his head toward the distant Port of Rome. "They see you crossing the Roman river. And another, not a Dane, asks for you by name."

Floki smiled again. "So my fame reaches even these southern waters. Who saw you by land?"

"Three horsemen. They rode to there," Hakon pointed down the strand, "and turned."

"Chased away by their own shadows. As you are by yours." Floki looked up, calmly, over Hakon's head. "Order the ships ashore, Sea-Friend. The child is ill and must sleep. We sail in the morning."

The two hulls were hauled back up onto the strand by their disgruntled crews while Floki waited, still sitting astride his mount with Eirik leaning groggily against his shoulder. Then, when the awnings were stretched over the lowered masts once more, he dismounted and carried the child up the gangplank.

At the top, he turned briefly to tell Gil and Ismail to stow their arms and gear and tend to the animals, and to ask Rachel to bring water and towels. Then he ducked beneath the shelter of the awning, Eirik clinging with limp arms around his neck.

Relieved of their loads, the ponies were turned out to graze the rough marsh grasses, though Gil had to drag Lionheart away from the wet, glistening hull of *Silver Dragon*, to which he had trotted as eagerly as to a waiting stable. *Tomorrow*, Gil said. *Night, and then morning*. Lionheart whinnied disconsolately. His pilgrimage done, he sniffed the air as if the cold, sweet winds of the North already blew. *Yeah. Me, too.* Gil patted his rump. His own eyes were already searching the misty sea, seeking a far horizon.

His chores done, he mounted the gangplank, glad to feel decking under his feet. Breathing in the ship smells of salt and weathered wood, Gil bent his head and stepped beneath the awning. In the dim light under the black cloth, Floki and Rachel knelt beside Eirik, who, sprawled on a bed of furs and cloaks, seemed hardly aware. Rachel held a leather bucket of water, while Floki gently washed each of the boy's skinny limbs.

Gil waited for further orders, but Floki never looked up, and eventually, he turned awkwardly and went back out into the bright sea light. Hakon came down from his own ship and climbed *Silver Dragon's* gangplank with his small wooden box of medicines that Gil already knew would be of no use.

Tiredly, Gil shifted his gaze to the shore. Caitilin had joined Janetta and Grimhildr and Percy kneading bread dough by the newly re-lighted fire. Ismail and Ragi threaded their way through the marshes carrying cut, dry reeds for the pony pen. In the distance, Erling, Bjorn and the two Shetlanders gathered driftwood. The rest of the crews of both ships sat in desolate clumps on the sand. Realizing suddenly there was no one in charge, Gil summoned two men from each ship to set a guard over sea and strand.

At dusk, the rain returned, damping the sand and splashing on the still grey sea. Their meal of fish and bannocks finished, the Northmen sought shelter in their black tents pitched between the hulls, or under the awnings.

Remembering the night before, Gil looked longingly at Janetta, but Grimhildr was already hurrying her away, with Caitilin, to the chaste shelter of a tent on the strand. Reluctantly, Gil joined his friends and the Irish boy beneath the awning, where they huddled at one end in silence, while Floki and Hakon tended the sick child at the other. Rachel sat, a little apart, with Percy curled up beside her; a sorrow in her eyes that made Gil turn his own away.

He slept, leaning stiffly against the strakes, and was awakened suddenly, in the darkest of the night, by a flurry of motion and a murmur of troubled voices. In the fluttering light of the oil lamp, he saw that Eirik was awake, trying to sit up, and being gently restrained by Floki.

The boy looked around wildly. "Was it because I took the bone?" he said in a small, frightened voice. "Is that why I'm sick?"

"No." Floki smiled and stroked his hair.

Eirik studied his own fingers, curling them. "Will someone take my bone when I die?"

"You do not die," Floki said. "Come. You sleep now, and in the morning you are better."

But Eirik just stared at him hopelessly. "I want Papa," he said.

"I take you to Papa."

"When?"

"In the morning. You sleep now and in the morning, we sail."

The boy shook his head, tears briefly brightening his fading eyes. "I want Papa."

The deck boards creaked under a heavy step. Gil turned and saw Bjorn standing bent over beneath the awning, a shining blade resting across his hands. Floki looked up. "I bring his sword," Bjorn said.

"No!" Floki crouched like a mother animal over the child. "Take it away. He does not die."

"Cousin," Hakon said gently. "It is so. He is a child, but he is a warrior. Let him die with his sword." Bjorn nodded, his big face mournful, and extended the weapon helpfully. Floki leapt up and swept the blade away with a slap of his bare hand, sending it clattering onto the deck. Bjorn stared, bewildered.

"But he goes to Valholl ...."

"He does not!" Floki shouted. "There is no such place!" Bjorn flinched and Floki's voice softened. "Please. Take it away."

Bjorn lifted the sword and backed off, holding it against his chest like a small child, clutching a toy. Floki turned in anguish to Rachel. "Bring me water."

"It won't *help*," she said.

"Bring me water! Clean, fresh water!"

Face wet with tears, she scrambled to her feet and followed Bjorn from the shelter, returning in moments with her leather bucket brimming. Floki was calm, then, kneeling over the child whose breaths were coming short and ragged and ever further apart. "Eirik," he whispered. He cupped water in his hand and poured it three times, softly, over the child's head. "I call thee, Eirik. *In nomine Patris ... et Filii ... et Spiritus Sancti* ...." His fingers trailed away and he smiled gently as the boy's eyes opened. "You are safe," he whispered, "None can harm you now."

Gil helped Bjorn dig the grave, on the site Floki had chosen, a small rise by the shore; the driest piece of ground they could find. A little salt-shriveled tree stood there, barely more than a shrub. All around was desolate marsh. While Bjorn brought tools from the ship, Gil waited, his hand on the little tree, his eyes on the sea.

A brown sail appeared out of the morning mist, small, and

rigged in the local manner. The Northmen stood up to watch it as it drifted lazily along the shore, then came about, heading back the way it had come. "Fishermen?" he said to Janetta, standing at his side, her arm around Percy who sobbed noisily into his sleeve. Gil looked uneasily toward the shrouded hull of *Silver Dragon*, where Floki kept watch over the dead child. Janetta took Percy away when Gil and Bjorn began to dig.

It was a hopeless place to bury anyone, with the water so near, and they could barely dig deep enough to protect the body from wild animals. When they were finished, Floki came from the ship with the dead boy wrapped tightly in his beautiful, fur-lined cloak. The crews of both ships trailed a respectful distance behind.

Hakon walked beside Floki, neither looking at him nor speaking to him. Gil thought of the boy's blood kin, so far from this rough burial; the old Norse Sea-King, from whose hall Floki had snatched the child, now bereft of the last of his sons; and his white-blonde daughter, Gudrun, who Hakon had pledged to wed. Hakon stood now, staring down into the muddy grave as if his own life lay buried there.

Without speaking, Floki stepped down into the grave, and laid the child down. His hands lingered, a moment, on the boy's shrouded head, and then he stood and climbed up, ignoring the help Gil instinctively offered. His face, gaunt with the weariness of three nights without sleep, was without expression. He put his arms around Percy whose sobbing was the only sound other than the wind, and said, "Where is Bjorn?"

The big Northman shuffled forward from within the gathering. He looked into the grave he had dug and rubbed the back of his hand across his nose. "I would have his sword, now," Floki said, "Not his brother's – that must go back to his father – his own. The sword I gave him."

Puzzled but obedient, Bjorn lumbered off, returning with the shorter blade that Floki had bought for the boy in Deer Bay. He watched while the earl climbed down again into the grave, laid the sword down beside the cloak-wrapped body, and again climbed out, this time accepting Gil's hand.

Floki stood rigid and silent as Bjorn and Gil shoveled muddy earth over the dead boy, and a dozen Northmen brought sea-washed stones up from the shore and weighted down the loose soil. Gil shut from his mind the boy's flaxen hair and bright, trouble-making eyes down in the black earth, dark forever. He glanced at Floki, standing yet with his arms around Percy, staring at the grave.

Percy squirmed and wriggled now to be free and Floki raised his head, as if awaking from sleep. He smiled at Percy and released him. "Go to the ship. Grimhildr will play King's Table." He nodded to her and then watched them go off together.

One by one, the Northmen turned and solemnly filed away. Bjorn stood with his shovel, staring at the little cairn of stones. "Is it so?" he said sadly. "Is there no Valholl? No land where warriors fight every day? No ale hall for heroes?"

Floki put a hand on the big man's shoulder. "Of course there is Valholl," he said gently. "Of course there is. Even Aidan says so."

A slow smile crossed Bjorn's sun-burned face. "*Aidan* says so." His thick moustache twitched upward with wonderment.

Floki nodded. "Yes. Aidan says so." Bjorn laid his shovel over his shoulder and strode with lightened step to the ships. Floki watched him go. "Only, he calls it hell," he murmured. "And I am in it." He smiled wryly at Gil and then suddenly he shook his head, his knees buckled and he collapsed on the ground beside the grave. Gil ran to help him, but he raised himself on braced arms, sat up, and waved him away. Leaning his head back against the little wind-swept tree, he said, "Leave me. I am well."

Gil turned to Hakon who looked down at his cousin with a mixture of sorrow and rage. "So you know, now," he said, "You are not Odin. You do not sit with the High Ones and choose who lives and who dies."

Floki looked up and met his furious gaze. "I make this right," he said.

"You make this *right*?" Hakon's eyes narrowed in disbelief. "The child is *dead*, cousin." He flung his hands in the air. "Get up. The wind rises. We leave this hellish shore."

"I must carve the runes," Floki said. "Warrior, bring an

oar, a good oar, with a broad blade." Gil turned to obey and Hakon closed a hand on his shoulder and hauled him back. Gil stiffened and jerked free of his grip. "Sail if you wish, Sea-Friend," Floki said quietly. "I do not leave this grave unmarked." He straightened and then climbed again to his feet. "You grieve, cousin, I know. Not for the child, but for his sister, and the marriage you would make. You shall have this. I make it right."

"You make *nothing* right!" Hakon exploded. "Indeed, you make everything wrong." His hands balled into fists. Gil stepped suddenly in between them.

"Leave him alone," he shoved Hakon angrily aside. "Just go. Leave him."

Hakon glowered at Gil and once more at his cousin. He looked up at the sun. "Terce," he said. "The third hour. By the sixth hour, we sail. With or without you."

"Bring the oar," Floki said to Gil.

It was nearly the ninth hour when Floki finished the runes. And though the ships were launched, the animals loaded, and all but a few of the Northmen aboard, Hakon did not sail. Gil sat with Floki while he carved the runic letters, which, like those on the wooden passport in his pocket, Gil could not read. That, the earl had scrawled in a hurry to keep Gil safe in Deer Bay. Now, he worked slowly and patiently, cutting each line with care, and for once, he seemed glad of Gil's company.

"Why do we stay in the world, Change-Thing?" he said. "Would you not rather chase mice and sleep in the sun? Would I not rather swim in the green sea? Why do we stay?"

"For love?" Gil ventured.

"For love," Floki said. He smiled sadly, and turned the carved oar blade to Gil and read aloud:

Eirik

A King's Son

"That's great," Gil said, and suddenly, for the first time, he was crying.

They stood the oar up at the head of the cairn, burying the

sawn-off shaft deep. Gil stepped back a few paces and studied it, pleased with how straight it stood, how clearly outlined against the blue sky, so that any who passed would see.

Floki pressed more stones into the soft earth around the base of the shaft, and then, his work done, sat down again on the ground, leaning his head against the sturdy oar.

Gil glanced uneasily down the misty strand to where the ships rode at anchor. There was no sign of Hakon. But he saw, then, a man walking toward them. Big and powerful, with a shield at his back and a sword at his side, he strode purposefully, scanning both ships and shore.

Against the hazy sun, he was but a silhouette, and yet, familiar. So familiar that the guard Gil had set had let him pass. They knew him: he had sailed with them across the British Sea, his deadly feud with their earl abandoned for pilgrimage.

"Floki!" Gil whirled.

"I see him." Floki raised his head slightly, his eyes narrowed against the sun.

"It's ...."

"Padraic Njalsson. I know." He stood up but did not move from Eirik's grave. Barefoot, and armed only with the small knife with which he had carved the runes, he watched the Irish warrior approach.

Gil's hands closed in impotent fists. "How did he find us here?"

"Odin's will," Floki said.

"Odin's *will*?" Gil stared. "You don't even believe in Odin. You –"

"Ah, my wise helmsman," Floki smiled. "He knows what I believe when I do not know, myself."

Gil shook his head fiercely and drew his sword. "I'll hold him," he cried insanely. "Get to the ship. Get your sword!" He ran forward. The old warrior strode calmly closer, his grey hair blowing across his weathered forehead. His cloak, fastened at one side in the Irish manner, was adorned with a silver pilgrim's badge. Seeing Gil coming, he laughed, a hearty, good-natured laugh and held up both hands, empty of weapons.

With one, he swept Gil aside as he might a playful puppy.

The other, he extended to Floki. To Gil's astonishment, Floki clasped the offered hand and welcomed the Irishman with a warm embrace. Padraic Njalsson hugged him like he would a son, and then stepped back holding him yet at arms' length.

"Ah, young lion. As dark as a moor from this sun, but I know you yet. And so, now, does half of Rome." He smiled broadly, "Your fame spreads ever further." He looked back at Gil. "And you train the cub well." He laughed again, but his eyes then fell on the fresh-dug grave and at once his face grew solemn. "A sad sight, here," he said, and he crossed himself. "Who lies buried?"

"A child."

Padraic Njalsson closed his eyes briefly and shook his head. "Ah. A child." He looked kindly at Floki. "It is hard to lose a child." His eyes strayed to the grave. "I lose two. A girl. And then later, a boy."

Floki nodded. The animation with which he had greeted the Irish warrior faded and he knelt wearily again beside the grave marker. Padraic Njalsson lowered himself to the ground beside him, studying the runes distractedly. Floki said, "He was not mine to lose."

"Ah." Njalsson rubbed his bearded chin. "This is indeed hard." His eyes returned to the Norse runes. "Was this the hostage? The boy from Norway?"

When Floki didn't answer, Gil said, "Yes."

The Irishman bowed his head. "A fine child. This land is hard on children." He sounded weary himself and he said, "Hard on all. A far shore."

"A far shore," Floki said quietly.

They sat a while in silence. Gil looked at the sun and the ships. The Irishman spoke again, his words measured. "My pilgrimage is done, young lion, and I would return north." For a moment, Gil thought he would ask again for passage, as he had at the pilgrim port of Dofras, and that this would all end in peace and good humor. But then, and sorrowfully, the old warrior said, "There is now this matter of the vow."

His gaze fixed yet on the child's grave, Floki made no response. Padraic Njalsson put a comforting hand on his arm. "Come, now," he said gently. "Send the lad to your ship for sword and shield and we will finish what is between us."

Floki looked up. His eyes swept sea and strand as if seeing them for the first time and returned to the waiting Irishman. "You finish it. I do not care."

The old man sat back, his face lined with dismay. "I cannot do that," he protested. He looked to Gil as if for help, then back to Floki. "Be reasonable, young lion. You know I must keep this vow. I am sworn on my life to kill you." He drew his own sword and laid it across his knees. "Look! See how highly I regard you. Fine Saxon steel. I purchase it carefully in Rome."

Floki glanced at the blade. "Then use it carefully."

Padraic Njalsson threw his hands in the air. He looked again at Gil and then at the sky. "Meet me with steel, Floki Magnusson. I am not an executioner."

"You keep your vow. I pay my debt. How I do so is not your concern."

Padraic Njalsson sheathed the sword and buried his head in his hands; then looked up, straight at Gil. "Can *you* not reason with him?" he cried indignantly.

How? Gil groaned inside. *He's as crazy as you are.* He covered his own face with his hands, but a shout from the shore caught his attention. Hakon, Bjorn and half a dozen of Floki's crew were running toward them while, behind, armed men poured off both ships to meet the wall of mounted knights thundering up the sands.

Suddenly alert, Floki took it all in in a glance. "Go, helmsman!" He thrust Gil toward the ships. "Now!"

He half-turned back to the child's grave, but Padraic Njalsson caught his shoulders in his big hands and shouted. "Yes! And you!" His frustration exploding in action, he wrenched the young Northman around and flung him bodily at Bjorn. Then, with a grunt of satisfaction, he drew his sword. Gil's was already in his hand as he ran beside the big Irishman toward the battle unfolding on the shore.

Armored and mounted, the attacking knights pursued their advantage, driving the Northmen back toward the surf. But then the Irish warrior was among them, more vigorous than a man half his age, springing up to drag one knight from his saddle, slicing another's arm to the bone with his new Saxon steel.

At the edge of the surf he paused long enough to join Floki's determined captors in the act of throwing him aboard his own ship. Laughing, knee-deep in surf, he shouted, "You give me passage across the British Sea, I give you passage across this! I too pay my debts, Floki Magnusson!"

Then he plunged back into the battle, beating back the dozen attackers trying to board, while Gil scrambled up the side and took the helm. "Take her out! Take her out!" Njalsson shouted over his shoulder.

"Come with us!" Gil called as the wind filled the sail. But the Irish warrior only laughed again and shook his head. And, as the last of the Northmen scrambled desperately aboard, and the ships gained way, he was still fighting, gloriously and joyously holding his strip of Roman sand.

Then there was clear blue water between them and the strand, and then the strand itself was a far, pale strip, fading into mist. Floki crouched on the deck, beneath the dragon's tail, his eyes on the vanishing shore, where Eirik's grave-marker dwindled to a smudge of charcoal against the sky.

Rachel knelt beside him and laid a slender arm across his shoulders. "Leave me," he said, without turning.

"No."

Mist rolled across the far strand, wiping the horizon clean. Floki stared into its nothingness. Then he turned suddenly and caught Rachel in a savage embrace, burying his tear-streaked face against her throat. She closed her arms around him and looked up to his stunned watching crew. Her eyes darkened with cold fury. "Have you no work to do?"

Gil snapped his gaze back to the sea ahead of his prow. The Northmen hastened to real or invented tasks. Rachel wrapped her arms tighter around Floki and lowered her head, shielding them both with the curtain of her beautiful hair.

The sun sank toward the sea, casting a golden sheen over the waves. With *Sea-Raven* in her familiar place off his steering board, Gil drove his ship toward the last light in the west. Beyond, somewhere, lay Halfdan's Island Mountain, the first landfall on the long sea-road home.

As darkness fell, he saluted Hakon, signaling they would sail on. The night was clear, the wind steady from the south. They rode a fine broad reach under a starry sky. Ulf came and sat beside Gil. Nodding toward Floki, sleeping in Rachel's arms, he said mildly, "Shall I wake him? Or do you know the way?"

Gil searched the sky, picking out familiar stars, unrolling his mind-map of the course they had sailed. "I know the way," he said, and it was only half a lie. Ulf wandered off and lay down beside the formidable bulk of Grimhildr. Gil's eyes traced the dark outlines of shaggy dozing ponies, the black tent where Caitilin and Janetta comforted Percy, the open deck where all else slept.

Small fish jumped before his questing prow. Something blue-green and sparkling lit the tumbling bow wave. Their wash, eerie and enchanting, glowed behind them, and above. Frigga bore her spindle through the Southern sky. Alone at the helm with the Northmen's gods, Gil sailed on.

CHAPTER EIGHT

"You go too fast!" Janetta cried.

Gil kept his eyes on the golden strip of sand and laughed. "Ragi! Ismail!" he shouted to his friends manning the sail. "She's luffing." He pointed to the slight ruffling of the tight-stretched cloth.

The boys adjusted the sheets and the tacking spar again and the edges of the bellying sail grew taut. Gil felt the small lift of the dragon prow and saw the bow wave rise. *Silver Dragon* surged forward, leaving Hakon's ship yet further behind.

"No, really," Janetta nudged his shoulder. "It is too fast."

"I'll remind you of that the next time you're galloping down some cliff face or something."

"I do not ...." she began.

But Rachel said suddenly, "She's right."

"Oh, not you, too," Gil sighed. His eyes swept the far shore, rapidly coming closer. It was their first landfall in three days. Their last, a desolate strand on the wind-swept Frankish coast, had offered little comfort.

Indeed, the whole way north from the Great Pillars was a gale-battered misery. And the Roman Sea, before, had been as fierce as any northern waters. Their gentle outward passage seemed now a dream. Rain slashed down endlessly. Nothing aboard remained dry. The ship stank of wet wool and wet ponies, and the beasts' pitiful grunts and neighs filled the air as they struggled to keep their footing on the pitching deck. Percy's green parrot clung, wind-battered and miserable, to a thrumming stay.

Seasickness afflicted even the heartiest, and in one day-long storm, only Floki and Gil remained immune. Each landfall brought a weary struggle for fuel and fodder, dreary, hissing fires, and suppers of half-cooked fish. Or, too frequently, no food at all. The men sank into morose gloom, missing their women and children, and muttering of sea-beasts and angry gods.

When, eight days beyond the Pillars, Gil spotted a distant sail, he watched it benignly, glad of its remote companionship. They had been so long alone on the grey winter seas. But Floki rose from his place at Gil's side with a look in his eyes that Gil hadn't seen since Rome. "Helmsman, we pay courtesy." He signaled to Hakon the change of course.

Sea-Raven drew alongside and Hakon shouted, "Enough. It is late. We have our own troubles. Leave him to his."

"His troubles relieve us of ours," Floki returned.

They closed in on either side of the stranger. Irons flew, ropes tautened. The ship, a Danish knarr en route to Hedeby, wallowed between them like a broken-winged gull. Richly laden, but lightly crewed, she gave up her cargo of silks and spices and her treasure kist of Arabic coins without a fight.

Gil watched dispassionately as Bjorn and Ulf hauled the plunder aboard his storm-battered ship. Their own treasury was nearly empty. They needed resources to buy fodder and food. He waited until the trapped knarr was set free, and then turned his dragon prow north. Pity was a luxury for the longhouse fire.

The light was fading as they made camp on another lonely shore, and he shut from his mind the Dane and his crew, doing the same somewhere down the coast, with their long journey now fruitless and nothing ahead but the bleak struggle home. His own weary oarsmen had a cask of wine for the night and silver for the markets of Dublin. Buoyed with the rewards of their hard winter's work, they rose cheerfully the next morning and left Francia behind. Even the harsh, three-day crossing of the British Sea, on a course far to the south of Dofras, couldn't blunt their enthusiasm. The wind carried a clear, cold scent, sleet rimed the sail: they were homeward bound.

Now, Kernow lay before their prow, its rugged peninsula stretching across the horizon. Cliff-fringed, with small narrow coves, its steep shores rose from white crescent beaches to green winter heights. It looked dry and inviting after so long at sea.

The sooner their keel rested on sand, the better.

Gil gauged the distance, judging when to bid Ulf loose the oar. The sturdy farmer watched him warily, in a way he would never have watched Floki. *Tough*, Gil thought. *I'm at the helm.*

"It *is* too fast," Janetta said again.

Percy wriggled in between her and Gil and shouted, "Faster! Faster!" in Gil's ear.

"*Heard* you," he grinned.

"She *is* right," Rachel said. "There are rocks there," she pointed. "And there."

"But there aren't rocks here," Gil said patiently. Sometimes the Northmen muttered that women were bad luck on a ship. He was beginning to understand why. He sighed again as he looked over his shoulder. *Sea-Raven* had dropped back further still. But Erling was always cautious; and Hakon was worse.

Still, Gil's eyes flicked instinctively to the earl, sitting alone on a sea-kist, just below the curving dragon prow. Wrapped against the weather in his rough pilgrims' garb that, without his fine cloak, he wore now of necessity, he ignored the approaching shoreline, his attention fixed on Janetta's psalter resting on his knees. Gil's eyebrows made a wry arch and he grinned at Janetta. "Your student doesn't care," he said, with another grin for Rachel.

Though weeks had passed since the earl approached Janetta with her prayer book and announced that he, too, would learn to read, the image of Floki Magnusson with a book still jarred. That the Northman might be weary of board games and bored of fishing, Gil could indeed understand. The long winter sailing offered always too much excitement, or too little; days of exhaustion and peril interspersed with days of discomfort and tedium. And, of the two, the last was worst.

He himself had played all the rounds of King's Table he could abide. And yet, between shifts at the helm, he still succumbed numbly whenever Ismail or Ragi brought out the board; there was so little else to do.

The men struggled to fill their time mending gear, telling old stories again, and dreaming of home. Grimhildr, and the girls, spun yarn from the fleeces of stolen sheep, and made endless lengths of braid on tiny hand looms crafted by Ciarnan of wood and shell. Every man's tunic was adorned at neck and sleeves. Lionheart had braid around his halter. But still the winds blew against them and the days stretched on. If there were a book aboard other than Janetta's Latin psalms, Gil himself would have welcomed it.

The limits of their library seemed not to worry Floki, however. Whenever he was free, he could be found studying the leather-bound psalter. At intervals, he would rise and return to Janetta for further instruction, folding his leonine length to sit meekly cross-legged before her slight, imperious form. Gil shook his head and smiled again.

"Why do you laugh?" Janetta cast a quick protective glance toward the earl in the bow. "He learns very quickly. He is clever."

"*Floki*?" Gil's grin widened.

"He speaks four languages, Gil," said Rachel. Gil shrugged, his eyes on the sea and the graceful curve of the strand. "And the poems?" she persisted.

He thought suddenly of the beautiful lament for the boy, Eirik, which Floki had recited on a Moorish shore, composed, like all his long, elaborate verses, entirely in the silence of his mind. He raised his gaze a moment from his course and met her eyes. "Yeah, that is pretty smart," he conceded.

Then he looked ahead again and saw the ripples, a ruffled line barely visible in the dark blue sea. A memory tugged. *Not there.* Then the sun broke through and he caught the glint of yellow sand beneath the waves. On his feet in an instant, he shouted, "Loose the sail!" But it was far too late.

When they hit, it was like hitting a wall. The tiller slammed into Gil's chest, flinging him backward off the steering board, and with a splintering crunch, the oar tore free, snapping the stout withy binding it to the hull. *Silver Dragon* slewed, out of control, swinging broadside to the seas, lurching onto her load-board.

The ponies squealed as water poured over the submerged rail. Percy and Rachel sprawled on the deck and Janetta tumbled into Gil's arms. Every man on board lost his footing. Except the earl. Floki sat yet on his sea kist, his feet firmly planted, and one hand closed in his iron grip on the rail. With the other, he turned a page of his book and studied it, without looking up.

Gil staggered to his feet as the ship settled back on an even keel, wallowing in the chop, water sloshing across her deck. He stared up her chaotic length, where men shouted and scrambled for oars. *He knew. The bastard knew. And he didn't tell me.*

Floki closed his book. He stood and sauntered down the wet deck, neatly avoiding flailing oars and frantic seamen, and stopped briefly to query Janetta about some matter of the text. Then he climbed up onto the steering board, where the tiller flapped like a dying fish, surveyed the golden plume of churned sand and mud stretching behind them, and turned to Gil. "When I wish you to plough, helmsman," he smiled slightly, "I set you ashore with a beast in harness."

He leaned down and handed Janetta her precious book. "I keep it dry," he said, with a nod toward Gil, "though he does not make it easy."

Then he stepped back and took the helm, lightly turning the disconnected oar. "This part is difficult," he said, as he coaxed the ship around until her prow again faced the shore. Oarsmen had taken their places. Ragi and Ismail waited expectantly. Gil looked warily at Floki, and then, with the words catching in his dry throat, ordered his friends to drop the sail.

Floki nodded approval as the yard slid down the mast and oars dipped into the sea. "Come," he beckoned, and stepping back, returned the tiller to Gil's hands. "Think, now, helmsman, you are on the little skiff, sailing to the Holy Isle."

Something painful and homesick lurched in Gil's chest. *If only.* Floki stepped behind him, speaking over his shoulder, his voice patient and soothing. "You have raised the steering oar, *as men do,*" he said dryly. "And now you steer, light, light, with just a loose oar. And see," he pointed to the dragon prow, aligned again toward the strand, "Even now she answers."

And even now he teaches me, Gil thought, with humble respect. His hands were shaking with relief and yet a small part of him wished the earl would fly into a temper and throw him in the sea, as he deserved.

Sea-Raven came up astern, as they limped towards the shore.

"What befalls you?" Hakon shouted, standing up on the rail. "Do you ground her?"

Floki saluted his cousin cheerfully. "No, Sea-Friend. We make that trail of mud for you. That you may find your way and not be lost."

Hakon looked back at the stained water and up at the heavens. He scratched his head with the hand not gripping a shroud. "Lost? Why should I be lost? The day is for once calm, the sky clear …."

"Sea-Friend," Floki called gently. "I jest."

Hakon threw both hands in the air, teetered dangerously on the rail, and grabbed again at the shroud. "I have enough of your jests! Is this, too, a jest; that you are now rudderless and we are yet weeks from home?"

"Nothing aboard a ship cannot be mended." Floki smiled, watching Hakon's own sail come down, his oarsmen dipping their blades. And then, with another smile for Hakon's angry crew, said, "And if the journey is so long, yet, one night more will make little difference. Come, there is light enough to hunt; we will feast tonight and drink ale." Both crews looked more cheerful then, as, under oar, the two ships beached on the sandy shore.

Gil watched miserably as *Silver Dragon* was dragged up the strand, revealing the damaged steering oar. He waded into the surf, determined to punish himself further with the sad sight, but Floki drew him back.

"I have to see," Gil insisted.

"Later. Now, you serve us all better unloading the beasts and taking your bow to the hill. Rachel," he beckoned, "Go with him, my fine huntress. And you," he quickly pointed at Ismail and Ragi. "Let us see who is first to the feasting."

Gil looked once more back at *Silver Dragon's* stern, reluctant to leave his wounded ship. But Floki gave him a friendly, but uncompromising shove toward the gangplank and pony pen, where Lionheart was already whickering his desperation for land.

Down on the strand, he had his hands full, with bow and quiver and his bucking, kicking pony. *I know you're happy,* he assured Lionheart. *Can't you say it, like, calmly?* Lionheart did two jumps and a little shimmy in answer. Gil grabbed the pommel of his jousting saddle with one hand, and with the other hauled the pony's head around toward the steep sand bluffs above the beach.

"Isn't he pretty, with all his braid?" Rachel pointed happily at Lionheart's decorated bridle.

"Gorgeous," Gil muttered. The three Hrolf's Isle ponies were already trotting obediently toward a narrow defile, where a stream ran down between dunes. Gil, on Lionheart, followed in little jumps and bucks until they had mounted up to the grassland topping the bluff.

Inland, thickets and forest cloaked a gentle hillside, promising game. Though, from the sea, they had seen distant smudges of wood smoke, here there was no sign of habitation at all. Exchanging smiles of delight, they cantered over the grasslands, where birds soared and hares bounded and spring flowers bobbed in the soft sea wind.

"Heaven!" Rachel cried, pulling up her sweating pony at the edge of the wood. She swung her bow forward, laying it ready across her saddle. Gil looked up at the sky, judging the light. They were yet far to the south of their Northlands home, where winter lay long and night would yet fall early.

"We've got at least an hour. We'll go in pairs and meet up here."

Ismail grinned at Rachel. "I go with the huntress, so I do not come back empty-handed."

Gil thought that unlikely, in any event, but turned Lionheart to the right, as Ismail rode left. Reluctantly, Ragi followed, his eyes straying to the bright flash of Rachel's hair, disappearing into the forest.

It was old woodland, virgin and untouched, the open forest floor carpeted with dead leaves. "Perfect," Gil murmured, slowing Lionheart to a trot, and then a walk, as they approached a clearing where some old forest giant had fallen. Sun-dappled meadow grass surrounded the decaying trunk and two roe bucks grazed in innocence. Alerted by scent and sound, they flung up pretty heads and bounded free. Lionheart ran after before Gil's heels touched his flanks.

Then they were racing, ducking, and laughing, through the low bare branches, their hill ponies deer-like in agility, a forest hunt as sweet as in Caledon. Gil was almost sad to end it with an arrow, when the time came. Ragi downed his quarry, too, and with the two bucks draped across their saddles, they turned, trotting easily back the way they had come, following their own trail of churned leaves and broken branches.

The open grassland was in sight beyond a last fringe of trees when Gil saw the Hrolf's Isle ponies. Rider-less, heads down, they grazed the rough grass at the forest's edge. Lionheart whinnied a greeting. "Where are they?" Gil murmured. Then he glimpsed the splash of bright color on the forest floor. Red as russet autumn in the brown winter leaves, it brought his heart into his throat.

"Rachel!" Ragi gasped.

Gil jumped down from his saddle and ran, bursting desperately threw a thicket of willow into a little clearing at the edge of the wood. Ismail and Rachel's mounts grazed yet contentedly, oblivious of the two forms on the ground. "Rachel!" he shouted. "Ismail! Are you all right?"

In a flurry of movement, both boy and girl sat up, wide-eyed with surprise. Ismail grinned loopily. Rachel glared, quickly re-pinning the straps of her tunic. "And why shouldn't we be all right?"

"We finish hunting," Ismail pointed helpfully to their tethered ponies, laden with furred and feathered game.

"We've been here, like, forever," Rachel added. Ismail shrugged and grinned.

"Right," Gil said, feeling his sea-weathered face turning pink. "Sure." He nodded, "Just what I'd do ... well, not with you, of course." He grinned lamely and shrugged, suddenly aware of Ragi, stiff with rage, at his side.

"Oh, do shut up, Gil." Rachel turned away and reached for her pony's reins. In the same instant, Ragi leapt down from his own mount and lunged for Ismail, drawing his sword.

"Hey!" Ismail's good-natured face registered surprise, and then wary good sense, as he jumped back out of the way. "I not fight with *you*," he said, holding up both hands. "You my friend."

"She is mine," Ragi cried hoarsely. "*Mine!*" He swung the sword and Ismail dodged again.

Gil tackled Ragi, grabbing him around the waist and hauling him back. Ragi lashed out with his free fist, breaking Gil's grip and turning again on Ismail. The African boy still held up his hands, but a warning look came into his eyes.

"Ragi," Gil said, "Be careful."

But suddenly a flash of steel came out of nowhere, as a sword blade clashed down on Ragi's, nearly striking it from his hand. "What?" he cried, looking up at Rachel in amazement. She raised the blade with which she had struck his own and tapped it against his chest.

"I am not yours," she said clearly. "Nor am I his." She glanced at Ismail, who looked crestfallen, but did not argue.

Ragi stared at her for a long while. Then he sheathed his sword and said stiffly. "No. You make sport with us both, but you save yourself for the earl."

Rachel lunged forward, thrusting her sword blade up beneath his lightly bearded chin. "*I do not*," she hissed. "And you will never, ever, say that again." She jabbed angrily, drawing a speck of blood. Then she whirled and swung the sword toward Gil and toward Ismail. "Any of you!"

They stared, shocked into silence, as she sheathed the blade and stalked to her pony. Jerking free the knot that tethered her hunting trophies, she flung a cluster of wood pigeons at Gil, and four bloody hares at Ismail. Then she swung herself aboard the big Hrolf's Isle pony and kicked it vengefully into a run.

The hoof beats faded, out in the open grassland. Gil turned warily to his two companions. "I guess we, like, don't say that again?" he ventured. Ismail looked at Ragi and the tall young Northman looked back.

"Friends?" Ismail said with a hopeful smile.

Ragi nodded wearily, and after a long pause, took Ismail's proffered hand.

Rachel was nowhere in sight when they reached the camp on the strand. But Floki was rubbing down her sweating pony with a tuft of dried grass. He met Gil's uneasy greeting with a raised eyebrow. "My hawk returns early."

Gil shook his head and muttered. "Don't ask." The earl's light laughter followed him as he ran down the strand to inspect his damaged ship.

Neither Hall, Hakon's carpenter, nor Brynjolf, Floki's smith, looked pleased to see him. Hall was short and stocky with an enormous beard like Erling's and a normally cheerful face, now darkened by ill-humor. "I do not expect, helmsman," he said grimly, as he displayed the detached steering oar, "Since you are not a master wood worker, as *I am*, that you understand with what care this was crafted. Let me explain."

Gil listened, flinching occasionally as the Shetlander described every step of the oar's construction, his stubby fingers jabbing at the splintered wood, the broken withy, the sheared iron bolt, as he spoke. That all of it was too firmly implanted in his mind, already, was information he thought better than to volunteer. But as his tormentor was joined by the smith, Brynjolf, with his own diatribe, Gil was far away, on a hillside on Hrolf's Isle, testing *Sea-Raven's* new-made steering oar with master shipwright, Eyolf Grimsson.

"He'd kill me," he muttered.

"Who? The earl? I do not know why he has not," Hall replied mildly. "It is a mystery."

But all of Floki was a mystery, Gil thought, since the day they left that sad Roman shore; his unshakeable calm, his whimsical scholarship, and most of all, the insane vow he made that very first night, to bind himself in slavery to the old Norse sea-king, as reparation for the loss of his son. On that, as on all else, he was as impossible to rile as a holy Ab and as immoveable as a rock cliff in the sea.

And the calmer he became, the more Hakon Sea-Friend's protests beat like a futile surf against that stone.

Replete with roasted game, the Northmen gathered in good cheer around the fire, telling stories and listening dreamily to the Irish boy's magical harp. Floki studied his book in the firelight. Gil sat in the shadows with his arms around Janetta. Only Hakon still glowered at him and lamented the two lost days.

Floki raised his eyes from the psalter and offered his cousin more ale. "Are there men," he asked, with a quick glance at Gil, "Who make no errors?" Hakon shrugged. Floki smiled. "Helmsmen do take risks. Ships do ground. A day comes, perhaps, when this happens, and I am not there. Should he not learn, now, when it is safe?"

"Safe?" Hakon exploded. "What is safe?" He glowered again at Gil. "We are yet weeks from home. Frigga's spindle sinks low to the sea. What of the spring ploughing? Do these things no longer matter?" His eyes narrowed as Floki turned a page of the psalter. "Or have you grown too holy to care?"

Floki smiled without looking up. "And are there no ploughmen in all the Shetland Isles?" He paused and turned another page. "Or do they need you for the horse?"

Gil giggled and quickly covered his mouth, but laughter spread lightly around the fire side. Hakon's black brows lowered and his dark eyes flashed. "And do you find in those pages a remedy for this wind that never turns, cousin?"

"I think not, Sea-Friend," Floki said mildly. "But I am a poor scholar."

"Then leave your book," Hakon growled. "And return to your fathers' ways. We have had nothing but misfortune since you turned from them."

Floki closed the book. He looked up, and for a moment, Gil saw the old Floki back again. But his voice was still calm when he spoke. "Say nothing, Sea-Friend, that you will not defend with steel." Hakon made a fist, but turned aside and slammed it into his own palm. "Neither Odin, nor the White Christ, brings these storms," Floki said with his gentle smile. "Only winter."

He stood up. "Still, we do sail north and soon we sight the Sudreys and Yula's Isle. But, before, there is Eire. Where are my men of Ireland?"

Ciarnan stepped boldly forward at once. Niall left his harp and shyly followed. Floki addressed them in their own Irish tongue, turning first to the boy harper. "We are but two days from Dublin. And Tara lies only a day's ride further. I will take you home, myself. Though there is no father to welcome you, there will be kin."

Gil thought of his own father, Lance'lot, far away in the forests of Francia. He closed his fingers, by habit, around the seeing stone in his pocket, which, like Floki's passport, he always carried. He might never meet his father again, but at least he knew he was there.

The Irish boy blinked, his eyes full of homesick yearning, but he said, "I cannot go to my home. Not before Caitilin returns to hers." Floki tilted his head quizzically. "It is by my playing she is taken from there," Niall said. "It is my duty to protect her."

"You were but a prisoner, yourself," Floki reminded him. Then he smiled suddenly, his gaze drifting to the shy Irish girl, sitting beside Rachel at the fireside. "But other men have found love in imprisonment." He glanced at Hakon. "Perhaps you would return to Tara with a bride?"

Niall shook his head and said with surprising dignity, "I am betrothed to one there who is but young. It was my father's wish and I shall obey."

"A fine humility before a father," Floki said, with another gentle smile. "You will stay with me, as you wish." He turned then to the boy-monk, Ciarnan, standing before him in his Viking tunic and britches. "Will you return to your father in Ireland? Or your foster-fathers on Hy?"

Ciarnan shook his head. "I will stay with my earl."

Floki smiled. "If your earl should want you."

Ciarnan flushed red in the firelight. "I have proved my worth, on the ship, and with my sword! I am the equal of any of your warriors!"

Floki laughed. "Yes. And the equal of myself in vanity." He studied the young Irishman and nodded. "For now, you will stay. But come summer, you will return to Eire and make obeisance to your father. And he will decide your future, holy or profane."

He smiled again, but Ciarnan said only, "I will return and pay a son's courtesies. But I will decide my future. I, alone."

Floki nodded quietly. "My equal indeed," he said, and this time he did not smile. "Perhaps by summer you will have learned respect for your father. And for your earl."

"What earl?"

The whole company turned. Hakon had stepped a few paces back from the fire and stood glaring over it at his cousin. "What earl will be there to hold him to this promise? You? You will be in Norway, a slave to that old liar of a sea-king." He stalked a few paces away, toward his ship, and then turned and stalked back. "Only, you will not. Because he will have you slaughtered. And not pleasantly."

"That would be foolish," Floki said mildly. "I am young, strong, a swordsman without equal. I am of great value."

"Yes," Hakon muttered. "Though at times only you think it. But you are indeed of value. To me, to your father, to your household, and to the girl you claim to love."

Again, Gil saw anger flicker in Floki's eyes. But the brief spark died, and when he spoke again, he said reasonably, "She is young. She will wait for me."

"Seven years? You indeed value yourself highly."

"She will wait."

"Where? When your enemies lay waste to Hrolf's Isle? What of your household without an earl, Floki?"

"They have my father."

Hakon shook his head. "An old man."

"An old man who would lay *you* in the dust, my kinsman." Floki paused and then said lightly, "But there will be no need of that. For you will rule Hrolf's Isle with him. You, and your wife; that beauty with the warrior eyes I saw in a Northern hall."

"And I will wed this woman with my cousin a slave in her father's household?" Hakon turned away to stalk off again but turned at once back. "Only that will not happen."

Floki laughed. "Decide, Sea-Friend. I can have but one of these dire fates."

"Well, it will not. He will kill you."

"I think not. But if so," he said, again reasonably, "There will be no need for recompense, so you can still wed. Blood for blood, Hakon. I have killed his son."

Hakon's face paled. "Illness killed the child."

"An illness he would never have met, had I not brought him there."

"Odin's will," Hakon said sadly.

"My will, Sea-Friend. Mine alone."

Hakon stood staring at his cousin. Then he came back to the fire, sat again, and dropped his head into his hands. "I will not have this," he said, the words muffled. "You will not do this for me."

"Then that is well," Floki said easily. "For I do not do it for you, Hakon. I do this for the old king. I must. I have taken his last son. He is aged and will fail and his household will turn on him, like all good Viking kin. His son, who would protect him, is dead. I must do this now."

The winds were kinder, two mornings hence, when they sailed from Kernow. Rounding its southernmost promontory, they turned to the north, caught a good south-westerly, and by dusk were in sight of the green hills of Ireland.

Gil signaled Hakon and set a course for a wide silver strand, conscious of every man's eyes upon him. His heart thudded as he fought his own fearful urge to drop his sail, far out to sea. But he held his nerve and beached his ship beautifully. Floki never looked up from his book.

The next day, they came to Dublin. Floki and Hakon, with minds again on their Northern farms, sought out ironmongers and grain merchants to haggle for seeds and tools. Gil spent his share of the treasure from the Danish knarr on a chain of silver and glass beads, with a pendant cross that reminded him of the clasp of Aidan's holy book. He fastened the chain beneath Janetta's dark hair and banished the uneasy thought that it might indeed be such a thing, plundered and re-worked.

Turning to face him, Janetta touched the cross and chain and they tinkled pleasantly against the necklace of red and white stones he had bought at Hrafn's Ayre. "Am I beautiful now?" she smiled playfully.

He studied her, pretending uncertainty. "It isn't gold, like the necklace from your dowry," he said. "Maybe I should fight Floki for that."

"*No!*" she cried, horrified.

"What?" he grinned. "Do you think he might beat me?"

"Yes," she said truthfully. "Besides, I do not want it. It is but a measure of my father's wealth. This," she touched it again, "is a measure of your love. Were it base metal, or clay, or even wood, I would love it just as much." She paused and said solemnly, "I will wear it all my days. I will wear it in my grave."

"Don't say that!" Gil cried.

"But it matters not, surely," she said. "I will be then with Our Lord."

But you won't be with me, he thought in silent anguish.

She smiled and blithely took his hand. "Listen," she said as the chains tangled again. I am like Grimhildr, weighed down with jewels."

"As long as that's the *only* way you're like Grimhildr," he laughed ruefully. But as they went on down the wooden walkways of Dublin's market, he liked that she jingled beside him, adorned with proud trophies, like a true Viking wife.

They sailed early the next morning, reaching the open sea under oar, as the winter sun was rising. Floki set Gil a new course, north by east, and returned to his studies.

The day was fine, the wind steady behind them. The dragon prow surged over long, breaking seas, rising and falling like a cantering charger. At sunset, Ciarnan, riding high up the mast, spotted land. Within minutes, it was visible to all, a soft blue outline against the dimming sky. Gil looked to Floki, but the earl remained absorbed in a game of King's Table, with Ulf.

The land ahead grew nearer, low at the shorelines, but rising to hills inland. On either side, lay open sea: an island, Gil saw, larger than those that lay off Kernow, smaller than Halfdan's Island Mountain. Mist drifted across its highest peak. Lower down, he could see individual boulders on its rapidly approaching shore. "Floki," he called uneasily.

Setting aside his board, the earl rose at last and joined Gil at the helm. He looked ahead, thoughtfully. "Do you see it, Helmsman?"

"Do I *see* it?" Gil said incredulously, "Of course I …"

"Ah, good. I wish that you not crash into it." He grinned and

Gil managed a wry smile. "I would go that way," Floki pointed over the steering board. Then, as Gil changed course, he raised his voice so all could hear. "It is Mona. A fine island, with a fine hall, renowned for the splendor of its feasting board."

A happy cheer swept the crew. "Indeed," Floki continued, "Its chieftain, Gudlief Egilsson, is yet another of my many kin." He paused and smiled. "So we will go armed."

CHAPTER NINE

Gudlief Egilsson's hall was fine indeed, a stone-built longhouse with a sweeping turf roof, shuttered windows and roof beams boasting bright-painted dragon finials. Colorful rune-stones stood either side of the broad door. Peat smoke hazed the air above green, fertile fields.

On the strand below, nousts hollowed from the shingle held five resting longships. Four more hollows lay empty and smaller craft were scattered on the sand above the tide line. Surrounding the longhouse, sturdy barns and stables spoke of prosperity; the waiting ships, of secure defense.

Gil steered toward an empty noust, with *Sea-Raven* following off his load board. *Silver Dragon* rode grandly landward, her full shield-racks and golden pennant declaring her no humble merchant's knarr, but an earl's ship, the man beside her helmsman in ragged pilgrim's cloak, a chieftain of equal rank.

The sail was lowered and the crew took up oars, and with steering oar safely raised, they slipped into their mooring. "Fine ships," Ulf said, nodding to the resting fleet.

Floki smiled. "Yes. And I think their keels are rarely dry." He raised his eyes to the green pastures, dotted with black beasts. "Ireland must be empty of cattle."

"And sheep." Gil grinned, pointing higher, where flecks of white brightened the moorland. "But maybe he's just a good farmer. Maybe they're all his."

"He will be a good farmer," Floki agreed. "He is my kinsman. But he will also ply the family trade." He laughed good-naturedly. "Look, he sends us welcome."

A cluster of figures appeared before the longhouse and flowed down the broad path between the sentinel rune-stones.

Women in bright tunics and shawls, children carrying flowers and cakes, an old man with a cask of wine; they gathered on the strand around the tethered ships, waving and shouting happily.

Gil smiled and waved back, but when he turned to Floki, he saw the earl carefully checking the bluffs above the hall. He touched Gil's arm and nodded slightly, "There. And there." Gil looked up and saw, well camouflaged in dull, grey cloaks, the watching guards who had alerted the household to their arrival, when they were yet far out to sea.

Floki returned his attention to the people on the strand. "A pretty welcome," he said mildly. "My kinsman has charm." He looked up, then, to the open door of the longhouse where a tall, rangy, red-headed man had appeared with a beautiful dark-haired woman at his side. Two young children clung to the woman's apron. Four more followed their parents to the shore. Five well-armed warriors trailed a few discreet steps behind.

"Come," Floki slapped Gil's shoulder. "We accept. But we are pretty, too, with swords and shields." He lifted his own from the shield rack and flung it over his back. Behind him, his crew did the same, standing briefly aside while their earl and his helmsman descended the lowered gangplank, and then quickly following, fanning out along the strand. To their left, *Sea-Raven's* crew formed their own protective arc behind Erling and Hakon. The Shetlander stood quietly watching as Floki stepped forward to meet their host.

Gudlief Egilsson was dressed like a Northman, in a fine blue tunic over close-fitted britches. But the cloak flung over his left shoulder was woven of multi-colored wool, in the manner of Caledon, and fastened with an Irish silver pin. He had braided two plaits in his red hair and his beard was neatly trimmed. When he greeted Floki, the words were Norse, but the accent so strange that Gil struggled to understand.

The two men embraced like affectionate brothers and Floki beckoned Hakon, who greeted his fellow kinsman more soberly, briefly gripping his hand. Gudlief beckoned the old man with the wine cask forward. A pretty young girl appeared with three silver goblets. Wine was poured and Floki linked arms with his kinsman, and, laughing and looking into each other's eyes, they drank a toast. Beside them, Hakon sipped his own wine thoughtfully.

The children stared at Floki and a small girl poked Gil's leg and ran, shrieking, behind her smiling mother. Floki looked up to the ship and beckoned Grimhildr. Shepherding Rachel, Caitilin, and Janetta before her, and with her sword strapped firmly at her side, Grimhildr descended to the strand. Percy followed, clutching the tails of her headdress with one hand and his treasured green parrot with the other.

Gudlief Egilsson's children ran to him, shouting in a mix of Norse and Irish, and reaching out for the bird. "It's mine," Percy said solemnly, allowing each of them in turn to touch a wing. "It was mine and Eirik's. Now it's mine."

One boy, fair, and bolder than his brothers and sisters, tried to clasp it in both hands, until his mother restrained him. He ran and tugged at his father's tunic. "Papa, I will have the shiny bird. It is mine." Gudlief cupped a big hand around the boy's fair head fondly and drew him back.

"It is his, little Viking. I will bring you one of your own."

"When?"

"One day."

"Soon," the child said stubbornly, "Or I sail for one myself." The adults all smiled, but Gil thought painfully of Eirik on his far, windswept shore.

Gudlief laughed as he turned to Floki, "You have been to southern lands."

"To Rome," Floki said. "My foster-brother and I make pilgrimage." He smiled innocently at Hakon but surprise still registered on the Shetlander's open face.

Gudlief Egilsson studied them both. "A noble journey," he said finally, with his own bland smile. He raised his eyes, taking in all the sixty men on the foreshore. "Come. We will celebrate your safe return. You, cousins," he nodded graciously to Floki and Hakon, "and all your brave oarsmen. My hall is spacious and many of my warriors at sea. Come, there is room for all."

Broad smiles broke out on sea-weathered faces, but to Gil's surprise, Floki held up a hand and shook his head. "You are too generous," he said simply. "It is winter's end and men and beasts feel want. A few will join you gratefully; the others, as gratefully, take the hospitality of your good shore." And though Gudlief urged him, protesting a fine harvest and full barns, Floki would not relent; and his own disappointed crew knew better than to object.

With a slight smile, Gudlief acquiesced. "Pilgrimage has deepened your humility," he said. "But come," he gestured lightly toward a sturdy wooden structure set beside a flowing burn, a short distance from the hall. "Refresh yourselves before we feast. You *will* accept water, good cousin?" he added with another smile.

Gil was glad when he and Ismail were both chosen for the feast, as well as a further half dozen of their crew and an equal number of Hakon's. Grimhildr, the three girls, and Percy went off with Gudlief's wife and her children, but Bjorn and Erling and the greater part of the company remained with the ships. And when Ragi and Ciarnan led the ponies down the gangplank, Floki directed them to return the animals to their pen, rather than set them loose to graze.

"Am I missing something?" Gil murmured to Ismail, as, clutching clean trousers, tunics, and shirts, they followed the earl and Hakon to the building by the burn. It was a well-built structure, bigger than it had looked from below; the size, at least, of the ruined longhouse at Cille Aidan. And unlike the wash houses of Saint Peter's *piazza*, it sheltered a hearth fire; sweet wood smoke drifted above the turf roof.

There were no windows, and when they entered through a single narrow door, the only light was the ruddy glow of the flames in the stone-lined fire pit that ran the length of the single open room. Blackened iron cauldrons of water hung steaming over the fire, and brimming wooden buckets stood on the warm hearth stones. "*Warm* water!" Gil murmured to Ismail.

"Warm house!" Ismail grinned, looking around. Benches lined the pine-planked walls as in a feasting hall, though spread not with furs and cushions, but with crisp-folded linen towels. "And soap!" he pointed gleefully at a wooden dish laden with grey, flat cakes.

Gil drank in the warm pine scent and the heady luxury

awaiting them: to scrub with real soap, not a fistful of seaweed; to wash the salt stickiness from his hair and comb the tangles and worse from its straggly length; to be really warm and really clean! Having so long bathed with a grim sluice of icy spring water, if, indeed, he bathed at all, it was paradise.

Scratching his itchy head in anticipation, he pulled off his salt-stiff tunic, his stained shirt, and pony-furred britches, and kicked loose his boots and grubby socks. Floki and Hakon, stripped naked already, tipped streams of warm water over their heads, scrubbing their bodies with the rough, grey soap.

Gil and Ismail copied them, stopping sometimes to just stand soaking up the caress of warm, pine-laden air. The soap stung Gil's eyes and reddened his skin, but he scrubbed all the harder, lids squeezed shut. He heard the door open and then close again, as someone entered, and felt a brief draft of cold air. Then a soft, feminine voice offered, "I wash your hair?"

"Wha ...?" Gil's eyes flicked open and he stared, mindless of the soapy sting. A sweet-faced young girl, maybe Caitilin's age, smiled helpfully, holding up a full water bucket. "Towel!" Gil gasped at Ismail. Ismail stuffed one in his hand, busy shielding himself with another. The girl waited patiently, while Gil wrapped it around himself. "It's okay," he muttered. "I'll do it."

She looked disappointed, but she turned away and approached Hakon. Another girl, as young and as pretty, was already soaping Floki's yellow mane. Neither he nor Hakon had bothered with a towel. Clutching his own strategically, Gil was reaching for a fresh water bucket when the door opened again.

A large, unsmiling woman, with loops of thick brown hair beneath a white headdress, stamped in and slammed the door behind her. "Wash hair," she announced, closing on Gil.

"No, I'm fine!" he protested, gripping his towel with one hand, and rubbing soap in his hair with the other. She shook her head; baffled less, he realized, by his alien accented Norse, than by his reluctance.

"Wash hair!" she repeated and, shoving up her sleeves, bared arms that would grace an oarsman. Clutching a hank of it, she jerked his head under a stream of water, the way he might if he'd decided to wash Lionheart. Spluttering, he came up for air, lost his grip on his towel and scrabbled for it desperately. She pointed down and said, "Hah!" before continuing his punishment. Detaching a stout bone comb from a chain at her belt, she hauled its fierce teeth through the knots and snarls, oblivious of Gil's howls.

Ismail stood, towel-wrapped and laughing until she turned her attentions to his own curly mop and did the same to him. After that trial, Gil relaxed and let one of the young girls plait his wet hair into neat braids, as he sat on a bench by the fire.

One by one, all their party were attended until, their task done, the girls and their chaperone retreated out the door, she as humorless as ever, and they still giggling with only half-averted eyes; their shy, admiring glances not just for the handsome young earl, but for Gil and Ismail as well. Wondering what he was supposed to say to Janetta, Gil wrapped himself tighter in his towel, shook water from his new braids and settled, wonderfully warm and clean, on a bench with the other men.

Ulf got up and poured cold water on the hearthstones and the air filled with sweet-smelling steam. "A fine host, your kinsman," he said to Floki and Hakon. The rest of the company nodded respectful appreciation.

"From which line does he descend?" asked Arnkel Fish-Tail courteously.

Towels around their waists, Floki and Hakon settled on benches and commenced an elaborate discussion of their complex family tree, tracing their bloodlines back to Norway, seeking the ancestor common to themselves and Gudlief Egilsson.

As names and connections, both lawful and illicit, were tossed back and forth over the fire, Gil sat with his wet head against the hot pine planks, dozing sleepily. The door opened again in a burst of cold sea air and an old man with a huge grey moustache came in, carrying an armful of fresh firewood. Spreading it along the flames, he then settled on a bench, cheery and red-faced, in all his clothes, and joined in the debate.

Seeming to know as much about his earl's family as they, he

announced, "Olaf Gunnarsson was sire to all. He was wedded to Kjartan Thorstein's daughter, Bergljot, but took to bed the daughter of Hrodny, the servant maid, from whom descends Kol who fathered Hallgrim, who fathered Einar who fathered Magnus and Gunnhild. But Gudlief descends from Bergljot, herself." He sat back and folded his arms with authority. "And holds the true line."

Hakon seemed about to argue, but Floki only nodded to the old man and said, "No doubt you are right, grandfather. The memories of the old are the finest."

Pleased with himself, the old servant stood up and, collecting two empty wooden buckets, said, "I bring fresh water."

When the door closed behind him, Floki rose from his bench and circled the fire to sit beside his cousin. He rested a hand lightly on the Shetlander's shoulder and said amiably, "Hakon, my kinsman, you have a fine ear for the truth, but no imagination. I would learn more from this good man who loves to talk. Please be silent, now, when I speak." He tightened his grip suddenly, and then released it, and returned to his place.

The old servant came in again, with his two buckets brimming and poured icy burn water over the hearth. Clouds of steam hissed up to the smoke-blackened roof. Gil's nostrils stung in the rush of piney heat. Ulf groaned contentedly and stretched his hairy legs toward the fire.

"Grandfather," Floki addressed the old man through the haze. "I would learn a new thing from you."

Beaming with pleasure, the servant set down his buckets, wiped sweat from his thick moustache, and settled comfortably on a bench. "What now would you learn?" he asked proudly.

"I would learn of a ship," said Floki.

"A ship is it?" The man nodded wisely, as if every ship on every sea was within the scope of his knowledge.

"Yes," Floki leaned forward, his face suddenly troubled. "A ship from Shetland. *Dawn Star*, she is called. Crewed by men of Shetland and captained by a chieftain of the Horse Isle, Arnfinn, son of Thorfinn, himself a Shetlander."

Gil listened dreamily; more names he did not know, more tangled blood ties; but he looked up sharply when Hakon straightened suddenly on his bench. "Cousin?" he protested, "I know not ...."

Floki ducked forward, scooped water from a bucket with his cupped palm and flung it across the fire. "Wake yourself, cousin. You dream and hear nothing of what I say!" He laughed, and the old man at his side laughed, too, but Hakon nodded abruptly and said nothing.

"Ah, this ship. Yes, I think I know of her," the old servant said. "A fine ship."

"Very fine. And fine men. Hence my concern," Floki leaned closer. "She sails with us, you see, to Rome, but on our return we are driven apart in the Roman Sea. And we have not seen her since. Have you word of her?"

The old man paused, his face clearly troubled as he strained his memory. At last he shook his head sadly. "No. We hear nothing of this third ship. Only the two that lie safe on our shores this night."

Floki shook his own head sorrowfully. "I fear her lost," he said then. "If one as wise as you in the traffic of these seas has had no word." The old man sighed agreement and respectfully rose to leave. "Thank you, grandfather," Floki said, distractedly staring into the flames. He remained like that, lost in sorrowful thought, until the old servant went out and softly closed the door. Then he looked up, met Hakon's baffled gaze, and laughed aloud. Hakon shook his head.

"What ship is this?" he said. "And why do you laugh? A lost ship is no cause for mirth."

"That is so, were there a ship," Floki said cheerfully. "But there is no ship."

Hakon looked more baffled. "Then why ask the old man this question?"

"I wish to learn if he has heard of her," Floki smiled.

"But there *is* no ship," Hakon said. "There is no third ship. And you, yourself, say it. How can he know of a third ship that does not exist?"

Floki's smile took on a wry twist. "Cousin," he said quietly, "How does he know of the two that do?"

The question hung in the steam-hazed air. In the quiet

that followed, Ulf nodded slowly. Floki's eyes held Hakon's. "Who seeks us, cousin?" he said. Abruptly, he turned to Gil. "Helmsman. Tell us."

"Jocelyn Guidbairn," Gil said. "The Golden Knight."

Floki smiled a brief acknowledgement and then looked up, his gaze sweeping the company, and then returning to Hakon. "The sea-road is harsh," he said, "The winds, ever against us, slow our passage. Our friend returns, overland, before us. And in his graciousness, he wishes to learn of our welfare and asks everywhere for word of us. Indeed, so great is his concern, perhaps, that he places a fine price on our heads?" He grinned at Hakon, "And so the old man, and indeed all this household, hear of our two ships." Floki paused and added innocently, "But somehow the others neglect to say."

He leaned forward. "Now, cousin, how hungry are our kinsman's beasts? How hungry his warriors, despite his fine board? We share a few drops of his blood, but he has six children who share it all. How hungry are they?"

Hakon shrugged. "They look well-fed to me. I see no sign of this hunger …."

Floki looked up at the sooty roof-beams. "And I see no sign of poetry in you, my plough horse of a brother. Oh, do not be outraged. You are as solid and faithful as the rock cliffs of Shetland, cousin. And I love you for it. But you are also just as thick. We play King's Table, Hakon!"

He threw his hands in the air and turned to Gil. "Helmsman, do *you* take my meaning." Guiltily, Gil nodded. Floki smiled. "Good! So you will not despair of what I ask of you next," he said with a mysterious grin.

Outside of the wash house, the night was bright with stars. Firelight glowed from the longhouse windows and voices and harp song drifted out into the night, and with it, the rich scent of roasting meat. Skin tingling yet from the heat, and aware suddenly of how hungry he was, Gil turned toward the waiting feast. Floki's hand on his shoulder drew him back. "Come with me to the ship. We must bring gifts to so fine a hall."

On the strand, the campfires were already burning, with stews of dried fish and barley bubbling in the cauldrons. They smelled good, too, and Gil felt less guilty about the feast. He waited at the foot of *Silver Dragon's* gangplank until Floki descended it, carrying lengths of silk from the plundered knarr, and a rich silver brooch from Dublin, for the chieftain's beautiful wife.

They climbed back up the starlit strand to the twin rune-stones flanking the longhouse door. Gil stopped to stare at them, fascinated. Firelight from within revealed serpents and dragons and fantastical beasts, twined around Christian crosses, saints and angels; the carvings highlighted in red, yellow, and blue. "All the gods, old and new," Floki laughed lightly, "My kinsman takes no chances. Are you hungry, Warrior?" he asked then, cheerfully.

"Starving," Gil said.

"Good. There will be many mice."

"Mice?" Gil stared blankly at the rune-stone. "He serves *mice*?"

Floki laughed delightedly. "No," he said, still laughing. "He serves beef and mutton and game. But you will not need those." He leaned closer to the rune-stone and tapped the colored carving of a magnificent sinuous cat.

"Now?" Gil glanced despairingly at the lighted hall. "*Here*?"

"No. Not here. There." Floki gestured to a long, low building. "In the stables, just beyond. I wish you to watch the horses. Do not fear; there will be no need to count. I only wish to know one thing: if any come, while we feast, and ride out."

"That's all?" Gil said sniffing hungrily at the tang of roasted meat. "Couldn't I eat first?"

"Of course you can eat. As I tell you, there will be many mice. Come, now," Floki said encouragingly. "Cats have no need of beef or game. Cats have mice."

"Oh, great," Gil groaned.

"Should even one horse be ridden out, you must come at once to the hall."

"Me? Or ...."

"Cat must come. A messenger from my camp would arouse suspicion. Look," Floki pointed, "the window shutters stand open. It is a mere hop for a cat. Only, do not hop onto the feasting board. It is not courteous. Come to me, quietly, as only a cat can."

"And what do I say?" Gil demanded.

Floki's eyes narrowed. "What do you *say*?" he asked with thinning patience. "You say meow, idiot." He slapped Gil's still wet head, turned away toward the hall, and then turned back.

"Warrior, I recall something. Stables have mice and rats and they also have cats. And, as you learn to your great interest in Rome, cats, like men and women, come in two kinds." He paused thoughtfully. "You are not to involve yourself with the other kind. Not in any way. Indeed, you are to be a monkish cat." He paused again, "Lest," he added grimly, "it fall upon me to do with you that thing we do with the cattle. When we wish them to live in innocence?" He tapped the knife at his belt. "Understood?"

Gil winced. "Understood," he muttered.

Floki flashed his white smile. "That is good, then. A good night to you, helmsman!" He strode jauntily to the open door of the longhouse, and Gil stamped off to the dark bulk of the stables, hunkered low against the starry sky.

Inside, amid the warmth and smell of beasts, it was so pitchy dark that he'd be lucky even to see another cat, much less know which kind he was seeing. Invisible horses stirred nervously at his presence. By habit, he spoke in his inner pony voice, *It's okay. I won't hurt you. And in a moment I'm going to vanish, anyhow.*

Scraping a circle in the hoof trodden dirt, he stumbled blindly within and grumbled the blessing. The last words ending in a feline hiss, Cat stepped from the circle and shook himself all over. His fur was inexplicably, and unpleasantly, ruffled and tangled, and he groomed himself carefully until it again lay smooth. Satisfied, he looked around the stable and its occupants that had emerged out of the darkness. His flattened ears rose up to a thousand wonderful sounds, and he opened his mouth, slightly, to better catch the rich blood scent of prey. *Supper,* he purred.

And then he saw her, standing right in front of him, by the hoof of a dozing horse. His tail swished with interest at the slight female scent, but it was a different kind of interest. Not like he felt for the black enchantress of Rome, but a sort of cozy kindness. Concern pricked his ears and raised his tail. *Don't stand there. You'll get stepped on.* She was smaller than the hoof. *There won't be anything left. Get over here, idiot,* he growled.

She looked up. Tiny bright eyes met his, brimming with admiration. On dainty paws, she ran to greet him, leapt onto his back, and sank claws into his neck. With a yowl, he shook her off. *Go play with something. I've got hunting to do.* He trotted down the central aisle of the stable to a promising heap of straw.

The first mouse almost walked into his mouth. Starving, he gobbled half before he looked up and saw her, a paw's length away, waiting with those irritatingly appealing eyes. *Fine. Have it. I'll get more.*

He left her daintily nibbling its wet glossy innards, plunged back into the straw, and slaughtered a second. It was almost too easy.

But then there was a new kitten, same size, same round eyes. He dropped the mouse in front of it and, with a weary meow of protest, went back to the straw. Fortunately, it was well stocked.

The next mouse was a claw swipe away when two balls of fur leaped over his carefully positioned paw and pounced uselessly on the place where the quarry had been.

After that, the hunting got harder. Whenever he closed in for the kill, a rustle or a stupid little squeak of a meow sent his prey fleeing. A quick snarl over his shoulder cleared the deck. But a moment later, the two were back, with a friend.

Hackles raised, head at an ominous tilt, Cat swatted the nearest. Then he sat down and licked disconsolately at his shoulder. There were kittens everywhere, four at least; one, conveniently, for each paw. Dimly, Cat suspected there were more. Driven on by his empty stomach, he resumed hunting, and when the stable door creaked open, he hardly noticed, though the kittens scampered away into dark recesses.

A light, held in a man's hand, bobbed down the aisle and then settled, high up, on a hook by a stall. Cat ignored its wavering shadows as the man moved around the horse in the stall. His attention focused on the thin, dark thread of a rodent tail, he gathered himself on his haunches. Pouncing savagely with both forepaws, Cat caught and dispatched the tail's owner in a brutal instant. He was crunching satisfyingly into its skull, when he thought of Floki.

Should a horse be ridden out .... Reluctantly, Cat released his barely tasted supper, raised his head, and glimpsed the heels of a horse, clopping after the fluttering lamp, into the night. The stable door swung shut and it was dark again, though not so dark that he failed to see the pile of kittens squabbling over his mouse. With a petulant slap of his paw, Cat sent them tumbling as, still hungry, he loped to the door, squirmed under it, and turned his nose to the lighted hall.

Three bounds from the stable wall, he froze. A new feline scent twitched his whiskers, the rank and threatening stench of tom. An involuntary yowl rose up his throat. Sinking low, he slunk, belly to the ground, toward his too distant goal.

Halfway there, it caught him. The scuffle of paws behind was the only warning he had. Spinning at the last instant, he met the onslaught with teeth and claws, eyes squeezed safely shut, ears tucked back, strong hind legs scrabbling to protect his underbelly.

Three times his size, and twice his age, the tom was formidable: Bjorn and Floki Magnusson rolled into one; a feline chieftain, a Viking of a cat. Teeth sank into his forepaw, crunching down to the bone. Claws raked his striped forehead and shredded one ear.

He broke free, ran, and was re-captured. Rolling and tumbling, he escaped again. Youth, and fear lent him the advantage of speed. Then the wall of the longhouse loomed before him, blocking his flight. With teeth slashing at his tail, Cat took to the air in a leap that surprised his opponent no more than it astounded himself.

Five, six times his height: it gained him the un-shuttered window, and he flew through it. Clearing the sill, and clearing the shoulders of seated men, he landed, four paws splayed, in the center of Gudlief Egilsson's feasting board. Shouts of alarm turned to laughter. Fingers pointed, children shrieked. Stunned, Cat sat down beside a platter of venison. He shook his head, spattering blood from his raked ear. "Oh, he is hurt!" the chieftain's wife cried.

"He will hurt more in a moment," the chieftain growled, rising to his feet and calling for the servant. Cat shook his head again and stretched his neck to sniff the venison.

A hand closed on his scruff and he sniffed a familiar human scent. "Do not trouble the old man," Floki said lightly. He lifted Cat by his loose neck fur with one hand, and casually picked up a piece of venison with the other. "See? He does good work in your stables and comes to his chieftain for reward." He held Cat and venison higher and the hall filled with laughter.

Gudlief Egilsson smiled. "Reward him, kinsman," he said, "Or my children will disown me." He laughed, too, then, his arm around two of his daughters. The youngest was seated beside him, in Janetta's lap, reaching out for Cat. Janetta restrained the child gently, her own eyes fixed fearfully on Cat. Cat blinked friendship, but his mind was on the venison just out of paw's reach. He hung stiffly, nose straining for the meat, as Floki carried him from the hall.

Outside the longhouse, Floki dropped both Cat and venison in a perfunctory heap, while he unbuckled his sword belt. Cat had just sunk grateful teeth into the meat when he was snatched up again and tossed unceremoniously through the circled leather. A moment later, Gil was standing looking sadly down at the muddied venison. "Why'd you throw it on the ground," he cried.

Floki shrugged. "You do not care before."

"I care now! I'm starving! And now I can't eat it."

"Then you are not starving. So, now you can speak, tell me what you learn."

Gil resisted the desire to speak with a fist, and said, "A man took a horse out." He shrugged. It seemed insignificant. He rubbed his bloodied ear and flexed his sore arm. "He was probably riding home early."

"No," Floki said quietly. "He was not." He looked down at the campfires casting leaping shadows around the beached hulls of *Sea-Raven* and *Silver Dragon*. "Go, now," he said. "Tell Erling to float his ship, and our oarsmen to float ours. Masts raised and sails unfurled and rowing benches full. I will follow with our people as quickly as I can with grace. And then we sail."

"Sail?" Gil looked forlornly at his ruined supper and then up at the star-studded sky. "It's the middle of the night!"

"Thank you for that wisdom, helmsman. *Yes*. Now go. And do not delay."

Bare masts probing the starlit night, the two ships rode gently in the shallows, as Floki hurried his party down the strand. Gil carried Janetta to the gangplank and went back for Caitilin. Ragi and Ismail raced each other to help Rachel, who ignored them both wading through the small waves herself.

When all were aboard and the gangplanks drawn up, they set out, silent, but for the light splash of oars, leaving their campfires burning on the strand. A few ship's lengths from the shore, they caught the wind and the sails rode, ghostly, up the masts. Heeling before a good westerly, they turned their prows to the open sea.

The campfires and the lighted longhouse windows dwindled to points of red-gold and winked out. Then, far above, a new ruddy glow rose to the sky. Gil stared at it. Floki stepped to his side. "The ward fire," he said. "He summons his chieftains. Ships and warriors answer his call."

"*Why?*" Gil whispered.

"Blood silver," Floki smiled slightly in the starlight. "The pretty children will know no want, helmsman. My kinsman sells us to the Golden Knight."

CHAPTER TEN

The ward fire was a far red eye behind their stern when Floki joined Gil on the steering board. "I bring you supper," he said cheerfully. He held out a stale bannock wrapped around a slab of salted herring. Gil eyed it dismally in the starlight. "It is good," Floki grinned. "If you are starving." He reached for the tiller. "I take her, while you feast."

Gil sat on the bench, munching grimly. The fish tasted like a piece of cold sea, the bannock, like leather. Floki sat beside him, his hands light on the tiller. "She sails well. A good wind." He seemed in high spirits.

Gil grimaced. "Any wind away from here is good." Floki laughed. "Aren't you even angry?" Gil said.

Floki shrugged. "Why be angry? Gudlief gives us a fine feast. And we hear the talk of the islands. It is a good night."

"And we even get away before he murders us! Great host, your kinsman."

Floki laughed again. "He is no worse than many, Warrior." He paused, "And he is useful. Now we know who are our foes."

"Who?" Gil said.

"Everyone. There will be a fine price on our heads. Almost as much as I am worth." He sounded pleased.

Gil grimaced again, finishing his meal. "That's, like, good news?"

"Any news is good if you hear it first. Now, there are no surprises."

"And no refuge."

"Ah, but there is." Floki looked ahead into the empty night. "I know a hall whose chieftain none can turn." He smiled suddenly and laid a hand on Gil's shoulder. "Well done, this night, helmsman. As quick away as a raiding party. Now, sleep. I take her into morning."

Gil slept a watch and woke without prompting at first light. Floki was still at the helm, though Ulf had risen, and sat companionably beside him, chewing a dry bannock. Dawn showed a dim expanse of grey sea, beneath low grey clouds. *Sea-Raven* rode a whispering wake off their steering board. A low line of darker grey, barely distinguishable from the sea, lay ahead of their prow.

Gil said, "Another island?"

Floki shook his head. "Galloway. From hence a man might ride to Caledon. Though, I would take the sea road, were it me."

Gil stared at the distant shoreline, his mind filled with memories of the great forest and of ruined Camelot. His gaze fell to the tent where Janetta slept beside Rachel and Caitilin, and he thought of the Mews Tower garden, where first they met. After so long away, to so many far places, it seemed more dream than reality and his heart ached with yearning for the innocence of that time and place.

Ulf rose and returned with two more bannocks, offering them to Gil and Floki. Before Gil could take his, Floki brushed it aside. "Loose the sail," he said to Ulf. "We break our fast with friends." He pointed to the shoreline, growing closer in the strengthening light. Gil saw a strand, white and shining in the dawn, and a lumpy range of hills against a brightening sky.

Ulf rose and released the reef knots that had tamed the sail for their night passage. The dragon prow lifted with the dawn breeze. White caps splashed the grey sea as the morning wind rose. Gil glanced behind at *Sea-Raven*, as her own sail billowed free.

Floki turned *Silver Dragon* windward, losing speed until his cousin's ship came up beside them. Then he waved and pointed to the land. Even in the dim light, Gil could read the displeasure on Hakon's face.

"What now, cousin?" the Shetlander shouted. "More kinsman?"

Floki laughed and shook his head. "Friends," he called, turning *Silver Dragon* again to catch the wind.

But when they drew close enough to make out the scattering of little buildings above the strand, Gil doubted Hakon would be any more pleased. "It looks like Cille Aidan," Gil murmured, "Except for that," he pointed to a high, round tower rising above the more familiar circular cells and rectangular chapel. "A *muinntir?*"

Floki nodded. "It is. Though older than Lindisfarne and older than Hy. It is the prayer house of Ninian, the Ab of the Picts. Aidan calls it *Candida Casa*, the White Hut."

Gil studied the *muinntir*; the steep-roofed church, the cells and barns, and the strange round tower, all fashioned of weathered wood or grey stone. "It's not white," he said.

"No. That is not the meaning, but pure; like to the White Christ, who is its lord."

Across the narrowing sea, a bell began to chime, sweet in the cool, crisp air. Gil pointed again. "It's a bell tower! Like Rome."

"Yes. And a watchtower, too. Also like Rome," Floki added drily. "But these are peaceful men. Come, we put them at ease." He looked up the deck to Ciarnan, cloak-wrapped, leaning sleepily against the rail. "Man of Hy," he called. "Fly my pennant."

Ciarnan climbed to his feet, and fetched the pennant, neatly stowed in a sea-kist in the bow. With a grin, he tucked it inside his belted tunic and scampered lightly up the swaying mast. Balanced on the yard, he fastened the pennant in place and let the rolled cloth flutter free.

Catching the first rays of the rising sun, it snapped and rippled, golden against the pink-streaked sky. On the shore, the bell chimed twice more and then fell silent. Dark figures emerged from huts and chapel and hastened to the strand. Two separated from the others and ran to a small skiff, beached above the tideline, dragging her seaward and into the light surf. Floki nodded approval as her slender mast was raised, and her sail caught the wind. "Good launch," he smiled "They could be Northman."

He stepped back from the tiller and handed the ship over to Gil. Then he stood up on the rail, watching the skiff approach. When they were close enough to see the sailors' friendly salutes,

Floki glanced up at his pennant. "You see, Warrior? It is not just for my vanity."

"I never said," Gil muttered.

"No," Floki jumped lightly down to the deck. "But you think it." He grinned and cuffed Gil's head.

A shout came, then, from over Gil's shoulder. He turned and saw Hakon standing up on *Sea-Raven's* rail, waving an arm, the hand clenched into a fist. Floki smiled. "My cousin would speak with us," he said. "Head up."

Gil turned into the wind and, sail flapping above them, they waited as *Sea-Raven* drew alongside. Clutching a shroud, Hakon leaned out over the sea, bristling with annoyance. "So, it is Hy, again!" he shouted. "More prayers and more plotting. I have enough of your churchmen, cousin. *There* is where we belong!" He flung an arm out northward. "In the Northlands. On a Northman's farm. Under the Northmen's gods!" Jabbing furiously with his pointing finger, he lost his balance, and slipped from the rail, splashing, thigh-deep, into the water. Still clinging to the shroud, he kicked out with one drenched leg, and with Erling's help, hauled himself back on board.

Floki leaned solicitously toward his damp cousin and smiled, "Or in a Northman's sea?" Then he straightened up and his smile vanished. "I choose this harboring, Sea-Friend. Sail where you wish." He turned his back. "Helmsman," he addressed Gil, "Take her in." With his face obscured from his cousin, he grinned cheerfully.

But Gil himself hesitated then. His hands on the tiller, he looked out from beneath the luffing sail, at the little skiff bouncing bravely across the waves. "Floki, we can't do this," he said.

Floki's eyebrows rose. "Helmsman?" he said pleasantly, leaving a careful space for Gil to reconsider.

"But he's right!" Gil cried. "It *is* like Hy. And Guidbairn will hear we were here and burn it, like he burned Hy. We can't do this to them!"

Floki smiled then and shook his head. "No, Warrior," he said mildly. "He is now a good Christian king."

"You *believe* that?"

"I do not. But in halls and longhouses of these isles, he has proclaimed himself so. He has repented his sins and made his pilgrimage. He cannot go back, now, without losing honor."

"Honor? Jocelyn Guidbairn?"

"It is a pretense, most certainly. But a pretense by which he holds his crown." He laughed lightly, "Take heart. Ninian's house will be spared. He has all the wide world to kill us in."

Gil winced. "Of course. He has Yula's Isle. He knows we'll come for Danni. It's another trap."

"Yes, Warrior, it is. But we know that now, and that is all the difference. And we will know more." He waved an arm, encompassing the waters around them. "Between this land and Eire lies so narrow a sea that, were the day clear, from that tower's height you would see the Irish shore. And these," he nodded toward the skiff with its bright white sail, "are seamen, like the brethren of Hy. All that sails between these lands will be known by these watchful monks. I would have that knowledge, before we sail on. Now," he said and the fingers laid on Gil's arm had a touch of steel, "do as your earl asks, and take her in."

Chastened, Gil swung the tiller and headed *Silver Dragon* down the wind. The brothers' little skiff jibed about and came alongside as Gil turned landward. Floki greeted its sailors in Irish and then in Pictish, a language Gil had heard only on Shony's tongue.

The boatmen, grey-robed and cowled, shouted back in Norse, which at least Gil could understand, "Welcome, Floki Magnusson. A good dawn that shows your sail." Gil smiled, leaning on the tiller, intrigued and baffled as always by the web of unlikely alliances through which Floki moved.

Escorted by the skiff and a halo of crying seabirds, he ran *Silver Dragon* smoothly onto the sands. Three ships' lengths off his steering board, *Sea-Raven* followed, Erling, cautious as always at the helm, Hakon, silent at his side.

The Ab greeted them on the strand; a youthful, powerfully built man with a sea-weathered face, a luxurious brown beard, and a smile of such cheerful welcome that even Hakon smiled in return. He spoke hesitant, accented Norse, lapsing often into Irish or Latin. But Gil understood enough to know they were being invited to breakfast and joined happily in transporting their own contribution – casks of Dublin meal and salt herring – to the refectory.

Within, he enjoyed his first hot meal in days, a soup of cabbage and barley that tasted like heaven. Sleepy and replete, he was jarred awake by prayers at the meal's end and stumbled wearily out into the weak sunlight to face the day's work. But Floki's hand on his shoulder stopped him, turning him, with Hakon, Erling, and Ulf, toward the low round Chapter House, instead. Inside, amid the solemn circle of senior monks, he felt young and ill at ease with the respect accorded him, helmsman to the earl.

The talk was soft-voiced and thoughtful, slipping from language to language. Floki listened intently. Hakon sat with folded arms, his eyes distant. Struggling to understand the shifting tongues, Gil still learned all he needed to know: that a splendid warship had passed, four days hence, accompanied by two others, only slightly less grand, all flying a pennant "as golden as your own." The Ab smiled broadly at Floki. "Though never so regal."

Floki grinned in return and nodded to his cousin. Hakon looked studiously down at his rope-scarred hands. Then Floki raised a new question and the discussion slipped into Irish as the Ab deferred to an elderly monk.

The old man listened with care and then slowly shook his head. Floki swept the assembled company with his intense gaze and repeated his query to each of the monks. Gil caught only the name, in Irish, of Yula's Isle, but the monks nodded understanding. Then, one by one, they shook their heads. With a shrug and a faint smile, Floki turned and bowed his own head to the Ab, and given permission, rose to leave. The Ab rose, too, as the monks filed out, followed by their Northern guests. Then he joined Floki and the two left the Chapter House together.

Fires were burning on the strand between the beached ships, and both crews were stretching awnings over lowered masts, and pitching tents. On board *Silver Dragon*, the ponies whinnied and stamped, eager for land. Catching sight of Gil, Lionheart reared and snorted indignation at his abandonment.

Floki tapped Gil's arm. "Let the beasts stretch their legs. I would stretch my own, now, alone, with the good father." He walked off with the Ab and then turned and called back, "You may take your lady with you, if you choose."

If I choose! Gil grinned and ran toward the gangplank. He collected Ragi, Ciarnan, and Ismail, and prised Janetta out of Grimhildr's suspicious care. Together, they led the prancing animals down onto the sands. The boys mounted the Hrolf's Isle ponies bareback. Gil and Janetta rode tandem on Lionheart. Janetta wrapped her arms around Gil's waist and her bare legs around Lionheart's warm flanks. Pressing her face against Gil's shoulder, she sighed happily and they set off at a canter down the strand.

Ahead, Floki walked, head down, beside the Ab, as he had walked beside Aidan the day they left Hrolf's Isle. Hakon watched from the deck of *Sea-Raven*, his dark face grim. When they called a greeting, he made no reply.

"I think Hakon wearies of the sea," Janetta said, looking over her shoulder.

Gil laughed. "I think he wearies of the earl."

Janetta was silent. "But the earl is his cousin. And more. His foster-brother. How can he weary of his own kin?"

Gil shook his head. The wind tore at his hair; the cold salt air stung his face. He felt happy and free and young, with the pony's hooves pounding the strand and Janetta's warm arms holding him so tightly.

He slowed Lionheart to a trot and said, "Hakon blames Floki for everything that's gone wrong since Rome. Everything since Eirik died," he added quietly. He glanced back at the earl and the priest, far behind now, and then forward to the heels of the Hrolf's Isle ponies, kicking up clods of wet sand. The boys raced, whooping and shouting. Gil slowed Lionheart more, looking for a place to turn aside.

Janetta said, "If that is so, then that is not fair. It is not the earl's fault that the storms come and the journey is so hard."

Gil stared over Lionheart's ears and said, "No. It's mine."

"What?" She leaned forward, her breath warm by his ear.

Gil shrugged. "It's my fault. Because of Rome. Because I

killed that man in Peter's Church."

She drew back, releasing her grip around his waist. He reined Lionheart to a halt. "Do you believe that?" she whispered.

"No." He twisted around and looked into her eyes. "But you do." He paused. "I hadn't any choice!" he said fiercely. "Oh, let's get out of here!" He turned back and kicked Lionheart, harder than he needed. *Sorry!*

Lionheart's ears went flat. He jerked his head up, yanking the slack reins from Gil's hands and leaped into a gallop, nearly unseating them both.

Janetta shrieked with happy excitement and wrapped her arms around Gil again. Gil caught up the reins, and, struggling to regain control, turned the pony up a sandy gully. Lionheart just ran faster, jumping over the lip of the gully onto the grassland beyond.

Gil gave up trying to stop him and hunkered down to enjoy the ride. It was a fair long while before the steepening hillside took its toll and the pony's pace slackened. Sweat-soaked and puffing, he slowed to a trot, and then a walk, and finally a halt. Gil dropped the reins onto his steaming neck.

Pleased with yourself? Next time you're too tired to climb something, I'll remember this.

Lionheart blew air through his nose and nuzzled Janetta's leg. "Oh, he is splendid," she cried. "See how far we have come!"

Gil sat back and looked down the hill at the distant strand. The ships were hidden by dunes, just their masts rising above. The *muinntir* cells huddled, barely visible, around their chapel. Only the round tower stood out against the sky. He let his gaze shift seaward, seeking the mist-veiled Irish coast, and then turned to look inland, imagining he could see beyond the Galloway hills, all the way to the Mews Garden of Camelot.

Janetta's gentle hand touched his arm. "You are troubled. Why?"

He smiled and shook his head. "Because you're still angry with me."

"I am not angry. I am sad."

Gil ran his fingers through his tangled hair and looked back at the *muinntir* below. "I know I can fix this," he said, almost to himself. "All I have to do is go down there and go to a priest and say I'm sorry I killed that man."

She nodded, her eyes shining with unspoken hope. He punched his fist into his palm. Lionheart jumped and jumped again when he shouted, "But I won't do it, Janetta. Because I'm not sorry. It was him or Floki, and I'd do it again! No matter how much blood I shed in Peter's fucking holy church!"

Her face paled. Then, without a word, she slid down from Lionheart's back and walked away. "Janetta," he shouted, but she kept walking, down the hill, toward the far grey buildings. "Right. Fine. Go. Go be a nun or something!" He dug his heels into Lionheart's furry flanks and slapped the reins against his neck. *You want to run? So run!*

Lionheart shimmied sideways, making an odd little grunt of resistance. Gil kicked harder. Lionheart reared, and he clung on, fingers knotted in mane, legs clamped around slippery flanks. *Don't you dare.*

Lionheart bucked anyhow, a powerful double jump, ending in a twin-heeled kick. Gil slid half to the ground and hauled himself up again with arms strengthened by months at sea. *You tried that at Einar's Holm, the first day I saw you. AND it didn't work.*

Lionheart snorted with frustration and shook his furry mane. *Try this.* He shimmied once to the left, once to the right, spun in a circle, reared so high that Gil felt his legs slide to the vertical, came down, bunched his feet, and then snapped his hind legs out, quick as a bow shot.

Gil flew over his head, somersaulted mid-air, and ploughed face first into a gorse bush. Flailing amid the thorns, he heard a thunder of departing hooves and a distant cry of alarm. When, scratched, bruised, and furious, he struggled to his feet, Lionheart was standing a hundred paces down the hill, grazing placidly beside Janetta.

"Are you hurt?" she called, sounding more dutiful than concerned.

"Not as hurt as he's going to be when I catch him!"

Janetta looked from Lionheart to Gil and then back to Lionheart. Then, clutching the pony's mane, she leapt up onto his back and gathered the reins. "Then you do not catch him!"

She spun Lionheart about and slapped his haunch, and with a snort he galloped homeward, head held high. Gil stared after them, astounded. Then, grinning good-naturedly, he folded his arms and waited for Janetta to soften and return in tearful remorse.

But pony and rider kept their determined course, dwindling to a bouncing dot on the horizon. At last, torn between outrage and grudging admiration, he set out on the long walk home.

Rough ground that had flown beneath the hooves of a galloping hill pony, proved slow going on foot. Far down the hill, the *muinntir* bell rang Saxt. Gil could just make out the tower, a dark smudge against the sky. He trudged on, clambering through bogs and jumping water courses.

The sea hung mockingly distant on the horizon. The *muinntir* buildings remained stubbornly far away. The bell rang None, sounding little closer. When, weary legs stiffening with the cold, he at last stumbled through the line of dunes onto the strand, the light was fading into dusk.

Cooking smells, mingling with the smoke of driftwood fires, cheered him slightly. He spotted Percy, studiously stirring the contents of a black cauldron, his parrot perched on his shoulder. The bird's green feathers shone, unearthly bright, in the gloomy air.

Grimhildr and the three girls kneaded dough by the fire, patting out rounds and spreading them on the hearth stones. Rachel and Caitilin waved cheerfully, both struggling not to giggle. Janetta's dark head remained bent over her work.

Gil hurried by them. He passed Ismail, Ciarnan, Ragi, and Niall sitting cross-legged amidst a circle of young *muinntir* brethren, mending a fishing net spread out between them. Aboard *Sea-Raven*, Hakon, Erling, and Hakon's carpenter, Hall, worked at something in the bow. The incoming tide was lapping at the ships stern and Gil quickly looked to see that *Silver Dragon* was secure above high water.

She looked different in the dim light and he realized, suddenly, that the awnings were down again. Ulf and Arnkel Fish-Tail sat astride the lowered mast and yard, unfurling the sail. Gil's heart sank. Another night sailing? But all the rest of the camp looked comfortably settled. He shrugged warily and shifted his gaze landward.

Two men with long robes whipped by the wind, herded five shaggy cows back up the hill. The cattle lowed, lamenting their warm milking shed. An answering whinny came from a grass-covered dune, nearer the shore. "Right," Gil said calmly, and ignoring the warmth of the fires and the promise of dry clothes in his sea-kist, he strode purposefully up the strand.

Lionheart had, as usual, maneuvered himself into the best bit of grazing, keeping the Hrolf's Isle ponies at bay with a flash of his big white teeth. He had even found a little tree for shelter, against which he was rubbing his haunch as Gil approached. Gil moved in between and shoved the haunch out of the way. Lionheart turned his head and whickered, hopefully nuzzling Gil's pocket.

In your dreams. Gil pushed the muzzle aside. *You dump me in the middle of nowhere and go off with Janetta and you want treats?*

Lionheart lowered his head and planted both forefeet firmly. *You left the herd.*

SHE left the herd.

The skin on Lionheart's neck twitched in a nonchalant pony shrug. *I like her.*

I like her, too. I don't leave YOU in the middle ….

She gave me a bannock.

A bannock? I've fed you from Hrolf's Isle to Rome and back and you leave me for a bannock?

And she combed my tail. She took the burrs out. He whisked it proudly. It did look less of a mess than usual. Though a burr or two certainly remained.

If I even think about combing your tail, you bite me. That's why it always has burrs.

SHE took them out.

Oh, Saint Janetta! Gil grabbed a hank of tail and plucked at the offending shrubbery. *Look, I'm …ow!*

Clutching bloody fingers, he stared in disbelief. Lionheart lowered his head. He fluttered his ears back and forth in what might have been an apology. *It tugged.*

Okay. I will leave you with your burrs until your tail gets so gross it rots and falls off.

Lionheart shivered. *I want my tree.*

HAVE IT! Gil shoved him back into his scrub willow and stamped away. "I hate ponies!" he shouted into the sea wind. "I hate churches!" he glowered at the White Hut, and then turned and glared malevolently at the campfire. "And I hate women!"

"Ah, that is indeed sad," said a cheerful voice at his ear. Gil gasped and whirled. The Ab was standing just behind him, leaning on the crook with which he had shepherded the cattle. Than an arm swept out of the dusk, enfolding his shoulders in the rough fabric of a ragged pilgrim's cloak.

"Be careful," Floki said, "Soon you hate ships as well, and there is nothing left to live for." The Ab laughed softly. "I think my helmsman and I will speak," Floki said then, and the smiling monk stepped aside, bowed, and let them go.

Gil looked back as Floki led him away. "He didn't really understand what I said, did he?"

"Every word," Floki grinned. "Only the last worries him. My friend, you are not happy. Come," he tightened his grip around Gil's shoulders. "We will drink ale."

Gil had a feeling that was the last thing he needed, but he numbly followed the earl up *Silver Dragon's* gangplank. Ulf and Arnkel were still busy with the lowered mast and yard. "Day is done, my friends," Floki said, and, recognizing a dismissal, they got down and trooped off the ship.

Gil watched enviously as they joined the gathering around the fire, but he took the place Floki indicated, on a sea-kist in the stern. The sail, half unfurled, fluttered, ghostly, in the light of the newly risen moon. Gil studied it, and then raised his eyes and saw the other thing that was different about the ship. "Floki!" he cried. "The figurehead's gone!"

The earl looked up from retrieving the ale cask. "My dragon is weary," he said mildly. "He would sleep a while." Then he laughed suddenly and shoved the ale cask aside. "Ah, now, here is something better."

He returned to Gil carrying a smaller cask and two silver wine goblets. "My cousin spends his time well, in the Port of Rome. And his silver." He filled the goblets from the little cask, pouring a liquid as pale as the moonlight. Handing Gil one, he drank from the other, himself. "Good. It is good. Drink!" he urged.

Gil sipped warily. The wine tasted as warm and sweet as the Roman vineyards they had left so far behind. He gulped the rest down. Floki refilled his cup and then sat back, turning his own in his hands. His eyes on the barren prow of his ship, he said, "Tell me."

Gil was uncomfortably silent. Then he blurted, "It's Janetta."

"How strange," Floki said solemnly. "I thought perhaps you had fallen for Grimhildr at last."

Gil choked on his wine. Wiping his mouth, he said vehemently, "She can't forget what happened in Rome. I keep telling her I didn't have a choice. I *had* to kill that man in Peter's Church."

"Since it was my back spared the sword, I do not argue."

"But *she* does!" Gil cried and then closed his mouth quickly. "I mean … it's not like she doesn't care. She kind of likes you." Floki smiled and sipped his wine. "She says you're a good man." Floki smiled again.

"You do not agree?" he said innocently.

Gil looked at his hands. "Well," he said slowly, "You're no worse than me."

"Do not flatter yourself. I am much worse than you." Floki lifted his goblet and studied it in the moonlight. "Warrior," he said then, "if there is no sanctuary, even in the Church, where can a man find peace?"

"Guidbairn doesn't deserve peace," Gil returned at once.

"What man does?"

Gil leaned back, and swayed suddenly from tiredness and the wine he should not have drunk. "I don't know," he said dully. He looked up and met Floki's cold, clear gaze. "She says she loves me, but she wanted me to go back to the priests, even though we'd both be dead."

Floki smiled and nodded. "I do not think you die, if you go here to the priests."

"Should I?" Gil said uncertainly.

"Warrior!" Floki laughed "I am but a humble farmer from

the Northlands. What do I know of such things?" He finished his wine and set the goblet down and said then, "She would win you the White Christ's kingdom. Is that not love?"

Gil thought for a long while, and then looked up and again met Floki's eyes. "It's not enough," he said.

Floki laughed delightedly. He accepted Gil's empty goblet and stowed it and his own with the wine cask. Still laughing, he said, "You are a hard man to please, Gil Lake of Tir nan Og. But come," he sat beside Gil again. "We talk of this world's matters now. A very important matter, on which rests all our delights; fine ships, fine horses," he paused and smiled, "Fine women." Gil shook his head, baffled. "Farming," Floki smiled again. "'Tis not the sword that holds the earldom, but the plough."

He held up both hands suddenly. "A Northman has two homes, as he has two hands. The ship," he waved one hand, "And the farm," he waved the other. "A man must be master of both. Gladly would I teach you, but now I go to Norway. So this falls to Ulf. The farm that will be yours adjoins his own. He, with Grimhildr, will farm both. You will work for them; your labors for their knowledge. This is fair exchange.

"Two years, you are thrall to them; one year to learn, one to prove your learning." He spoke quickly, laying out the future as he had laid out Gil's path through the Roman marsh. "Your helmsman's wage buys seed and tools. I leave silver for cattle. Sheep, you steal."

Gil shook his head, but Floki waved away protest. "I know what troubles you, Warrior. There remains your vow to Aidan. I do not forget. I leave you *Silver Dragon*. Erling for your helmsman. I name men for the oars."

"I can't do this," Gil said painfully. "I can't do this alone."

"You are not alone. You make alliance with Hakon. His judgement is good. He is kind and generous. He is a peacemaker. Hakon is a fine earl for the longhouse. But he is not an earl for battle. He does not lead. Hakon will guard Hrolf's Isle. You will take ships to war." Gil shook his head again. Floki ignored him.

"First, to Francia. Again you make alliance. Your good father. Palamedes. The Men of the Forest." He smiled encouragingly and Gil returned a hopeless shrug.

"I can't. I'm not you. I'm just ...."

With a wry smile, Floki looked up at the Southern sky, where Frigga carried her spindle through the stars. "Gods of my fathers? I give this man silver and he objects. I give this man an earldom and he objects. Indeed, he refuses the Kingdom of Heaven!" He looked back at Gil and slapped the wooden bench.

"Come. Enough of talk. Up." He dragged Gil to his feet and hurried him to the kist where each man had left his weapons, as on Hy. "Sword and shield," he said to Gil, as he retrieved his own. Quickly. The hour grows late."

"But the *muinntir* ...."

"We leave their bounds. Come." He ran lightly up the deck to the gangplank.

They slipped like two shadows from the camp. Only Lionheart noticed, catching Gil's scent and whinnying nervously. *Yes. I'm abandoning you. Goodbye forever.*

The campfires were hidden, the singing voices faint above the sighing of the surf, when Floki called a halt. Before them, a stone wall ran down from the pastureland, crossed the sands, and ended in the sea. Too low to thwart even a sheep, it seemed to have no purpose.

Far behind, the *muinntir* bell rang Compline. Floki nodded. "The brethren pray and sleep now. None will hear." He stepped over the wall and beckoned to Gil. "It is the *vallum*," he said. "We leave holy ground." He walked down the sands to the sea's edge, turned, and drew his sword. "Come," he beckoned Gil again. "Fight me for the earldom you would not have as gift."

"You're joking," Gil muttered.

"Not with a sword in my hand." Floki smiled, his eyes glinting moonlit ice. "Draw yours."

Hand shaking, Gil slipped his sword from its scabbard, the blade catching awkwardly on the wood. "Come," Floki beckoned again. Gil clenched his fist around the hilt, and shuffled forward behind his shield, the blade raised defensively before the earl's. Steel flashed in the moonlight, slamming it from his hand.

He stood rubbing his stinging fingers. Floki said, "I ignore that. Now pick it up and fight. I do not play."

Neither do I. Gil angrily snatched up the fallen weapon and ran at the earl, swinging wildly. Floki met the chaotic charge with one sharp blow, again taking the weapon from Gil's grasp. This time, the earl caught him with his shield arm, swung him around and held the razor edge of his sword against his throat. "You are dead, my friend." He let Gil go.

"Fine," Gil said. "Let's go home." He bent down for his fallen sword. Floki caught him by his long hair and yanked him upright.

"Once more," he whispered in Gil's ear, "And I lose my patience." With a savage jerk of his arm, he flung Gil to the ground.

Gil scrambled to his feet, his terrified eyes on the waiting steel. "Do not watch the blade, Warrior," Floki said mildly. "Watch the eyes. Do not I tell you?"

You do. Gil gripped his weapon furiously. *About a million times. Watch the eyes. The eyes tell the next move.*

He faced the earl, struggling to ignore the deadly blade, raised his gaze to Floki's face and feinted to the left and to the right. The icy eyes never left his own. "Save your dancing for the longhouse, friend," Floki smiled. "Fight."

Damn you, I will. Gil charged blindly, stumbling over a moss-covered rock. With an irritated shake of his head, Floki stepped forward to meet him. Gil's foot hit a tiny pool, and skidding on the tide-slicked weed, he slipped to his knees. Spurred by desperation, he slashed upward, below Floki's sword swing. His own blade caught Floki's tunic and slashed through the cloth.

The earl leapt safely back, with a small smile. "Very good."

Gil scrambled up. *Fine. Let him think I did it on purpose. I deserve a break.* His feet skidded again and he jumped quickly onto firm sand. The mound of rocks and treacherous wet moss lay between him and the earl. Gil stopped dancing, lowered his blade, met Floki's eyes, and shrugged. "*Now,* let's go home."

Floki smiled but shook his head. "Come."

Gil shook his own, positioning himself carefully, keeping the rock mound between them. "No."

"You say what?" Floki murmured.

"I say no. I'm cold. I'm tired. I'm hungry. And I'm sick of your games." *Watch the eyes.* "Stay here if you want to. I'm going home." He flung his shield over his back, half-turned, and saw the anger flare.

"No game, Warrior." Floki leaped for him and Gil flung up his shield again, and as the earl's foot slid on the moss, he jumped forward. Kicking out, he caught Floki's other leg behind the knee and twisted his own. They teetered together in a flailing embrace, and then Gil slammed his shield up under Floki's chin and sent him sprawling on the surf-beaten sand.

Floki rolled in an instant, freeing his sword hand, but Gil's blade was already at his throat. He smiled slightly, but his eyes kept their icy calm. "Do it, Warrior," he said. "And you are a young earl."

Gil shook his head in disbelief. Then he jumped to his feet and flung the sword, hard as he could, to the edge of the moonlit surf. "No!" he looked down at Floki, "I don't want your earldom! I don't want to kill you. You're my friend. I don't want anyone …." He stopped his voice breaking and then shouted hoarsely, "Why are you doing this stupid thing? Giving everything you've ever wanted to a stupid boy so you can go and get killed by that stupid old liar!"

Floki laughed softly and got to his feet. "Because," he said, "I am Floki Magnusson, and I pay my debts."

Gil stared at him and shook his head hopelessly. Then he, too, laughed. "No," he said. "You're not Floki Magnusson. You're Palamedes. Sir Palamedes of Camelot, chasing his Questing Beast. You're just the same."

An unfathomable look crossed the earl's face and Gil stepped warily back. But then Floki flung back his head and laughed again, with delight. "Oh, I am honored, honored," he cried. He threw an arm around Gil's shoulders and gave him an affectionate little shake. "Now come, my wise young friend. We go home. But first, take your sword," he shoved Gil gently toward the abandoned weapon. "You need it yet for Yula's Isle."

They crossed the *vallum* together and walked back along the strand, Floki's arm resting lightly on Gil's shoulders. Gil said suddenly, "In the Chapter House, you asked a question about Yula's Isle. In Irish. What was it?"

"A simple thing, Warrior," the earl said mildly. "I ask the

way to the Island Port, that the child, Caitilin, calls her home."
He paused and gave Gil a faint smile. "Each man assures me
that the place does not exist."

Gil drew in a breath. "Is she lying?"

Floki shrugged. "I would not think she could, Warrior. But
then, I know that they cannot." He smiled again. "No matter.
Soon enough, we learn the truth."

The camp lay ahead, the fires burning low. Floki stopped
walking. "Understand this," he said solemnly. "I pledge this
stupid thing, as you say it, now, before we sail on to Yula's Isle.
I win there the one I love and with my lass in my arms, I grow
weak. Hold me to this."

"Me?" Gil whispered.

"Who better can I trust, than the man who would not be
earl?"

Saluting the watching guards, they slipped back into the
camp, past the dozing ponies, the dwindling fires, and the
black tents pitched beside the ships. Percy's parrot woke and
squawked and slept again. All else was silence.

Shrouded again by her awnings, *Silver Dragon* bulked
before them. Gil followed Floki up the gangplank and ducked
beneath the black cloth. Within, the murky darkness was filled
with the grunts and sighs of sleeping men. He found his way to
his bedroll by long habit, stepping over Ciarnan, snoring on his
back, and creeping into his own place between Ragi and Ismail,
both buried in mounds of sheepskins.

Gil pulled his own bedding up over his damp clothes as
quietly as he could, but the mound on his left stirred. "Sorry,
Ismail," he mumbled under his sheepskin.

"It is me," said a sweet girl's voice.

"Janetta!?" He sat up straight, staring into the night.

"Hush. You wake the others." Her face was a pale smudge
in the darkness.

"Where's Ismail?" he said stupidly.

"Beside Grimhildr. We change places."

"Beside *Grimhildr*?"

"Please. I come to beg forgiveness."

"Oh, granted. Granted." He wrapped his arms around her

and felt her soft lips on his own. She pulled away.

"I go now, before she wakes."

"Oh, stay. Stay," he murmured, condemning his best friend to death by throwing axe. But she was already gone.

CHAPTER ELEVEN

They left the White Hut at dawn, with the psalms of Lauds still echoing in their ears. The wind was strong and offshore, and they raised sail at once. "See!" Erling shouted to the watching monks, "We also take holy vows!"

The brothers smiled and pointed at the masts. The longships' fine striped sails were gone, replaced by the patched and faded spares, kept in reserve. The dun-colored cloth was as drab as the brothers' habits, and on Floki's orders the yards were hoisted to only two-thirds of their normal height.

Stripped of her dragon figurehead, no pennant on her masthead, and no shields on her shield racks, *Silver Dragon* looked dowdy and unfamiliar, like her master in his pilgrim's robes. Beside her, *Sea-Raven* rode, dull as a merchant's knarr.

The Ab laughed, standing with his Northern guest, knee-deep in the surf beside his little skiff. "A fine humbling, Floki Magnusson. I would never know you."

"Nor will any other, my friend," Floki smiled. "A plain fish in a school of plain fish." He looked up at Gil, at the helm of his ship. "Take her out."

Gil signaled to his oarsmen, holding the ship in check, and to Ragi and Ciarnan to tighten the sheets. With barely an oar stroke, they were underway, slipping into the swell with the offended dignity of a knight's charger harnessed to the plough.

The burly Ab launched his skiff, and with Floki riding beside him and working the sail, shadowed the longships out into the brightening sea. Gil steered toward a distant blue headland, enclosing the *muinntir's* broad bay, while the little skiff darted like a sea bird in and out of his wake, glancing so close to his stern that he feared for his steering oar, until, with a peal of laughter, the monk whisked his craft away.

"Look, I clip her feathers!" the Ab pointed at the stern post, stripped of its glorious dragon tail. He darted off, then, to torment Hakon's steersman and Gil smiled, thinking of the light craft he sailed in the wild tide race of the Holy Isle. *And Janetta, waiting on the strand.*

His eyes flicked to the rails of the pony pen, where she perched, as Danni once had, stroking Lionheart's neck. Lionheart whinnied with pleasure. *Fine. I'll give you to her. Good riddance.*

Dreamily, he imagined the summer heat of the barley harvest on Hrolf's Isle, and Einar's Holm as he had known it, and last, Cille Aidan, before it, too was a blackened ruin. *We'll rebuild it.* He, Janetta, Rachel, Ismail, and Danni, too, all together again. And yet, when he pictured it, he saw themselves as they were now, and Danni still the girl-child she had been, as if she alone had neither grown, nor changed.

The skiff bore down on them again, and Floki signaled Gil to head up. Turning into the wind, he heard the earl's light laughter as the Ab drew alongside. *Who is she, now, who has waited so long for him?* Gil thought sadly. *And who is he, who will leave her anyhow?*

The skiff slipped within inches of the heavy moving hull, her mast almost clipping their yard. The Ab took the sheets from Floki, and, balancing against the rail of the little boat, steered with the toes of his bare foot. Floki stood up on the rail, caught Bjorn's offered arm, and jumped aboard. With a cheerful "Godspeed," the Ab drew in his loose sail with one hand, and reclaimed his tiller with the other, and the skiff darted away.

"That is a fine seaman," Floki said to Gil. Then, raising his voice, he called, "Come to the Northlands, friend. I make a Viking of you!"

The Ab's laughter boomed over the widening sea between them. "Sooner I make a monk of you, Floki Magnusson!"

Floki leaned out over the rail and pointed to the sky. "Sooner, still, the moon fails!"

And, as the skiff dwindled to a white dot lit by the rising sun, and the waning moon slipped into the sea, they rounded the headland and entered the channel that would take them north and west to Yula's Isle.

The day was fresh, with high-flying clouds and a hint of spring warmth in the sun. The wind held brisk and steady, over Gil's shoulder, and even with their truncated sails, they made good speed.

At first, Floki directed him to hug the coast, and when Ciarnan, riding the yard on the earl's orders, spotted a sail, they sought shelter in a secluded bay.

The ship, a laden knarr, riding low in the water, passed by unaware on a southerly course, and they resumed their own. Leaving the land behind then, they set out into open sea. When next they saw sails, there was nowhere to hide.

"Four ships," Ciarnan shouted from the yard. "Tacking south."

Floki beckoned him down and stood up on the rail, peering ahead over their humbled prow. "What see you, helmsman?"

Gil stared through the sea spray on the blue horizon, at the four vessels crossing their own course on a broad reach. Their hulls were long and low, rising up at stem and stern. The tall masts bore bright colored sails. "Longships," he murmured. "Warships. Like ours."

"Not like ours," Floki said sharply. "We are but two common knarrs, sailing for the Sudreys. What is your course, helmsman?"

"Away from here," Gil muttered.

Floki laughed. "Wise helmsman." Then he shook his head. "But hounds do follow the hare that runs. We hold course." He looked over his shoulder, "But first, I speak with my cousin."

Gil headed up and when Hakon drew alongside, Floki stood up on the rail again, and addressed both crews. "There are too many of you and you are too handsome."

A wave of nervous laughter swept through the watching men. They stood facing their earl, their eyes straying to the approaching warships. "Which of us goes overboard?" Arnkel called.

"Myself of course," Floki answered. "I am the most

handsome." He grinned and then nodded to Hakon. "Him next. But first, arm yourselves, all of you."

"We fight them?" Bjorn's face broke into his huge smile.

Floki smiled back but shook his head. "If we must. But I trust not. All but six, on each ship, lie down flat on the deck, swords at your sides, shields beneath your heads. The six still standing," he pointed quickly to Arnkel, Svein Snaggle-Tooth, Ragi, Grimhildr, Ismail, and Brynjolf the Smith, "Cover them with the awning cloths."

He turned to Janetta, Caitilin, and Rachel, "Into your tent, and keep silence. Hakon Sea-Friend," he raised his eyes to his cousin, "the same on *Sea-Raven*. Do as I do and do not speak."

Hakon stood up on his own rail, face dark. Floki's lips quirked in a smile. "Now take care, brother."

"Floki, there are four of them and I wager well-armed. If we turn now, we may yet outrun them."

"With these scraps of sails, we do not outrun them," Floki answered.

"And whose idea was that?"

"Mine. Like all good ideas. They are not out a'viking, cousin. Look, see the pennants." Gil peered again through the mist and glimpsed a flicker of gold catching the sun on one mast, and then another. "What use have they for two farmers' knarrs?" Floki said. Hakon stared blankly. "Cousin," Floki said gently, "Just do what I say."

Reluctantly, Hakon stepped down from the rail and turned to direct his crew as Floki had asked. On board *Silver Dragon*, men were already retrieving their weapons and stretching themselves out on the deck.

Ragi and Svein dragged the black awning cloth over them, Percy giggling wildly and clutching his fluttering parrot as it covered his head. The girls retreated to their tent and secured the flaps. Grimhildr tucked Ulf in tidily beneath the awning cloth and then rose and stepped carefully over the hidden men. Folding her hands primly, she took a seat on a sea kist before the mast. "Good," Floki said. "We keep our cargo dry."

Gil nodded. With only her master and helmsman on the steering board, a crew of five scattered down the laden deck, and a humorless merchant's wife in the bow, the longship suddenly resembled one of the many trading vessels they had passed on their journey. He raised his eyes to the approaching ships. They had turned onto a leeward tack and the gold pennants were clearly visible. "Is it him?" he said quietly to Floki.

Floki shook his head. "You see his ship at Mont Tombe. It is twice that length. These are his henchmen."

"Looking for us."

"No," Floki smiled slightly. Sitting down on the bench, he pulled the cowl of his pilgrim's cloak up, covering his bright hair and half obscuring his face. "Looking for Floki Magnusson, that scoundrel of a Viking." He sighed, hunched over against the wind. "Ah, would I were home already, with Hildigunn."

"Who?" Gil took his eyes from the sea a moment and stared at the earl.

"My wife, helmsman. Mother of my six children." He looked up sideways. "Have you lost what little wits you possess, Oleif?"

"Who? ... Oh. Right. Got it." Gil nodded and returned his gaze to the approaching ships. They had adjusted their course, so it would now cross their own. "Am I married too?" he asked.

"Yes, sadly. To that terrible scold, Thora. More's the pity." Floki paused. "Hail them."

"What?"

"Wave. Come now, we are long at sea. The sight of such noble ships is a pleasure."

"If you say so." Gil raised one hand in a cautious wave. A figure beside the helmsman on the nearest craft returned the wave. Gil saw their sails shift as they again adjusted their course.

"Good. They seek to know us better."

Wishing he shared his earl's confidence, Gil said, "What do I do?"

"Hold course, and when I say, head up and wait." When they were a few ship's lengths from the leader, Floki murmured, "Now." And as Gil swung the tiller, he said quietly, "You are Oleif Gunnarsson, sailing home from Dublin, to the Sudreys. Your cargo is seed, leatherwork, and ponies."

"Ponies?"

"Those things. Furry, with ears," Floki pointed at Lionheart and his companions. "Oleif, you have the brains of a gnat, but you are a good helmsman. And yes, a silver ring to win Thora's favor. Not that it will work."

Head buzzing with his new identity, Gil said suddenly, "What if they board us?"

Floki cast him a sideways glance. "Fight like the devil himself. And I see you in Valholl." He looked up then and gave the master of the approaching ship a cheerful smile.

Ragi and Svein loosed the sail, and it flapped clumsily. *Silver Dragon* swung crosswind and wallowed in the chop, drab as a gull in yearling plumage.

The warship drew alongside, a glorious peacock. From stem to stern, her upper strakes were painted in blue and green. Her sail was checkered, red and white, and her figurehead of a snarling wolf glistened black, silver, and gold. Her three companion ships, closing around them as Floki smiled and waved, were equally splendid. Men, dressed in fine Frankish tunics, gathered along their rails.

"What ship?" the master called across the small gap of sea between them. The words were Frankish-accented Norse, the tone, commanding.

Floki raised his head and smiled. "Forgive me if I do not rise, sir. I have taken a chill and my legs are weakened." He hunched over, molding his graceful height into the posture of a weary, older man. "She is *Summer Dawn*, sailing from the Sudreys. We buy these ponies in Dublin. Now we are seeking a goat."

"A goat," the master repeated. He narrowed his eyes, studying Floki and his ship. Then he nodded sharply at *Silver Dragon*. "She has fine lines for such a trade. The lines of a Sea-Stallion, not a knarr."

"She is a warship, in truth," Floki said innocently. Gil stifled a gasp as the man shot Floki a quick suspicious glance. Floki smiled in return. "Our fathers went a'viking in their youth."

The man shook his head, a frown of disdain crossing his face. Then he smiled wryly, raising his gaze to take in Hakon and *Sea-Raven*, as well. "And are your fathers proud of sons who sail for goats and ponies?" Laughter from his watching crew swept across the sea.

"They are not proud," Floki kept his smile. "They are dead. We choose a peaceful life." He shrugged philosophically, "But the old ships have their uses."

The master shook his head again and laughed. Then he, too, shrugged, with a touch of scorn and turned to his helmsman.

"And you, sir," Floki called after him, "What brings your fine ships to our islands? A tale for my Hildigunn's hearth, no doubt? Though it is not my affair," he added.

The man paused, considering. "No. It is not. But I will tell you. We seek the Viking, Floki Magnusson."

"*Floki Magnusson,*" Floki echoed. He shivered and clutched his tattered cloak tighter.

The man leaned closer, over his rail. "Have you seen him?"

"Praise God and his Holy Mother, I have not." Floki crossed himself, and then said solemnly, "I wish you success, sir, in your bold quest. May you find him."

The master of the warship laughed and as his helmsman turned the vessel back to their course, he shouted cheerfully, "And I wish you success in yours. May you find your goat!"

"May we, indeed," Floki whispered as Gil turned their prow again north.

At sunset, they were once more in sight of land. A dusky blue line off their load board marked the distant Irish shore, while dead ahead lay a long dark promontory, their last landfall before Yula's Isle. The roar of the surf on its fine white beaches carried far out to sea. Its low hills were heather clad and desolate.

Above, the sky had cleared. The wind, falling light, backed to the north. Directed by Floki toward a pristine curving strand, Gil aligned the bare stem post with a convenient tree on the shore. Eyes alert for rocks or shallows, he headed in.

By dusk, the hulls were safely above the tideline and the awnings draped over lowered masts. But there was no comforting flicker of flames and no promising scent of wood smoke. "Do you think they'll come back?" Gil said, as Floki ordered a double guard.

"No. They seek that Viking scoundrel, now, to the south. But I think they are not alone. If a farmer from the Northlands summons seven ships, how many more answer to a king?"

As night fell, and they munched disconsolately on stale barley bread and cheese, clouds rolled in, blotting out the stars. When Gil woke at grey first light, the awning above his head sagged with a weight of snow.

"Would that I were home already with Thora," Gil muttered as he tramped out with Ismail to bring in the tethered ponies.

"With *who*?"

"Thora. My wife."

"You crazy?"

"No. Married. To Thora the Scold."

Ismail grinned. "You crazy. Too many days at sea."

They found the animals snuffling for frozen grass, under a layer of white. Lionheart shook a resentful mane, showering Gil with ice crystals.

Don't look at me, North Pony. You're the one who wanted to go home. My hooves are cold.

All the way home to your snowy tree. Gil untied Lionheart and one of the Hrolf's Isle ponies, while Ismail took the other two. They trudged back through the snow, bemoaning the fireless camp and their grim breakfast of soggy bannocks. "Hey, remember the day we sail past Africa?" Ismail said dreamily. "And we swim and lie in the sun?"

Gil clapped freezing upper arms with colder hands. Lionheart snorted at the shaken lead rein. "Oh, do I!"

"Would that I were home again with Fatima." Ismail grinned. "*My* wife. Fatima the Ferocious." He looked up. "You in trouble, I think."

Gil raised his gaze and sighed. "When am I not?"

Floki was standing just above the tide line, within a circle of men. "Helmsman," he called, with strained patience. "We await you."

"Go." Ismail took Gil's two pony leads and shoved Gil toward the earl. Gil hurriedly joined the group on the foreshore. Hakon was there already, with Erling, and two of the older Shetlanders, dour, quiet brothers called Helgi and Bard. Ulf stood beside Floki, with Arnkel Fish-Tail, his thumbs hooked into his sword-belt, and Svein Snaggle-Tooth, scratching his disheveled beard.

Grimhildr followed Gil into the circle, shepherding before her the Irish girl, Caitilin, and the boy, Niall, with the High-King's harp slung over his shoulder. Both boy and girl looked frightened and confused, surrounded by sea-worn, unkempt Northmen.

Floki acknowledged Gil's arrival with a wry smile. "Other men can tend beasts, helmsman." He knelt then, and with a piece of driftwood began drawing a long, curving line in the snow. The line circled around and joined itself, enclosing a snowy interior within a waving, indented boundary. "What see you, helmsman?"

Gil studied the drawing. "If that's water," he poked the snow outside the drawing, "Then, an island. A map of an island. Yula's Isle?" he guessed.

Floki smiled again and drew a fish beside his island. "That is water. And this is, indeed, Yula's Isle, as I know it. "It is one island, but nearly two. Here," he touched the map with his driftwood pen, "The waters of a sea loch run between these two headlands, so far that the land is near divided. Here," the driftwood traced a new line, "the land is higher, but most is low. Fine farmland, turf for the fires, fish in the waters, seabirds on the shore. It is a good island. Perhaps the best."

He looked up and his eyes settled on Gil. "But there is a price to pay for such bounty. The seas of Yula's Isle are fierce. Here," he touched one headland, "I think the fiercest I have seen. And here," he quickly drew the coast of a neighboring island, "Between Yula's Isle and this, the Deer Isle, runs a tide as swift as any I know." He let his gaze pass across the faces of all the watching men. "Many fine ships are driftwood on these shores. Many fine seamen leave their bones amid the weed." He paused, and they all watched him uneasily, the wide-eyed Irish children clutching each other's hands.

"Good!" Arnkel Fish-Tail grinned, "We have good fortune, and our enemy founders here, first!"

Erling shook his head. "Do not wish shipwreck on another, lest it come to yourself."

Arnkel laughed boldly. "Surely the White Christ will protect us, now our earl reads his holy book?" There was laughter, then, from all but Hakon, who looked away, his brooding eyes on the grey horizon.

Floki turned back to his map. "There is a hall here," he marked a small square at the head of the sea loch. "I know its earl, a good, fair-minded man." He paused, looking briefly at Caitilin. "There are shielings in the hills, and, too, prayer houses along the shores. Old, and most abandoned. But some remain. The earl is a pagan, but he leaves them in peace."

He paused again, thoughtfully, and then spoke directly to the girl, "This is the only hall I know, its chieftain, the only earl. Is this your father's house?"

She stared at the map and then at Floki. Then she covered her face with her hands and shook her head.

"No?" Floki's voice remained mild, but his eyes narrowed.

"No." Then she murmured something else, so softly that the Irish words eluded Gil.

Floki reached out to her. "What say you?"

The *file's* son stepped protectively in between. "She says her father is not a pagan."

Floki smiled gently at both children. "Very well." He reached again to Caitilin, drew her toward him, and pointed to the map. "Show me where lies your father's hall."

"Floki, she is a child," Hakon scuffed the snow with his boot, "What does this mean to her?"

Floki shrugged and smiled again, his gaze never leaving Caitilin's face. "You are indeed young, as my cousin says. Perhaps you have never left your mother's side?"

Her eyes suddenly flashed and she gave Hakon an angry look. "I have," she said proudly. "I have travelled to Eire for my betrothal. My husband is also young," she gave Hakon another resentful look, "And so we must wait to marry."

"No doubt he waits eagerly," Floki said. "For so lovely a bride." She looked down and her cheeks reddened.

"I have travelled further still," she said, "My father's sister bides at Urchard in Glen Alban. There, too, I have journeyed."

"And now, to Holy Rome as well," Floki laughed softly. "Far indeed from your mother's side." He pointed again to his map in the snow. "Show me the port from which you sail."

She knelt down beside him then, her fear vanished, and taking the driftwood from his hand, marked a small cross in the snow, within the boundaries of his map. Exclamations of puzzlement came from all around and Hakon said sharply, "There is no point to this, cousin. She has no understanding."

Floki ignored him and leaning close to the girl said, "I see no water there, child. How is this a port?"

She looked up in surprise. "But there *is* water. You have not drawn it." She crouched over the map, and in the center of an expanse of snow, drew a long oval. With a quick smile for Gil, she added a fish.

"A loch," Floki said. "Very well. But a port?"

She drew then a long line from the head of the sea loch, stopping just short of the oval. Then, beside her fish, she added two small circles.

"Islands?" Floki said.

Caitilin smiled; it had become a child's game. She drew then a large, solid square on the largest island and added a peaked roof. "My father's hall," she said, and then added, "In truth, my uncle's, but they are close and share a hearth." She sat back on her heels. "This is my home. The Island Port of Yula's Isle."

Floki nodded. Hakon said, "You cannot sail from there."

"But I can and did!" She moved closer to Floki who had become her ally. "Here," she drew a line from the island, down the length of the loch and drew a boat shape on it. "Here the small ships go back and forth. Here," she drew a dotted line, "Men walk or ride and beasts carry goods. It is not far. And here," she drew a row of boats at the top of the line that joined the sea loch, "are the nousts my uncle builds for the big ships. Here, they come with goods and with friends, and with all the great earls, when my uncle's council meets."

"Up the river?" Floki tapped the line.

She nodded.

"Sometimes, in summer, they drag the ships here, and here." She marked two places and Gil saw that she knew her river well. "But most often not. And then," she traced the river line down to the sea loch, "They come to the Loch of the Waiting and when the tide is right, out to the open sea."

"I know that river," Floki said quietly, "And I know that loch. I have waited for its tide, too. It would be as she says." Hakon glowered. Floki again ignored him. Leaning close to the child, he said, "Does your uncle not fear for his ships? So long in such narrow waters?"

"But who would there be to fear?" she cried innocently, "All the lands around are his. My uncle rules all of Yula's Isle and islands and lands far beyond. All the chieftains are loyal and fierce in his defense. Who could harm us here?"

"Who indeed," Hakon said abruptly. "Cousin," he stepped back from the circle. "We must speak."

Floki stood and said softly to Caitilin, "Stay with Grimhildr." He beckoned Gil and Erling and they followed Hakon a short distance down the strand.

Hakon glanced back and said, in a whisper, "She is lying."

Floki shook his head. "The child could not lie if the devil himself demanded it."

"It is a trap!" Hakon hissed.

Floki smiled and said patiently, "Of course it is a trap, Sea-Friend. But that does not mean she lays it."

"What matter who lays it? The jaws close on us the same." Hakon shook his head fiercely. "The sea loch itself is a trap. And the river?"

"She says her uncle holds it secure."

"Indeed. Secure for Jocelyn Guidbairn, with whom he strikes a fine bargain." Hakon cast a furious glance back at the group on the shore. "And who *is* this uncle who rules all of Yula's Isle?"

Floki was silent. He looked at the girl, crouched by his map in the snow, and then out to the sea beyond the dark headland. "I know only one earl on Yula's Isle," he said thoughtfully, "and he rules no more than an eighth of the island."

"Well, let us go to him, if you trust him, and learn what he knows of this earl of whom no one has heard."

"I do trust him," Floki said mildly. "He is a good and decent man. But old, and no longer strong. I do not bring our troubles on his head." He paused. "When we were boys, Sea-Friend, I thought Redbeard and your father ruled all the Northlands. So fine and powerful are a father and an uncle in the eyes of a child."

Hakon nodded. "Perhaps you still see with the eyes of a child." He leant close to his cousin, "She has been the prisoner of the *Golden Knight*, Floki. Do you doubt his power to bend her will to his?"

Floki studied Hakon in silence, and then turned and walked back to the others. Kneeling again in the snow, he placed his big hands on Caitilin's shoulders and looked into her eyes. "Child, I thank you for all you tell me. But now I ask one more question. Think carefully of your answer, for the lives of all here depend upon it." She nodded fearfully. Floki said, "Is it true?"

Her eyes opened wide. "Why would I say it, if it were not true?"

Floki shook his head, still holding her firmly. "Perhaps," he said slowly, "Another has spoken to you? Perhaps sworn you to secrecy?"

"No," she said in a tiny voice, lip trembling. Floki gave his cousin a bitter look but went on. "Caitilin," he said urgently, "If you have been threatened, you must tell me. Name the man, and I will kill him. I will protect you. But I cannot if you do not tell me the truth."

"But it is the truth!" she cried. "I have no other truth to tell." Tears filled her eyes and she struggled to free her hands to cover her face. Floki released her and gathered her into his arms, holding her close against his rough cloak as she sobbed. He looked up at Hakon, over her shoulder.

"That is enough for me, cousin. If not for you, then set your own course." He stood up, his eyes on the Shetlander's dour, kindly face. Hakon shook his head, ran a troubled hand through his tangled black hair and looked away.

"As you say," he said, with another shake of his head.

Floki smiled wryly. "I thank you for your trust, cousin. I work hard for it." He turned back to the frightened girl, watching him like a small, captured animal. "One last question," he said gently. "Just one, and I trouble you no more." He looked down at his map again. "Is there no other port, Caitilin? None closer to your father's hall than this?" He touched the river where it flowed into the Loch of the Waiting.

She shook her head. "Only the Port of the Hunters," she said innocently.

Hakon spun around, eyebrows arching in exasperation. "And where is that?" he cried. She shrank back and Floki gave his cousin a warning look.

"It is only small," she whispered.

"Show me," said Floki.

She bent over the map, glancing warily at Hakon and pointed to the strait between the two islands. "The strand is narrow, and the shores are steep. But it is only a short crossing to Deer Island. My uncle keeps boats there to take men to the hunting. But all others come the other way," she insisted. "It is better."

Indeed it is," Floki smiled. "But not for us."

———

At the first sight of Yula's Isle, Floki had the men arm themselves as before, and when they were close enough to discern trees and outcrops, he ordered them under the awning cloths.

This time, however, he let Caitilin remain in the open air, seated between himself and Gil on the steersman's bench. "One of my six children, Oleif," he smiled. Then, to the girl straining for a view of her home island, he said, "You can go to the rail, but hold tightly." She climbed up, carefully, onto the topmost strake, both hands gripping a shroud, and Gil thought her convincing as a merchant's excited young daughter on her first voyage from home.

But, although she sought them eagerly, there were no ships to convince. Nor was there sign of habitation other than an ancient fortress, crumbling to ruin, and two small chapels, one with a tall stone cross, like on Hy. "Where's all the great farmland?" Gil asked curiously.

"To the west. I take you the Viking way," Floki smiled. "Where a man might hide a ship." He leant forward then, peering at the grey shore. "Though, were it me, I would hide it better than that."

"What?" Gil's eyes swept the shore, falling readily on the beached longship sheltering in a small, sandy cove. Its high stern was clearly visible above the rocky promontory that concealed the rest of the hull. "They're not even trying," he said.

"They are lazy. Hauling her up properly is too much work."

Caitilin came down from the rail, her face troubled. "Surely, they are pirates," she said. "Why would my uncle's ships rest there, when they have their own fine harbor?"

Floki smiled. "No matter, child. I know who they are." His eyes were already scanning the horizon. "There," he said to Gil, showing him the top of an inland hill. Squinting, Gil made out a small dark knob on the skyline. "Wood for the ward fire," Floki smiled again. But I think they do not light if for two merchants' knarrs." He pointed to the top of a farther hill. "Another. And there will be others. They will be seen far off. The island is not high."

"It's high there," Gil gestured to two conical hills dominating the horizon ahead. "Those are mountains."

"They are. But they are not on Yula's Isle. They are on the Deer Isle beyond. A sound lies between, narrow and fast. Soon we enter it."

Gil felt already the tug of the quickening tide, nudging the steering oar. The coast off his load board passed faster. The shore of the Deer Isle grew closer as the strait narrowed. "Look!" Caitilin suddenly cried. But Gil had seen it already, a blue wisp of smoke rising from trees near the shore.

"A ward fire! They've seen us!"

Floki laughed. "Who lights a ward fire in a wood?" His eyes swept the coast. "But a campfire, yes."

"My uncle's huntsmen," Caitilin turned to Gil with shining eyes. "Perhaps he is there. Perhaps my father! Please, take us across. It is not far."

Floki regarded her gravely. Then he said, "Soon, child. But not now. We would not impose on their hospitality." She looked stricken, but the earl turned to the nearer shore of Yula's Isle. "There, helmsman. That small cove beneath the waterfall. Can you take her in there?"

Warily, Gil assessed the unpromising shore. Steep cliffs

rose up along its length, broken by occasional gullies cutting shadowy courses into the hillsides. Water tumbled down the one Floki had chosen, onto a crescent of shingle bordered by rocky promontories. The beach seemed hardly big enough for the skiff Gil had sailed to the Holy Isle. "Is there room?" he said doubtfully.

"You are helmsman."

Gil looked over his shoulder to *Sea-Raven*, following, with Erling's usual caution, well behind. No help there. The current tugged urgently; he had moments to decide. "Going for it," he muttered. He signaled Ragi and Ciarnan, manning the sheets, and shouted for oarsmen.

The black awning cloth erupted as hidden sailors leapt to their feet and ran for oars. Gil swung the tiller, jibing *Silver Dragon* around, and ran downwind for the shore. Nearer land, the racing tide was stronger. He leaned all his weight on the shuddering steering oar, fighting to hold his course. Black rock jutted either side of his path. He shouted to his load board oarsmen to dig deep and pulled desperately on the tiller. The ship heeled hard, the prow swung around, and they tore past the rock barriers with barely an oar's length to spare.

Behind the curved arm of the promontory, the cove was broader than it had appeared, and calm. The rush of water fell silent and the hull settled on an even keel. Arnkel freed the rudder and *Silver Dragon* rode up onto the shore, grounding gently on gravel. Gil released the tiller from still shaking hands and sat down heavily on the bench. He heard the earl's soft laughter over his shoulder. "You are better than you think you are, my friend."

When both ships were secure above the tideline and the masts lowered, Floki ordered the figureheads replaced and the yards rigged again with their fine bright sails. Gil watched uncertainly as the dragon raised its glittering head. The promontory, though thick with trees, was still an imperfect screen. And the shingle of their harbor showed signs of casual use; charred driftwood and scorched rocks marking old camp sites.

Floki saw his uneasiness and smiled. "Send Oleif back to his merchant's scales. We are Northmen, again." He beckoned Gil inland toward the waterfall. "Come. We stretch our legs."

Gil found himself stretching not just his legs, but his arms as well, as they scrambled up the natural rock staircase beside the thunderous linn. Stopping at last on a narrow, dripping shelf, Floki turned to look out across the strait. Gil took a firm grip of a heather root and did the same.

They had climbed something less than a hundred feet, but the Deer Isle lay, now, spread out before them, revealing a wooded shore rising gently toward the rugged hills beyond. Inland, among the trees, the coil of wood smoke had been joined by two more. The scene was peaceful and untroubled, the only sign of life a white bird that rose from the tree shrouded camp, circled once, and struck out on a sure, straight course to the south.

In the foreground, the faint, but unmistakable outlines of three beached ships stood out against the pale shore. Whoever had left them clearly had little to fear. "Caitilin's uncle," Gil said. "Out hunting."

Floki watched the white bird thoughtfully and more thoughtfully, still, when a second rose to follow the first. "Out hunting, indeed, but I think not the deer."

Gil gave him a puzzled look. Floki gestured to the distant shore. "We are far from that strand, Warrior. Skiffs to ferry huntsmen would elude our eyes. These are warships. And the one in the center, twice the size of our own." He looked down to *Silver Dragon*, resting on the shingle below. "Bring me my hawk."

While Floki waited, Gil descended the rock staircase and returned with Rachel. Eager, as always, for the chance to fly, she boldly outpaced him on the climb and flopped down, rosy-cheeked, at the earl's feet.

He unbuckled his sword belt, looped it again in his hand and dropped it on the ground beside her. "Pretty Hawk," he said, "I would know of the camp across the water. Who is hunting and what their quarry. Fly, but not too near. Huntsmen may have hawks of their own."

But they saw no hawks, other than Rachel, darting, swift

and brown, out across the water to the wooded island beyond. When she had dwindled to a speck and then vanished from sight, they sat down on the ledge to wait.

Gil studied the Sound below, gazing back the way they had come, and then out to where the waters, lit by late afternoon sun, flowed to the Western Sea. Splashed with white caps and crossed by tidal bars, they were, but for the crowds of sea birds, empty of life.

"Where are the ships?" he said suddenly. Floki raised a questioning eyebrow. "This great chieftain, Caitilin's uncle … if those aren't his men," Gil shrugged toward the encampment across the Sound, "Then where is he? Wouldn't he send someone to check them out? And that other ship we passed. Does he let just anyone light ward fires?"

Floki leaned his head back against the moss-covered rock and gave Gil a faint, appreciative smile. Then he said, "My lands in the North are mine in name and mine in practice. But they are not mine, in truth. I hold them for an earl in Norway, a very powerful man."

Gil nodded. "Aidan told me that," he said.

Floki smiled more openly. "It is no secret. And should that earl, who rarely visits, find some urgent business on Hrolf's Isle, some business that is not my affair, would I raise objection? Or would I perhaps take my skiff to the Holy Isle, to fish?"

Gil laughed. "Knowing you, you'd raise objection."

Floki grinned. "I might. But since it would cost me Hrolf's Isle and possibly my life, it would not be wise."

Gil studied the distant warships. "So, Caitilin's uncle and father are looking the other way."

"Perhaps."

"She's so proud of them," Gil said sadly.

"Even evil men have good children who love them," Floki said. "And they are perhaps less evil than trapped."

"Okay," Gil said slowly. "But where are his chieftains' ships? The seas around Hrolf's Isle are always full of ships. Your chieftains are always coming to see you."

"Perhaps he lacks my charm," Floki smiled, but then he said, "You are wise, helmsman. There is something here that baffles.

The girl is truthful; I rest my life on it, but her truth is not the truth of the monks of the White Hut. Nor is it the truth of the old man of the Loch of the Waiting. Where are the warriors of this mighty earldom? It is as if they walk as ghosts among us and cannot be seen." He looked up. "Ah, my hawk returns."

Gil shaded his eyes, at first seeing nothing. A lifetime of distant seascapes had given the Northman matchless vision. "There," Floki pointed helpfully, "In a line above that tree." At last, Gil's eyes caught the dark fleck winging toward them.

"She's really moving," he said admiringly.

Floki laughed, relaxed now that she had appeared. "Ducks fly faster, but they are less fierce." He paused then and his laughter faded. "She veers."

Gil, too, had seen the change of course. A moment earlier she had flown, straight as a bowshot, toward them. Now, she angled away to the south as if retracing in the air, their journey over the sea. "What's she doing?" he cried.

"She has lost her way." Floki's voice was calm, but Gil saw the fear in his eyes, that she would vanish into the vastness of the sky, and never return to him.

"Not Rachel," he said desperately.

"All creatures err." Floki followed her aberrant flight and whispered, "Here, Pretty One. I am here." She flew on, and they watched helplessly. Then suddenly he grabbed Gil's arm, nearly unbalancing him on the narrow ledge. "Yes!" he cried joyfully. "Look! She hunts!"

A white speck had appeared against the dimming sky, and the dark pinpoint that was the hawk closed on it. Floki embraced Gil's shoulders, laughing again, and Gil grabbed at the rock face. "Remember where we are!"

"Ah, yes." Floki released him. "I forget these things." The hawk was upon its quarry, circling once above and then stooping in a flash of sunlit wings. White feathers exploded and fell like snow, and then she was streaking home to them, her prey safe in her savage grip.

Floki held up his arms, hands clasped in a triumphant circle. The hawk swept through them, trailing a flurry of white down, and Rachel stood before him, a blood-spattered dove in her hands. Its pretty white head hung limply, its ruffled wings, awkwardly splayed.

"Did I ask that you should hunt?" Floki said.

She regarded the dove sadly, though Gil, remembering his venison, wasn't sure if she was sorry it was dead, or sorry she hadn't eaten it when she had the chance. "No," she said. "You asked me to learn of the camp across the water." She raised her eyes from the dove and met his. "Under the trees stands the pavilion I saw in Rome. On the strand lies the ship we saw at Mont Tombe. And," she held out the dove, "I brought you this." She touched the bird's scaly grey feet. On one was wound a strip of leather, not long and trailing, like the jesses of a hawk, but a neat package, snugly tied.

"Ah, clever Hawk," Floki murmured. He carefully unwound the leather and freed the ink-scrawled vellum within.

"Are you glad, now, I hunted?"

"Very. Read it to me."

She smiled benignly. "When you say thank you."

His eyes widened with amazement. She fingered the vellum. "I thank you," he said evenly. "Now *read it*."

Rachel screwed up her face and regarded it for a very long while. "The Latin's terrible."

"Pretty One!" Floki waved an exasperated arm. Gil glanced, alarmed, at the cliff. "My concern is not the scholarship but the meaning!"

Rachel smiled again. "'Flames await ....'" She paused. "Or, 'Await flames.' You see it *could* be either."

"Yes," Floki breathed. "It could indeed. Or both." He looked up from the vellum and met Gil's eyes. "His ward fires are in place and his warriors await the signal that we are in the trap."

"Only, we're not," Gil said.

"No. We are not. And now, my friends," his gaze swept both their faces, "We light him a ward fire that the Angels of Heaven see."

CHAPTER TWELVE

Gil cracked his fire striker against the flint for the tenth time and at last a tiny spark caught in his nest of new wool. "Quick!" he cried. Ismail was already teasing fresh strands across it. The spark flared a moment, and then went out. Gil rocked back on his heels and groaned in despair.

"Try again," Ismail smiled encouragingly. "It almost worked."

Gil sighed. He looked up at the rock shelf roofing the shallow sea cave in which they crouched. Water dripped continuously from the mossy stone. Tongues of rising tide damped the sand floor. "If I can light a fire here, I can light one anywhere," he said.

"Don't say!" Ismail grinned. "Next, he asks you light it under sea."

Gil wiped a hand over his soaking hair. "You mean we're not?" he raised the fire striker once more. The crack of steel on flint echoed beneath the low roof, piercing the ongoing thunder of the nearby waterfall like a hammer blow on an anvil.

A shower of sparks flew, and Ismail rushed to shield them with his hands. The wool smoldered and flared. Gil added dry bracken and the pine needles and cones. Flames rose and grew and Ismail fed them eagerly with the driest of driftwood.

Gil sat back again, stroking the dragon heads trimming the fire striker, and then, with a nod of satisfaction, replaced the tool and the flints in the leather pouch tied to his belt. The driftwood crackled and flamed. Smoke swirled beneath the low, wet roof, vainly seeking an exit. Gil rubbed his stinging eyes and coughed. "Oh, great."

Brief daylight flickered as Floki pushed aside the dripping

ferns at the cave's entrance and crawled in under the overhang. "Good," he said, kneeling beside them. "You have a fire, and a ship's length away, I see no smoke."

"No," Gil said cheerfully. "Every bit of it's in here."

"That is as it should be. I hear your fire striker on the shore, but there," he waved a hand vaguely toward the Sound and the Deer Isle, "Over wind and tide, I think they hear nothing. This is well. But still, we must take care."

He left them then, and Gil and Ismail took turns, each with muffled face, feeding the growing fire, while the other crouched at the cave entrance breathing in gasps. Then Floki returned with Ulf and together they stretched sail cloth over the narrow entrance, blocking out the daylight and with it, any semblance of fresh air. The earl tossed Gil and Ismail wet rags to cover their faces and nodded, covering his own. "Better." Coughing, Ulf crawled out and Gil watched enviously. But Floki remained with them, stacking more wood on the fire until a red glow brightened its core.

Gil looked at it dismally and said, "We should have kept the dove. We could have cooked it." Ismail laughed but Floki only smiled and shook his head. When they had returned with Rachel's prey to the camp, Percy had cried, insisting with his own inexplicable logic, that it was his green parrot's friend and they must bury it, like they buried his own friend, Eirik, in Rome. And so, after much ceremony, organized by Percy and carried out by Floki, the bird rested now beneath a mound of pebbles and seashells, while Percy carved his own mysterious runes on a driftwood cross.

"When a loss is too great for us," Floki said, laying more wood on the fire, "We grieve for something small."

"Is so," Ismail agreed. Gil nodded grudging acceptance, his mind on the last hot meal he had tasted. Who would have imagined he'd grieve one day for monastic soup? He looked up at the barely visible ceiling.

"Maybe we could smoke some fish?"

The ferns rustled and Erling appeared, crawling under the sailcloth curtain, with two small leather sacks in his hand. "Ah, it is Loki," Floki grinned. Gil gave him a blank look and he added, "The fire-bearer," and reached for the first sack. Inside, snug in its nest of straw, was the small metal box which carried fire from hearth to hearth. Floki took the lid from it, and with tongs improvised from two green twigs, lifted glowing embers from the center of the fire and dropped them inside, packing the box to its brim.

He fastened the lid again, replaced the box in its straw burrow, and tied the leather sack. He reached for the other, but Erling held it yet and said formally, "Hakon Ragnvaldsson requests I tell you this: That you return, or not, from this venture, is your own affair. But *this*," he tapped the box firmly, "returns regardless."

Floki took it, smiling to himself, and said, as he filled it with embers, "Tell my dear cousin that my wraith will return with it, and bear it behind him 'til the end of his days. He will be called Hakon the Haunted."

The boys' laughter dissolved in fits of coughing, and they rubbed their streaming eyes. But Erling slowly and solemnly shook his head. Floki shoved the filled fire boxes at him. "Erling! It is a jest! Gods of my fathers!" He looked up at the smoky roof. Then he turned to Gil. "Never sail with my cousin. Dreariness afflicts his ships until men forget how to laugh." He slapped Gil's arm. "Well done. Now get water and put this fire out."

"Put it out?" Gil groaned. But Floki was already ducking beneath the sailcloth, following the fire-bearer from the cave. Clothes reeking of smoke, and faces smudged with soot, Gil and Ismail crawled out after him, into the fading daylight.

"Hey, you African," Ismail grinned.

Gil wrinkled his nose, "Hey, you smoked herring."

They found leather bailing buckets aboard the beached ship and hauled them, brim-full, back into their cave. Wet rags pressed against their faces, they ceremoniously doused their hard-won fire. Steam hissed up, and a wall of heat hit them, like in Gudleif Egilsson's wash house, as coughing and choking, they scrambled back out beneath the sailcloth and ferns.

Outside, clouds had thickened and light rain damped the sand. Armed and ready for battle, *Silver Dragon's* crew waited on the shore. Arnkel held a sack stuffed with dry bracken; Ragi, a thick bundle of driftwood, and Ulf, a creel over-flowing with pinecones soaked in carpenter's pitch. Hakon stood slightly apart, with Erling, who held the two fire boxes, wrapped protectively in a fur.

Gil looked around for Floki and saw him then, sitting with Percy by the burial mound of the dove, talking softly to the boy, while Percy nodded solemnly and stroked the green parrot he held in his arms. The Northmen watched, shifting their weight from foot to foot and eying the darkening sky.

"It is slack tide, cousin," Hakon shouted. "If you are to go, go now."

Floki rose then, smiling cheerfully and crossed the strand to join them, with Percy clinging tearfully. Janetta ran from where she tended the ponies, and gently detached the boy, and with a motherly arm around his shoulders, led him away. Gil suddenly imagined a day when the child she comforted would be his own, and love for her rose up in his chest, so fierce that it hurt.

"Helmsman?" Gil wrenched his gaze from Janetta and back to the earl, standing before him. Floki smiled. "Yes. She is very lovely. But we have work, my friend." He waved airily toward the rock-bound entrance to the cove. "That pretty thing you do today? You do it now, in darkness."

"It will be impossible," Hakon interrupted, "When the tide turns."

Floki turned to his cousin as if only just noticing him. "Ah, now the gods are both with us. Loki bears fire, and All-Wise Odin commands the sea." He covered one eye and grinned at Hakon. "I go now and return with your firebox. And your helmsman."

"And who takes us home, if you do not?"

"You, cousin," Floki said with another smile. "As fine a helmsman as any. If timid."

"At sea," Hakon growled, "timid is part of fine."

Floki nodded, then, and suddenly grew serious. "I leave my people in your safe hands, Hakon Sea-Friend. If you see three fires, all is well. If not, sail before dawn."

He turned abruptly then and addressed his crew. "Three ships lie on the farther shore. We go now to burn them. We cross under oar, masts down and sail furled. The strongest men on the oar." His gaze flicked quickly from Bjorn to Ulf and roved over a dozen more. "And the fleetest," he marked out Ismail, Arnkel, Gil, and Ragi, "to go ashore."

Bjorn scowled, "No battle?"

Floki smiled fondly. "No battle. They far outnumber us. We must be swift, and we must be thorough. Ashore and away before they see the first flames. Nothing, come morning, but black keels and white ash. They are stranded, or we are dead men."

"They have other ships," Hakon interrupted. "One, on this very coast. And four more with whom you make sport. Whose masters may rethink your pretty story and return."

"They may. But they are a day's sail south. And the lie-a-bed keepers of the ward fire," Floki shrugged a shoulder toward the beached ship they had passed, "seek us in another place. There is time, still, to return our young hostage to her people and re-claim our own. And then, cousin, we raise sail for home."

A look of wistful longing flitted across sea-weary faces. Floki smiled and nodded. "Yes. Home. You have sailed far, far from where we began. Farther than ever intended. And all with no more complaint than women at the milking. I thank you."

He paused solemnly. "What I ask now is dangerous work. So late in the journey, so close to home. Should any man choose to stay with Hakon, he is free." He stepped back and turned away, allowing them space to desert him.

No man moved. When the earl turned again and saw them all standing there yet, he laughed delightedly. "Ah, what better men are there, than men of the North?" He ran toward his ship. "Come. To work!" Cheering, they all followed, loading their sacks of kindling and the precious fireboxes aboard, and then hauling the heavy hull back into the waiting sea.

Hakon and his crew watched, the older men grimly, the younger, envious. Barely visible in the dusk, the girls stood silently beside Grimhildr as the ship was readied for raiding. But when Gil tossed his length of rope aboard and mounted the gangplank, Janetta broke free and ran to his side. Throwing her arms around his neck, she kissed him boldly on his mouth, a long, long kiss which, despite the laughter and jeers of his shipmates, he had no wish to end.

"A warrior is not delayed by women, helmsman." Floki's hand closed roughly on the scruff of his neck. But his eyes were full of laughter as he dragged Gil away.

Gangplank drawn up, the ship slipped into open water under softly dipping oars, as low and as secret as the dragon she was named for. Gil peered past the figurehead, seeking the mouth of the cove. Night had fallen; moon and stars were hidden. Deprived of their lace of tidal foam, the rock barriers were nothing but shadows. "I can't see them," Gil muttered.

"Hush. Listen." Floki, at his shoulder, tapped his left ear. "You hear them." Over the splash of the dipping oars, there was still a low murmur of small waves. "When eyes fail, use ears."

Gil leaned on the sound, keeping it safely at bay until the stern had cleared the last of the nearest rocks. Releasing his breath, he raised his head and peered forward into blackness. Fear rose again. "I can't see anything."

"Can you see the Deer Isle?" Floki said mildly. Gil made out a dim mass against a murky sky.

"Yes, but …."

"Can you see the water?" Blacker than island or sky, the Sound lay before him, flecked with dim splashes of white. Gil nodded hopelessly. "Then it is not so that you see nothing. There is always light at sea. And there, now, helmsman, our friends provide a beacon."

Gil followed the line of the earl's outstretched arm. A ruddy light flickered, vanished, and re-appeared on the dark hillside above the shore. "It is their campfire, through the trees. Steer for it, but do not stare at it; it will make the darkness darker. Gil aligned the dragon's head with the flickering light and looked quickly back to the night sky. "You are well now?" Floki asked.

Shaking, Gil murmured, "I'm well."

"Good. Now we talk." Floki raised his voice and called, "My runners?"

Ismail, Ragi, and Arnkel shipped their oars, rose from their benches, and joined Gil and the earl in the stern. Floki sat beside Gil, on the steersman's bench. The three young men crouched on their heels in a ring, around them.

"Soon, we come to the Deer Isle," Floki said. "There we stand off. Erling takes the helm. The oarsmen turn her and wait. We wade ashore." His gaze crossed each of their faces. "Five men. Two fireboxes. Three ships. The outlier," he indicated left, "to Ragi and Arnkel Fish-Tail. The near," He gestured right, "to the Saracen and my helmsman. The center, I take. I owe her master some fire; he burned my father's house."

Ismail and Ragi nodded. Arnkel grinned, a pale glimmer of teeth in the darkness. Floki said, "Together, we board and set out our kindling. Add anything you find – sails, oars – and spread your embers, saving one third each. Bring the fireboxes to me and return to the ship. I light the last fire and follow." He paused. "If we are discovered, to sea at once. No one waits for me. Erling knows."

They all nodded warily. Arnkel said, "The guards?"

"They must die. There will be, I think, two. He feels safe, making camp so far from the strand. You and I will deal with them. If four, then my Saracen takes the third, my helmsman and the Man of the High Island, the fourth."

Gil took his eyes from his course and stared at the earl's shadowy face. Floki reached behind him, suddenly, and mimed a sword cutting his throat. "Like this, Warrior. No sound."

Released, Gil looked back at the black sea, his fear of it eclipsed by a greater fear. *Please. Let there be only two.*

But, when they drew close to the Deer Isle's shore, there was no sign of any guard at all. The rise of the land hid the campfire now, and the rain fell steadily. Through it, the shoreline appeared a blurred pale band between forest and sea.

Gil scanned it for any sign of life. The three beached hulls bulked darkly in the foreground, cloud diffused moonlight glimmering on gilded prows. Lowered masts and stacked oars were silhouetted against the pearly sky. On either side, low mounds of sea-washed rock formed natural citadels; the place any master would mount a guard. Gil's eyes went instinctively to each but no luckless warrior hunched there, cloak-wrapped against the rain. He raised his gaze to the dim shoreline beyond and saw nothing.

Floki rose, stood up on the rail, and called softly for raised oars. In the stillness, as they drifted, no sound came but the lapping of waves. He stood a long while, listening, and searching the dim strand, and then stepped down and sat again beside Gil. "That is arrogant, even for him," he said.

"No guard?" Floki shook his head. Gil again scanned the shore and whispered, "Maybe it's another trap."

"Warrior, he sails with an army. If he knew we were here, would he lay a trap in the night, when he could cross the Sound in daylight, put every man to the sword, and return to his feast in peace?" He laughed softly. "No. He has set his snare in the Loch of the Waiting, and waits, himself, in comfort." He tapped the tiller. "Take us in." Then he ran lightly through the ranks of oarsmen to the bow, and leaned over the rail, sounding the depth with an oar. Yards from the shore, he raised the oar, and as Gil turned the ship, jumped down into the shallow sea.

With the prow again facing Yula's Isle and the oarsmen softly countering the shoreward drift, Gil relinquished the helm to Erling. Holding his kindling and firebox high, he slipped down into the water, with Ragi, Ismail, and Arnkel, and followed the earl ashore.

In silence, they separated, each running to their assigned task. For Gil and Ismail, it seemed almost too easy. The gangplank of their ship awaited them. The deck was littered with potential tinder: sacks and lengths of rope, rolled awning cloth and the loosely furled sail. Overall, was a surprising stench of spilled ale. Gil thought grimly what Floki would say if he ever left *Silver Dragon* in such a mess. Signaling silently to Ismail, he set down the firebox and emptied the first sack of kindling onto the deck.

The rain had stopped and the clouds thinned. A shaft of moonlight broke through, momentarily, lighting the strand with threatening clarity. Keeping their heads low, they worked quickly, building a frame of driftwood around pitch-soaked bracken and pinecones. In the very center, a thick nest of horsehair, plucked conveniently from Lionheart's tail, lay ready for the embers.

Ismail rimmed the driftwood with lengths of weathered

rope, scoured from the deck. Gil lifted a dozen oars down from their rack and piled them, crisscross, around the whole construction. Spotting a crumpled heap of awning cloth beneath the lowered mast, he crossed the deck and gripped it with both hands.

It was heavy and stank of ale, and something else, like sour milk. Wrinkling his nose, he jerked hard. It snagged and he jerked harder. And then, from beneath its dark folds, a groan arose and two hands, ghost-white in the veiled moonlight, reached out and pulled it back.

"Ismail!" Gil's whisper sounded like a shout in his own ears. He covered his mouth, staring at the fumbling hands. "There's ...." Then the cloth rose up and slid aside, and Gil was looking into a stunned, sleep-befuddled face, as young and terrified as his own. With a grunt, a second face appeared, and an arm, reaching for a weapon. *The guards. The guards!*

"Yours," Ismail whispered hoarsely. He jerked his head toward the first man, as, sword in hand, he dove for the second. Gil stood paralyzed. The man scrabbled drunkenly at his belt. "Gil!" Ismail hissed, "is not game!" Bright metal flashed before Gil's eyes and something cold thudded against his cheek, breaking his stunned trance.

Suddenly his left arm was around the vomit-caked face, jerking the head back, and his sword was in his right. The fine-tooled blade seemed to know what to do, itself. *Like this. No sound.*

But there was sound, the hissing and splattering of hot blood spattering the deck and he'd remember it all his life. He dropped the man's twitching body. The lolling head thudded against the deck. Blood ran warm and wet down Gil's hands as he sheathed his sword. He raised them slowly to his face.

"Gil?" He looked up. Ismail shook his head sadly in the moonlight. "The fire," he pleaded. "Or there is no point."

Jarred into welcome action, Gil dove for the waiting firebox, unwrapped the fur, and opened the leather sack. Pulling his sleeves down over his bloody hands, he lifted the hot metal box from the straw, knelt by their waiting tinder, and raised the lid. The embers glowed red, fanned by the fresh night air. He drew a deep breath and tipped a careful portion into the wad of horsehair. Before he had lidded the box again, smoke was rising. *Oh, burn, burn. Let it be for something.*

At once, flames flickered. The bracken crackled and caught. The pitch-soaked cones flared blue and yellow. Then the dry wood sparked and flamed and the deck was alight with a yellow glare.

The two dead guards sprawled, dark, blood-soaked mounds, beneath their awning cloth. Gil caught the end of it and jerked it free. "You don't need it now," he muttered, flinging it into the rising flames. It caught, too, and the coils of rope, and then the oars began to char.

"Good," Ismail nodded. "Good. Is safe to leave." Gil wrapped the firebox again in the sack and the fur, and they ran for the gangplank. The fire licked the loosely furled sail and sparks rose into the night as they raced down to the strand, running with their gift of fire, to the earl.

Beyond the black hull of the Golden Knight's galley, the outlying ship blazed into light. Arnkel and Ragi appeared, running to join them. Floki emerged suddenly from the shadows, grasped both fireboxes, and blended back into the night. Gil turned and ran to where his own ship waited, afloat on a fire-lit sea.

Arnkel and Ragi were already scrambling aboard, hauled up by oarsmen whose monstrous shadows danced across the waves. Close on Ismail's heels, Gil plunged into the water, washing the dead guard's blood from his hands as he waded to the ship. He splashed his face and the dull ache of his cheek flared into fiery pain. Salt burning in the wound, he hauled himself, gasping, aboard, and staggered on shaky legs to the helmsman's bench.

Erling stood yet on the steering board, the tiller braced against his sturdy hip, his gaze turned over his shoulder, to the burning ships. Flames soared up from the deck of the galley, racing down its length, as Floki's expert fire took hold.

Gil searched the shoreline for the earl and glimpsed a moving shape between the ships. Erling punched his arm and grinned. But then suddenly there were two shapes, weaving in and out of the shadows and shouts of anger and alarm. The ringing clash of steel cut through the roar of the flames.

"Take her out!" Erling swung around to face the sea. "Take her out!" Oars dipped and the ship surged forward.

"Wait!" Gil jumped up from the bench.

Erling thrust him aside. "He tells me no."

Gil lunged forward, wrestling Erling out of the way, and grabbed the tiller. "I am helmsman of this ship and I tell you yes." He leaned hard on the steering oar, swinging *Silver Dragon* parallel to the burning shore.

Beard bristling with outrage, Erling thudded into his shoulder. But then a happy cheer arose from the oarsmen. Silhouetted against the firelight, Floki appeared, running down the strand. He bounded through the shallows, jumped for the moving stern, and was hauled aboard. As Gil swung the ship back out to sea, he climbed to his feet, mounted the stern rail, and stood leaning against the dragon's tail, watching the rising flames.

"A high price you pay, my friend," he murmured, "For a farmer's roof." He turned and gave Gil a grim smile, but the smile faded at once and he reached to touch Gil's face. "Who wounds you?"

Gil winced and pulled back. "The guards were on the ship," he said. "Two of them. Asleep. Drunk." He paused. "They're dead."

"I see." Floki looked quickly to Ismail, who nodded affirmation, and returned his gaze to the receding shore. The fires had taken firm hold; the ships were alight from stem to stern. Thick black smoke darkened the already dim sky, and rolled seaward, bringing with it a stench of pitch and burning wool, and something more familiar, the scent of charring meat.

Floki turned back to the boys, his face strained in the lurid light. "These guards on the ship, they are truly dead when you leave?"

Gil nodded shakily.

Ismail said, "Very dead."

"Good," the earl said quietly. The stench strengthened and Gil suddenly understood: flesh, alive and young like his own an hour before, was roasting now like game in the flames. He covered his mouth, threw the tiller at Floki, and flung himself, retching, at the rail. After a long while, he straightened, wiped his face with a sodden sleeve and staggered back to the helm. But Floki summoned Erling, who, with a black look at Gil, took the steering oar. Then he led Gil to an empty sea kist, went to his own, and returned with a stoneware jar. He turned Gil's face to the flickering light. "I tend this now."

"It doesn't matter," Gil said. "It's nothing."

"Small wounds fester and men die of them." Floki poured liquid from the jar and with gentle fingers spread it over the wound. It stung and then it felt cool and pleasant. "They are dead, those two," he said. "You dying from this 'nothing' will not make them otherwise."

"They were really young," Gil burst out. "Like, my age. They'd just drunk some ale and got under a cloth to keep out the rain." He shook his head miserably.

"Stay still." Floki studied the wound in the faint light of the distant fires. "You look like a Northman, now." Then he sat back. "This night," he said, "I kill a man older than my father. An old, lame man they send for more ale ...." He smiled sadly. "But if I do not, he raises the alarm, and my people die." He looked straight into Gil's eyes. "This is the world, Warrior."

"I hate it."

Floki smiled again. "Do you? Even though it holds the girl you love?" He looked back at the flames on Deer Isle. "In the old days," he said softly, "We send our chieftains to Valholl aboard a burning ship. You give them an honor they never expect." He rested his hand briefly on Gil's head, the way Aidan would, and sat in silence beside him as the oarsmen bore them on, across the Sound.

The tide had turned, and their helmsman was working hard to keep his course. Floki watched him, and then said, "I leave this ship with Erling Maiden-Face. Why, when I return, are you at the helm?" His voice was as soft, still, but Gil was suddenly very aware he was not sitting beside Aidan. With a wary glance at the sea, he said, "He wouldn't wait for you."

"I tell him not to."

Gil muttered, "I wasn't leaving you."

Floki gave him a small smile. "That is kind. In your kindness, you forget something."

"Not to disobey your orders," Gil said numbly.

Floki shook his head, still smiling. "I am a selkie, Warrior. You leave me, I just swim." He laughed and stood up. "Now take the helm from Erling and take us in. It is dangerous," he pointed to the white foam of running tide, rimming the promontories. "And you are the better man."

The stamping of horses and the jingle of harness awoke Gil at dawn. He sat up quickly, pressing a hand against his throbbing face. The dim light beneath the awning revealed empty bedrolls neatly stowed. He stood quickly and, hunched beneath the dark cloth, hurried out to the open air.

The day was calm and fair, the sun not yet up. Smoke still stained the sky above Deer Isle. Around him, the Northmen were breaking camp and preparing the ships for launch. Saddled and bridled, the four ponies drank from the pool beneath the waterfall, while Janetta held their leads.

He turned to join her, but Floki appeared with Hakon and together they studied his wound, and after washing it with spring water, anointed it again with the contents of the stoneware jar. Gil reached up to touch his face, but Hakon slapped his hand away and said gruffly, "You are pretty no longer, but it will heal."

Still, Janetta seemed not troubled at all; glancing proudly at his fresh-won scar as, together, they led the ponies back to the camp. This was her world and this time he had broken none of its rules.

Floki lifted Caitilin up onto the smallest of the Hrolf's Isle ponies and while Hakon stood watching, instructed Rachel and Janetta to ride either side of her, and Niall, the *file*'s son, to ride with his harp, behind.

Percy ran from his dove-shrine, begging Floki to take him, too, to find his sister. Floki listened gravely and said, "But who is to guard Bjorn, now that Eirik is gone? He is my best oarsman and must not be stolen away. There is none, now, but you." Percy thought carefully and then, with great solemnity stepped to the side of Bjorn Break-Neck and took the hem of his tunic in one hand.

Floki summoned Gil and Ismail then. "We walk ahead; you are my guard." Gil nodded, dimly aware that the order was significant; that men on foot had peaceful intentions, a girl attended by young women was treated honorably, and that, in this dangerous world, such things mattered.

Hakon gave a weary shake of his head. "Again you travel with children," he said, "And to the hall of a man of whom you know nothing."

"I know this," Floki said with a cheerful smile. "Should this man have chosen to look aside from our troubles, he can forget he ever saw us. He cannot forget sixty men."

"He can forget you even more easily if you are dead."

Floki smiled again. "Sea-Friend, were the skies to open and manna fall, as in Aidan's holy book, you would expect poison. *Why* should he wish to kill me? I bring him his daughter! A father's gratitude is greater shield than a hundred warriors. Besides, if he is a third as powerful as the child says, what use are sixty weary men? And if he is a third as fine as the child herself, he will welcome me as a brother."

Hakon laughed. "Perhaps like our brother, Gudleif Egilsson?" He glanced uneasily at Caitilin, and then leaned close and whispered, "A noble daughter may have an ignoble father, as you and I both know. Take a guard, cousin," he pleaded. "Take men."

Floki stood between Gil and Ismail, with a hand on each of their shoulders. "These are men, Sea-Friend," he said quietly.

But the girl, who sat the while on her pony, with head meekly bowed, suddenly looked up with anger flaring in her eyes. "He needs no guard at all!" she cried. "My father and uncle are noble men. They will welcome your cousin with fine courtesy, and send horses to bring you to their hall, and warriors to guard your ships. You will feast like kings and leave laden with gifts."

Floki smiled and shook his head. "Hunted men make unlucky guests, child."

"But he is much in your debt," she insisted.

"No more than I in his, should he lead me to the lass I seek."

"You will find her at his hearth," she said simply. "For surely he has taken her into his household as you have taken me into yours, and fostered her, as you have fostered me." Tears shone suddenly in her eyes and she turned her face away.

"Surely," Floki answered, as if by saying it, he could make it true. He turned abruptly to his young guards. "Find us a way up the bluffs. Ponies do not climb cliffs."

Gil and Ismail ran ahead along the narrow strand, until they reached a place where the steep bluffs shallowed and a deer path wound up a wooded slope. Ducking beneath branches, and clambering over fallen trees, they led the sure-footed mounts up from the shore. Soon they had re-joined the burn of the waterfall and were following it up a green valley between low hills.

Behind them, the sun lit the mountains of Deer Isle above the stubborn grey smudge of smoke. Ahead lay the blue waters of the loch from which the little river flowed, and, in the distance, a small stone building with a steep, heather-thatched roof.

"The chapel!" Caitilin cried joyously, "The ruined chapel. I rested there often with my cousins, coming home from the shielings." She stood up in her stirrups, staring at the building. "And look, someone has roofed it now, to make a better shelter."

But when they drew closer and could see the building clearly, Floki said, "Are you sure, child? To my eyes, that is an old roof."

She stared at the moss-grown thatch, sagging at the eaves, and nodded uncertain agreement. "But it was not there before. Not a year past, the walls stood open to the sky. And look!" she cried again. "The round pen where we kept lost lambs – it has a roof now, too."

At the edge of the tumbling burn that ran behind the chapel, stood a circular stone hut with a small hat of thatch, like at Cille Aidan. Beside it, cabbages grew in a patch of tilled ground. "Someone's living here," Gil said.

"I will see." Floki walked forward and Gil hurried at once to his side. "I think I am safe enough here," he smiled, but he let Gil stay with him. Bowing his head beneath the low lintel, he entered the little chapel, with Gil just behind.

Inside, it was dark, except for a thin bar of sunlight slipping through a narrow window, but they could see at once the building was empty. There were two tables at the far end, niches in the walls for holy vessels, and a single oil lamp, burning in the shadows. With the rush of the burn recalling the murmur of the sea, Gil could have been in Aidan's lost church. He half expected the crow, Feannag, to appear, or the Noble Cat to leap through the window to the broad window ledge.

Floki crossed himself and stepped out into the morning sunlight. With Gil again shadowing him, he walked around the chapel to the circular hut by the burn. It, too, was empty. But at the familiar sight of desk and prayer book and hanging lamp, Gil felt a lurch of homesickness for a place that was now only blackened stone.

Floki stepped back from the low door and returned to the waiting riders, gathered together under Ismail's watchful eyes. Looking up at Caitilin, he said simply, "This is no shepherd's shieling, child, but the home of a priest. All his things are here, and no doubt he is not far."

She looked puzzled for only a moment and then she smiled happily. "Surely my uncle, for the sake of his soul, has given it to a hermit. Is it not his duty to provide for the church?"

"No doubt it is," Floki agreed amiably.

She turned her gaze from the chapel to the way ahead. Gil looked back at the sagging roof as they passed, and despite her innocent confidence, he felt a nudge of doubt. He stepped close to the earl and said softly, "Could there be, maybe, another chapel that she's remembering? Like, she's mixed them up? It's easy to get lost here." He looked out over the featureless marshland and low heather hills, one much like another.

But behind him, Caitilin cried out once more, "And there is *An Cailleach*!" She stood up again in her stirrups and shaded her eyes. "See, there, at the height of that hill."

An ancient stone monument, like Odin's Stone on Hrolf's

Isle, stood dark against the morning sky. *"An Cailleach,"* he said, "The Old Woman?"

Caitilin nodded happily. Then she looked solemn and said, "Our nurses told us she was a real woman, once, who lost a child on the hill, taken by wolves or drowned in a bog. And she looked for it so long she turned to stone. See how she appears to search, even now?"

Gil studied the monument, which had indeed the hunched shape of a woman in a shawl.

Caitilin added, "They said it would happen to our mothers, if we strayed from their sides." She shrugged cheerfully, "We did not believe them." Smiling, she urged her pony forward.

Striding ahead, with Gil and Ismail, Floki said, "It is the landscape of her childhood. She cannot be wrong."

Gil thought then of a place he had almost forgotten, the Lookout Rocks by the river at Greene Mountain Falls. And Danni, with her freckles and her swinging dark braids. He looked up at *An Cailleach*, seeking her lost one, as they sought theirs, realizing suddenly that she might be only a mile or two away.

When they stood at the foot of the standing stone, Caitilin sat with her arms wrapped around herself, trembling, as if she could not believe she was really there. "We are halfway, now from the chapel to home. And from that height," she said, of a larger hill ahead, "we look down on all the White Hollow. The Loch. And the Island Port of Yula's Isle."

The land steepened and with the summit in sight, Floki's own eagerness overtook him, and he caught hold of Caitilin's reins and began to run up the hill. Gil and Ismail ran too, and the other ponies clattered along behind them, Lionheart snorting with excitement as Janetta urged him on.

"There!" Caitilin cried. "There by that copse is the very place I saw her; the slave girl, in her chains."

Floki stopped, breathing hard, staring at the little clump of rowans, as if Danni might yet be standing there. But nothing moved but a small flitting bird, and there was no sound but the soft island wind. Gripping the reins again, he ran on.

Gil caught up with him, just below the summit, and they

crested the hill together and looked down on the marshy valley beyond. A sheltered loch nested within it. Longer than it was broad, it was hemmed in, to their right, by low hills, and to their left, opened out into a sea-lit distance. Blue and grey beneath racing clouds, its waters lapped gently at two small, grass-grown islands snugged close to the far shore. A heron stood on a single leg beside the smaller, and above the larger, a hawk soared in solitude. All else was utterly still.

Shaking his head, Gil turned to Caitilin and the earl. Floki held the pony's reins yet in one hand, and with the other, gripped the animal's shaggy neck, as if he needed its strength to stand. "Child?" he whispered, looking up at the girl. She stared past him, small and frail and terrified.

"It is gone!" she cried. "My father's hall is gone!"

CHAPTER THIRTEEN

They descended the hill, in numbed silence, broken only by the sobs of the desolate girl. Floki walked beside her, leading her pony and she clung to its mane, staring at the green empty islands across the water as he circled the head of the loch, seeking the narrowest crossing. When they reached the shore, she cried out again, "Where is the causeway?"

Floki looked up at the girl and said quietly, "The loch is shallow, child. We need no causeway."

"But who has taken it away?" She turned from the earl to Gil and Ismail, as if one of them might have the answer, and something half-remembered tugged at Gil's mind.

Floki shook his head and led the pony into the water. It was thigh-deep on Gil, at the most, and leading Lionheart, who protested he would drown and fish would eat him, he followed the earl to the opposite shore.

The island was low and green, fringed with marsh grass. Small, hummocky rises gave the only elevation. The hawk circled, hunting. The heron stood, untroubled. Just when Gil was certain no human hand had ever touched this place, they came upon a small circle of mossy stone, long overgrown. It was the size and shape of the foundation of his own cell at Cille Aidan, but if a hermit-priest had lived here, he was long gone.

The circle stood at the highest point of the island, and from it, nothing was hidden. Caitilin slipped down from her pony and turned slowly, looking all around. "All is gone!" she cried. "Everything! Here should stand the chapel. And there," she flung out a small hand, "The stables and byres. And there, there," she pointed to a long rise, "My uncle's Great Hall. And beyond, on the small island, the Hall of the Chieftains. And all is gone! Some terrible king has come with his warriors and left not a stone upon a stone!"

Floki stepped forward and carefully wrapped his long arms around the girl, and holding her thus, said, "This is not possible, child."

Gil's eyes swept the surrounding landscape, bewildering in its very simplicity of stone and grass and water. "We *must* be in the wrong place. This can't be the island she remembers."

"But it *is*," Caitilin insisted. "I played on this shore with my cousins, every day." She pointed to a modest beach, "There, we built harbors for the boats our fathers carved. And there," she waved her hand toward a smooth rock, "The laundry women came to wash our linen. I know it so well."

Floki lifted her chin so she looked into his eyes. "I have burned households, Caitilin. Fire is a fearsome weapon, but it does not consume stone. Even had each wall been razed, the rubble would remain."

"Then some witch has come and magicked it all away!"

"Child," he said sadly, "No witch in all the world has such power."

She looked up at him with innocent trust and said, "Then what, sir, has happened to my home?"

"I have no answer," Floki said simply. "I do not know."

Caitilin's gaze swept the barren island desperately and suddenly Gil saw her as someone else; another young girl in a landscape inexplicably changed. He spun around, facing the others, still mounted on their ponies, "Rachel! The day you came to Cille Aidan? The road by the Great Stones you thought had been taken away?"

She studied him uncertainly, her smooth brow furrowing, and then suddenly she pressed her fingers to her lips and nodded vigorously. "Like Caitilin's causeway!" she gasped. She looked intently back to the water they had crossed. "The White Hollow," she murmured, and then louder, "Oh! Oh, Gil! I know where we are. The White Hollow. Finlaggan. We're at Finlaggan."

She jumped down from her pony and ran to Caitilin's side. "No one has harmed your uncle's hall," she said joyfully.

"No warriors. No witch. No one has taken it away. It isn't here because no one has built it yet."

"But surely it stands a hundred years!" Caitilin cried. "My great-grandfather raised its walls."

"He will," Rachel said. "And there will be a great earldom here and your uncle will be Lord, indeed of all the Isles."

Caitilin bit her lip doubtfully and shook her head. Floki said, "Pretty Hawk, this makes no sense."

"But it does," said Gil quietly. "Because we are the ghosts."

"What say you?"

Gil smiled and shrugged. "It's not them who walk as ghosts among us. We are the ghosts who walk among them."

Floki regarded him in silence, a rare confusion in his eyes. "What kind of men are these, that we walk among them and yet see none?" He flung out his arms. "Where are they?"

"Here," Gil said. "Just like we are. But across the sea no man can sail, in Time Yet to Come. They are in our future. We are in their past. Maybe hundreds of years in their past."

"Men do not live hundreds of years. If this is so, why are we not dead?"

"To them, we are."

Floki narrowed his eyes. "And they to us?" he said.

"They aren't born yet."

"Warrior," Floki rested his hand on Caitilin's shoulder, "This child has seen twelve summers. And you tell me now, her father is yet unborn?"

"My father will not be born for a thousand years," said Rachel. "And nor will I. But I am here."

Floki stared at her and shook his head. "Are you a ghost? Are you all ghosts? Am I dead, that I walk with ghosts? No. I am alive and so are you. Men do not walk through time."

"Finn MacCoull did this." They all turned, surprised, to the *file's* son, Niall, who sat so quietly on his pony that Gil almost forgot he was there. "That is why his harp is called Time-Heddler." The boy stroked the strap of the instrument slung over his shoulder. "It draws time apart, so men can pass through."

"A story," Floki said gently.

"I saw him." The *file's* son was as calm as he was certain. "When my father played at the High-King's hearth, I saw, come into the Hall, a man, dressed in the old way, with a sword yet blooded from battle at his side. It was Finn MacCoull, fleeing his enemies. He sat amid the warriors and spoke with the king, who was his great, great grandson, and then the music ended, and he was gone."

Floki smiled. "Children at the hearthside grow sleepy. And with their heads full of warrior's tales, they dream of heroes. We have our stories, too, of men of old who did what no man living can do."

"I am living," Gil said. "And I have done this, too." He looked up at Niall, "When you played your harp, outside the gates of Rome."

"You were there?" Niall said wonderingly.

Gil glanced quickly at Floki, who nodded, and then he said, "Yeah. I was there … sort of … hidden." He looked back at the earl. "And while he played, I passed through time, to Tir nan Og. And even there, I heard the music and when I fled the Golden Knight, I followed it back to Rome."

Floki studied him thoughtfully. Then, with a wry smile, he said, "Even cats dream."

"Yes. Of mice and rats. But they don't bring dream-mice home in their claws. Or scraps of cloth."

Floki was silent. He looked away across the grassy island, to its small companion, and watched as the heron speared a fish. "And this earldom we cannot see, this, too, is in Tir nan Og?"

"No," Rachel said. "It's long before that. As far from Tir nan Og as the Great Pillars are from Rome. There's nothing left of Finlaggan in Tir nan Og, but grass and stone." She paused and rested a hand on the moss-covered boulders of the hermit's cell. "It is, again, like this."

"That cannot be," Caitilin whispered. "It is so great that every chieftain comes there, and priests and bishops, too. It is the center of the world."

Floki drew the girl close to him and sat down with her on the overgrown wall of the lost hermitage, and with his arm yet around her, he looked out over the silent grey waters of the loch. A small bird flew up from a scrub of willow, twittering in protest, her beak stuffed with grass. Floki laughed gently. "Men give their lives for earldoms, Caitilin, and in the end, a small bird inherits all."

Defeated, he stood and stepped back to placate the nest-builder. Then he led the girl back to her pony, lifted her to the saddle, and took the reins in his hand. "Come. To sea, and home."

"But will you not take me to my father?" she cried.

Floki looked up into her eyes and shook his head sadly. "He is beyond my reach, child, and my lass with him." He returned his gaze to the untroubled waters of the loch. "I have sailed every coast of these islands. I have sailed to Norway and to Francia. I have sailed to Rome. But on this Sea of Ghosts, I cannot set a course. Come," he said again, "I take you to the Northlands. You will be my daughter, now." He turned to lead the pony away, but Gil stepped in between and laid his hand on the bridle.

"I can set a course," he said.

Floki paused and smiled gently. "You are a fine helmsman, my young friend. But this is beyond mortal men." He moved to step past.

Gil kept his grip on the restless pony. "Caitilin," he said urgently. "The day you saw the slave-girl here; tell us what happened."

"I have told you. I sought a lost cow and met a strange man …."

"Before that. What did you hear?"

"I have told you that also. There was music. Beautiful music of a harp, but I saw none, nor any harper."

"No. But you see him now." Gil turned to Niall, sitting awed and uncertain, on the big Hrolf's Isle pony. "You must play for us," he said. "You must play for us here, as your father played for Finn MacCoull at Tara."

With a curt shake of his head, Floki reached to free the bridle from Gil's hand. But Gil held firm. "For what purpose do you ask this?" the earl said tiredly. "The boy plays his harp in every camp from Rome to these shores. Men sleep and men dream.

None leaves his place." He paused and added drily, "Not even a cat."

"But none has paid the wage," said the *file's* son.

Floki turned to the boy, his eyes suddenly alight with laughter. "Indeed, I have not! And for such sweet music. Forgive me! Such an earl who lets his poet go hungry!"

The boy shook his head innocently. "I am never hungry," he said. "You have been most generous. And I am only a cowardly boy who owns neither harp nor music. It is not myself who must be paid, but the harp. Those who would cross time, must pay Time-Heddler's wage."

Floki fell silent, studying the Irish boy. "Ah," he said then, "the ferryman's coins."

Niall nodded. "My master in Francia was both powerful and cruel, but even he must pay."

Floki looked to Gil and then back to Niall. "Then I will match his price," he said. "Whatever it might be. I pledge Hrolf's Isle and all my lands, to cross this sea."

"But there is no need," the *file's* son smiled shyly. "The smallest silver coin is enough. But silver must be paid." Hesitantly, he held out his hand.

With a startled shrug, Floki reached to his belt and then he laughed softly. "Good harper," he said, "Aboard my ship is a treasure chest of silver. But I travel, here, a farmer, without finery or purse." He raised his sun-browned arms, bare of bracelets, as always when he took that humble guise, and touched his unadorned throat. "It seems humility does not suit me," he smiled. But then his finger brushed the leather thong he always wore around his neck. "Ah," he said softly, "There is this."

He unfastened the thong and drew forth from his tunic the small leather pouch holding the amber necklace he carried for Danni. "A dowry for a bride," he said, and without hesitation withdrew the necklace and placed it in the Irish boy's hand. "Play for me, now, that I might bring that bride home."

Niall looked down at it, glowing like a pool of sunlight in his palm, and sadly shook his head. "It is very beautiful," he said. "But it is gold."

Floki smiled slightly. "This is so," he agreed.

"But it is silver that must be paid," the boy said. "Only silver." He held out his hand to give back the necklace, the fingers splayed, as if afraid to grasp such a treasure. "A king's crown, were it gold, could not pay the wage."

Floki closed his fist around the amber cross and suddenly laughed. "I think the gods amuse themselves with me," he said. He looked up at the sun, and back to the Irish boy. "Give me the horse," he said. "I ride for silver."

The boy obediently dismounted, but Gil said, "There's no time. It'll be dark."

"And no need." Janetta jumped down from her pony, too, and ran to the earl. "I have silver." She unclasped the necklace Gil had given her in Dublin and held it out to Niall.

Floki stepped between and gently turned Janetta's hand aside. "No," he said. "You do not surrender that."

"It does not matter," she said. "It is but a sign of love and love outlasts all earthly things."

Floki shook his head again and Gil's heart ached with sadness as Janetta draped the cross and chain around the boy's neck and fastened the clasp beneath his wind-tangled hair. "Does this pay the wage?"

Niall nodded solemnly. He slipped the harp from his shoulder, unbuckled its leather casing, and lifted it free. Then he sat down on the broken wall of the hermit's cell with the old harp resting between his bony knees.

As always, Gil was surprised how small and plain it was, without carving or decoration, its only beauty the luster of the ancient, darkened wood. "You must take the ponies away," Niall said. "Lest they be frightened of what they see."

Rachel helped Ismail lead the animals to the far side of the island. When they returned, the Irish boy gathered them all within the small protective circle of the ruined cell and had them stand in a ring, all facing outward, each holding the hands of those beside them. When all were in place, he fell silent. His young face stilled and grew solemn and his voice, when he spoke, had lost its boyish shyness.

"My father teaches me," he said, "That time is as a tide-race around us, forever flowing. And men and women are but seabirds, upon it. All our kin, our grandfathers before us, our children's children beyond us, are always there, forever flying, forever calling. You will hear them, even see them. You must turn away, although you see terrible things. Or beautiful things. Close your eyes, your ears, your hearts, to all but the one you seek. Only then, and not before then, let go your companions' hands." Then he sat back, and closed his own eyes, and began to play.

The harp notes, at first as soft as distant birdsong, grew in strength and beauty. Gil felt the familiar dreamy peacefulness descend, as when Niall played beside their campfires. Sleep tugged at his eyelids and his mind drifted. *Danni.* He focused on the grey waters of the loch. *Only Danni.*

Waves rippled and broke. The hawk soared, riding the wind. The heron fished. *Nothing's happening,* Gil thought. *It's not working.* Then he saw that something veiled the heron; a mist that rose and softly swirled, as on the stillest of mornings. And though the breeze ruffled the heron's feathers, the mist only thickened.

Something moved through it, and Gil leaned toward it. His companions slipped from his consciousness. Floki's powerful grip on his left hand loosened. The cool touch of Rachel's fingers in his right grew insubstantial. Ismail, at Rachel's right, and Janetta and Caitilin in the ring behind him, seemed only shadows.

He realized then that he could see through the hawk and though it yet flew, it had become translucent, like water, clearly showing the low hill beyond it. The music swelled and the images in the mist took blurred but solid form, and he thought of the mysterious windows of Merlin's Tower. Then Rachel cried out beside him and before him the loch and hills vanished.

In their place stood a row of weathered stone houses on a cobbled city street. High above their red-tiled roofs, a distant church tower floated, pale, against a blue summer sky. Each house had a small hedge-sheltered garden and on the gate of the nearest, a bow of faded yellow ribbon fluttered like a sad little flag.

The door of the house opened and a bearded, grey-haired

man stepped out. Gil took in his strange, drab clothes: *Not a Northman.* Then their strangeness resolved into familiarity, with a jolt. *A jacket. He's wearing a jacket. And a tie ….* The man tilted his head as if listening to a faraway sound, his intense dark eyes searching the empty street.

"I'm here!" Rachel cried out. "I'm here!" She tugged at Gil's hand and tried to run forward.

"Don't let go!" Remembering the fatal power of the Underwater Bridge, he pulled her back fiercely into the ring. And then, as quickly as it had formed, the vision vanished into the mist, even as new shapes thickened and took form.

"It was my father," she whispered. "My father. And he's still looking for me." Then she gripped Gil's hand harder and with tears running down her cheeks, stared resolutely into the swirling currents of time.

Fascinated and terrified, Gil watched a whole landscape emerge: a rocky, surf-pounded shore, a gale-lashed sea, and a ship; a scrap of sail aloft, rowers battling at the oars, and at the helm, a steersman with wind-whipped beard and a mane of wild grey hair.

"Einar!" Floki gasped. The sea rose and thundered all around them, the roar of wind and tide drowning all sound but the delicate notes of the High-King's harp. Waves breaking over the struggling ship drenched their faces.

Real water. Gil shook his head to clear his vision.

The ship was yards from them. The old man looked up, eyes widening with astonishment. "I take her, Einar!" Floki wrenched his hand from Gil's grip and lunged to leap aboard.

"No!" Gil cried. "It'll take us!" The earth beneath his feet lost all solidity. He was falling, and then swimming, his freed left hand flailing in the sea, only Rachel's slim fingers keeping him from being swept away.

Before him, the longship struck rock, splintering strakes and shattering oars. Then, even as she foundered, and the sea closed over the old steersman's head, the vision mercifully faded, its waters receding like a tide.

Dry ground grew firm beneath Gil's feet. He turned and saw that Floki yet stood beside him, held safe by the lifeline of

Janetta's small white hand. "My grandfather," he said numbly. "I let my grandfather drown."

"It's years ago!" Gil protested. But there was no years ago – no past, no future, only the present spanning all.

The mist swirled, parted, closed in again and became rain; a torrential, grey wall splattering drenched red earth and pounding the metal roof of an open-sided hut. Two children crouched on their haunches, a cloth held over their heads as the downpour drummed on their frail shelter. "Ismail!" Janetta cried behind Gil, "She is so like you!"

Stunned, Gil realized that, facing opposite ways, they yet saw the same vision: the girl with her watchful, too-wise eyes, the image of his African friend. "Maryam!" Ismail cried, "Hassan! Wait for me. I come back."

The girl looked up, startled and then wondering, and as the mist closed in, her dark face broke into Ismail's wide, white smile. "Wait ...." Ismail called again, but the vision had vanished and the only sound remaining was the ethereal music of the harp.

Its tempo quickened and the flow of time grew faster, sweeping savagely around them, like the tide-race of the Holy Isle. Sunlight flickered into starlight, summers flashed into snows. Images crowded forward; men and animals, ships and armies, knights, herdsmen, farmers, monks; as if all who had ever lived and ever would live, were passing before their eyes.

Like Merlin's Tower. Gil thought again of the eerie forbidding windows of Time Past, and Present, and Time Yet to Come, as mysterious and compelling and as impossible to decipher as this ... until the Golden Knight held up his small, hollow stone. The stone! Merlin's seeing stone, given to him by his father in the forest of Francia – the stone that raised the Rainbow Bridge. Like the key to the door of the Indian Kettle pool, the stone would lead him to Danni. He eased open his fingers, clenched around Rachel's hand.

"Gil!" she cried, tightening her grip.

"Trust me." He glanced sideways. Her eyes were terrified, but with a small, frightened nod, she agreed. He felt the tug of the Time-Race even before their hands parted, but just as they did, he darted his arm through hers, linked their elbows, and with the fingers of his freed hand wormed the precious seeing stone from his pocket. Raising it awkwardly to his eye, he peered through the circle at its center. "Danni," he murmured, "Show me Danni."

At once, the mist vanished, and she appeared, with Percy beside her on the Lookout Rocks in Greene Mountain Falls. Face sun-browned, hair in plaits, thumbs hooked into the pockets of her jeans, she glared stubbornly at his own young self. Short and slight, in jeans and tee shirt, he held in his hand the hollow white stone.

The Stonepecker cawed from a tree branch. The river ran high and fast. The whirlpool of the Indian Kettle waited below them: three children caught in an eddy of time – the moment on which everything turned.

He'd raise the stone. He'd see Janetta. He'd argue with Danni. She'd throw the stone and Percy would make his fateful leap … he watched, barely able to breathe. *Don't*, a voice whispered, deep in his heart. *Don't look. None of it will happen.*

Don't look?

Give the stone back to Percy.

And never see her? Never meet her? Never ride with her through Camelot? Never helm a longship, with her at my side?

You will never have known her. She will vanish like a dream at dawn. Stay safe in the world where you belong.

Gil smiled. *And Arthur will sleep under Eildon until time ends.* He shook his head and leaned toward the vision. "Go for it," he whispered to the boy on the riverbank, and the boy raised the stone to his eye.

The harp song faded to a single perfect note. The Time-Race stilled. They stood in silence. "Slack water," said Floki. And then pitch-black darkness fell.

Gil's old terrors rushed in; the Turnip-Head Tomb, the bone-filled Roman catacomb, the Indian Kettle's swirling black heart. But then his eyes caught a tiny flicker of yellow flame, hanging, it seemed, in mid-air. His mind leapt to Cille Aidan. "A church!"

"It is our chapel!" Caitilin cried joyfully. "We are home!" She pulled away from the circle and ran, boots scuffing a stone floor. A door-hinge creaked in the darkness and brilliant sunlight flooded in, lighting the altar and paling the flame in its sanctuary lamp.

"Wait, child," Floki lunged for her, but already she was running out the door. Gil and Ismail broke from the ring, following the earl into a bright autumn day. Three steps from the chapel door, they stopped, staring up in astonishment.

Before them, where there had been only marsh grass, a great stone hall stood three floors high, glazed windows reflecting loch and sky, steep roof glistening with recent rain. Byres and outbuildings surrounded it, and peat smoke rose from its chimneys. Men and women in strange fine clothes gathered in the cobbled yard below.

Doves fluttered and hens and geese scattered before shouting children. Horsemen clattered over the stone causeway joining island to shore. The green fields beyond were dotted with black cattle, the low surrounding hills now purple with heather in bloom. Splashed with white horses and brightened by distant sails, the long loch sparkled beneath a wide blue sky.

Near to the shore, a small, graceful longship approached a waiting pier. Men with ropes and boat hooks hurried to greet her, while others, with swords and helms and the uncompromising stance of guards, lined the cobbled pathway to the hall.

The sail slid down and oars flashed, guiding the ship in. She appeared more a pleasure craft than a warship; the men and women on her deck dressed as splendidly as for a king's court. But each man was fully armed, warriors still beneath their finery.

Behind the ornate figurehead stood the undoubted chieftain; a great wolf of a man with ruddy hair and beard, a sword in a silver-trimmed scabbard and a tall grey dog at his side. Before him, a young woman in a fur-hooded cloak bent to stroke the dog. Resting his hands protectively on her shoulders, the chieftain scanned the approaching shore and then turned suddenly to the man beside him.

Younger, leaner, and darker, but with the same fierce features, his companion stepped abruptly to the rail as startled shouts rose from the gathering outside the hall. "There!" Ismail cried, as Caitilin appeared, darting across the courtyard, intent on the shore and the ship. Floki followed, red tunic and yellow hair bright splashes of color, weaving through the milling crowd.

They broke into the open together, running down the stone path. The guards paused only an instant to stare at the young warrior in ancient dress, then reached for their swords. Ismail grabbed Gil's arm. "We not leave him alone!" And together they ran to defend their earl.

Plunging into the crowd, Gil was aware of Janetta and Rachel close behind and aware too of the unending note of the High-King's harp, still sounding in his ears, though Niall had not left the chapel. Men and women scattered before them and children shrieked and pointed and ran away. *We walk as ghosts among them ....*

Ahead, Caitilin and Floki had reached the guards. Thrusting the girl safely behind him with one hand, Floki drew his sword with the other. Disarming two men, he kicked a third out of his way and broke through to the pier. The outwitted guards turned on Gil and Ismail, blocking their way with a line of steel. Over their heads, Gil saw a huddle of seamen with raised boat hooks barricading the lowered gangplank.

Floki swerved without breaking stride, sheathed his sword, swept Caitilin up in his arms and leaped six feet of open water. Clearing the ship's rail, he landed lightly aboard, a stride from the astounded chieftain. Setting Caitilin down on her feet, he held up empty hands in the brief moment before a dozen warriors fell upon him in a fury of fists and boots.

Caitilin's cry of dismay and the protests of the young woman were lost in their outraged shouts as they battered him to his knees. Forgetting sense, Gil charged his captors, was floored by a boat hook over his shoulders, and dragged brutally to his feet. Arms wrenched behind his back, he watched helplessly as Floki's attackers threw him full length on the deck and drew their swords.

"No!" The woman in the fur cloak broke free from her protector, rushed forward, and flung herself down beside Floki, shielding him with her outstretched arms. "Do him no harm!"

The hood of her cloak slipped back, revealing the glossy dark hair piled high on her head, and the defiant tilt of her chin. But it was by her sheer fearlessness as she glared up at the stunned warriors that Gil recognized her; the same bold, unthinking courage with which, long ago, she jumped into the Indian Kettle whirlpool. "Danni!" he cried.

A rough hand clamped over his mouth. "Silence!"

The warriors on the ship edged away, uncertain eyes on their earl. Then the lean man pushed through them and stood before the chieftain, with Caitilin clinging to him, her arms around his waist, her tearful face pressed against his shirt. "Free him, Brother," he said quietly. "He brings me my daughter." He shook his head, "We do him grave wrong."

Caitilin looked up. "He is my *friend*, Uncle," she sobbed.

The chieftain turned from the girl to Danni. Kneeling now respectfully before him, she spoke in the same Irish tongue, "Foster-father, this is my beloved. We are pledged. Have I not told you he would come for me?"

The chieftain nodded solemnly, his great beard brushing his chest. "Many times," he agreed. "Many times." He looked down at the battered, bloodied man at his feet and said, "Is this true?"

"It is true," Floki answered, so quietly that Gil could barely hear him. The chieftain leaned down and offered his hand. Floki took it, sat up slowly, and got painfully to his feet. Danni rose to hers, wary eyes on her foster-father's face.

His fierce features softened and he said, "He is safe, now, daughter." He bowed his head to Floki, "I am shamed, young warrior, that you should come to us with noble purpose and be so ill-used." He cast a black look at his own warriors and they shuffled uncomfortably backward.

But Floki said at once, "It is no shame for warriors to defend their earl. My own," he glanced wryly at Gil and Ismail yet pinned on the pier, "Would do the same, were they free."

The chieftain looked down a moment and roared, "Release them!" Instantly freed, they bolted up the gangplank, with the girls behind them.

"And the fault is mine," Floki said then. "I come too hastily

into your company." He nodded to his assailants whose faces
broke into relieved, grateful smiles. "But my ship lies on a far
strand and time is short."

Even as he spoke the words, Gil heard the note of the harp
strengthen and swell and another note join the first. Janetta's
hand grasped his, and he realized that all of them were hearing
it at once.

"Your ship ...." The chieftain studied Floki, as if assessing
his strange clothing and his Norse-accented Irish. "Whence
come you?" he said.

"A far land," Floki turned to look at Danni, "And she, a land
farther still."

She met his gaze, her young body yearning toward him, her
eyes bright with tears. And Gil knew in that instant, seeing her
beside him, so grown and so beautiful, with all the grace of
a sea-king's daughter, that the only land she belonged in now,
was his.

The chieftain nodded. "What is your name, young warrior,"
he said.

Danni proudly answered, before he could speak, "Floki
Magnusson."

The chieftain raised bushy eyebrows in surprise. Then he
turned back to Floki and with a gruff laugh, said, "Your father
had a fine ear for the sagas."

"You know my father?" Floki said uncertainly.

The chieftain shook his head. "But I know the tale. And
he did right to give you a hero's name. You are a hero to my
fosterling. You have kept faith many seasons, as indeed has she.
I offer her many a fine match, and she refuses all."

He looked then, sadly, at Danni. "And now I must lose her."

She returned a stricken glance, realizing suddenly that what
she had longed for would bring its own sorrow. The chieftain
smiled. "Go to him, daughter," he said.

She turned to Floki and they fell into each other's arms,
clinging and kissing and stroking each other's faces in an
embrace that lasted so long that time might as well have stopped.

But it hadn't, Gil knew, because the music of the harp was
growing stronger, more intricate, and more beautiful, and when

he raised his eyes to the great hall he saw above it, wheeling in the air, the faint transparent outline of the hawk. "Floki," he muttered.

"I know, Warrior." Floki released Danni and raised his eyes, also, to the sky. "The tide turns."

The chieftain smiled broadly. "There will be other tides. Two each day until the moon fails. This night, you sleep in my hall. First," he touched Floki's battered face with a father's gentle hand, "We tend the wounds you did not deserve. And then we feast, in honor of this betrothal. I send you to that far land with gifts befitting a son."

Floki shook his head. "Only this gift, I beg you." He drew Danni close. "Nor is there time for feasting. We sail a sea few men can sail; its tides obey no moon." He smiled gently at the chieftain's puzzled look, and said, "Bid your fosterling farewell. We must go."

Danni stepped forward and put her arms around the chieftain's neck and drew his wolfish head close. Then, with a tearful kiss, she turned away. Floki took her hand, and together they ran from the ship.

Gil hurried Janetta before him and with Ismail and Rachel at his side, ran after them. The gangplank already felt strangely hollow beneath his feet. The great hall above grew misty and insubstantial. The song of the harp was all around them, and the startled, shouting crowd produced no sound, as through them Floki and Danni ran, she so dark and he so fair, and both with bold, unearthly grace, fairy visitors from a longhouse tale.

Ahead, the walls of the chapel thinned to a grey veil through which the *file's* son and his enchanted harp were clearly visible. Images grew in the circling mist, striving to take form. But only a few more steps remained, and they would be safe. Safe, and all together, at last, for the first time since they parted in the Forest of Pentecost.

Floki and Danni reached the chapel, the walls mere shadows now. He turned and drew Janetta in beside him, and Ismail, too. "Helmsman!" he called. "Faster!"

"Any faster and I'd fly," Gil panted, leaping up the little rise. And then he heard Rachel's cry.

"Gil!"

He whirled. "I'm here!" She was but feet away. "Come on."

"The children, Gil!" she cried. "The children. They are *there*!"

The children. Rachel's vision in the museum. The vision that brought her to Cille Aidan. The vision in the flames in the Forest of Pentecost. The vision in Deer Bay. Rachel's children. And now he saw them, too.

There were three, crowded together in an open casement window; a boy and a girl of six or seven, reaching out to him, dark eyes imploring. And a smaller child with black curly hair and round baby cheeks. Eyes squeezed shut, she raised chubby arms in infant trust. Its frame already charring, the window was a dark oasis in a wall of fire. Smoke thickened the air. The roof above was ablaze. "Turn away!" Gil cried. "Turn away!"

"I cannot!" And nor could he. She jumped and he jumped with her, and in an instant, he was kneeling in a black night, on the grimy cobbles of a city in flames.

Chapter Fourteen

Manure smeared his hands. He raised them, wiped them on his tunic, raised his head. Rain slapped his face. The air was filled with smoke. Somewhere, horses were neighing and he felt their panic. *Fire. Fire.*

Skidding on the filthy cobbles, he staggered to his feet. The night sky flickered red and black above a black, rain-drenched alleyway. Sparks exploded across leaning roofs. Distant shouts and thudding feet jarred his memory. The stench, the midden stench of habitation, after the clean air of the sea; a town, an angry crowd – *Deer Bay*. In an instant, he was back there, running through the narrow streets, pursued by Pock-Mark and the mob. Running for his life.

"Rachel!" he called urgently. Mind racing, he turned, seeking her. She stood just feet away, transfixed, her face raised. Following her gaze, he saw the fiery glow high above the rooftops, a great wooden tower, ablaze.

"It's Deer Bay, Rachel." He ran to her side, catching her arm. "We're back in Deer Bay!"

"I know," she said softly, "And I know when." Startled, he turned to her, but an explosion of flame and sparks wrenched both back to their purpose. At the end of the alley, the glow of fire fluttered with movement, figures, silhouetted in the night, running toward a burning house. Shouts rose above the howl of the wind. "There!" Gil cried.

The alley was narrow, with a gutter at its center brimming with filthy water. He splashed through it, feeling his way along the dark walls into the glare of the firelit street beyond.

At once, he knew where he was. To the left lay the square of the slave market. To the right, twisting streets led to the Roman Wall. Up there was the gable end that had taken an arrow – an arrow meant for him. In his mind, he yet saw its quivering tail. Over there, he had rolled the barrels of flour. And there, right across the street, was the open pen from which he had freed the ponies, sending a wall of thundering horseflesh down on Pock-Mark.

The houses were different; taller, grander, with glazed windows and tiled roofs. But the open space remained, though half-filled now by a low building that bore its own glow of fire. *Tame fire.* A blacksmith's forge. Horses, tied within and sensing the wilder fire without, neighed in panic, hooves thudding against confining wood.

Gil's eyes swept the tall house fronts on either side and through the smoke and sheets of rain, saw the children's window, their small figures barely visible, their cries drowned by the tumult in the street. "Come on!" he called to Rachel, "They're still there."

She was running, already, joined by a crowd of hurrying figures; men and women, shouting and pointing. Relief surged in Gil's heart. *Stay there*, he willed the children. *We're coming.*

He reached the house. Its lower windows were tightly shuttered, its sturdy door, set at the top of a flight of stairs, firmly closed. Shadowy shapes bulked before it. The rain whipped down incessantly. All was noise and chaos and yet, through it, somehow, the beautiful notes of the High-King's harp played on, the music swelling and urgent.

Ignoring it, Gil raced to the foot of the steps, mounting the narrow flight to the waiting door. Two men were there before him, wrenching at the latch, kicking and pounding. Gil dove in to join them, thudding his shoulder against solid oak. A voice shouted in his ear, the words an alien jumble; Frankish, Saxon, a little Norse. Grasping for meaning, he turned, and a fist, its meaning unequivocal, thudded into his jaw.

"Wha – ?" Stumbling backward, he slammed into something soft and outraged. Perfumed, female hands slapped against each of his ears. Then the man who had punched him grasped his tunic front with both hands and hurled him down the steps.

"I'm trying to help!" Gil protested.

"We were here first!"

"Find your own Jew-house!"

"*What?*" Gil stared. Rachel was beside him, pulling at his sleeve.

"Get back, Gil. They're looters."

Two women pushed past them, laughing, as the assault resumed. "They say the chamber pots are gold!"

The door gave way, splintering on its hinges. The crowd howled triumph and surged up from the street. Rachel dragged Gil aside as pounding boots trampled wood and glass. He stared up at the window where the frightened cries were as faint as the distant harp.

"But there's children!" he plucked at the sleeves of the jostling mob. "Get the children out first!" Smoke poured from the open door, even as the boldest pushed in, emerging moments later with objects of blind choice: furnishings, plates, whole chairs, and cupboards. Trundled down the steps, the goods formed an impassable river. "The children," Gil protested impotently.

"Jew children." The woman with perfumed hands shrugged, righteously clutching a silver bowl.

"No better than the infidel!" shouted a sweating man.

"Another door," Gil cried to Rachel. "Find another door." He turned back to the street, seeking some way to the rear. An angry oath stopped him, as an enormous black-haired man lunged out of the crowd, blocking his path.

A blacksmith's stained leather apron strained over the man's massive chest. Huge arms bare, he gripped an iron-headed mallet with both hands and clambered up the steps. "Get out of there!" He kicked a man and a woman aside. "Thieving scum! Out of there! Out!"

"They're usurers!" cried a voice from the crowd. "They make their money from sin."

The blacksmith swung his mallet over his head. "If it's a sin for them to lend it," he roared, "then it's a sin for you to borrow it." He pointed an angry finger at a man below. "Which you do every year!"

He turned to Gil, thrusting the mallet in front of his face.

"Get out and learn better than your elders."

"I'm not stealing," Gil cried. "It's them."

"Always it's someone else," the blacksmith growled, but Gil shook his head, and, ducking away from the mallet, caught the man's mighty arm. "There're children up there. Please! Help me get them out."

The blacksmith looked up and his ruddy face paled in the firelight. "Aaron! Rebecca!" he shouted. "Come to me!" He held up his great arms. "Jump!"

The children cried and shrank back, the girl holding her hands over her face. Only the baby seemed willing, in her innocence, to obey.

"It's too high," Rachel moaned. Gil rushed to the wall.

"Help me up," he called to the blacksmith. "On your shoulders. I'll climb."

The man shook his head. "You won't reach." He glanced down and tapped Gil's sword hilt. "Can you use it?"

"Oh, yes."

"Hold them off." The blacksmith gestured to the half-cowed mob. And as Gil, sword in hand, took up a position at the top of the steps, he bolted into the night. With Rachel beside him, her own blade ready, Gil faced the sullen looters.

"Why let it all burn, boy? When we could all be rich as Jews?"

"He's one of them. Look at him. That's no Christian face. And her. A Jewess, I swear by God's Mother."

Gil moved closer to Rachel. "If they rush us," he murmured, nodding to his left, "Take those two. I'll take the rest."

The crowd muttered, stirred, pushed each other; edging forward. Then, from the cobbled yard of the blacksmith's forge, arose a frantic neighing, the clatter of shod hooves, and the rumble of iron clad wheels. Heads tossing, eyes white with panic, a harnessed pair of huge grey horses burst from the yard. A crude, heavy wagon thundered behind, with the blacksmith standing aboard, driving them on with a cracking whip.

The wagon careered through the crowd, scattering even the boldest. The blacksmith hauled back on his reins, halting his team at the front of the burning house.

Gil ran down the steps and caught their bridles. *You're safe. You're safe. I'm here.* Immediately, the animals calmed, their fire-lit eyes turning to the silent voice. "Hold them." The blacksmith threw down his reins, and stretched up on the wagon's flat bed, reaching again to the window.

"Jump, now, Aaron. I'm here," the big man pleaded. "Rebecca! You show him." They edged forward, but suddenly a flaming timber broke from the roof-tree and slid down the tiles, cascading in a bright fire-fall, onto the horses' backs. They reared and bolted, and by the time Gil halted them, the wagon had lurched from beneath the window and the children had disappeared. A moan came from the crowd, a thrill of cold excitement.

"They're gone!" Rachel cried.

Gil turned to the desperate man on the wagon. "Another door? Is there another door? A window even?" The blacksmith shook his head.

"Only to the scullery, off my courtyard. Tiny, lad. Two panes. You'd never fit through. And you'd never find the room, if you did." Rain and tears runneled the soot on his face. "You'd only die with them in the flames."

Gil shook his head. "I'll fit," he said. He sheathed his sword. "Rachel, stay with him." She stared and then suddenly her eyes lit with hope.

"Stay low!" she called, as he ran.

"I will!" he shouted back. "Very low." The blacksmith jumped down from the wagon, to stop him, but Gil dodged away, laughing. "And I won't die!"

In the blackness of the courtyard, he felt his way along the gable wall of the house until his fingers found wood and glass. The window: two panes as the blacksmith had said, set low, barely chest height, four hands' breadths at the most in width. Locking it into his mind map of the courtyard, he left the wall and stumbled across the rough cobbles to the blacksmith's open shed.

Lit by the dying fire in the forge, tools stood in careful alignment along an inner wall. He chose a sturdy hammer and returned to the courtyard. Something solid and metallic caught his boot and he fell to his knees. Clutching the hammer in one hand, he felt the obstruction with the other. Smooth and cold, it curved away beneath his fingers: a wheel. The empty iron rim of an unfinished cart wheel. Perfect. Adding it to his mind map, he crossed again to the window, found it first try, raised the hammer, and swung hard.

The glass shattered with a tinkling crash and he hacked at the frame, clearing the shards away, and then the wood. Stretching out his hands, he nodded grim satisfaction. Enough for a child. Just.

A sudden burst of cold air rushed past his face, sucked into the building by the heat of the fire above. He dropped the hammer, dashed for the cart wheel and leaped within, the blessing already on his lips and his lips already furred.

Whiskers sprang out into the air, trembling with awareness. Before him, the metal wheel rim rose as a rampart and the cobbles swelled into boulders. The darkened courtyard blazed into focus, every wall and roofline clearly defined against the stormy sky.

A dozen smells assaulted his twitching nose and he crouched low, tail swishing: smoke, mouse, cheese, milk, horse, rat, bird, smoke. The crackling of flames within the ancient timbers filled his wide cupped ears. And cries; small cries. Mice and rats seeking escape, but something else. Lost young-thing cries. Kitten-cries. Ears flattening, he dashed to the wall and leaped for the window, bounding through the empty frame into the smoke-filled darkness beyond.

Inside, he skidded to a halt on the stone floor, caught in a web of scents: meat, fish, milk. *A scullery. And a dairy*, his boy mind reasoned. *Food*, his Cat mind returned. As boy, he had forgotten how long since he'd eaten. Cat never forgot.

This house is burning, he reminded his feline self.

Not down here. His nose turned of its own volition toward a huge wheel of cheese. But then the cry came again from above. Kitten-thing in trouble. Human kitten-thing. Staying safe where its mother left it. *Only she hasn't come back.*

With an angry flick of his tail, Cat abandoned the cheese and ran on low, cautious paws into the room beyond. The smoke was thicker there, roiling along the ceiling. Tables and chairs loomed above him. Beyond, a staircase rose to the burning upper floors. Again he heard the flames crackling in the timbers.

Ears flat, he fought his fine wise instincts, and pulling his whiskers in tight and squeezing his eyes half shut, bolted across the room to the smoke-filled stairs.

When he reached the top, he smelled them: the pleasant young-human scent of children, the sweet milkiness of the baby. A surprising protective urge rose in his feline heart. *Kittens. They ate your mice and ruined your hunting and bit your tail out of sheer stupidity, but still … and even a human kitten was a kitten.* Tail swishing, he went on, following scent and sound.

Their whimpers led him up another flight of stairs, down twisting, smoke-veiled corridors, to a small chamber, high at the front of the house. Still, when he entered it, the room, even to cat eyes, looked empty.

Something moved in the furthest corner. Hackles rising, Cat crept closer. Cloth, a curtain, fallen from the open window, and beneath it, lumpy shapes. Breathing. He stretched out his nose and sniffed. The cloth jumped and Cat scuttled back. A small sob rose from beneath the curtain. They were there, seeking a final refuge. He could hear the littlest one's hopeless mother-chant. *Come back for me. Come back.*

Stiff-legged, Cat stalked forward, wormed beneath the heavy cloth and butted his head against a small tear-soaked face. She cried out, just once, before she wrapped her arms around him and buried her face in his fur.

A purr arose, utterly unwilled, even as he struggled to free himself. "There is a cat!" cried the boy. "A cat has come in." He reached out, too, and the bigger girl threw the curtain aside, staring at Cat in the flickering firelight. The baby squealed and held him desperately. But Cat was smooth and slippery and slid from her grasp. With a cry of dismay, she fastened both fat hands on his tail.

Cat yowled, but neither scratched nor bit. Carefully, he stepped away. The child followed, still gripping his tail. Jaws clenched with distaste, Cat continued on light, determined paws, toward the door.

"Say-Say!" the older girl cried. "Sarah! Come back!" But the baby was Cat's. Clinging devotedly, she padded behind him, into the corridor. Cat heard frantic feet following. And then suddenly the boy shouted, "It is helping us. It leads us! It leads us out!"

After that, it was easy. Low to the floor, they scuttled after him, and with the infant's hands still tormenting his sensitive tail, Cat led them on, down the stairs, beneath the smoke clouds of the lower rooms, past the wonderful cheese, to the low scullery wall.

With a yowl, he broke free, jumped to the stone sill, looked over his shoulder to see they followed and leaped out into the room.

The girl came first, reaching back for the baby, and the boy, last of all. Behind them, the fire roared as the roof timbers crashed down. Cries of dismay rose from the front of the house. Cat streaked across the cobbles, waving his offended tail, and dashed into the street, with the children at his heels.

Laughing with relief, Rachel scooped him up in her arms, while the blacksmith swept all three children into his. Cat purred briefly, but the notes of the distant harp, tugging dimly at his feline consciousness, grew more urgent, even as they dwindled and faded. He yowled and wiggled to be free.

"Where is the boy?" The blacksmith set the children down. They shook their heads. The baby reached for Cat with her chubby hand. Her brother said, "We see no boy."

Alarm crossed the big man's face and he turned back to the courtyard. The children cried out, stretching terrified arms to him, and Rachel said, "Take them away. I'll wait for the boy." Cat yowled again, and twisting his supple neck, sank teeth into Rachel's arm. She dropped him like a furry brick. Landing on four stiff paws, Cat ran for the courtyard.

"I must find the boy!" The blacksmith raced after him.

"Don't bother!" Rachel cried vehemently, rubbing her arm, "He'll be *just fine.*"

Five bounds took Cat to the cart wheel, shining dully in the strengthening firelight. With the blacksmith's boots thudding on the cobbles behind, he leaped into the metal circle. And then, suddenly, he was standing there; a boy in Viking clothes, cheeks scorched, hair frazzled, face to face with his stunned pursuer.

The man stared at him and then looked all around him, as if seeking some hiding place from which he could have emerged. He shook his head, returning his gaze to Gil, standing within the cart wheel. At last, he said, "But where is the cat?"

Gil pointed over his shoulder. "They can move fast, when they want."

The man peered behind him and slowly nodded. His eyes swept the courtyard, settling on the tiny window, pulsing red with the fire within. "But how ...?"

"Bigger than it looks," Gil grinned lamely. The blacksmith looked from Gil to the window and back to Gil. Again he searched the courtyard with baffled eyes.

"What are you?" he said quietly.

Gil grinned again. "Skinny?"

The blacksmith nodded slowly, seeing the impossible and deciding to accept it. He reached out his hand. "Come with me, whoever you are."

Back in the street, the children, huddled together yet beside Rachel, cried out at the blacksmith's return. "Adam, Adam! Mistress Gower left us. And the maids and servants ran away!"

"No matter," he folded them back into his great arms. "I am here."

"Where are their parents?" Rachel whispered.

"Safe. Beyond the Walls on business, when it began. Which was good fortune. The others," he nodded grimly down the street where more houses were now ablaze, "took refuge in the Tower. And now it, too, is burning."

He looked beyond the rooftops, where distant flames flared like a torch in the night. "What men do in the name of God, would make God weep." He laid a heavy hand on the mane of one big grey. "I choose horses," he said. "They are gentle and kind."

Gil smiled. *You don't know Lionheart.*

He helped the big man lift the children up into the flat bed of the wagon. Gathering some sacks from behind the driver's bench, the smith wrapped them in them, as best he could. Then he beckoned Gil and Rachel.

"Come with me. My sister has a farm in the country. Where they do not yet sell their neighbors for thirty pieces of silver." He smiled sadly and stretched his big hand down to help them up.

Gil returned the smile but shook his head. "We have a place to go," he said simply. "Friends to protect us."

The blacksmith looked doubtful. "You are certain, lad? With a mob," he said grimly, "no one is safe." He looked back at the courtyard of his forge. "I would take even that cat, if I could. It is a fine cat."

"A very fine cat," Gil agreed.

"Splendid," Rachel murmured, holding her arm.

They stood side by side, as the blacksmith called up his horses and the wagon rumbled away down the cobbled street, into the smoke shrouded night. Gil turned to Rachel with a happy grin. "That," he said, "Was worth doing. Whatever happens next."

"Good," said Rachel. She stepped closer, nodded slightly, and punched him in the jaw.

Gil reeled. It was at least as hard as the looter's punch, and better aimed. "What did you do that for?" he cried.

"*You bit me.*"

"*I* didn't." Gil rubbed his jaw, swelling now on both sides. "It was …."

"*You,* Change-Thing." Rachel grabbed the front of his tunic and pulled his face down to hers. "I have talons and a beak that could tear your throat out," she hissed. "Have *I* ever bitten …."

"He was stressed. Cats get stressed."

"I'll stress his arse if he ever bites me again!" She shoved him away.

"Rachel …."

"I didn't even eat the damned dove!"

"Rachel, the harp …."

"Oh, what about it?" she snapped.

"I think it's stopped."

"What?" Anger forgotten, she caught his hand, her eyes widening with fear. He strained his ears. A note came and another, so faint and far away he was uncertain they were real.

"We have to get back. Now."

She nodded. "But how? Where do we go?"

"Anywhere else but here," Gil said. "Here come our friends." Dark shapes flitted in the shadows; the looters, returning like carrion crows to a carcass. One man held up a flaming brand, shouted and pointed at them.

Gil gripped Rachel's hand and ran, as once in another Deer Bay, he had run from another mob through the same twisting streets. Only, this time, there was no Floki Magnusson to rescue them.

"We'll come to the wall, like last time," Rachel gasped. "There's no way out."

Rounding a corner, Gil pulled her sideways into a darkened doorway. "Yes, there is," he murmured, reaching in his pocket for the small white stone. Shouts grew nearer. Boots thudded. Somewhere, a window shattered. He held the stone up, framing the darkness within its soft white glow. *Janetta. Show me Janetta.*

The mob burst around the corner; men and women holding torches, eyes glittering in their flickering light. "Jew-girl!" a woman shouted at Rachel. "Jew-girl! Jew-girl!" Others took it up, a mindless chant.

Gil pulled Rachel behind him. And then, through the center of the stone, he saw daylight, hills and sky, a hawk circling above. Before him, through a grey veil, he saw the hermit's cell and the *file's* son bent over his harp.

Floki and Danni appeared, running toward the cell, leaping its broken walls. Floki turned and drew Ismail and Janetta into the ring. Her eyes met Gil's. She reached out both hands.

"Helmsman!" Floki called. "Faster!"

Gil wrapped his arms around Rachel and lunged forward, straight at the crowd of leering, chanting looters, his eyes only on the vision within the stone. "Any faster and I'd fly!"

The mob closed around them, jostling and clutching. A hand gripped his cloak. Another caught his arm and the seeing stone almost slipped from his grasp. Then a length of timber cracked into his knees, his legs buckled, and he felt himself falling.

In a last desperate act, he thrust Rachel ahead of him, into the beautiful daylight, and, as the night engulfed him, let go of her hand.

CHAPTER FIFTEEN

F ace down on the cobbles, Gil steeled himself for the boots of the mob. *She's safe. Rachel's safe. The children are safe and Rachel is safe.* Maybe that was all that mattered.

Light flickered and pulsed in the night. More fires. *More destruction.* Yet, though hurrying feet surrounded him, and a jumble of voices sounded over his head, the blows did not come.

Cautiously, he raised his head, and then jerked back in alarm. Above him hung a huge, leering face: white, unnatural skin, a bright red nose, huge red lips, and a shock of bright orange hair. It seemed to glow, as if lit with an unearthly fire. Behind it, two yellow half circles made a strange halo.

He stared at them and then at the glowing face. *Clown. It's a clown.* And the circles. Arches. Yellow arches. *Golden* Arches. He raised himself on his elbows. "It's a McDonald's. I'm *home* ... somewhere."

The crowd surged, oblivious of him, shouts and laughter, a babble of clipped English words. *They talk like Rachel.*

A pair of trainers and two jeans clad legs appeared a foot from his face. "Cheer up, mate." The voice, slurred and friendly, was addressing him. With a grunt, the speaker squatted down on the cobbles. A brown glass bottle was thrust before Gil's face. "Have another."

Gil smiled slightly, wincing as he did, and sat up, gently pushing the bottle away. "Thanks. I'm fine." He was used to longhouse drunks. He turned to look around and his new friend saw his face. "Hey, man," he murmured kindly, "someone's done a right job on you."

"Rachel," Gil muttered, touching his face. Her punch had

re-opened the sword slash from Deer Isle. Fresh blood smeared his fingers.

"Your girl did that? Cool chick!" The drunk grinned and made mock punches. "Dunff, Dunff." Gil tried to match the grin. The bottle was offered again. "Have a swig, mate. Mine dumped me, too. Said I was drunk. Two beers." He grinned again. "Well, maybe a few more."

Dodging the bottle with a smile, Gil assessed his companion. Dark, straggly hair. A narrow face. A wisp of unshaven beard. Young. Too young to be that drunk. Floki would send him back to the women. But kind.

The drunk boy got to his feet, stumbling twice before he managed it, and stood swaying and offering Gil his hand. "May as well finish what we started." He nodded to a brightly lit building across the street.

Its doors, of colorful glass and shining metal, burst open and a cluster of young people stumbled out into the night. Boys and girls in jeans; the girls with skimpy tops in spite of the rain. Gil's companion lurched toward them, still beckoning him. But, kneeling yet on the cobbles, his eyes on the broad glass window of the McDonald's, Gil froze.

Just above the clown face, someone had pasted a piece of paper, facing out to the street. White, with a shaded border, it had the words MISSING and HAVE YOU SEEN THIS PERSON? spelled out in black letters, faded brown by the sun. The picture below was also faded, a girl with intense dark eyes and a braid of thick hair. A young girl, in a school uniform jacket and tie – the young girl he met, long ago, at the Wandering Pool of Cille Aidan. "Rachel," he whispered. "It's Rachel."

"Come back, has she?" his friend crowed happily. "Ah, they all crawl back." He turned staggering and pointed to the crowd of young people. "That her? The blond?"

Gil shook his head, pushing the stumbling youth aside as he got to his feet, staring still at the poster in the window. Below the picture was a police phone number and details, Rachel's height and weight and age: fourteen. *Only she's not. She's nearly sixteen, now.* And her name. *Rachel Weintraub.*

He shook his head again and said the name aloud. "I never

knew her last name." In their world, where so few used them, it
had never mattered.

The drunk boy was tugging at his arm. He'd pulled a small,
shiny rectangle from his jeans pocket and was waving it in Gil's
face. "Whass-er number? Send'er text." Gil stared at the thing
he was holding, trying to identify it. Past and present merged in
a jolt: Rachel mourning the little white rectangle snatched from
the Wandering Pool. *My phone. I've lost my phone. I want to call my
Dad.* "Phone," he whispered. "It's a phone."

The little rectangle made a musical note. The boy stabbed it
with his finger, blinked and then howled, "Ah, shit, man. That's
not on." He turned to Gil, thrusting the phone's screen before
his eyes. "She's shagging my best mate."

The crowd of young people straggling across the street
surrounded the boy. A big youth with close cropped hair laid
an arm over his shoulders. "Always told you she was a cow." He
offered the boy a drink from his own bottle. Turning to include
Gil, he stopped, stared, and then laughed raucously. "Hey,"
he beckoned his friends, "Will you look at this? It's Thor!"
He released the boy and stepped close to Gil. He was half a
head taller and a lot wider and his grin was openly belligerent.
"Where's your hammer, Thor?"

Thor. Floki told stories about Thor. "Odin's son?" Gil muttered.
"Right?"

"You should know, mate."

"Hey *like* the threads." Someone tugged at his tunic. Another
prodded his sheepskin boot. Gil stepped back.

"Leave him alone," a girl said quietly. "He's just a games-
nerd. They're okay." The big youth gave Gil a shove. Gil ignored
him, turning to the girl.

"Where are we?" he said urgently. "Is this Deer Bay ... I
mean York?"

"It's York," the girl said. Under all the make-up, her face was
kind. Even motherly. "Are you on holiday?"

"York, England?" said Gil.

"No," the big youth pushed his face in between them. "*Noo
Yawk,*" he laughed coldly. "Check your plane ticket, mate."

Check your plane ticket. Rachel said that. She thought she was here.

And now I'm here. In England. "I haven't got one," he muttered.

"Thor doesn't need one," a lanky blond boy shouted. "He's a superhero." He lurched forward, a fist extended, and one leg raised. "He can fly! See," he straightened up. "He's even got a cape!" He grabbed one end of Gil's wet cloak and held it out. "Fly, superhero!"

"Hey!" Gil's friendly drunk staggered close. "Check the sword!" He leant over, peering at the weapon in its scabbard, belted around Gil's waist. "That real, mate?"

The crop-headed youth swaggered up to Gil again. "Show me your sword, Thor." Gil ignored him again. He looked at Rachel's picture and then back at the circle of young people.

"Does anyone know this girl?" he said.

"Not anymore." The swaggering youth's laugh was cold. "Nobody knows *her* anymore." He reached again for the sword. Gil swerved away.

"Some perv got her." The kind faced girl shivered. "They're everywhere, pervs."

Gil shook his head. He remembered the vision in the time-race, Rachel's grey-bearded father, coming out of his front door. "There's a house," he said. "With a yellow ribbon on the gate. She lived there. Does anyone know where it is?"

The girl shook her head. "Everyone had yellow ribbons out for her." She shrugged. "They're all gone now. They're not even searching …."

"I said show me your sword, Thor." The youth lunged to take the weapon. It was in Gil's hand before he even thought, the tip an inch from the youth's throat.

"No."

The girls screamed. With a clatter of heels, they backed hurriedly away. The blond youth followed but Gil's friendly drunk swayed forward, "Cool, man," he gave Gil an encouraging smile, "He's just joking."

Gil kept his eyes on the shaven-headed youth, who held his ground. Then, with a careful show of nonchalance, the boy stepped back out of range of the sword, drew a phone from his pocket and flipped it dramatically open. "Deal with you," he grunted.

Gil strode forward and pressed the sword tip against his chest. "Give me the phone," he whispered. "Now." The youth's face turned red. For a moment, he hesitated. Gil pressed the point harder. With a wince of outraged pain, the youth flung the phone at Gil. Gil caught it with a quick left hand, surprising even himself.

"Thank you." He nodded once to his staggering friend and bolted, shoving his way through the terrified boys and girls, and out into the street. Weaving wildly, dodging moving cars, he raced blindly into the wet, noisy night.

Shouts and curses followed him, but the voice in his own head was louder. *I'm in a foreign country. No plane ticket. No money. No passport. And I've broken the law.*

Sirens were sounding already when he found what he sought: a dark, silent place, alone. A narrow walkway led between a church and a high stone wall. Sheathing his sword, Gil ducked within and followed the lane into a shadowy refuge. Behind a wrought iron fence, huge old trees, still bearing summer leaves, overhung a grassy rectangle broken by heavy dark shapes. Gravestones. A church graveyard. Gil slipped the phone into his pocket, placed his hands high up on the ornate fretwork and vaulted the barrier. Landing lightly on the soaked grass beyond, he crouched beside a stone cross and drew out the phone.

Its small, bright screen glowed like a fallen star. He studied it only for a moment, before memory came racing back. *Google.* He tapped in 'Rachel Weintraub. York. England.' Before he finished, links were piling in.

News stories. Pictures. Interviews. Police statements. GIRL VANISHES ON SCHOOL OUTING. MUSEUM MYSTERY. WHERE IS RACHEL? "An address," he muttered. Give me her address. He flicked from screen to screen. His finger paused. SCHOOLFRIENDS HOLD CANDLELIT VIGIL. Five girls in uniforms, like Rachel's; three holding candles in jam jars. Two tying yellow ribbons to a lamppost. More ribbons, candles. *There.* The house. Her house. The gate; the big yellow bow still fresh and bright. But where? He searched vainly for a street sign, something, anything … and then he saw it, right at the edge of the picture, on the corner of the neighboring house; a white, lettered board. With thumb and forefinger, he grew the picture and the words expanded; became legible: SAINT MARY'S B&B.

A name. At last. But would there be only one? He shrugged. He had nothing else. A link came up at once. In moments he had a map and a road name for the GPS. Phone yet in hand, he vaulted the graveyard fence and ran out into the bright, wet streets.

The sirens were closer, and once he glimpsed flashing blue lights. He plunged into the crowds of young revelers and raincoat clad tourists. One or two stared; most barely noticed him.

At a wide crossroads, he paused, looking quickly around. A pale square tower loomed high above the roof tops, bathed in flood lighting. A church. A *muinntir. Our minster,* Rachel had called it. *And it's eight hundred years old.* But standing where Deer Bay's *muinntir* had stood. Down a long street, he saw a glint of moving dark water. The river! His route took him toward it, and nearing its banks, he looked over his shoulder and saw another lighted building. A castle, coldly glowing where he had seen a torch of flame. His mind map began to form, merging with the small blue square.

I know this. I know this. The river was narrower and there were bridges across it, carrying cars and buses, but beyond was the bend he remembered. *We tied up here ... somewhere.* He watched the endless flow of traffic; white headlights and red taillights making a river of their own. Everywhere, there was light. Everywhere there was noise.

A yearning swept over him for the dark, silent nights, the star-crowded skies, the splash of oars, and the creak of timbers and rigging ... the low laughter of the Northmen around the campfires ... the fire lit faces of his friends. An emptiness swallowed his heart.

They're all dead, now. All of them. A thousand years ago. "Janetta!" he whispered. *She is bones and dust. Unless I return.* He pushed his flagging legs harder, boots pounding the concrete. The way back. He had to find the way back. And there was one: the museum in York where Rachel saw the amber necklace, and the children in the fire.

The traffic thinned and the streets grew quieter. The sirens, too, fell silent. Relieved, he made his way down peaceful lanes lined with tidy houses. Curtain windows glowed softly behind small, hedge-bordered gardens. Here and there were signs with pretty house names – "Rosedew," "Minster View" – and offers of Bed & Breakfast. *Breakfast.* The word itself gnawed as his empty stomach. He tried not to think how long it had been since he'd eaten, even as he hastened his pace once more.

He turned a corner and the GPS beeped triumph. Before him, a white board on the wall of a tall brick building proclaimed "Saint Mary's B&B" in ornate black lettering. On the gate of the neighboring house, the bedraggled yellow bow hung limply in the rain.

Panting with exhaustion, Gil opened the gate and staggered up the path to the door. Beside it, light shone dimly through thick curtains screening a large bay window. On the door frame, below a brass plate engraved with the name Professor P. Weintraub, was a small lighted button. Gil reached to press it and in the same moment heard the sirens he was sure he had left behind.

"How?" he cried, despairingly. "How did they know where to find me?" And then, with a groan, "Because I told them." He'd asked a street full of people for Rachel's address. Blue lights flashed at the far end of the street. He'd made a trap for himself and run right into it.

Jerking his finger back from the bell, he looked wildly over his shoulder. *Run. But where?* There was nowhere to go, even if he had time. And he hadn't. With a hopeless shrug, he pressed the lighted button and then hammered with his fist on the door.

He heard steps approaching behind it, light and quick; not an old man's steps, though through the time-race of Finlaggan, Rachel's father had seemed old. *Let it be him.* Gil hammered again on the door.

With a sharp click, the heavy latch shifted and the door opened, letting a wedge of light out into the night. A sturdy safety chain rattled taut, securing the narrow gap. "Yes?" the voice was tired, cautious, but gentle as well. "Can I help you?"

"Please," Gil blurted. "I have to come in." He caught a

glimpse of the man's face, half in shadow, the grey beard, the tired lines, and the piercing dark blue eyes. Rachel's eyes.

"Why?" the man said quietly. "Who are you?"

"I'm Rachel's friend," Gil said.

The man's face drew back, the expression instantly changed. "No. You are not. I know her friends. I don't know you." The gap narrowed to a slit. Gil thrust his fingers into it. "Be careful!"

"I'm not from here," Gil said. "I'm her friend from where she is now."

The man sighed. "Please," he said softly. "Don't torture me. I'm sure you are having a wonderful game, but this is *real*." He sighed again. "Sometimes I think you young people don't know the difference anymore."

Startled, Gil shook his head. "I'm not playing a game."

"Then why are you dressed like that?"

"They're my clothes. I don't have ...." Gil heard the sirens again, close. "Please, I'll explain," he said desperately. "Look, see, I won't hurt you." Throwing his cloak back, he quickly unbuckled his sword belt with his free hand, and laid it down at his feet, the way Floki did to show he meant no harm.

The man shrank back. "Is that *real*?"

"I won't use it."

"Move your fingers, I'm closing the door." Gil jammed his boot toe into the gap.

"Please," he begged, "I need your help."

The man hesitated, fear and fatherly compassion warring in his eyes. He looked up from the weapon on his doorstep and said, "What is your name?"

"Gil Lake."

"Fine. Show me some ID."

"I don't have ...."

"No. You don't do you." The man tilted his head wearily, but said, "Alright. Show me Rachel's number on your phone."

"This isn't mine. I stole it."

The man's eyes widened. He leaned back into the shadow, shaking his head. Down the street the sirens suddenly burst into life. "And I suppose that's the police, after you?"

"I think so," Gil said.

The man laughed suddenly, a small, tired laugh. "No ID. A stolen phone. A deadly weapon. And the police on your trail. And I'm supposed to let you in? Full marks for *chutzpah*, Gil Lake. Now go away." He shoved Gil's foot with his own.

"Wait!" Gil cried. He leaned against the door jamb, pressing his boot into the gap with all his strength. Something hard in his pocket ground into his hip, and suddenly he remembered what it was. "Wait!" he cried again. "I have this!"

With desperate fingers he dug out the small piece of wood Floki had given him in Deer Bay. Dirty and weathered from its long journey, it was still clearly marked with the Northman's carved runes. "I have this," he cried again and thrust it through the door. The man brushed it aside. "No. Take it," Gil pushed it into his hand.

Reluctantly, the man closed his fingers around it and raised it to the light. "And what is this supposed to be?" he said wearily.

"A message ... a sort of passport?"

"And what does this message say?" The man turned it, studying it distractedly.

Gil shrugged. "I don't know. I can't read it." But suddenly the bearded man wasn't listening to him. Eyes intent on the carved wood, he fumbled glasses from the pocket of his jacket and set them on his nose.

"My God," he whispered. His head came up, eyes wide beneath the distorting lenses. "Where did you get this? Did you steal this too?"

"No!" Gil protested. "He gave it to me. Floki gave it to me."

The man took off the glasses, twirling them in the fingers of one hand, while the other clutched the carved wood. "Floki Magnusson. Floki Magnusson gave you this?"

"*Yes*," Gil's voice rose in spite of himself. Over his shoulder, he heard car tires approaching, a slowly moving car. Blue lights pulsed over the hedges. The man looked up and then reached a decision with surprising assurance.

"Right. Well I won't get any sense out of you standing out here. Pick that up, before you come in," he indicated Gil's sword belt, "It's rather a dead giveaway, isn't it?"

Gil nodded. Warily removing his foot from the door, he

crouched, and lifted the weapon. The door pushed closed for a heart-stopping moment, and then re-opened without the chain. A hand gripped his shoulder and hauled him in. The latch clicked shut as, outside, the car came to a halt.

"I'll have that," the bearded man reached for the sword belt. In the dim light of the entranceway, he looked small, old, and slight. Gil handed over the weapon with a reassuring smile. The hand on his shoulder directed him down a hallway, into a darkened room, as the bell rang behind them. "I'll have to talk to them. Stay here, until I come back."

Gratefully, Gil sank down on a small, ornate chair and dropped his head into his hands.

Voices murmured down the hall, and the latch sounded as the front door closed again. Gil looked up as his protector re-entered the room, holding a phone in one hand. "They're gone," he said sternly. "You have five minutes to tell me the truth, or I call them back." He paused, stepping back quickly as Gil got to his feet.

"Before we start," he began again, "My name is Phillip Weintraub. I am professor of Medieval History at the university. I have a PhD in Christian Mysticism, a reasonable knowledge of Latin, Greek, Anglo-Saxon, and Old Norse, and a black belt in karate. Just so we understand each other. And," he added, "I've locked your sword in my study for safekeeping."

Gil nodded. Phillip Weintraub was short, with a stoop to his narrow shoulders and a small pot belly. The hand holding the phone was shaking. Scrunching himself down to be the same height, Gil said, "I have a knife, too. Do you want it?" He pulled back his cloak to reveal the sheathed blade at his belt.

The professor laughed, a light, whimsical laugh. "Well, full marks for honesty, too. This is absurd," he said, lowering the phone.

"Only," Gil said, "If you can give it back later, please. It was my father's." Hunger and exhaustion suddenly overcame him. He felt his lip tremble and bit down hard.

Phillip Weintraub leaned toward him, reaching out an instinctive, compassionate hand. "No. Keep your knife." He shook his head, looked around the dimly lit room and offered

Gil one of two armchairs by a glowing coal fire. "Please, sit down." Hesitantly, Gil obeyed. The professor took the opposite chair, and sat facing him, the rune-carving in his hands.

"Now," he said, with a small patient smile, "You did *not* get this from Floki Magnusson, in spite of what is written on it. Floki Magnusson, if he was a real person at all, lived over a thousand years ago. It is, however, a superb reproduction. The Old Norse is accurate to the period, the runes are exactly right. Somebody who knew what they were doing made this."

He turned it admiringly in his hands, scholars delight briefly overcoming tiredness and sorrow. "How, indeed, had they even *heard* of Floki Magnusson? The saga is obscure. Fragmentary. Nothing extant beyond two fifteenth century copies in Reykjavik. Nothing in English translation at all." He shrugged, "Some other time, I might like to know who that person was. But right now, I want just one answer. Why have you come to me? What have I to do with this story of a semi-mythical nineth century Viking that you turn up at my door? With this?"

"Rachel's with him," said Gil.

The professor stared for a moment, then closed his eyes and sat shaking his head, the little carved piece of wood dangling, forgotten from his fingers. "If you could *know*," he said slowly, "How much this nonsense hurts. The mediums. The mystics. The frauds. And now," he opened his eyes again and met Gil's gaze with frightening intensity, "The internet gamers.

"My beautiful daughter, my only child, vanishes, inexplicably, and without a trace ... if you could *only* understand."

"I do understand," Gil said quietly. "My father went missing kayaking on the river and they never found his body." He paused and added with dignity, "And I'm not playing any kind of game."

Phillip Weintraub's face softened and his eyes grew suddenly warm, like Rachel's when she was helping someone. "Oh, I *am* sorry. I am *so* sorry." He looked down at the runes, shaking his head again, and then looked up and smiled suddenly. "Do you know, I'm hungry," he said. "How about you?"

Gil's stomach ached at even the thought of food. "Starving," he said honestly.

The professor stood up. "Come to the kitchen. We'll raid the fridge." He looked happy, as if Gil was his own kid, needing feeding.

In the bright lighting of the kitchen, he stopped and stared. "My God, young man, what's happened to your face?" He reached a tentative hand to Gil's bruised and lacerated cheek.

Gil shrugged. "This side," he touched his left cheekbone, "was a looter in Deer Bay. This," he touched the crusted scab, "was a sword fight on Deer Isle. And this," he gingerly felt his right cheekbone, "was actually Rachel."

"Rachel? *Where*?"

"*Here*," Gil said. "Well, not here. Or, yes here, but not now. We were together in Deer Bay rescuing the children … her children … the children she saw in the museum … in the fire …" Aware he was babbling, Gil stopped, and said only, "We were here."

Rachel's father came close, peering carefully at Gil's eyes. "I seem old to you," he said. "But like everyone old now, I remember the 'sixties."

"It's not drugs!" Gil threw his hands in the air. "You sound like Dr. Fairchild!" The professor looked puzzled. "My *shrink*. Yeah, I may be crazy. I may be a Change-Thing. I may walk through time. But I don't do drugs!"

"What's a *Change-Thing*?"

"You don't want to know." Gil looked away. His gaze fell on a framed photograph set on one of the kitchen counters across the room. "It's Rachel," he said.

The professor studied him carefully. "It's Miriam," he said. "My wife." His eyes slid to the photograph by long habit and he smiled slightly. "Fortunately, Rachel took all her looks from her mother."

"Her eyes are like yours."

"Yes." Phillip Weintraub shook his head and brushed a hand across his face. "And everyone who follows Facebook, or watches television, or reads a paper, would know the color of Rachel's eyes."

"That's not how I know," Gil said simply.

The professor looked away and said softly, "You cannot know how much I want to believe you."

"Don't let yourself believe me," Gil said, "Until you're sure it's true."

"Because it hurts so much if it isn't?"

Gil nodded. The professor laid Floki's rune carving on the table. "You are an unusual young man. We'd better do something about your face. That's a nasty cut, however you got it."

"It's okay," Gil said. "Floki and Hakon put something on it."

"Hakon?" The man's eyes opened wide. "Hakon *Sea-Friend*?"

"Yes!" Gil said, surprised.

"His cousin."

"Sort of more than a cousin."

"I know. His foster-brother. Where are you *getting* all of this?" Rachel's father looked up at the ceiling and recited, from memory:

"'In chains, bold Sea-Friend
Wins a sea-king's daughter.'"

Gil smiled. "That's Floki. He's always making up poems."

The professor nodded. "He, or someone, anyhow, was very much a poet." He raised the rune-stick. "You don't know what this says?"

Gil shook his head. "But I know it works. People run a mile."

"I'm not surprised." A small smile quirked the corners of Phillip Weintraub's mouth. Tracing the carvings with his finger, he read:

"This idiot belongs to Floki Magnusson
Harm him, and you die."

Gil winced. "And *that's* Floki, too."

"The word isn't exactly idiot, but near enough ...."

"Oh, near enough," said Gil.

Phillip Weintraub smiled. "I think we'll have that food."

He opened the refrigerator door and peered inside, collecting bread and roast meats, milk, cheese, and fruit, and a half a chocolate cake. Gil watched, mesmerized by the sight of so much food. Rachel's father spread it all out on the kitchen table and began slicing bread for sandwiches. "It's like a great feast," Gil murmured.

"Oh, hardly," the professor laughed. But he seemed pleased. And, though he had said he was hungry, he did not eat, only sat gently twisting a silver bracelet on his wrist, as Gil devoured everything in sight. "More?" he said, smiling.

Full for the first time in what felt like weeks, Gil shook his head. "Thank you. It was wonderful."

"Oh, a pleasure. A pleasure. To have someone young in the house again ... all my friends are old. Can't eat this. Can't eat that." He laughed again.

When he rose to clear the dishes, he took the bracelet off, tugging it, with difficulty, over his knuckles. "It was my wife's," he said, laying it down beside the rune-stick. "I gave it to her." Gil nodded. It was a simple silver band, plainer than those the Northmen wore, but it was marked, like the rune-stick, with letters. These were English and easy to read. *And All Shall Be Well.* Gil sat up straight, reached to touch the silver band, and then quickly drew back his hand.

"It's all right," Phillip Weintraub's voice was gentle. "You can look at it." He lifted it and placed it in Gil's hands. "Julian of Norwich. I'm rather fond of her. Wrote a book about her, actually." He sounded boyishly proud. "And all shall be well, and all shall be well ...."

"And all manner of thing shall be well," Gil finished.

The professor drew back. "Now you *are* a surprising young man." Gil shook his head, turning the bracelet to see all the words. "It's Rachel's message. To you. It's her message to you. She wrote it on a piece of vellum in Aidan's scriptorium." Phillip Weintraub's thick eyebrows rose at Gil's use of the word.

"His *scriptorium*?"

"Where he wrote books. By hand." Gil's words tumbled over each other in his haste. "She wrote it on the edge of something. She called it margin-something."

"Marginalia."

"She said it was where we get history."

Rachel's father nodded and then laughed softly. "I never thought she listened to me."

"Oh, she listened." Gil looked up and locked his eyes with those of the older man. "I asked how it would get to you, and

she said, 'Who knows where it will be, in a thousand years?'
And she just dropped it on the floor."

The professor nodded, "Of course. Of course."

"But I *moved* it. I came back. Cille Aidan was gone, burnt,
everything ruined, but I found one book and Rachel's message
and I put it in the book ...."

"Whose book?" Phillip Weintraub's hands closed on Gil's
and the bracelet.

Gil shrugged. "Aidan's. He had lots of books. I couldn't read
them."

"No. They would be in Latin. Or Greek. Perhaps Hebrew."
He looked away into the night as if he could see the scene Gil
was describing. After a long silence, he said, "It's in the British
Museum."

"Rachel's message is in a *museum*?"

The professor nodded. "It's called the 'Seville Anomaly.'
After the book it was found in; a very old copy of Isidore of
Seville, probably originating in Iona. A single page, with some
rather amateurish calligraphy, recording those words. Those
words of Julian of Norwich who post-dates the Iona library by
some five hundred years. A total anachronism and an obvious
fraud. But, and here's the puzzle – a brilliant fraud. The vellum,
the ink, everything about it, date to the late nineth century. And
no one can figure how it was done. So why does some genius
create a brilliant fraud, and then blow it out of the water with
that utterly anachronous phrase?"

"Because the genius was Rachel. And actually," Gil said,
defensive of his friend, "Her calligraphy was pretty good."

"Oh, forgive me," Phillip Weintraub smiled gently, "It's
a technical criticism. Of course it was good. Far better than I
could do, anyhow." He closed his eyes. "She always was good
with her hands."

He was silent for a long while. Cautiously, Gil said, "Mr. ...
Professor ...."

I think Phillip will do."

"Phillip, I have to get back there. And you have to help."

The professor rested his cheek against one hand, his blue
eyes intent on Gil. "Tell me how," he said.

Gil studied his face, solemn and bearded like a professor should look, and yet somehow he reminded Gil of Crazy Ivan. *The way he listens. Like kids are as smart as he is.* He took a deep breath. "Time doesn't work the way we think it does," he said.

"How so?"

The old-fashioned clock on the wall struck midnight, the chimes loud in the quiet house. Gil waited until they fell silent. "It's like a sea ...." he began.

When he finished, the hands on the clock stood at three. On the table before him, amid a new collection of plates and cups, and the last remnants of the chocolate cake, the rune-stick and the silver bracelet lay side by side, together with Merlin's seeing stone.

Phillip touched one and then another. "A sea no man can sail," he mused. "And yet, you have. And so has my daughter." His face was etched with weariness. "To know that she is alive ... such joy! But so far, so far away."

"And so close," Gil said softly. "Twice we were within a mile of here. And then, from Finlaggan, we even saw you."

"Saw me?"

"You came out of your front door. I think you heard something. You seemed to be listening."

Phillip turned away. "My ears trouble me." He tapped one. "A ringing. Tinnitus it's called. I've had it for years."

"But it wasn't a ringing this time, was it?" said Gil. The professor looked wary. "It was music, wasn't it? Harp music."

Phillip leaned back in his chair, ran his fingers through his hair, and then cautiously nodded. "Beautiful. Beautiful harp music." He paused. "I thought I was going mad."

Gil smiled and shook his head. "It was Time-Heddler. The High-King's Harp."

Phillip's eyes grew bright. "The harp that draws apart the threads of time. What a marvelous idea. Do you know," he leaned forward, animated, "I have a friend, a particle physicist ... the things they work with these days! He'd love to talk to you."

He toyed with the rune-stick, the bracelet, and the stone, re-arranging them thoughtfully. "All right. I understand that time is, let us say *thinner* in places. The whirlpool in your river. The waterfall in the forest."

"And the museum."

Phillip nodded. "And the music of the harp somehow thins it further, and this," he lifted the hollow seeing stone and held it briefly to his eye, "Is like a window. Or even a door. But how does it *work*? What is the mechanism?"

Gil was quiet, thinking, for a long while. Then he said slowly, "I think it's love. I think it works by love."

Phillip's eyebrows rose startlingly high. "Love? And *how* …?"

"Aidan told us the stone shows us the treasures of our hearts. It shows us what we love. So," he paused, thinking of Jocelyn Guidbairn, "If that's gold and power, that's what you see. That's where it leads you. But if you're like Rachel and what you love is helping people, then it shows you people needing help. Like the children in the fire."

"Ah," Phillip said, "What a thought. And yes, that is my Rachel. Into the fires of hell, if need be."

"That's what it was like," Gil said. "Everything burning."

"1190," said Phillip. "The massacre of the Jews." He paused. "We must, in history, try never to judge the people of the past by the standards of the present … still," he said quietly, "it was a savage event."

"But there was the blacksmith," Gil said.

"Indeed there was. One of the Just." Phillip smiled at Gil's puzzled look. "One of the Twelve Just Men always in the world, for whose sake the Lord spares mankind his righteous wrath. An old tradition." He smiled again, "I like to think there are a few more than twelve."

He laughed lightly. "So Rachel saw the children. Ismail saw his brother and sister. And Percy – ah, Percy – Percy saw his beautiful cup." Phillip smiled whimsically, "The Grail-Knight's cup. I have friends who would *love* to talk to him!" He twirled his glasses, his eyes twinkling. "And you saw the girl from Camelot." Gil nodded. "The girl you love."

"I didn't say that."

Phillip laughed. "You have said it all night. Well, we must

get you back to her. Not good manners to keep a lady waiting."
He excused himself and left the kitchen. When he returned, he
was wearing his overcoat and carrying Gil's sword belt. "I think
you will need this."

"Where are we going?"

"To the museum."

"But it's three in the morning. Won't it be closed?"

"It will." Phillip's smile broadened. "But I am a trustee. And
I have this." He reached into his pocket and drew out a ring of
keys.

Imbued with a boyish excitement, the professor hid Gil in the
shadows of the hedges, as he backed his car out of his driveway.
The street was silent, the windows of the houses darkened. A
single, confident cat watched from a gatepost.

The rain had stopped and the sky was clearing. River mist
haloed the distant Minster tower. Phillip beckoned Gil and
bundled him into the passenger seat. Spreading a picnic blanket
over his head, he whispered conspiratorially, "Just in case we're
stopped."

Gil thought that a bit unlikely. There wasn't a car on the
road, and he suspected the police had gone home to bed. But
he stayed dutifully under the blanket as the professor drove
through the sleeping city.

When the car drew to a slow halt, he was almost asleep
himself. A large building bulked in the shadows of tall trees.
Phillip led Gil to a side door and unlocked it with familiar ease.
"Sometimes," he said, as they stepped into a quiet corridor
stacked with cardboard boxes, "I come here almost as late as
this. To work. Or sometimes just to sit and think. People imagine
it a frightening place at night, with the bones and the grave
goods all around. But the dead are kindly company. They've
seen everything and felt everything. They know how hard life
is."

He stopped then, at the foot of a broad staircase. "This is all
storage, down here. Up there are the exhibits. The room where
Rachel was last seen is just through to the left." His voice broke,
"I do avoid it. I know it's cowardly, but my mind invents such
terrible scenes ... what happened there ...."

"I'll go alone," said Gil.

"You will not," Phillip replied instantly.

Gil looked up the stairs to the dim, night-lit rooms above. Throwing his cloak back to free his sword arm, he quickly drew the weapon, as before any battle, holding it first up to the light and then polishing the steel against the rough leather of his boot. Grit and grime affected balance.

"That looks rather deadly," the professor said.

"It is."

Something dawned in Phillip Weintraub's eyes. He nodded slowly. "I see." Nodding again, he said, "We do not judge the past by the present," and gave Gil his gentle smile.

At the top of the stairs, Phillip flicked a row of switches. Soft lights glowed within glass cases in each of the next rooms. They crossed the first quickly and turned left. At the threshold of the next, the professor halted. His face was pale, and the hand on Gil's shoulder trembled. "Just beyond," he murmured. "Just beyond."

Gil stepped through the doorway, and then behind him, heard a startled cry. He whirled, hand on sword hilt. But Phillip's face was alight with happy amazement. "I hear it!" he cried, "I hear the harp!"

Then, Gil heard it too, and in the same moment, he saw, sealed in a case halfway across the room, the golden chain with its gold and amber cross; as perfect and shining as when he first saw it, held up in a triumphant Viking's hand. "It's there!" he cried to Phillip. "It's there." He pointed, and then reached into his pocket for the seeing stone. But Phillip suddenly caught his arm.

"Here, take this with you." He pulled the silver bracelet from his wrist, and thrust it over the knuckles of Gil's rough, calloused hand. "For Rachel. My answer. My answer to her message."

Gil smiled and threw both arms around the older man. "Thank you for believing me." Then he raised the hollow stone. Daylight flooded through it, brightening the dim room. Gil saw sky and water, the circling hawk. Then the low grassy island of Finlaggan and the ruins of the hermit's prayer house. He hastened toward them, but Phillip cried, "Wait! How much time has passed? What if he's sailed without you?"

Gil grinned and shook his head. He ran to the vision, turning at the last minute to wave goodbye. "He can't sail without me," he called. "I'm his helmsman!"

Chapter Sixteen

"Helmsman!" Floki called. "Faster." He was laughing, his arms yet around Danni, who he turned to kiss.

"Any faster and I'd be flying," Gil gasped. The stone yet in his hand, he felt his feet touch solid ground. Gratefully he fell to his knees on the grass within the ruined cell. The music dwindled to silence and the *file's* son rested his quiet hands on the strings.

"We are safe!" Janetta threw her arms around Gil weeping. "We are safe."

Gil caught his breath and looked up into her eyes. "I'm sorry … I stumbled … the time-race."

"Why are you sorry?" she said.

"I'm so late."

She shook her head. "But we are all together. You were just behind Rachel. And she, just behind us."

"But I was there all night."

Floki raised an eyebrow. "Where, Warrior?"

"Deer Bay. York."

"With me," Rachel said.

"No," Gil got to his feet. "I fell. The time-race took me. I was in York in *our* time." He paused. "I was with your father."

"My father!" She hesitated, as Phillip had done, caution tempering the yearning to believe.

"Warrior," Floki said. "This is not possible. I never lose sight of you. I see you always, running. Too slow," he said drily. "But running."

"It *is* possible," Rachel stepped close to the earl. "We were together in Deer Bay. I was with him."

"You are always in my sight."

"Was I?" she whispered. She turned uncertainly from Floki to Gil. "Did we dream?"

"Dream?" Gil met her puzzled gaze, then looked slowly around. Floki watched him curiously. Ismail gave his lopsided grin. The *file's* son smiled shyly. Gil raised his eyes to the sky. The hawk circled, the same pale sun touching its wings. At the water's edge, the heron speared a fish. Beyond, Lionheart grazed contentedly among the ponies, oblivious of his absence. Nothing had changed.

Could I have dreamed it all? He looked down then at Niall, cradling the worn old harp against his chest. *A music so sweet … that time stands still … and a man can be in two places at once ….*

Gil held up his arm, silver glinting against the sun-browned skin. "No dream," he said softly. Working the silver bracelet over his knuckles, he slipped it gently onto Rachel's wrist.

She stared at it in joyous amazement. "It's true! It's true!" She showed the bracelet to Ismail. "My mother's," she said, laughing and then suddenly crying. More man now than boy, he stepped protectively to her side.

Gil looked up to Danni, his childhood friend, a grown woman in the arms of her nineth century love. Then, resting his rough seaman's hands on Janetta's shoulders, he bent his head and gave her a lingering kiss. As Aidan had foretold, long ago, they who had come to this world as children, were children no more.

"Helmsman."

"I know. The tide." Gil smiled wryly, released the girl in his arms, and went with Ismail to collect the beasts. Setting Janetta up on Lionheart's back, he followed the earl and his lady to the marshy island shore.

Lionheart balked at the edge. *It's wet.*

It's water.

My feet are sinking.

Janetta stroked his furry neck. "Poor Lionheart."

Lionheart flicked a mournful ear. *Poor Lionheart.*

Gil gave him a savage tug. *Poor Lionheart, my ass.* The pony splashed into the loch, still grumbling, but Gil's mind was already far away, on his waiting ship, his unfinished quest, and the cold Northern seas of home.

About the Author

Alison Scott, the daughter of two writers, Alexander Leslie Scott, master of the western detective novel, and artist turned short story writer, Lily Kay Scott, was born in Manhattan. Her brother, Justin Scott, is a master of thrillers, mysteries, and sea stories, including the Isaac Bell Adventures. A Junior Year Abroad from her American university took her to Scotland, where she met her future husband, Clement Skelton- -an actor, playwright, film cameraman, Battle of Britain Spitfire pilot, and monster hunter. She had her first baby while living on the shores of Loch Ness.

From an apprenticeship in Gothic romances, she went on to publish her first hardcover novel, A World Full of Secrets, writing as Alison Scott, while her husband became C.L. Skelton, writing successful family sagas. After she was widowed, she continued writing while raising their two sons, Professor Alasdair Skelton, geologist researching in climate change, and actor and gardener Justin Skelton.

As Alison Scott Skelton, she has published several works of contemporary and historical fiction in the US and Britain; among them, *Different Families*, *A Murderous Innocence*, *Saving Grace*, *An Older Woman*, and *Family Story*.

The Warriors of Tir nan Og, the six-book series that opens with *The Underwater Bridge*, is her first work for a young adult audience.

Curious about other Crossroad Press books?
Stop by our site:
https://www.crossroadpress.com
We offer quality writing
in digital, audio, and print formats.